生活實用度100%，就算考試也能從容應戰，
專為深受「讀」害的你而寫的教戰手冊，
過去無法搞定的所有文章閱讀，現在開始一本快速掌握！

本書使用方式

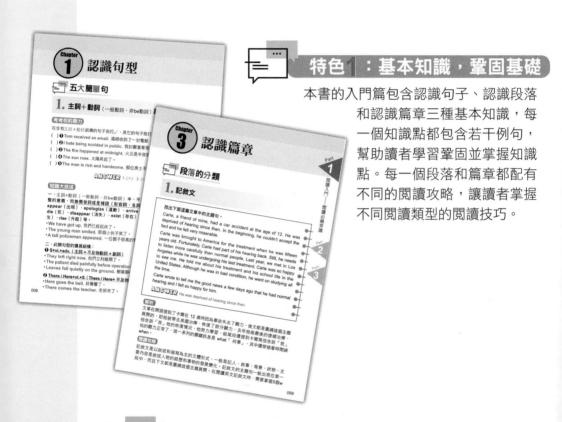

特色1：基本知識，鞏固基礎

本書的入門篇包含認識句子、認識段落和認識篇章三種基本知識，每一個知識點都包含若干例句，幫助讀者學習鞏固並掌握知識點。每一個段落和篇章都配有不同的閱讀攻略，讓讀者掌握不同閱讀類型的閱讀技巧。

特色2：化繁為簡，閱讀精華

入門篇的「Pass 掉句子不必要的成分」是本書的精華所在，在複雜的句子結構中去掉附加訊息就可以得出句子的核心內容。本書詳細介紹了「不必要的成分」的分類，使得讀者可以快速分辨需要篩選的部分。

Chapter 1 英文原著

少年維特的煩惱

①In other respects I am very well off here. ②Solitude in this terrestrial paradise is a genial balm to my mind, and the young spring cheers with its bounteous promises my oftentimes misgiving heart. ③Every tree, every bush, is full of flowers; and one might wish himself transformed into a butterfly, to float about in this ocean of perfume, and find his whole existence in it.

④The town itself is disagreeable; but then, all around, you find an inexpressible beauty of nature. ⑤This induced the late Count M to lay out a garden on one of the sloping hills which here intersect each other with the most charming variety, and form the most lovely valleys. ⑥The garden is simple; and it is easy to perceive, even upon your first entrance, that the plan was not designed by a scientific gardener, but by a man who wished to give himself up here to the enjoyment of his own sensitive heart. ⑦Many a tear have I already shed to the memory of its departed master in a summer-house which is now reduced to ruins, but was his favorite resort, and now is mine. ⑧I shall soon be master of the place. ⑨The gardener has become attached to me within the last few days, and he will lose nothing thereby.

補充單字片語

- solitude [ˈsɑlɪtjuːd] /n./ 單獨，孤獨，幽靜
- bounteous [ˈbaʊntɪəs] /adj./ 大方的，慷慨的

句構分析

① In other respects I am very well off here.
介系詞+名詞　主詞 be動詞 副詞 形容詞 副詞

語法分析 這句話是談段的主旨句。後面的幾個句子都是在具體細述感受愉快的原因。

② Solitude in this terrestrial paradise is a genial balm to my mind, and the young
主詞　　　　介系詞+名詞　　be動詞 述語　　介系詞+名詞　　主詞
spring cheers with its bounteous promises my oftentimes misgiving heart.
介系詞+名詞　　動詞　　　　　　副詞　　受詞

譯 這片樂園的寧靜是醫治我心的靈丹妙藥，圍繞的溫暖春光充滿了我這顆時常焦慮懷疑的心。

③ Every tree, every bush, is full of flowers; and one might wish himself
主詞　　　　動詞　述語　　主詞 助詞　　受詞
transformed into a butterfly, to float about in this ocean of perfume, and find his
受詞補語　　介系詞+名詞　　　　　　介系詞+名詞　　動詞
whole existence in it.
受詞　　　介系詞+代名詞

譯 每一棵樹，每一片灌木叢都開滿了鮮花。讓人想變成一隻蝴蝶，飛翔在花的海洋中，去盡情地吸露吸蜜。

語法分析 該段句是由and連接的兩個並列句。Every tree, every bush, is full of flowers是一個主詞+動詞結構的簡單句。第一個and後面的句子：主詞是one，其後有兩個並列的動詞，其中一個是 wish，另外一個是find。

④ The town itself is disagreeable; but then, all around, you find an inexpressible
主詞　　　　動詞　述語　　副詞　　　　主詞 動詞　　受詞
beauty of nature.
介系詞+名詞

譯 城市本身不討人喜歡。但是，周圍的一切，你會發現一種無法形容的自然美。

⑤ This induced the late Count M to lay out a garden on one of the sloping hills
主詞　動詞　　受詞補語　　　　受詞　　介系詞+名詞
which here intersect each other with the most charming variety, and form the most
形容詞子句　　　　　　　介系詞+名詞
lovely valleys.

譯 這促使後來的伯爵在一座斜坡上布置了一座花園。這裡的景色與最迷人的景色相交叉，形成了最美麗的山谷。

⑥ The garden is simple; and it is easy to perceive, even upon your first entrance,
主詞　　動詞 述語　　　主詞 動詞 不定詞　　　　　　　介系詞+名詞
that the plan was not designed by a scientific gardener, but by a man who wished
介系詞+名詞　　　　　　　　介系詞+名詞 形容詞子句
to give himself up here to the enjoyment of his own sensitive heart.

譯 花園很簡單，即使在你第一次進來的時候，也很容易察覺到這個平面圖不是由一個科學園丁設計的；而是由一個想在這裡享受自己敏感內心的人。

⑦ Many a tear have I already shed to the memory of its departed master in a
受詞　　　助詞 副詞 動詞　介系詞+名詞　　介系詞+名詞 介系詞+名詞

特色3：英文原文，化簡分析

「英文原著」、「美語演講」、「新聞報導」、「公告信件」均是英文原文，使用「Pass掉句子不必要的成分」來分析句子結構，在最大程度上讓讀者體會閱讀的樂趣。

特色4：閱讀實踐，牢牢掌握

實踐篇針對各類考試題型，透過「選詞填空」、「匹配段落大意」、「句子連貫與銜接」、「推敲細節」來充分學習篇章，在這些文章中，讀者可結合基本知識和閱讀技巧來整體把握篇章，並從細節處理解篇章。

Preface 前言

為準備各種英文考試，我們必須培養良好的英文閱讀能力。如果平日養成閱讀英文原著、文學名著、報章雜誌、信件等習慣，將所學的英文落實在日常生活中，對於準備考試必定大有幫助，尤其是全民英檢、多益考試、研究所考試、雅思、托福等，考題內容通常包含許多冗長、複雜的句型。而培養英文閱讀能力是有技巧的。為了讓廣大讀者學會快速理解英文閱讀的技巧，我們特地編輯本書，與讀者分享訣竅。

本書包含三部分，分別為「閱讀入門」、「閱讀提升」、「閱讀實踐」。在「閱讀入門」中，我們從簡單的句型文法著手，協助讀者先了解句型的結構，為大家打下閱讀的基礎。該部分包含一個重要的閱讀技巧，即「Pass 掉句子不必要的成分 」，這部分是全書的精華所在，旨在幫助讀者面對冗長、複雜的句型時，能快速掌握句型的主幹。學會句型之後，接著學習段落和篇章的類型，此能協助讀者對段落和篇章有一個明確的概念，進而能以結構拆解段落和篇章。

在「閱讀提升」中，本書透過四個不同的章節（「英文原著」、「英文演講」、「新聞報導」、「公告信件」）共 52 篇英文原文，協助讀者化繁為簡，學以致用，進而快速掌握文章的核心內容。在「閱讀實踐」中，本書從全民英檢、雅思和托福的題型著手，收錄 49 篇閱讀理解文章，讓讀者進行實戰練習。

本書的使用對象不僅僅是需要參加考試的英文學習者，也包括對英文名著和小說感興趣的讀者。我們相信，本書呈現的閱讀知識和技巧將有助讀者讀懂並理解複雜的長篇英文文章。

Contents 目錄

Part 1

閱讀入門——
閱讀必備常識

認識句型

五大簡單句

1. 主詞＋動詞（一般動詞，非be動詞）結構

考考你的眼力

在含有 主詞＋動詞 結構的句子前打✓，其它的句子前打×。

(×) ❶ Tom received an email. 湯姆收到了一封電郵。

(×) ❷ I hate being scolded in public. 我討厭當著眾人面前遭到責備。

(✓) ❸ The fire happened at midnight. 火災是半夜發生的。

(✓) ❹ The sun rose. 太陽昇起了。

(×) ❺ The man is rich and handsome. 那位男士不僅很富有，而且很英俊。

ANSWER 1. (×)　2. (×)　3. (✓)　4. (✓)　5. (×)

知識大放送

一、主詞＋動詞（一般動詞，非be動詞）中，不及物動詞本身就可以表達完整的意義，而無需受詞或是補語（形容詞、名詞）。常見的不及物動詞有：**appear**（出現）、**apologize**（道歉）、**arrive**（到達）、**come**（過來）、**die**（死）、**disappear**（消失）、**exist**（存在）、**fall**（落下）、**happen**（發生）、**rise**（升起）等。

• **We have got up.** 我們已經起床了。

• **The young man smiled.** 那個小伙子笑了。

• **A tall policeman appeared.** 一位個子很高的警察出現了。

二、此類句型的擴展結構：

❶ S+vi.+adv.（主詞 + 不及物動詞 + 副詞）

• **They left right now.** 他們立刻離開了。

• **The patient died painfully before operation.** 病人在手術前已痛苦地死去了。

• **Leaves fall quietly on the ground.** 樹葉靜靜地飄落在地上。

❷ There / Here+vi.+S（There / Here+ 不及物動詞 + 主詞）

• **Here goes the bell.** 鈴聲響了。

• **There comes the teacher.** 老師來了。

- **There stands a little girl.** 有個小女孩站在那裡。

❸ S+vi.+to do（主詞+ 不及物動詞 +to 動詞）
- **We began to do homework.** 我們開始寫作業。
- **The secretary forgot to take the meeting minutes.** 秘書忘了帶會議紀錄。
- **They stopped to buy some fruits.** 他們停下來買了一些水果。

隨手練一練

一、找出下列句子中的主詞和動詞，並翻譯整個句子。

1. To my surprise, he resigned last month.
2. My mother forgot to turn off the lights.
3. I drive to pick up the clients.
4. He wants to go out for a walk.
5. The young girls laughed loudly outside.

二、找出下面這段話中主詞＋動詞（一般動詞，非be動詞），後面無需受詞或補語結構的句子。

Jack got up late this morning. He couldn't catch the bus, so he went to school on foot. He found that something happened on the way to school, because a lot of people gathered on the corner of the street. It seems that a traffic accident had happened. But Jack was in a hurry to go to school, so he did not stop to see what exactly happened. However, Jack still did not arrive on time, for he walked too slowly. Jack was given a telling-off by the teacher. The teacher asked him to write a self-review report.

<hr>

ANSWER

一、

1. **To my surprise, he resigned** last month. 讓我吃驚的是，他上個月就辭職了。
2. **My mother forgot** to turn off the lights. 我媽媽忘了關燈。
3. **I drive** to pick up the clients. 我開車去接客戶。
4. **He wants** to go out for a walk. 他想外出散步。
5. **The young girls laughed** loudly outside. 女孩們在外面大聲地笑著。

二、

Jack got up late this morning. He couldn't catch the bus, so he went to school on foot. He found that something happened on the way to school, because a lot of people gathered on the corner of the street. It seems that a traffic accident had happened. But Jack was in a hurry to go to school, so he did not stop to see what exactly happened. However, Jack still did not arrive on time, for he walked too slowly. Jack was given a telling-off by the teacher. The teacher asked him to write a self-review report.

2. 主詞＋動詞＋受詞結構

考考你的眼力

在含有主詞+動詞 (一般動詞，非be動詞) +受詞結構的句子前打 √ ，其它的句子前打 × 。

(×) ❶ The sun rises in the east. 太陽從東邊升起。

(√) ❷ Lily got a good score. 莉莉得到了一個好的成績。

(×) ❸ Did you get up late this morning? 你今天早上晚起嗎？

(√) ❹ She wants a window seat. 她想要一個靠窗的座位。

(×) ❺ The leaves fall in autumn. 樹葉在秋天落下 。

ANSWER 1. (×)　2. (√)　3. (×)　4. (√)　5. (×)

知識大放送

一、在主詞+動詞(一般動詞，非be動詞)+受詞結構中，動詞通常是及物動詞(vt)，動詞後的受詞可以是名詞、代名詞、動名詞、不定詞（to+V），或是子句。

- Mark has a red coat. 馬克有一件紅色的外套。
- No one would like to help him. 沒有人願意幫他。
- They like swimming in summer. 他們喜歡在夏天游泳。
- He wants to go to the library. 他想去圖書館。
- I will do what I have said. 我會做到我所說的話。

二、此類句型的擴展結構：

S + vt. + O + adv.（主詞 + 及物動詞 + 受詞 + 副詞）

- She finds an interesting book in the bookstore.
  她在書店發現了一本有趣的書。
- I want the present badly. 我好想要這個禮物。
- I finished the homework quickly. 我快速地寫完了功課。

隨手練一練

一、找出下列句子中的主詞、動詞、受詞，並翻譯整個句子。

1. I don't know what he did.
2. Where can I find the wallet?
3. You forgot to buy a bag of salt in the supermarket.

4. My dad will drive my mother to the airport.

二、找出下面這段話中主詞＋動詞＋受詞結構的句子。

My father is a math teacher. He teaches grade 4 and grade 5 all the time. He likes his students very much. My father works late sometimes. Last year, one of my father's students got the first prize in the math competition. My dad was so happy that he praised the student many times in class. My father often guides my study at home.

ANSWER

一、

1. **I don't know what he did.** 我不知道他做了什麼。

2. Where can **I find the wallet?** 我在哪裡可以找到錢包？

3. **You forgot to buy a bag of salt** in the supermarket. 你忘了在超市買一包鹽。

4. **My dad will drive my mother** to the airport. 我爸爸會開車帶媽媽去機場。

二、

My father is a math teacher. <u>He teaches grade 4 and grade 5</u> all the time. <u>He likes his students</u> very much. My father works late sometimes. Last year, <u>one of my father's students got the first prize</u> in the math competition. My dad was so happy that <u>he praised the student</u> many times in class. <u>My father</u> often <u>guides me</u> at home.

3. 主詞＋連綴動詞＋主詞補語（形容詞、名詞）結構

考考你的眼力

在含有主詞＋連綴動詞＋主詞補語（形容詞、名詞）結構的句子前打✓，其它的句子前打✗。

(✓) ❶ **His elder brother is an English teacher.** 他哥哥是一位英語老師。

(✗) ❷ **My sister can't speak English.** 我妹妹不會說英語。

(✓) ❸ **The cat has white and black fur.** 這隻貓有白色和黑色的毛髮。

(✗) ❹ **These books turned wet after the rain.** 下過雨後，這些書變濕了。

(✗) ❺ **I want to become a teacher.** 我想成為一位老師。

ANSWER 1. (✓)   2. (✗)   3. (✗)   4. (✓)   5. (✗)

主詞+連綴動詞+主詞補語（形容詞、名詞）結構中的連綴動詞不能表達完整的句意，其後需接主詞補語來補充說明，這類主詞補語主要有名詞和形容詞。連綴動詞可根據含義的不同而分為表示狀態、表示結果或轉變的連綴動詞。

一、表示狀態的主詞+連綴動詞+主詞補語（形容詞、名詞）結構：

表示狀態的連綴動詞有：look（看起來）、appear（顯得）、seem（看起來）、feel（摸起來）、taste（嘗起）、smell（聞起來）、remain（仍然是）、sound（聽起來）、stay（保持）、keep（保持）

• **The desk looks very old.** 這張桌子看起來很舊。

• **Only the fish tastes delicious on the table.** 桌子上只有這道魚嘗起來很可口。

• **The coat feels like satin.** 這件外套摸起來很像綢緞。

二、表示結果或轉變的主詞+連綴動詞+主詞補語（形容詞、名詞）結構：

表示結果或轉變的連綴動詞有：be（是），become（成為），grow（成長），go（變得），turn（變得），prove（證明）

• **The little boy wants to become a scientist in the future.**
這個小男孩將來想成為一名科學家。

• **It gets darker and darker, but his parents haven't come home yet.**
天越來越黑了，但是他的父母還沒有回家。

• **Maple leaves turn red instead of yellow in autumn.**
楓葉在秋天變紅而不是變黃。

隨手練一練

一、找出下列句子中的主詞、連綴動詞、主詞補語(形容詞、名詞)，並翻譯整個句子。

1. They grew apart after graduation.
2. He says, "My mother is an art teacher."
3. Several young men are interested in playing basketball.
4. Her father is fifty years old, and looks very young.
5. Her voice sounds very nice.

二、找出下面這段話中主詞＋動詞（一般動詞，非be動詞），後面無需受詞或補語結構的句子。

There was a suitcase at the door last night. It was missing this morning because my mother brought it to the airport. My mother is a manager of a food company and she often goes on a business trip. Since she was promoted to manager, she has become busier. I hope my mother can accompany me as often as possible.

ANSWER

一、

√1. **They grew apart** after graduation. 畢業後他們的關係疏遠了。

2. He says, "**My mother is an art teacher.**" 他說：「我媽媽是一位美術老師。」

3. **Several young men are interested in playing basketball.** 他們中的幾個年輕人對打籃球很感興趣。

4. **Her father is fifty years old**, and **looks very young.** 她爸爸 50 歲了，看起來很年輕。

5. **Her voice sounds very nice.** 她的聲音聽起來很好聽。

二、

There was a suitcase at the door last night. <u>It was missing</u> this morning because my mother brought it to go to the airport. <u>My mother is a manager</u> of a food company and she often goes on a business trip. Since she was promoted to manager, <u>she has become busier</u>. I hope my mother can accompany me as often as possible.

4. 主詞＋動詞＋雙受詞

考考你的眼力

在含有主詞＋動詞＋雙受詞結構的句子前打√，其它的句子前打×。

(√) ❶ These students bought their teacher a batch of flowers.
這些學生給他們的老師買了一束花。

(×) ❷ His father asked him to do homework first. 他爸爸要求他先寫作業。

(×) ❸ We call the boy little Tom. 我們稱這個小男孩為小湯姆。

(×) ❹ The man behind the tree saw his son coming out the school.
在樹後面的男人看到他兒子從學校出來了。

(√) ❺ My brother gave me a bottle of juice. 我哥哥給了我一瓶果汁。

ANSWER 1. (√) 2. (×) 3. (×) 4. (×) 5. (√)

知識大放送

在主詞＋動詞＋雙受詞結構中，動詞後一般接間接受詞和直接受詞來使句意表達完整。其中，間接受詞一般指代表人的受詞，而直接受詞指代表物的受詞。

一、間接受詞位於直接受詞前

可用在此結構中的動詞一般有：give（給）、buy（買）、show（指示）、bring

（帶來）、get（幫某人弄到）、pass（遞給）、pay（支付）、tell（告訴）、teach（教）等。

- **The woman always buys her daughter beautiful skirts.**
  這位女士總是給她女兒買漂亮的裙子。
- **Can you bring me a comic book?** 你能幫我帶一本漫畫書嗎？
- **Get me a cup of coffee, please.** 請給我一杯咖啡。
- **Her mother teaches her English and her father teaches her math.**
  她媽媽教她英文，她爸爸教她數學。

二、間接受詞位於直接受詞後
❶ 在此類結構中，間接受詞前加介系詞。

(1)間接受詞前加介系詞for
可用在此類結構中的動詞有：buy（買）、make（做）、play（演奏）、choose（選擇）、do（做）、order（訂購）等。

- **He made a kite for his youngest daughter.** 他為小女兒做了一個風箏。
- **I think you can choose the red coat for your mother.**
  我覺得你可以為你媽媽選這件紅色的大衣。
- **He played the piano for his girlfriend again and again.**
  他一遍遍地為女朋友彈鋼琴。

(2)間接受詞前加介系詞to
可用在此類結構中動詞有：give（給）、bring（帶來）、tell（告訴）、sell（賣）、leave（留給）、show（出示）、write（寫）、send（送給）等。

- **I will bring my notebook to you tomorrow.** 我明天會把筆記電腦帶給你。
- **The owner of the house sold it to a couple.** 房子的主人把它賣給了一對夫婦。
- **He remembered that his father left some money to him.** 他記得父親給他留了一些錢。

❷ 直接受詞是 them 或 it
- **Maybe he won't lend it to us.** 也許他不會把它借給我們。
- **The rich man bought them for his wife.** 這個富人為他的妻子買下了它們。
- **You must order it for one of your friends.** 你一定要為你的一位朋友訂購它。

三、雙受詞和受詞補語的區別
在主詞+動詞+雙受詞結構中，兩個受詞是並列的；而受詞補語是對受詞所做的補充，受詞和補語之間有主詞與受詞的邏輯關係。

- **They elected me the monitor.** （受詞補語）他們選我當班長。
- **He showed the card to the clerk.** （雙受詞）他向店員出示了卡。

一、找出下列句子中的主詞、動詞，標明間接受詞和直接受詞，並翻譯整個句子。

1. Before going out, he did the housework for his mother.
2. The old man returned the wallet to the guy who lost it.
3. Jack wrote his friend an e-mail after he won the game.
4. He would pass it to me if necessary.
5. The waiter got the customer a cup of hot water instead of beer.

二、找出下面這段話中的主詞＋動詞＋雙受詞結構的句子。

James is writing a report. His boss, Julia, gave him a schedule form. James received it and had a conversation with Julia. They talked about the products sales of last month. James showed Julia the data on his computer and Julia wasn't satisfied with them. James explained the reason to her. They decided to have a meeting next Monday. James said he would hand the report to her as soon as possible.

ANSWER

一、

1. Before going out, **he did** the housework for his mother.（間：his mother，直：housework）出門前，他為媽媽做了家事。
2. **The old man returned** the wallet to the young man who lost it.（間：the young man who lost it，直：the wallet）老人把錢包還給了年輕的失主。
3. **Jack wrote** his friend an e-mail after he won the game.（間：his friend，直：an e-mail）傑克贏了比賽後給朋友寫了一封電郵。
4. **He would pass** it to me if I need.（間：me，直：it）如果我需要，他會把它遞給我的。
5. **The waiter got** the customer a cup of hot water instead of beer.（間：the customer，直：a cup of hot water）服務生給客人拿了一杯熱水而不是啤酒。

二、

James is writing a report. His boss, <u>Julia, gave him a schedule form</u>. James received it and had a conversation with Julia. They talked about the product sales of last month. <u>James showed Julia the data</u> on his computer and Julia wasn't satisfied with them. <u>James explained the reason to her</u>. They decided to have a meeting next Monday. James said <u>he would hand her the report</u> as soon as possible.

5. 主詞＋動詞＋複合受詞

在含有主詞 + 動詞+複合受詞結構的句子前打✓，其它的句子前打✕。

( )❶ **I won't allow you to go ranning when it rains.** 我不會允許你在下雨的時候跑步。

( )❷ **He wants a car model.** 他想要一個汽車模型。

( )❸ **The teacher lets two students read the text.** 老師讓兩位學生讀課文。

( )❹ **Do you really like the movie made by the famous director?**
你真的喜歡這位知名導演執導的這部電影嗎？

( )❺ **They often called me "fool" when I was five years old.**
我五歲的時候，他們經常叫我「傻瓜」。

ANSWER 1. (✓) 2. (✕) 3. (✓) 4. (✕) 5. (✓)

受詞 + 受詞補語就是複合受詞，在主詞+ 動詞 + 受詞 + 受詞補語結構中，受詞補語的作用是讓整個句子的意思更加完整。動詞在這個句型結構中也可稱為「不完全及物動詞」（除了需要受詞外，還需要補語才能表示完整意思的動詞）。

「不完全及物動詞」有：call（稱呼）、wish（希望）、keep（保持）、let（使）、allow（允許）、want（想要）、feel（感覺到）、find（發現）、make（使）、ask（要求）、tell（告訴）、think（認為）等。

• **I wish you a happy life!** 祝你們生活愉快！

• **They want us to follow their order completely.** 他們要我們完全聽命於他們。

• **My parents always tell me to study hard.** 我父母總是告訴我要好好學習。

一、受詞補語的構成

❶ 在此類結構中，能充當受詞補語的一般是名詞、形容詞、副詞、分詞或片語、介系詞片語和不定詞 (to + 原形動詞)。

• **Most people consider his behavior immoral.** 多數人認為他的行為不道德。

• **My mom told me not to ride a bike on the street.**
媽媽叫我不要在街上騎自行車。

• **When we got there, we only found a baby crying.**
當我們到達那裡時，只發現一名嬰兒在大哭。

• **The clown made the children very happy.** 小丑讓孩子們很開心。

• **My parents asked me to wait for them.** 我爸媽叫我等他們。

❷ 句中有使役動詞 make（使）、let（讓）、have（讓）及感官動詞 see（看到）、hear（聽）等時，to 必須省略。

- She had her husband buy the movie ticket for her. 她叫先生幫她買電影票。
- Who made him clean the whole yard? 是誰叫他打掃整個院子的？
- The headmaster let three Chinese teachers organize the exam.
  校長讓三位語文老師籌備這次的考試。

二、主詞 + 動詞 + it + 形容詞 + to + 真正受詞

❶ it 放在受詞的位置，則受詞補語一起放在後面。

- I think it hard to learn two foreign languages at the same time.
  我認為同時學習兩種外語很困難。
- They all believe it difficult to make the dream come true.
  他們都相信實現這個夢想很難。
- Someone said it unlikely that they will finish the task.
  有人說他們不太可能完成這個任務。

❷ 現在分詞或片語是真正的主詞時，如果其補語是 no point, no use, no sense, useless, senseless 等，it 作虛受詞。

- He felt it useless trying to explain it to his wife.
  他認為跟妻子解釋這件事情是沒有用的。
- She considered it no use arguing with her boss.
  她認為跟上司爭辯是沒有用的。
- I found it senseless that this celebration was full of controversies.
  我發現這個慶祝活動充滿爭議，是很沒意義的。

 隨手練一練

一、找出下列句子中的主詞、動詞、受詞、受詞補語，並翻譯整個句子。
1. Their wonderful performance made all the audiences laugh.
2. All her friends thought her mad for giving up such a good job.
3. Only Amanda heard someone singing.
4. My mom always asks me to keep my room clean.
5. We believe it necessary to make a plan first.

二、找出下面這段話中的主詞 + 動詞 + 複合受詞結構的句子。
Climate change has an increasingly negative impact worldwide. The United Nations encourages every country to take measures. In our country, everyone is told to protect environment and not to litter. Teachers ask us not to use disposable chopsticks. Now, our parents and teachers often praise us for our behavior.

複合句

1. 名詞子句

考考你的眼力

在含有名詞子句的句子前打√，其它的句子前打×。

( ) ❶ I don't know what he is doing. 我不知道他在做什麼。

( ) ❷ Did you see the man who is in red? 你看見這個穿紅衣的男人了嗎？

( ) ❸ He mentioned the fact that you made a mistake. 他提到你犯錯的事實。

( ) ❹ It's a pity that she missed the game. 遺憾的是她錯過了比賽。

( ) ❺ If they don't agree, we will cancel the contract.
如果他們不同意，我們就取消契約。

( ) ❻ What they are holding is a litter bin. 他們拿的是廢紙箱。

( ) ❼ He got up early so that he could catch up with the bus.
為了趕上公車，他起得很早。

( ) **❽ The woman wears a colorful coat, which attracts people's attention.**
這位女士穿了一件鮮艷的外套，吸引了人們的注意。

ANSWER 1. (✓) 2. (✗) 3. (✓) 4. (✓) 5. (✗) 6. (✓) 7. (✗) 8. (✗)

知識大放送

名詞子句分為主詞子句、受詞子句、同位語子句和述語子句。（述語：用以描述主詞的行為或狀態，常用動詞擔任，一般置於主詞之後。）

一、主詞子句

顧名思義，主詞子句就是在句中充當主詞的子句，這類子句的引導詞有：關係代名詞what, whichever, whoever, whatever，連接副詞when, why, how, where，以及連接詞whether和that。

❶ that引導的主詞子句這類子句可以用it來代替真正的主詞（that子句），作為虛主詞。that子句要放在後面。如果that引導的主詞子句位於句首，that不能省略。

• **It's true (that) they realized their goal within three months.**
  他們在三個月內實現了目標，這是真的。
• **That he was absent from the meeting is a rumor.**
  他缺席會議的事情是個謠言。

❷ whether 引導的主詞子句whether引導的主詞子句通常位於句首，也可以用it作虛主詞，而whether子句置後。

• **Whether he can pass the exam is unknown yet.**
  他是否能通過考試還不得而知。
• **It's doubtful whether the team can win the final fame.**
  這支隊伍能否贏得決賽，仍有相當疑慮。
• **Whether the city should develop tourism is not decided.**
  這個城市是否要發展旅遊並還沒有決定。

❸ 連接代名詞引導的主詞子句

• **What they said is against the chairman's idea.**
  他們說的話與主席的想法相反。
• **It is important to review what you learn in the class.**
  你把在課堂學到的東西再覆習一次，這很重要。
• **You should forget whatever you saw yesterday.**
  不管你昨天看到什麼，都應該把它忘掉。
• **Whoever is late will be scolded by the teacher.** 無論誰遲到都會被老師罵。

❹ 疑問副詞引導的主詞子句

• **When the man was killed was a mystery.**
  這個男人什麼時候被殺死的，成了一個謎團。

- **Where they will spend their honeymoon is known by all.**
  所有人都知道他們要去哪裡度蜜月。
- **How to make a complete song is very difficult for her.**
  如何製作一首完整的歌曲對她來説非常困難。

❺ 用 it 作虛主詞的主詞子句
- **It's necessary that we should prepare for the coming holiday.**
  為即將到來的假期做些準備是有必要的。
- **It is thought that there are 200 countries in the world.**
  人們認為世界上有兩百個國家。
- **It is said that the president will visit another country next month.**
  據説主席下個月要訪問另一個國家。
- **It must be pointed out that these data are useless for research.**
  必須指出的是這些數據對研究沒用

二、受詞子句
受詞子句是在句子中充當受詞的子句，它的引導詞有：從屬連接詞that, whether, if；關係代名詞what, who, whom, which；連接副詞when, why, where, how。

❶ 從屬連接詞引導的受詞子句
- **The tall player said (that) he had won five championships.**
  這個高大的運動員説他已經贏了 5 個冠軍。
- **I don't know whether it will rain or not.** 我不知道是否要下雨。
- **We wonder if you could change a seat with us.**
  我們想知道你能否和我們換座位。
註：whether 和 if 引導受詞子句時，有時可以互換，有時只能用 whether，而不能用 If。

❷ 關係代名詞引導的受詞子句
- **I don't care what they said.** 我不在乎他們説了什麼。
- **It's very important who will teach Grade 5.** 誰教 5 年級都很重要。
- **She would like to choose whichever has a beautiful diamond on it.**
  她會選擇上面有鑽石的任何東西。

❸ 連接副詞引導的受詞子句
- **Only the professor can explain how to do the experiment.**
  只有教授能解釋如何做實驗。
- **Can you tell me where I can find the correct answer?**
  你能告訴我在哪裡可以找到正確答案嗎？
- **They haven't decided when to start the huge project.**
  他們還沒有決定什麼時候開始這個巨大的工程。

❹ 受詞子句的特殊情況：
如果主要子句是一般現在式，且主要子句的主詞是第一人稱，其後動詞是感知動詞（think, believe, suppose, consider, expect, imagine 等），那麼子句的否定詞需要移動到主要子句中。

- **I don't think you are doing the right thing.** 我認為你做得不對。
- **I don't believe you have failed the exam.** 我不相信你考砸了。
- **We don't expect they can run the restaurant well.**
  我們預料，他們無法把餐廳經營好。

三、同位語子句

同位語子句是對修飾的名詞進行解釋説明的子句，其引導詞有：連接詞that, whether；關係代名詞what, whatever, which, who, whom；連接副詞how, when, why, where。

下列抽象名詞後常常跟同位語子句：
idea（主意）、answer（答案）、fact（事實）、news（消息、新聞）、belief（信仰）、order（命令）、suggestion（建議）、advice（建言）、problem（問題）、promise（承諾）等。

❶ 連接詞引導的同位語子句

- **He remembered the matter that someone broke the window.**
  他記起了有人打碎玻璃的事情。
- **Did you hear the news that he was admitted by one of the top universities in the UK?** 你聽説他被一流大學錄取的消息了嗎？
- **No one gave any advice about whether the meeting should be held continuously.** 這個會議是否要繼續舉行，沒有人給出任何建議。

❷ 連接代名詞引導的同位語子句

- **They have no idea what they can do to help the poor.**
  他們不知道能做什麼來幫助窮人。
- **She always buys clothes that are inexpensive.** 她老是買平價的衣服。
- **She made me believe what she said was true.**
  她讓我相信她所説的話是真的。

❸ 連接副詞引導的同位語子句

- **The police had some cases where the so-called evidence was incorrect.** 警方有些案件的證據是不正確的。
- **Double Tenth is the day when we celebrate our national birthday.**
  十月十日是我們慶祝國家誕辰的日子。
- **Do you have any idea when the exhibition will start?**
  你知道展覽什麼時候開始嗎？

❹ 同位語子句的虛擬語氣用法

如果同位語子句修飾的名詞是表示「建議、勸告、命令」等名詞時，子句的動詞用虛擬語氣，即should + 動詞原形，should可省略。

- **He suggested that I (should) write a thank-you letter.**
  他建議我寫一封感謝信。
- **Their advised that we (should) leave for New York was refused.**
  他們提出我們應該前往紐約的建議被否決了

- **The boss made the order that all the staff (should) not be late every day.** 老闆下令每一位員工每天都不能遲到。

四、述語子句

述語子句一般是用來修飾主詞的，對主詞的特徵、狀態進行描述，多用在連綴動詞之後。

述語子句的連接詞有：連接詞that, whether，連接詞組as if, as though，連接代名詞who, whom, whose, what, which，連接副詞when, why, how, where, why, because。

❶ 連接詞引導的述語子句

- **It seems that they are going to merge with another company.**
  他們似乎要和另外一家公司合併。
- **The problem is whether we can invest in real estate without risks.**
  問題是我們能否無風險地投資房地產。
- **Her thought is that she could borrow some money from her friends.**
  她的想法是她可以從朋友那裡借一些錢。

註：引導述語子句時，whether 不能用 if 代替。

❷ 連接詞組引導的述語子句

- **It looks as if it is going to rain.** 看起來好像要下雨了。
- **It looks as if the children dislike him.** 看起來孩子們好像不喜歡他。
- **It sounds as though someone is running towards the classroom.**
  聽起來好像有人在向教室跑過來。

❸ 連接代名詞引導的述語子句

- **This is what I want to do in the future.** 這是我將來想做的事情。
- **This is whom my friend talked with yesterday.** 這就是我朋友昨天交談的人。
- **This is whose book I want to borrow.** 這就是我想借的那本書。

❹ 連接副詞引導的述語子句

- **This is where she will work.** 這就是她將要工作的地方。
- **That is why you are not allowed to enter the hall.**
  那就是你為什麼不能進禮堂的原因。
- **The problem is when they can afford a house.**
  問題是他們什麼時候能　買得起房子。

❺ 述語子句的虛擬語氣用法

如果述語子句修飾的主詞是表示「建議、命令、勸告」的名詞，那麼子句的動詞應用虛擬語氣，即should + 原形動詞，should可省略。

- **The man's order that everyone (should) not be allowed to leave the building was neglected.** 這位男士命令，每個人都不能離開大樓，被忽視了。
- **The teacher's advice is that we (should) practice a lot.**
  老師的建議是我們應該多做練習。

- **His plan is that we (should) spend the holiday at seaside.**
  他的計畫是我們到海邊度假。

隨手練一練

一、找出下列句子中的名詞子句，並翻譯整個句子。
1. I think he should be responsible for this accident.
2. The elder advised that they should irrigate the fields at once.
3. Whether he will come is not my concern.
4. His father gave him advice before death that he should be patient.
5. The trouble is that our car is running out of gas.

二、找出下面這段話中的名詞子句。
Due to serious environmental pollution, many countries have taken strict measures, such as plastic and vehicle limit order. Some people think that this is not very helpful to protect the environment, because many people will not abide by the law. Some countries have imposed serious penalties on those who violate the plastic limit order so as to reduce pollution. The problem is that this can't improve the environment fundamentally. Some experts gave the suggestions that advanced countries should develop new technologies to create alternative energy sources. Whether it can be successful depends largely on the country's comprehensive strength.

ANSWER

一、
1. I think **he should be responsible for this accident**.
   我認為他應該為這次事故負責。
2. The elder's advised **that they should irrigate the fields** at once.
   這位年長者的建議是他們應該馬上灌溉農田。
3. **Whether he will come** is not my concern. 他是否會來不是我所關心的。
4. His father gave him advice before death **that he should be patient**.
   父親生前經常建議他要有耐心。
5. The trouble is **that our car is running out of gas**.
   麻煩的是我們的車子快沒油了。
二、
Due to serious environmental pollution, many countries have taken strict measures, such as plastic and vehicle limit order. Some people think <u>that this is not very helpful</u> to protect the environment, because many people will not abide by the law. Some countries have imposed serious penalties on those who violate the plastic limit order so as to reduce pollution. The problem is <u>that this can't improve the environment</u> fundamentally. Some experts gave the suggestions <u>that advanced countries should develop new technologies</u> to create alternative energy sources. <u>Whether it can be successful</u> depends largely on the country's comprehensive strength.

2. 形容詞子句

在含有形容詞子句的句子前打√，其它的句子前打╳。

( ) ❶ He didn't notice the news that a factory exploded.
　　他沒有注意到這則工廠爆炸的新聞。

( ) ❷ No one saw the man who is in the picture. 沒有人看見照片上的人。

( ) ❸ My parents' suggestion is that I go to a local university.
　　我父母的想法是我應該上一所本地的大學。

( ) ❹ I haven't been to the place where he was born. 我沒有去過他出生的地方。

( ) ❺ I don't think the machine can work now. 我覺得現在這台機器壞了。

ANSWER 1. (╳) 2. (√) 3. (╳) 4. (√) 5. (╳)

知識大放送

在複合句中修飾名詞、代名詞或主要子句的句子就是形容詞子句，而被修飾的詞就是先行詞，通常位於形容詞子句前。引導形容詞子句的關係詞有：關係代名詞 who, whom, that, which, whose，關係副詞 when, where, why。

一、關係代名詞引導的形容詞子句
❶ 指人的關係代名詞引導的形容詞子句
- The headmaster who wears a beard is my father. 長着鬍子的校長是我爸爸。
- The girl whom I talked to yesterday just returned from abroad.
  我昨天交談的女孩剛從國外回來。
- I saw a little boy that was riding on an adult bike.
  我看見一個小男孩在騎成人腳踏車。

註：關係代名詞 that 和 who 在形容詞子句中做主詞時，可以互換。that 和 whom 在形容詞子句中做受詞時可以省略。

❷ 指物的關係代名詞引導的形容詞子句
- Did you see the tree that stands in front of our school?
  你看見我們學校前的那棵樹了嗎？
- He cancelled the meeting which was going to be held at six.
  他取消了要在六點舉行的會議。
- They decorated the house which was bought two weeks ago.
  他們裝修了兩週前買的房子。

二、關係副詞引導的形容詞子句
- I often think of the days when I spent the holiday in Paris.
  我經常想起在巴黎度假的日子。

- **He drove me to the airport where I will take the flight.**
  他開車帶我去了機場,我要在那裡搭飛機。
- **You'd better give the reason why you didn't pick him up at the school.**
  你最好解釋一下你沒有去學校接他的原因。

註:關係副詞有時可引導形容詞子句修飾一些抽象名詞,如 situation 情況、condition 情況、case 情況等。

- **They are in a situation where they are in danger.** 他們處於非常危險的處境。

三、介系詞＋關係代名詞引導的形容詞子句

如果關係代名詞在形容詞子句中充當介系詞的受詞,子句多由「介系詞 + 關係代名詞」來引導,這種情況也可用在關係副詞引導的形容詞子句中。

- **She forgot to bring a novel for which her classmate asked.**
  她忘記帶她同學想要的小説了。
- **Tom went to the library in which / where he met his old friend.**
  湯姆去了圖書館,在那裡他遇見了老朋友。
- **We will never forget the day on which they gave us a surprise.**
  我們永遠也不會忘記那天他們給我們的驚喜。

四、限制形容詞子句和非限制形容詞子句

在限制形容詞子句中,修飾的先行詞有限定的作用,若被去掉後,句子的意思會不完整;在非限制形容詞子句中,修飾的先行詞沒有絕對限定的作用,去掉後並不影響句子的意思。

❶ 限制形容詞子句

限制形容詞子句中的關係詞,在充當形容詞子句的受詞時可省略,可以使用 that。

- **He is the smartest man (that / who) I've ever seen.** 他是我見過最聰明的人。
- **This is the only kite that he made by all efforts.**
  這是他唯一盡全力製作的風箏。
- **It is a city that is famous for its tourism.** 這是一座因觀光業而聞名的城市。

❷ 非限制形容詞子句

非限制形容詞子句,它的關係詞不能是that,在作形容詞子句的受詞時不能省略,且who不能代替whom。

- **She left the banquet early, which is a pity.**
  她早早離開了宴會,這是一件令人遺憾的事。
- **The man married the woman, whom he knew for many years.**
  男士和女士結婚了,他認識她很多年。
- **He is a hard-working man, as is known to us all.**
  我們都知道,他是一個勤奮的人。

❸ 限制形容詞子句只能使用關係詞 that 的情況

(1) 先行詞是不定代名詞,或被 every, a little, no, some, little, few, much, any, each 等修飾。

(2) 先行詞既包含人，又包含事和物。

(3) 先行詞被序數詞、形容詞的最高級，或 the only, the same, the very 等修飾。

(4) 關係詞在形容詞子句中作述語。

- **He said something that is very important to the meeting.**
  他說了一些對會議非常重要的事情。

- **We saw the man and the dog that are walking towards us.**
  我們看見了向我們走來的這個人和這條狗。

- **There is no doubt that he is the last one that was praised by the teacher.** 毫無疑問，他是最後被老師表揚的。

- **The man is no longer the one that he was ten years ago.**
  這個人不再是十年前的他了。

❹ **關係代名詞 as 和 which 引導形容詞子句的區別**

(1) which 在形容詞子句中作指示代名詞，修飾前述的句子。

- **The department has been withdrawn, which is a good thing.** 這個部門被撤消了，這是一件好事。

- **More and more young men are unemployed, which is normal.** 越來越多的年輕人失業了，這很正常。

- **He can definitely get the highest score, which is beyond doubt.** 他肯定能得到最高分，這是毋庸置疑的。

(2) as 引導的非限制形容詞子句在複合句中的位置靈活，而 which 引導的非限制形容詞子句只能位於主要子句之後。

- **As is known to all, the Great Wall is a Chinese ancient building.**
  眾所皆知，長城是中國的古建築。

- **The shape of the moon is changeable, which is a natural phenomenon.**
  月亮的形狀是多變的，這是一個自然現象。

- **America, as we all know, is a developed country.**
  眾所皆知，美國是一個已開發國家。

(3) 先行詞被 the same, such 修飾時，只能用 as 來作形容詞子句的引導詞。

- **He said the same words as you said before.** 他說了和你以前說過同樣的話。

- **There is such a big pool as we can swim in.**
  有一個這麼大的水池，我們可以在裡面游泳。

- **Last year, I bought the same dress as you had.**
  去年我買了和你的裙子一樣的裙子。

隨手練一練

一、找出下列複合句中的形容詞子句，並翻譯整個句子。
1. They denied the fact that they made a mistake during the experiment.
2. The old man refused their help, which is quite strange.

3. Many people are not willing to return to the building in which they have worked.
4. Do you believe this person who always tells lies?
5. The way that you treat your child gives me a fright.

二、找出下面這段話中的形容詞子句。
Do you know your blood type? Blood means each individual's unique genes. As we all know, if people need blood transfusion due to accidents, the doctor will choose the blood of the same blood type. The patient's body will quickly accept the blood instead of rejection. That's the reason why the blood type is so important. Normal adults that have normal weight can donate some blood each year, but not all people are qualified for blood donation. Those who weigh less than 50 kg are not allowed to donate blood.

ANSWER

一、
1. They denied the fact **that they made a mistake** during the experiment.
他們否認了在實驗中犯錯的事實。
2. The old man refused their help, **which is quite strange**.
老人拒絕了他們的幫助,這很奇怪。
3. Many people are not willing to return to the building **in which they have worked**. 很多人不願意回到他們曾工作過的大樓裡。
4. Do you believe this person **who always tells lies**? 你相信這個總是說謊的人嗎?
5. The way **that you treat your child** gives me a fright.
你對待孩子的方式讓我感到害怕。
二、
Do you know your blood type? Blood means each individual's unique genes. <u>As we all know</u>, if people need blood transfusion due to accidents, the doctor will choose the blood of the same blood type. The patient's body will quickly accept the blood instead of rejection. That's the reason <u>why the blood type is so important</u>. Normal adults <u>that have normal weight</u> can donate some blood each year, but not all people are qualified for blood donation. Those <u>who weigh less than 50 kg</u> are not allowed to donate blood.

3. 副詞子句

考考你的眼力

在含有副詞子句的句子前打√，其它的句子前打×。

( ) ❶ You'd better take an umbrella in order to avoid the rain. 為了避雨，你最好帶一把傘。

( ) ❷ If you don't agree, they won't sign the contract.
如果你不同意，他們不會簽契約。

( ) ❸ I was talking online with my pen pal when my father came in.
爸爸過來的時候，我正在和網友聊天。

( ) ❹ I will remind you what you should do. 我會提醒你應該怎麼做。

( ) ❺ Although the meeting was cancelled, they didn't get off work on time.
雖然會議取消了，但是他們還是沒有按時下班。

( ) ❻ Mr. Smith told us he couldn't attend the activity because of the rain.
史密斯先生告知我們因為下雨，不能前來參加活動了。

( ) ❼ Some of the research projects were cancelled because they didn't have enough funds. 因為經費不足，一些研究被取消了。

( ) ❽ She often goes to the place where her grandfather lives.
她經常去爺爺居住的地方。

ANSWER 1. (×) 2. (√) 3. (√) 4. (×) 5. (√) 6. (×) 7. (√) 8. (×)

知識大放送

副詞子句，顧名思義就是在複合句中充當副詞的子句，其作用是修飾動詞、非述語動詞、副詞、修飾語或整個句子。引導副詞子句的詞一般是從屬連接詞和有連接詞作用的詞。根據子句表達的不同含義，副詞子句可分為八個類別，即：條件副詞子句、時間副詞子句、地點副詞子句、目的副詞子句、結果副詞子句、原因副詞子句、讓步副詞子句和狀態副詞子句。

一、條件副詞子句

引導條件副詞子句的詞主要有：if（如果），as / so long as（只要），in case（如果），on condition that（條件是），if only（但願），only if（只要），unless（除非），providing / provided that（假如）

❶ if 引導的條件副詞子句

if引導條件副詞子句時，子句的述語動詞通常只用一般現在式和現在完成式，其主句的述語動詞可用現在式、過去式和將來式。if引導的條件副詞子句可位於主要子句的前後。

- **If you have finished the work, you could leave as soon as possible.**
  如果你完成了工作，就可以盡快離開。
- **They won't go out if it continues to rain.** 如果繼續下雨，他們不會出去。
- **If they miss the train, I will drive them to the station.**
  如果他們錯過了火車，我會開車帶他們去車站。

❷ unless 引導的條件副詞子句

unless意為「除非」，語氣較強，相當於if ... not，有時兩者可互換。

- **You'd better work hard unless you don't want to pass the exam.**
  你最好努力學習，除非你不想通過考試。
- **He will solve the difficult problem if I can't.**
  如果我不能解決，他就會解決這個棘手的問題。
- **They can't get there before ten in the evening unless they take the plane.** 他們不可能在晚上十點前到達，除非他們乘坐飛機。

❸ as / so long as 引導的條件副詞子句

- **She can make her dream come true as / so long as she makes up her mind.** 只要她下決心，她就會實現夢想。
- **As / So long as you promise to give us a discount, we will increase the order.** 只要你們承諾 予我們折扣，我們就會增加訂單量。
- **They will deliver the goods at once as / so long as they receive the deposit.** 只要他們收到訂金，他們就會馬上出貨。

❹ on condition that, providing / provided that 等引導的條件副詞子句

- **Her mother will award her a car on condition that she will be admitted by a famous university.** 她媽媽會獎勵她一輛車，條件是她考上名校。
- **Providing / provided that it clears up tomorrow, they intend to go climbing.** 假如明天放晴，他們打算去爬山。
- **These books can be renewed for a further two weeks provided that no one else has reserved them.**
  如果沒有其他人預約這些書，你可以再續借兩個星期。

❺ if only, only if 引導的條件副詞子句

if only引導的條件副詞子句，通常要用虛擬語氣；而only if表示的是現實中的某種情況，位於句首時，主詞與動詞部分倒裝。

- **If only it would become cool.** 如果天氣變涼就好了。
- **Only if it is autumn can the leaves fall from trees.**
  只有到了秋天，樹葉才會從樹上落下。
- **If only I were smart enough.** 如果我夠聰明就好了。

二、時間副詞子句

引導時間副詞子句的詞有：when（什麼時候），as（當），while（而），after（在……之後），before（在……之前），since（自從），as soon as（只要……就），by the time（到……時），till / until（直到）。

❶ when, as, while 引導的時間副詞子句

- **When they came home, they found the key missing.**
  他們回到家的時候，發現鑰匙 了。
- **The bird flew away as the boy tried to hit it.**
  當小男孩試圖攻擊的時候，小鳥飛走了。

- **The cook is making cakes while the waiter is serving.**
  服務生在服務客人的時候，廚師在做蛋糕。

❷ after 和 before 引導的時間副詞子句

- **The tree grew fast after it was watered by the rain.**
  樹被雨水澆灌後生長得很快。
- **You should knock at the door before visiting someone.**
  拜訪某人前你要先敲門。
- **Someone cried out before we made the call.** 我們打電話前有人叫了起來。

❸ since 和 by the time 引導的時間副詞子句

- **Since he left the hometown, his parents have been looking for him.**
  自從他離開家鄉，他的父母一直在找他。
- **It's been five days since my wallet was lost.** 我的錢包已經遺失五天了。
- **We will design a unique wedding dress for you by the time you get married.** 你結婚的時候我們會為你設計一件獨一無二的婚 。

註：since 引導的時間副詞子句，常和現在完成式連用；by the time 引導的時間副詞子句，其主要子句通常用一般將來式。

❹ till 和 until 引導的時間副詞子句

- **He didn't find out the truth until he saw the diary of the dead man.**
  直到他看到了死者的日記，他才找到了真相。
- **She always felt lonely till / until she got married.**
  直到結婚前，她一直感到孤獨。
- **The man sat before the door till it was night.** 這個男人在門前坐著直到深夜。

❺ as soon as, the moment, the instant, the minute, immediately, directly, instantly 等詞引導的時間副詞子句

- **She got the bad news as soon as she got back home.**
  她一回到家就得知了這個壞消息。
- **These insects flew away the moment they were found by people.**
  這些昆蟲一被人們發現就飛走了。
- **The little girl turned shy the instant she saw the stranger.**
  小女孩一看到陌生的叔叔就害羞了。

註：在 hardly / scarcely ... when 和 no sooner ... than 引導的時間副詞子句中，如果 hardly, scarcely 和 no sooner 位於句首，那麼主要子句用倒裝文法。在這類結構中，子句通常用一般過去式，而主要子句通常用過去完成式。

三、地點副詞子句

引導地點副詞子句的詞主要有：where（哪裡），anywhere（任何地方），wherever（任何地方）。

❶ where 引導的地點副詞子句

- **Where there is a forest, there are animals.** 哪裡有森林，哪裡就有動物。

- **Where the meeting will be hold, the secretary can be seen.**
  會議在哪裡舉行，秘書就會出現在哪裡。
- **Where there is a new mall, these women will go shopping there.**
  哪裡有新的商城，這些女人就去購物。

註：where 引導的地點副詞子句常常和 there 構成 where ... there ... 結構，譯為「哪裡⋯⋯，哪裡就⋯⋯」。

❷ anywhere 和 wherever 引導的地點副詞子句

anywhere和wherever引導的地點副詞子句，可位於主要子句的前後。

- **Wherever they go, they always bring their belongings.**
  不管他們去哪裡，他們總是會帶著他們的行李。
- **Don't worry, you husband will take you anywhere there is a garden.**
  不要擔心，你丈夫會帶你去任何有花園的地方。
- **Remember to call you parents everyday wherever you are.**
  無論你在哪裡，記得每天和父母打電話。

四、目的副詞子句

引導目的副詞子句的詞主要有：so that（以便），in order that（以便），for fear that（以免），in case（以防），lest（唯恐）。

❶ so that 和 in order that 引導的目的副詞子句

so that引導的目的副詞子句只能位於主要子句之後，而且子句中的動詞常常包含語態動詞；in order that引導的目的副詞子句可位於主要子句的前後。

- **They had to work overtime this month so that they could finish the sales as scheduled.** 他們這個月不得不加班以便如期完成銷售量。
- **The hospital has increased 300 beds per floor in order that every patient has a bed.** 為了讓每一位患者有床位，醫院在每層樓增加了300個床位。
- **In order that the library can be built in three months, the government employed 100 workers.** 為了能在三個月內建成圖書館，政府雇用了 100 名工人。

註：so that 引導的是目的副詞子句，而 so ... that 引導的是結果副詞子句。

❷ for fear that, in case, lest 引導的目的副詞子句

在這類目的副詞子句中，子句的述語動詞常常用虛擬語氣，即「should + 動詞原形」，should可被省略。如果不用虛擬語氣，子句一般用現在式或過去式。

- **They prepared a large sum of money for fear that the project should fail.** 他們準備了一大筆錢，唯恐這個計畫會失敗。
- **You'd better tell him about your schedule lest he should be angry.**
  你最好告訴他你的行程，以免他會生氣。
- **Her mother bought her a small-sized computer in case she couldn't carry it.** 她媽媽給她買了一臺小型電腦，以防她拿不動。

五、結果副詞子句

引導結果副詞子句的詞主要有：so ... that 如此⋯⋯以至於，such ... that 如此⋯⋯以至於。

❶ so ... that引導的結果副詞子句

在so ... that 引導的結果子句中，so是副詞，其後修飾形容詞和副詞。

- **It's so cold that they stayed at home for the whole weakened.**
  天氣太冷了，他們整個週末都待在家裡。
- **The flowers were so beautiful that we picked many.**
  這花太漂亮了以至於我們摘了很多。
- **Their performance was so wonderful that all the audience applauded.**
  他們的表演如此精彩，所有的觀眾都鼓掌了。

❷ such ... that 引導的結果副詞子句

在such ... that引導的結果副詞子句中，such是形容詞，其後修飾名詞。

- **Little Tom has such a big apple that David wants to have one too.**
  小湯姆有一個很大的蘋果，戴維也想有一個。
- **There is such heavy rain that no one is walking on the street.**
  雨如此大，沒有人在街上行走。
- **Carrie thought of such a good idea that she took action at once.**
  卡麗想到了一個如此好的主意，她馬上行動起來了。

六、原因副詞子句

引導原因副詞子句的詞主要有：because（因為），for（因為），as（因為），since（因為），now that 既然。

❶ because 和 for 引導的原因副詞子句

because是所有原因副詞引導詞中語氣最強的，可直接回答why提出的疑問。for 引導的原因副詞子句一般位於句末，有時可以和because互換。表示非直接原因時，只能用for。

- **She didn't attend the meeting because she was on a business trip.**
  她因為出差而沒有出席會議。
- **It probably rained last night for the ground is wet.**
  昨晚可能下雨了，因為地面是濕的。
- **They didn't do the work well, because / for they had limited time.**
  他們沒有把工作做好，因為他們的時間有限。

❷ as 和 since 引導的原因副詞子句

as引導的原因副詞子句語氣較弱，一般位於句首，而since引導的原因副詞子句多表示已知的原因。

- **As it was Sunday, they didn't go to work.**
  因為是星期天，所以他沒有去工作。
- **I will tell you since you want to know.** 既然你想知道，我會告訴你的。
- **You should work carefully since it's working time now.**
  既然現在是上班時間，你應該認真工作。

❸ now that 引導的原因副詞子句

now that表示的是對方已經知道的原因，和since有相似之處。

- **Now that he decides to leave, let's hold a party for him.**
  既然他決定要走，我們為他舉辦一個聚會吧。
- **Now that you have a baby, you should take good care of him.**
  既然你生了孩子，你就應該好好照顧他。
- **Now that you are going to the library, take me with you please.**
  既然你要去圖書館，那就帶我一起去吧。

七、讓步副詞子句

引導讓步副詞子句的詞主要有：though（儘管），although（儘管），as（儘管），even if（即使），even though（即使），no matter + 疑問詞或疑問詞 + 字尾ever，whether ... or not（無論……都……）。

❶ **though 和 although** 引導的讓步狀副詞子句，though和although在一般情況下可互換，但是although比though更正式，通常指的是真實的情況，而不是假設。二者都不能和but連用，但是可以和yet連用。

- **Although / though the company offers good benefits, the man decides to resign.** 儘管這家公司提供較好的福利待遇，但是這個人還是決定辭職。
- **I don't believe him although / though he behaves like a gentleman.**
  雖然他表現得像一個紳士，但是我不相信他。
- **Although you don't agree, I will stick to my opinion.**
  即使你不同意，我也會堅持我的看法。

❷ **even if 和 even though** 引導的讓步副詞子句兩者通常可互換。

- **Even if / Even though she is a woman, she didn't enjoy the special treatment.** 即使她是女人，她也沒有享受特殊的待遇。
- **We can't pass the road smoothly even if / even though it has been repaired.** 即使道路修好了，我們也無法順利通過。
- **He refused to make an apology even if / even though he was wrong.**
  即使是他錯了，他也拒絕道歉。

❸ **as 和 though** 引導的讓步副詞子句

as和though引導的讓步副詞子句中，述語和副詞可置於句首，此時子句要倒裝。

- **A child as she is, she can sing many songs.**
  儘管她是個孩子，但是她會唱很多歌。
- **Tall though he is, he couldn't install the curtain well.**
  儘管他很高，但是他也不能把窗簾安裝好。
- **Say as they would, they didn't get the support.**
  雖然他們說了，但是沒有得到支持。

❹ **no matter + 疑問詞或疑問詞 + 子尾 ever** 引導的讓步副詞子句

- **No matter what you say, I won't believe you any more.**
  不管你要說什麼，我都不會相信你了。

- **Whoever you are, you can't disturb the students.**
  不論你是誰，都不能打擾這些學生。
- **No matter when you start, you should remember the correct process.**
  不管你什麼時候開始，都要記得正確的過程。

❺ Whether ... or not 引導的讓步副詞子句
whether ... or not 引導的讓步副詞子句，意為「不論……都……」，而且or not
有時可省略。
- **Whether you believe or not, he meant no harm.**
  無論你相信與否，他沒有惡意。
- **Whether you admit the crime or not, the police will investigate you.**
  無論你承認犯罪與否，警察都會調查你。
- **Whether he is a bad guy or not, he is their son.**
  無論他是不是壞人，他都是他們的兒子。

八、狀態副詞子句
引導狀態副詞子句的詞主要有：as（像），as if（好像），as though（好
像），as ... so（正如……）。

❶ as 引導的狀態副詞子句
- **He became an athlete as his parents wanted him to be.**
  正如父母希望的一樣，他成為了一名運動員。
- **These students are doing the experiment as the professor taught them.**
  這些學生正按照教授教他們的方法做實驗。
- **Children tend to speak as their parents do.**
  孩子們總是喜歡像父母一樣說話。

❷ as if 和 as though 引導的狀態副詞子句
- **It looks as if he wants to say something.** 看起來他好像要說什麼。
- **They looked worried as though the train had left.**
  他們看起來很著急好像火車已經離開了。
- **The baby walks as if she were a duck.** 嬰兒走起來像隻鴨子。

❸ as ... so 引導的狀態副詞子句
as ... so引導的狀態副詞子句一般具有比喻意義，as通常置於句首，表示「正
如……，就像……」。
- **As we respect our parents, so should we respect our teachers.**
  就像我們尊敬父母一樣，我們也應該尊敬老師。
- **As we protect the environment, so should we protect the earth.**
  就像我們保護環境一樣，我們也應該保護地球。
- **As the earth is to us, so is water to fish.**
  正如地球對我們是重要的，水對魚也是重要的。

 隨手練一練

一、找出下列句子中的副詞子句，並翻譯整個句子。

1. She has been practicing dancing for 12 years in order that she can become a dancing artist.
2. A huge wave hit before the boat reached the coast.
3. Though three colleagues helped him with the work, he didn't finish it in time.
4. Providing that this dress hits twenty percent off, I will buy it.
5. I will go wherever you go.
6. Teddy was so sad because his dad had refused his request.

二、找出下面這段話中的副詞子句。

A $100 million deal was created at the recently concluded New York auction. It was a palace painting of the fourteenth century. Before the auction began, it had attracted the attention of many art lovers and businessmen. When the host announced that it was the next auction, the audience was boiling. The seller started at a high price as people had expected. In order that it can attract more people to participate in it, the host also put forward idea of giving other auctions for free. The man who got the painting hired dozens of bodyguards to protect it after the auction ended.

ANSWER

一、

1. She has been practicing dancing for 12 years **in order that she can become a dancing artist**. 為了成為一名舞蹈家，12 年來她一直努力練習舞蹈。

2. A huge wave hit **before the boat reached the coast**. 在那艘船抵達海岸之前，一個巨浪襲來。

3. **Though three colleagues helped him with the work**, he didn't finish it in time. 儘管有三個同事幫他做工作，他還是沒有即時完成。

4. **Providing that this dress hits twenty percent off**, I will buy it. 如果這件衣服打八折，我就會買。

5. I will go **wherever you go**. 你去哪我就去哪。

6. Teddy was so sad **because his dad had refused his request**.泰迪很難過，因為爸爸拒絕了他的請求。

二、

A $100 million deal was created at the recently concluded New York auction. It was a palace painting of the fourteenth century. <u>Before the auction began</u>, it had attracted the attention of many art lovers and businessmen. <u>When the host announced that it was the next auction</u>, the audience was boiling. The seller started at a high price <u>as people had expected</u>. <u>In order that it can attract more people to participate in it,</u> the host also put forward the idea of giving other auctions for free. The man who got the painting hired dozens of bodyguards to protect it <u>after the auction ended</u>.

 # pass 掉句子中不必要的成分

1. 副詞修飾

考考你的眼力

在下面可去掉副詞的句子前打√，其它的句子前打×。

( ) ❶ **He runs quite fast.** 他跑得相當快。

( ) ❷ **His sister likes the flower very much.** 他妹妹非常喜歡這朵花。

( ) ❸ **They never play basketball in the yard.** 他們從不在院子裡打籃球。

( ) ❹ **Linda and Lucy seldom go to school by bus.** 琳達和露西很少坐公車去學校。

ANSWER 1. (√) 2. (√) 3. (×) 4. (×)

知識大放送

副詞在句子中具有強調和說明細節的作用，其實也是一種「不必要」的成分，去掉副詞後，句子的主幹會快速呈現。副詞主要有兩種形式，即以-ly作字尾的副詞和特殊副詞。

一、Pass 掉以 -ly 作字尾的副詞

- The coach asked them to get to the training ground (quickly).
  教練要求他們快速到達訓練場所。
- The young man admitted his error (frankly).
  這個年輕人誠實地承認了自己的錯誤。
- Climate change is (widely) considered one of the most serious threats to human survival. 氣候變遷被廣泛視為是對人類生存造成最嚴重的威脅之一。

註：有些以 -ly 結尾的副詞，如：hardly（幾乎不），scarcely（簡直不），rarely（很少地）等出現在句中不能被去掉，否則會改變句子的意思。

二、Pass 掉特殊副詞

除了以 -ly 結尾的副詞，還有一些特殊副詞，如：

程度副詞 quite（相當），very（非常），much（多），so（如此），pretty（十分）時間副詞 today（今天），yesterday（昨天），tomorrow（明天），tonight（今晚），already（已經），yet（還沒）

頻率副詞 often（經常），usually（通常），always（總是），sometimes（有時）

- The children like the amusement park (very much).
  孩子們非常喜歡遊樂園。
- The boss and the secretary decide to return (tomorrow).
  老闆和秘書決定明天返回。
- He said the little girl (always) stay up (late). 他說這個小女孩總是熬夜。

註：有些形容詞可用作副詞，如 late（晚地），hard（努力地），early（早地）。但是如 however（然而）、first（第一）、seldom（很少）、never（從不）等副詞在句中不能被去掉，否則會改變句子的意思。

隨手練一練

一、找出下列句子中可被 pass 掉的副詞，並翻譯整個句子。

1. He treated the foreigners very friendly.
2. They can hardly keep awake because they slept late last night.
3. It was so cold that no one would like to go out.
4. The woman never eats out because she is in very bad condition.
5. The sales manager has already been removed.

二、找出下面這段話中可被 pass 掉副詞的句子。

Lucy and Lily are twin sisters. They look very much alike, but they have the opposite characters. Lucy is very lively and she quite likes making friends. Lily is pretty introverted and she is always afraid to speak to strangers. But both Lucy and Lily are outstanding students, and they often get top two in the exams. Their mother is proud of them.

一、

1. He treated the foreigners **very friendly**. 他對待外國人非常友好。

2. They can hardly keep awake because they slept **late last night**.
他們很難保持清醒，因為他們昨晚睡得晚。

3. It was **so** cold that no one would like to go out. 太冷了，沒人願意出門。

4. The woman never eats out because she is in **very** bad condition.
這位女士從不在外面吃飯因為她的身體狀況非常不好。

5. The sales manager has **already** been removed.
銷售部經理已經被撤職了。

二、

Lucy and Lily are twin sisters. <u>They look very much alike</u>, but they have the opposite characters. <u>Lucy is very lively and she quite likes making friends.</u> <u>Lily is pretty introverted and she is always afraid to speak to strangers.</u> But both Lucy and Lily are outstanding students, and <u>they often get top two</u> in the exams. Their mother is proud of them.

2. 介系詞＋名詞／動名詞／名詞子句

考考你的眼力

在下面可以去掉「介系詞+名詞/動名詞/名詞子句」的句子前打√，其它的句子前打×。

( )❶ **The teacher has a question about how he can do it in such a short time.** 老師有一個疑問，他是如何在這麼短的時間內做到的。

( )❷ **The man in black is watching the ants.** 穿黑衣服的男子在看螞蟻。

( )❸ **I don't know how they got in.** 我不知道他們是怎麼進去的。

( )❹ **No one knows the reason why they were arrested.**
沒有人知道他們被捕的原因。

( )❺ **They have time to see a film.** 他們有時間去看電影。

( )❻ **The lawyer is not interested in accepting this case.**
這位律師對接受這件案子不感興趣。

ANSWER 1. (√) 2. (√) 3. (×) 4. (×) 5. (×) 6. (√)

知識大放送

一個句子的核心部分一般是主詞和動詞，而介系詞+名詞/動名詞/名詞子句構成的介系詞結構可以用來表示時間、地點、狀態、工具、方法、怎麼樣等細節，這些屬於次要訊息，在理解句子時，可透過去掉這些次要訊息來理解核心意思。

一、Pass 掉介系詞 + 名詞

❶ Pass 掉一般介系詞構成的介系詞片語

一般介系詞包含：in, on, with, by, at, of, for等。

- **The two sons (of Mr. Green) like to swim (in summer).**
  格林先生的兩個兒子喜歡在夏天游泳。
- **The little girl is sleeping (on the bed) and her mother is cleaning (in the living room).** 小女孩正在床上睡覺，她的媽媽正在客廳裡打掃。
- **Mom and dad are working hard to earn more money (for me).**
  媽媽和爸爸在努力工作為我掙更多的錢。
- **She always gets the highest score (in the class) (with her learning skills).** 她用自己的學習方法總能在班上得到最高分。
- **They must be playing the games (at home).** 他們肯定在家打遊戲。

註：① one of 後接複數名詞時作主詞時，應該把 of + 複數名詞 pass 掉。
② 當一些與介系詞搭配的數字片語與複數名詞連用時，可以不用被 pass 掉，如 hundreds of, thousands of, a number of。

❷ Pass 掉特殊介系詞片語

除了我們常見的一般介系詞外，還有一些是由兩個或以上的單字構成的介系詞片語或者特殊的介系詞與名詞連用的形式，如according to（根據，按照）、like（像）、including（包含）、in addition to（除……外）、as to（關於）、such as（比如）、along with（與……一起）、with regard to（關於）等。

- **Many people come to attend the meeting, (including businessmen, teachers, professors, and artists).**
  很多人來參加這個會議，包括商人、老師、教授和藝術家。
- **Lisa dares to go to a remote place (along with her friends).**
  和朋友一起，麗莎敢去偏遠的地方。
- **She likes all kinds of music (such as pop music, classical music and rock music).** 她喜歡各式各樣的音樂，比如流行音樂、古典音樂和搖滾音樂。
- **(Thanks to their help), we could get back to the office before the rain.**
  幸虧有了他們的幫忙，我們才能在下雨前回到辦公室。

❸ Pass 掉介系詞 + 被修飾的名詞

在介系詞+名詞的結構中，名詞前可放置形容詞或代名詞。

- **The car was stuck (in a big hole).** 這輛車陷入了一個大坑裡。
- **She is the highest girl (among those girls).** 她是那群女孩中最高的。
- **The flight was delayed (due to the quite heavy fog).** 因為大霧航班延誤了。

二、Pass 掉介系詞 + 動名詞

介系詞後還常接動名詞形式，但是動名詞後也常接名詞作動名詞的受詞，在閱讀中，除了pass掉介系詞和動名詞，還要把動名詞後的名詞一起去掉。

- **They entered the dead man's house (by breaking the window).**
  他們透過打破窗戶進入了死去男子的房子。
- **The man woke up (after having a bad dream).**
  男子做了一個不好的夢就醒了。
- **She had breakfast (before walking her dog).** 她出門遛狗前，先吃了早餐。

三、Pass 掉介系詞 + 名詞子句

相較名詞和動名詞，名詞子句是更長的細節表達，一般是由疑問詞引導的，但是語序是陳述句型。

- **I don't care (about where they are going).** 我不在乎他們要去哪裡。
- **The man had a question (about why there was a red shoe on the spot).**
  這個男士有一個疑問，為什麼現場有一只紅色的鞋子。
- **Are you interested (in making kites by yourself)?**
  你對自己製作風箏感興趣嗎？

 隨手練一練

一、找出下面句子中可被 pass 掉的介系詞構成的部分，並翻譯整個句子。

1. The children like to play games in the living room.
2. The man took a long travel along with his dog.
3. Maybe only the old woman knows about where the witch is.
4. The little boy was beaten by his father with a stick.
5. You will be fined according to the law.

二、找出下面這段話中可被去掉介系詞 + 名詞 / 動名詞 / 名詞子句結構的句子。

It is getting colder and colder. This year the Johns have enough coal for the winter. The book store operated by John has a good income in the second half of the year. John's wife, Mrs. Marie has worked as a nanny in a wealthy family for three months this year, and got a lot of money. Their son just graduated from a university, and soon found a well-paid job. As for their daughter, Grace won a scholarship of $3000 this year, which can be used to subsidize the tuition.

ANSWER

一、

1. The children like to play games **in the living room.**
   孩子們喜歡在客廳裡玩遊戲。

2. The man took a long travel **along with his dog**.
   這個人和他的狗進行了一次漫長的旅行。

3. Maybe only the old woman knows **about where the witch is**.
   也許只有這位老婦人知道女巫在哪裡。

4. The little boy was beaten **by his father with a stick**.
   小男孩被父親用棍子打了。

5. You will be fined **according to the law**.
   根據法律規定，你肯定會被罰款的。

二、

It is getting colder and colder. <u>This year the Johns have enough coal for the winter</u>. <u>The book store operated by John has a good income in the second half of the year</u>. John's wife, <u>Mrs. Marie has worked as a nanny in a wealthy family for three months this year</u>, and got a lot of money. <u>Their son just graduated from a university</u>, and soon found a well-paid job. <u>As for their daughter, Grace won a scholarship of $3000 this year</u>, which can be used to subsidize the tuition.

3. 非述語動詞

考考你的眼力

在含有非述語動詞的句子前打√，其它的句子前打×。

(　) ❶ The boss decides to employ more staff. 老闆決定雇用更多的員工。

(　) ❷ They have enough time to have a perfect wedding.
        他們有足夠的時間舉辦完美的婚禮。

(　) ❸ Living abroad for long time, she has led a very different lifestyle.
        長期生活在國外，她有非常不同的生活方式。

(　) ❹ The cat hidden under the desk is her pet. 藏在桌子底下的貓是她的寵物。

(　) ❺ Perhaps they are having a meeting. 他們可能在開會。

ANSWER 1. (×) 2. (√) 3. (√) 4. (√) 5. (×)

知識大放送

非述語動詞，即在句子中不能充當述語成分的動詞，有三種形式，即：動詞不定詞（to+V）、現在分詞和過去分詞。

一、Pass 掉動詞不定詞

❶ **to + 動詞原形構成動詞不定詞。常被放置在名詞和述語後，可作補語。**

- **They only have one minute (to prepare) for the meeting.**
  他們只有一分鐘的時間來準備會議了。
- **The children are very happy (to play the game).**
  孩子們玩這個遊戲很開心。
- **There are delicious dishes for them (to eat).** 有美味的菜餚在等他們吃。

註：只有修飾名詞、述詞和整個句子的不定詞才能被去掉，如果是述語動詞後的不定詞被去掉就不能成為句子了。

❷ **Pass 掉動詞不定詞的其它情況**

動詞不定詞結構在句子中還常用作目的副詞。

- **They went there on foot (so as to save money).**
  為了省錢他們步行去了那裡。
- **(To sell this dress), she definitely tried whatever she could.**
  為了賣出這件衣服，她的確用盡了一切的方法。。
- **(To pay for the credit bills), she took a part-time job.**
  為了償還信用卡帳單，她做了一份兼職。

二、Pass 掉現在分詞形式

❶ **動詞的現在分詞位於名詞後可作後置修飾語，如果分詞後有名詞，也要被 pass 掉。**

- **There are five monkeys (looking for food).** 有五隻猴子在找食物。
- **These women (wearing formal dresses) must be stars.**
  這些穿著正式禮服的女士肯定是明星。
- **He stood there (watching the film).** 他站在那裡看電影。

❷ **Pass 掉現在分詞的其它情況**

有時，現在分詞片語用逗號與主句隔開，此時，現在分詞片語表示的是主句的附加訊息。

- **(Knowing the bad news), he made a call to his friend.**
  得知了這個壞消息，他給朋友打了電話。
- **(Sleeping late last night), he couldn't get up this morning.**
  昨晚睡得晚了，他今天早上起不來。
- **(Though being washed by its owner), the dog barked all the time.**
  儘管正在被主人洗澡，這只狗一直在叫。

三、Pass 掉過去分詞

❶ **動詞的過去分詞置於名詞後可作後位修飾詞，分詞後如果有介系詞片語，也要一併去掉。**

- **The professor asked a question (answered by no students).**
  教授提出了一個問題，沒有人回答。
- **I don't like the cake (made by this bakery).** 我不喜歡這家烘焙坊的蛋糕。

- The policeman saw the thief **(hidden among the crowd).**
  警察看見了躲藏在人群中的小偷。

2. **Pass** 掉過去分詞的其它情況

與現在分詞相同，過去分詞片語用逗號與主句隔開，表示附加訊息，連同後面的介系詞片語一併去掉。

- **(Helped by a strange man), she felt very grateful.**
  被一個陌生人幫助了，她感到非常感激。
- **(Informed just ten minutes earlier), they had no much time left.**
  在十分鐘前才得到通知，他們剩下的時間不多了。
- **(Located in the center of the city), the building can be seen at first glance.** 這座建築位於城市的中心，一眼就可以被看到。

 隨手練一練

一、找出下面句子中可被 **pass** 掉的非述語動詞結構，並翻譯整個句子。

1. There is a park around the community for people to do exercise.
2. There are ten trains running at this time.
3. Insulted by someone, he decided to find a lawyer to file a libel lawsuit.
4. The woman wearing a gold necklace is Mr. White's wife.
5. They plan to collect more money to build a school.

二、找出下面這段話中包含非述語動詞結構的句子。

On the calm lake, two ducks are swimming leisurely. Suddenly, a duck swims in the opposite direction; maybe it finds something it is interested in. The other duck doesn't notice that its partner has left, and it keeps swimming slowly on the lake. The hunter hidden from behind the trees is very glad to see the this only duck is left alone, and he is ready to shoot it with his shotgun. At that moment, the duck that is far away suddenly quacks loudly from a distance, and the duck aimed at by the hunter swims as fast as it can and escapes the danger. The hunter sighs, "What a pity!"

ANSWER

一、

1. There is a park around the community for people **to do exercise**.
   社區附近有一個公園可以讓人們鍛煉身體。
2. There are ten trains **running at this time**. 此時有十輛火車在運行。
3. **Insulted by someone**, he decided to find a lawyer to file a libel lawsuit.
   被人辱罵了，他決定找律師提出毀謗訴訟案。
4. The woman **wearing a gold necklace** is Mr. White's wife.
   那位戴著金項鏈的女士是懷特先生的妻子。

5. They plan to collect more money **to build a school**.
他們計劃募集更多的錢來建立一個學校。

二、

On the calm lake, two ducks are swimming leisurely. Suddenly, a duck swims in the opposite direction; maybe it finds something it is interested in. The other duck doesn't notice that its partner has left, and it keeps swimming slowly on the lake. <u>The hunter hidden from behind the trees is very happy to see this only duck being left alone, and he is ready to shoot it with his shotgun.</u> At that moment, the duck that is far away suddenly quacks loudly from a distance, and <u>the duck aimed at by the hunter swims as fast as it can to escape the danger.</u> The hunter sighs, "What a pity!"

4. 連接詞＋主詞＋動詞

考考你的眼力

在含有連接詞 + 主詞 + 動詞結構的句子前打√，其它的句子前打×。

( )❶ **The door bell rang when they came back.** 他們回來的時候門鈴響了。

( )❷ **I said nothing.** 我什麼也沒說。

( )❸ **Even though he is a math teacher, he can teach Chinese well.**
即使他是一個數學老師，他也可以把語文教好。

( )❹ **Since you are right, you have the final say.**
既然你是對的，你就有最終話語權。

( )❺ **Why did you say nothing at the meeting?** 為什麼你在會議上什麼也沒說？

ANSWER 1. (√) 2. (×) 3. (√) 4. (√) 5. (×)

知識大放送

「連接詞 + 主詞 + 動詞」通常指的是副詞子句，副詞子句在句子中主要起的是副詞作用，修飾整個句子，在刪選的時候，注意要pass掉整個子句。

❶ Pass 掉副詞引導的副詞子句

• **(Although there is a flaw at the bottom of the cup), it was sold at a high price.** 即使底部有一點瑕疵，這個杯子也被賣出了高價。

- It rained (before the exhibition ended). 展覽會結束前開始下雨了。
- (As he is rich), many women want to marry him.
  因為他很富有，很多女人想嫁給他。

❷ Pass 掉子句引導的副詞子句

- (Even if you are very healthy), you should do exercise.
  即使你很健康，你也應該做運動。
- (Now that you are going to get married), why don't you hold a wedding?
  既然你們要結婚了，為什麼不舉行一個婚禮呢？
- (No matter what you are doing), you should stop to have dinner.
  不管你在做什麼，你都應該停下來去吃飯。
- The car stopped (in that it was running out of gas).
  車子因為沒油而停了下來。

隨手練一練

一、找出下面句子中可被 pass 掉的連接詞＋主詞＋動詞結構，並翻譯整個
　　句子。

1. They went for a picnic after the weather cleared up.
2. He didn't answer the phone when it rang.
3. Whether it is your mistake or not, it is not important.
4. You'd better leave early if you want to get the useful information.
5. Why don't you stop to enjoy the view now that you like it?

二、找出下面這段話中包含連接詞＋主詞＋動詞結構的句子。

A zoo was built in the centre of the city. Since it was opened, the zoo has attracted a lot of tourists. Many young lovers and newly-wed couples come here. But the zoo is most popular with children, because they love the animals. By the end of last month, the zoo has been visited by 10 million tourists. If you are over 70 years old, you can get a free ticket. The tickets are half price for children while the adult ticket is $70.

ANSWER

一、

1. They went for a picnic **after the weather cleared up**.
   因為天氣放晴了，他們就去野餐了。
2. He didn't answer the phone **when it rang**. 電話響的時候他沒有接。
3. **Whether it is your mistake or not**, it is not important.
   這是不是你的錯並不重要。
4. You'd better leave early **if you want to get the useful information**.
   如果你想得到有用的訊息，最好早點出發。
5. Why don't you stop to enjoy the view **now that you like it**?
   既然你喜歡為什麼不停下來欣賞風景呢？

二、

A zoo was built in the centre of the city. <u>Since it was opened</u>, the zoo has attracted a lot of tourists. Many young lovers and newly-wed couples come here. But the zoo is most popular with children, <u>because they love the animals</u>. By the end of last month, the zoo has been visited by 10 million tourists. <u>If you are over 70 years old</u>, you can get a free ticket. The tickets are half price for children <u>while an adult ticket is $70</u>.

5. 先行詞＋關係代名詞＋動詞

考考你的眼力

在含有<u>先行詞 + 關係代名詞 + 動詞</u>結構的句子前打✓，其它的句子前打✕。

( ) ❶ I never saw the man, who was a thief. 我沒有見過這個小偷。

( ) ❷ Do you know the accident which happened last night?
你知道昨晚發生的事故嗎？

( ) ❸ This matter has nothing to do with him. 這件事情和他無關。

( ) ❹ You are really a fool. 你真是一個傻瓜。

( ) ❺ What a big boat! 好大一艘船啊！

ANSWER 1. (✓) 2. (✓) 3. (✕) 4. (✕) 5. (✕)

知識大放送

「先行詞 + 關係代名詞 + 動詞」一般指的是形容詞子句。根據先行詞的不同和形式可把形容詞子句分為三類：指人的形容詞子句、指物的形容詞子句和介系詞 + 關係代名詞引導的形容詞子句。

一、Pass 掉指人的形容詞子句

❶ Pass 掉指人的主格的形容詞子句

• They have a daughter (who has a smart brain). 他們有一個頭腦聰明的女兒。

• No one has seen the girl (whose leg is injured).
沒有人見過這個腿部受傷的女孩。

• The factory will punish those (who steal the parts).
工廠會懲罰那些偷零件的人。

❷ Pass 掉指人的受詞的形容詞子句

- She is the woman (whom my father talked with yesterday).
  她就是我爸爸昨天交談的女士。
- The boy (whom I like very much) is my aunt's son.
  這個我非常喜歡的男孩是我姑姑的兒子。
- The man (whom you saw just now) is our new teacher.
  你剛才看見的人是我們的新老師。

二、Pass 掉指事和物的形容詞子句

❶ Pass 掉句子基本的形容詞子句

- He holds a book (which was written by Mark). 他拿了一本馬克寫的書。
- They went to the lake (which is famous for the clean water).
  他們去了那個因乾淨的水而聞名的湖泊。
- He will challenge the race (which might give him an award).
  他要挑戰這個可能會給他獎勵的比賽。

❷ Pass 掉非限制形容詞子句

- Most of the students didn't pass the exam, (which made the teacher disappointed). 大多數學生沒有通過考試，讓老師很失望。
- (As is known to all), the mountain is rich in mineral resources.
  眾所皆知，這座山裡有豐富的礦產。
- This is the first time our country hosts the Olympic Games, (which makes everyone excited).
  這是我們國家第一次舉辦奧運會，這使得每一個人都很激動。

三、Pass 掉介系詞 + 關係代名詞引導的形容詞子句

介系詞 + 關係代名詞相當於關係副詞。

- The elderly will definitely like the park (in which / where) they can go for a walk. 老年人肯定喜歡這座公園，他們可以在裡面散步。
- It's ten o'clock (at which /when they will leave for the airport). 現在 10 點了，他們要出發前往機場。
- We knew the reason quickly (for which / why he didn't win the race).
  我們很快就知道了為什麼他沒有贏得比賽。

隨手練一練

一、找出下列句子中包含的先行詞 + 關係代名詞 + 動詞結構，並翻譯整個句子。

1. Many roads are being repaired at the same time, which caused inconvenience for us.
2. The model that is super famous has been married.
3. Don't harm frogs which are helpful to the farms.
4. They went to the zoo in which his kids knew a lot of animals.
5. They young man whom they want to hire has rich working experience.

二、找出下面這段話中包含<u>先行詞</u>＋<u>關係代名詞</u>＋<u>動詞</u>結構的句子。

Evan was born in a small town in southern Italy. He grew up in a happy family. His parents were very much in love. He has two sisters and a brother; they are all the persons he loves most. When Evan was 18 years old, his parents died, which made him sad for two years. This is the reason why he later wrote a book to commemorate his parents. Now Evan is 30 years old, and he got married with a French woman three years ago and had a son. He loves his son who looks like Evan's father very much.

ANSWER

一、

1. Many roads are being repaired at the same time, **which caused inconvenience for us.** 很多路同時在修，給我們造成了不便。

2. The model **that is super famous** has been married.
   這個有超高名氣的模特兒已經結婚了。

3. Don't harm frogs **which are helpful to the farms.**
   不要傷害青蛙，牠們對農田有幫助。

4. They went to the zoo **in which his kids got to know a lot of animals.**
   他們去了動物園，他的孩子在那裡認識了很多動物。

5. The young man **whom they want to hire** has rich working experience.
   他們想雇用這個有豐富工作經驗的年輕人。

二、

Evan was born in a small town in southern Italy. He grew up in a happy family. His parents were very much in love. <u>He has two sisters and a brother, who are all the persons he loves the most.</u> When Evan was 18 years old, his parents died, which made him sad for two years. <u>This is the reason why he later wrote a book to commemorate his parents</u>. Now Evan is 30 years old, and he got married with a French woman three years ago and had a son. <u>He loves his son who looks like Evan's father very much.</u>

Chapter 2 認識段落

段落的分類

1. 首句即主旨句

> **考考你的眼力** 選出下面段落中的主旨句。
>
> Yesterday was the happiest day for me. First of all, it was my birthday and I received a letter informing me that I was admitted to Harvard University, which is good news for our family. Secondly, my father was promoted to the manager, which means that he can earn more money for my family in the future. Third, my elder brother whom I have not seen for about five years flew back from abroad to celebrate the good things with us. He has been in the military school abroad. Finally, my family and I had dinner and we ate cake together; what's more, I received a lot of gifts.
>
> **ANSWER** Yesterday was the happiest day for me.

閱讀攻略

這種段落通常第一句話就會說出作者的觀點，或者總結出主要的內容，後面的內容都是在論證這個觀點，或者對主要內容進行詳細的說明。第一句話是該段落的主旨句，如果是在考試中遇到這種類型的段落，考生應該細讀第一句話，略讀其他的細節句，務必讀懂主旨句。需要注意的是，論證觀點或者詳解內容時，該類段落通常需要一系列的連接詞，使得該文理清楚、內容連貫、脈絡分明。這些連接詞有：first，then，for one thing，for another，finally，besides，moreover，one another，still another，second，also等。

隨手練一練

找出下面段落的主旨句，以及連接詞。

More and more students major in computer science at the university. On the one hand, this is because of the fact that the development of computer technology and the network piques their interest in learning computer.

They believe that the knowledge and skills they learn can help them better understand how to operate the computer. On the other hand, office automation is one of the reasons that impacts this trend. People think that work related to computer will be paid higher, and that they can find a job much easier.

ANSWER

主旨句：More and more students major in computer science at the university.
連接詞：On one hand, On the other hand

2. 句尾即主旨句

考考你的眼力 選出下面段落中的主旨句。

Last week I was in hospital due to an accident. Mike came to help me with my schoolwork every day. He always explained to me patiently to make sure that I fully understood what the teacher taught in the class. Sometimes he brought food for me because my parents were busy. I couldn't thank him enough. Mike is glad to help anyone in the class. For instance, Linda used to lag behind the class and was scolded by the teacher. As her classmate, Mike helps her study every day. He also shared with her some learning skills. When Linda got a good score in the final exam, the teacher said it was all because of Mike. Mike also helps others when he is on his way home, for example, helping the elderly cross the road. Mike is really a helpful person.

ANSWER Mike is really a helpful person.

閱讀攻略

句尾即主旨句與首句即主旨句相反，其主旨句一般位於句末，起到總結前文的作用。在這類段落中，主旨前的內容都是圍繞該主題進行事例式展開。段落中一般會提及三件或更多的事例來說明主旨。在這類段落中，提及的事例之間是並列的關係，一般沒有連接詞，但這並不妨礙對主旨的理解。在閱讀這類段落時，注意仔細辨別句首和句尾的句子，正確判斷哪一個句子是主旨句。

 隨手練一練

找出下面段落中的主旨句，以及並列事例的關鍵詞。

David's family spent the day enjoying the scenery and attended the local special dancing party in the evening. David and his brother liked diving in the sea. And their parents liked sunbathing at the beach. They also tasted a lot of Hawaii's unique fruit. They booked two double rooms in the hotel that are nearest to the sea. The French window in the room is the best place for them to enjoy the night scenery. They stayed there for seven days, and David didn't want to go back to his country. On the last day, they bought a lot of local souvenirs at a duty-free shop. This trip to Hawaii is very memorable for David's family.

ANSWER

主旨句：This trip to Hawaii is very memorable for David's family.
並列事例：spent, liked, tasted, booked, stayed, bought

3 前呼後應主旨句

考考你的眼力 選出下面段落中的主旨句。

Mark Twain is a famous American novelist. Millions of Pounds is one of his greatest literary works. His another well-known book, The Adventures of Tom Sawyer, is included in many children's reading lists. Mark Twain is very good at writing satirical works. His novels range from long, medium, to short works that contain wisdom and a great sense of humor. As is known to all, Mark Twain is a very humorous person, and anecdotes about him can be published into a book. Mark Twain can be called Lincoln in the history of American Literature.

ANSWER Mark Twain is a famous American novelist.

閱讀攻略

在前呼後應文章中，段落的首句或前兩句一般是主旨句，後面的內容一般為細節、事例或數據分析，目的是對主旨句給予支持。在段落的結尾處往往會對整段話進行總結，與開頭的主旨句相呼應。在閱讀這類段落時，首先準確理解主旨句的意思，再仔細閱讀針對該主旨展開的細節訊息。但是，這類段落的主旨句仍然是開頭的主旨句而不是結尾的總結句。

 隨手練一練

找出下面段落中的主旨句和總結句。

Around 6 yesterday evening, an explosion occurred at a restaurant in downtown Chicago. When the explosion occurred, there were about ten guests dining in the restaurant, and that didn't include the restaurant staff. The explosion also caused serious damages to other businesses nearby, and a bar in particular was badly damaged. Although the fire caused by the explosion was quickly put out, there were still casualties. A French couple were seriously injured because they were close to the explosion. An investigation shows that the explosion was due to gas leakage. The explosion has drawn people's attention to gas leakage detection and the importance of safety precaution measures.

ANSWER

主旨句：Around 6 yesterday evening, an explosion occurred at a restaurant in downtown Chicago.

總結句：The explosion has drawn people's attention to gas leakage detection and safety precaution measures.

4. 並列型段落

考考你的眼力 選出下面段落中的羅列標記。

First of all, there is a big shoe rack behind the door, and every shoe rack on each floor is filled with shoes. Across the porch, we can see a large living room about 70 square meters, and its layout is quite unique. There are two long sofas in the center of the living room with a table in front of them. In the southeast of the living room are a dining table and six chairs. On the right side of the living room is a kitchen, and the cooking utensils inside are neatly placed. On the right side of the kitchen is a large refrigerator filled with food.

ANSWER First of all, Across the porch, In the southeast, On the right

閱讀攻略

並列型段落是按照某種分類特徵進行羅列描述的敘述結構，並沒有一個固定的主旨句。通常在文中有明顯的羅列標記，如順序、方位、時間等。羅列的每一項都是並列關係。因此，根據段落中的羅列標記可快速判斷段落類型，並且對段落

整體可分條列式的方式來理解，這有助於閱讀者從大段的文字中有條理地進行閱讀。

找出下面段落中的羅列標記和對應事物。

First, our company has transnational cooperation with multiple countries. Since 2005, we have established business partnerships with dozens of developing countries, which have significantly helped us import and export commodities. Second, we have been working on the development of cutting-edge technology to improve our life. The electronic products we produced are sold at home and abroad, and they have improved the speed of the Internet. Third, we are supported by abundant capital. Finally, we have been ahead of other local enterprises in human resources, which is because we provide excellent employee benefits.

ANSWER

羅列標記：First, Second, Third, Finally

對應事物：transnational cooperation, working on the development of high technology, supported by abundant capital, ahead of other local enterprises

5. 因果型段落

考考你的眼力 找出下面段落中的主題句。

Nowadays, more and more young people prefer working in the city. The elderly and children are mostly left in the rural areas, which results in desolate land. Desolate land is not conducive to the development of agriculture, but it is a fact that rural areas lack of labor force. So the government issued the policy of return for subsidies. People who are willing to return their hometown will receive government subsidies, and it helps to stop brain drain in the rural areas.

ANSWER So the government issued the policy of return for subsidies.

閱讀攻略

因果型段落分為兩種類型：先因後果和先果後因。總的來說，因果型段落的主題句一般出現在具有總結性含義的詞語後或者是段落強調的原因或結果，如：

so（所以），therefore（因此），in a word（總而言之），thus（因此），in summary / in conclusion（綜上所述），in short / in brief（總之）等。所以在閱讀此類段落時，可首先尋找結論句（主題句）。

隨手練一練

找出下面段落中的主題句和結果。

Since the mobile phone was invented, it has greatly changed people's lives. People enjoy more convenient and faster communication. In the past, people can only write letters to express their feelings, and to wait for a long time to receive a reply. Nowadays, people can use the mobile phone to communicate with anyone they want. With the development of network, people can do many things with mobile phones, such as shopping, paying, financing, reading news and so on. The mobile phone has not only saved a lot of time for people but also helped them work more efficiently.

ANSWER

主題句：Since the mobile phone was invented, it has greatly changed people's lives.

結果：People enjoy more convenient and faster communication.

The mobile phone has not only saved a lot of time for people but also helped them work more efficiently.

6. 轉折型段落

考考你的眼力 找出下面段落中的主題句。

The horsepower of a car equipped with Germany's new engine has the maximum speed of 300 miles per house. Moreover, it consumes less fossil fuel and produces much less vehicle exhaust emissions than other cars, which is obviously conducive to environmental protection. The company that produces this type of cars claims that the car is a symbol for environmental protection. As for the price, although it is more expensive than other cars, its overall price is still high. However, the car caused some consumers much dissatisfaction because of the tail noise.

ANSWER However, the car caused some consumers much dissatisfaction because of the tail noise.

閱讀攻略

在轉折型段落中，段落一般可分為兩個部分，即：轉折前和轉折後。而在這類段落中常會遇到表示轉折的詞：but（但是），however（然而），yet（可是），while（而），on the contrary（相反）等。有時候轉折前後的句子可能並無明顯的轉折詞，但前後表達的意思相反也是轉折。轉折型段落中的主題句一般是位於轉折詞後的句子，而並不是前面的內容。

找出下面段落中的主題句並**pass**掉主題句中不必要的成分。

This painting is a great artist's last work. It is well-structured and rich in images that brough out the details. There is a clean and tidy courtyard in this painting, with two pieces of lush pomegranate trees in front of the gate. The gate was open, while a man with grey hair sat in the chair viewing the scenery outside the wall. The painting was named "Life", which undoubtedly reflects a life that the old man yearned for. The artist was suffering from an illness before he died, so we can see from the picture that the strokes were not so strong. A few chicks around the old man shown in the courtyard add a lot of meaning to this painting.

ANSWER

主句：It is well-structured and rich in images that brough out the details.
Pass 掉形容詞子句後，重點為：It is well-structured and rich in images.

 # 段落的練習

分析下面的段落分別屬於哪種類型。

1. There are many books in my father's study room, including all kinds of subjects. They are neatly arranged in three rows on the shelves. There is also a big table in the study room, and my father often works there. There is only one computer on the desk, but my father never allows me and my sister to play on it. However, my father sometimes accompanies us to study. The study room is always clean thanks to my mother. She cleans it every day. I really love the study room.

2. Two female employees of the personnel department resigned to get married yesterday, and the personnel department became very busy. The personnel

manager, Peter, decided to post a recruitment ad on the Internet in order to hire at least two staff members. They require that the candidates should have two years of work experience or above, and shouldn't have any criminal records. The personnel manager hopes to complete the recruitment work in one week.

3. This book is of great significance to me. First, it is a gift my best friend Anna sent me ten years ago when I was in bed due to illness. At that time, I was very depressed and lost the desire to live. Anne gave me this book to encourage me to overcome the disease. Finally, I succeeded. Second, this book's author is my favorite novelist, and I have the similar experience with the protagonist inside, which tugs at my heartstrings. And the most important thing is that there is an autograph of the writer on the cover of this book.

4. There is a large stone gate at the park on which offers the introduction and a road map of the park. As you enter the park you can see a musical fountain. It will eject various shapes of huge water column with the music in the evening. There is a garden in the right of the fountain in which there are hundreds of flowers, including roses, peonies, tulips, lilies, roses and so on. These flowers bloom in different seasons, so people can come to take a look at them any time. In the left of the fountain is a large bamboo woods, and the bamboos have been at least 5 years old. In summer, people will definitely come here. The park is a place for relaxation.

5. For decades, the environmental pollution and climate change have a bigger and bigger impact on people's lives. Air pollution is a major problem of environmental pollution. Air pollution increases the probability of human suffering from respiratory diseases. According to incomplete statistics, there are about 1 million people worldwide each year suffering from respiratory diseases, even pulmonary tuberculosis. Extreme weather caused by climate change not only threatens people's life and health, but also destroys the ecological balance to some extent. In some areas with plantation, even the weather has changed.

6. Lily, your task is to make a statistical report within three hours, and give it to the sales manager. Linda, your work is to call 50 of the company's regular customers to collect feedback, and make a report. David, you need to drive Mr. Steve to the airport, and to purchase office supplies on the way back. As for Sophia, you will go along with me to attend the meeting. You should make a note of the meeting.

7. The electronic products indeed provide great convenience for us, making the dream of knowing the world in the room come true. We can do a lot of work by using a mobile phone, such as communication, ordering, traveling, shopping and so on. What's more, all kinds of electronic products make our

life more colorful. We can browse the information and watch a video without going out. However, the negative impact brought by electronic products should not be overlooked. The electronic games provided by developers make young people addicted to the games, and even abandon their studies. Browsing electronic pages for too long has made some people's eyesight decline rapidly.

8. Last August, a chemical factory was closed down because it was found dumping chemical pollutants into the river. In other words, the factory went bankrupt. Thus, thousands of employees in the factory were laid off. All these workers were young people living nearby the city, and they had to find a new job after the factory was closed down. But because there were too many people being laid off, they couldn't find a job in a short period of time. They also found that the factory they once worked for was one of the reasons for other companies to decide whether they would be hired.

9. The popularity of electronic books (e-books) is easy to understand. E-books are portable and easy to search. People can download all the books they want to read in a device, which saves a lot of time when handling books. According to a survey, 70% of people think that e-books make them want to read more than paper ones. In addition, many search engines can help us find the book we want to read. Although e-books are becoming more and more popular, they still leave some room for improvement.

10. How do we lose weight quickly and effectively? Many women would choose to eat less and do more exercise to stay in shape. Nutritionists believe that food calories and fat are key factors in gaining weight. To reduce calorie intake and eat less greasy foods can help lose weight. Having fresh fruit and vegetables instead of high protein and high calorie food is what we can do to lose weight. In addition to food, exercise is also very important. Doing exercise every day, such as jogging, walking, yoga, and dancing can help reduce body fat. A healthy diet combined with exercise will bring a better result.

ANSWER

1. 首句即主旨型段落

解析 該段落的第一句就是主旨句,即:爸爸的書房裡包含各方面的書。接下來都是在描述書房裡的事物,以及在書房裡發生的事。如:桌子、電腦、爸爸不允許我們在裡面玩、爸爸陪我們學習,書房很乾淨。段落的結尾則是對前面的內容進行了概括,即:我真喜歡這個書房。

2. 因果型段落

解析 該段落的第一句提到公司的兩名員工辭職了,後文緊接著提到人事部經理決定招聘至少兩名員工，並且提到了招聘要求，後文還提到人事部經理希望在一週內結束招聘工作，由此可知員工辭職是招聘員工的原因，該段落是因果型段落。

3. 句首即主旨型段落

解析 該段落的第一句提到了「這本書對我有很重要的意義」，接下來依次按照 First, Second, And what the most important 這三個方面來詳細陳述了這一主旨，而且結尾處並沒有對段落進行總結，由此可判斷該段落是總結型段落。

4. 句尾即主旨型段落

解析 該段落是對事物方位進行了描述，從公園的大門、公園內的溫泉、溫泉右側的花園到左側的竹林依次進行了詳細的描述，段落的結尾處「這個公園是一個好的休閒場所。」是對整個段落的總結，所以該段落是句尾即主旨句段落。

5. 前呼後應型段落

解析 該段落的第一句提到「過去十年，環境汙染和氣候變遷問題對人們的生活影響越來越大」，緊接著從空氣汙染致使了人們患呼吸道疾病的概率增加、極端氣候威脅人們的生命和健康、種植環境發生變化來進行了詳細描述，所以該段落是前呼後應型段落。

6. 並列型段落

解析 該段落的關鍵訊息是幾個不同的人物，即 Lily, Linda, David, Sophia，他們在接受不同的工作任務，彼此之間是相互獨立並列的關系，因此該段落是並列型段落。

7. 轉折型段落

解析 在閱讀該段落的前半部分時，很容易理解為破題型段落，因為前半部分從電子產品的具體用途對第一句作了解釋。在段落的後半部分出現了轉折詞彙 However，後文是對電子產品的負面效應進行了描述，所以該段落是轉折型段落。

8. 因果型段落

解析 該段落的第一句提到了工廠倒閉的事情，緊接著提到「上千名員工下崗了」，後面均是圍繞著失業員工尋找新工作的事情展開的，由此可判斷工廠倒閉是因，找工作是果，所以該段落是因果型段落。

9. 轉折型段落

解析 該段落主要描述了電子書的發展，前半段都是針對電子書籍的發展快以及發展成果來進行詳細描述，但是在後半段出現了明顯的轉折詞 Although，所以該段落是轉折型段落。在英語中 although 不能和 but 一起出現，但是翻譯成中文時，需把 but 的含義翻譯出來。

10. 句尾即主旨型段落

解析 該段落的第一句並沒有完全體現主旨，而第二句則是完全展開了後文，也是本段主旨句。而且段落的結尾一句是對第二句主旨句的高度概括。所以該段落是句尾即主旨型段落。

段落的分類

1. 記敘文

找出下面這篇文章中的主題句。

Carle, a friend of mine, had a car accident at the age of 12. He was deprived of hearing since then. In the beginning, he couldn't accept the fact and he felt very miserable.

Carle was brought to America for the treatment when he was fifteen years old. Fortunately, Carle had part of his hearing back. Still, he needs to listen more carefully than normal people. Last year, we met in Los Angeles while he was undergoing his last treatment. Carle was so happy to see me. He told me about his treatment and his school life in the United States. Although he was in bad condition, he went on studying all the time.

Carle wrote to tell me the good news a few days ago that he had normal hearing and I felt so happy for him.

ANSWER He was deprived of hearing since then.

解析

文章在開頭提到了卡爾在 12 歲時因為事故失去了聽力，後文都是圍繞這個主題展開的，即他被帶去美國治療，恢復了部分聽力，去年他做最後的復健治療，他告訴「我」他的恢復情況，他努力學習，結尾段還提到卡爾寫信告訴「我」他的聽力正常了，這一系列的關鍵訊息是 what「何事」，其中還穿插著時間線 when。

閱讀攻略

記敘文是以敘述和描寫為主的文體形式，一般是記人、敘事、寫景、狀物，主要內容是敘述人物的經歷和事物的發展變化。記敘文的主題句一般出現在第一段中，而且下文都是圍繞這個主題展開。在閱讀英文記敘文時，需要掌握5個w

和1個h，即5ws and 1h。5個w指的是何時（when）、何地（where）、何人（who）、何因（why）、何事（what），1個h指的是如何。這6個要素可幫助讀者快速理清事物的來龍去脈，從而理解整個故事。如果是故事類篇章，那麼需要讀者通過文章的細節來體會作者的寫作意圖。

註：記敘文的敘述順序有順敘和倒敘兩種，所以在閱讀此類篇章時要從事物發展的情節來理解。

 隨手練一練

找出下面這篇文章中的主題句和記敘文的要素。

Once upon a time, there was a king who had four daughters. All of them were old enough to get married.

The three elder daughters of the king were so beautiful that they were favored by the king and the queen. But the eldest daughter was very jealous; the second daughter had a very bad temper, and the third daughter was hypocritical. Thus, no one would like to marry them in this country. Finally, the king ordered the sons of the three ministers to marry these beautiful daughters. The king's youngest daughter had no beautiful appearance, and was often overlooked by the king and the queen. But the youngest daughter was very kind and hard-working, and all the young men in the country were willing to marry her. Finally, the little girl married the prince of another country.

A few years later, only the king's youngest daughter lived a happy life, and the three beautiful daughters often quarreled with their husbands. This story shows that personality is more important than appearance.

ANSWER

主題句：This story shows that personality is more important than appearance.

要素：1. 時間 Once upon a time; a few years later；2. 地點 the country；3. 人物 daughters；4. 事件 get married；5. 原因 The three elder daughters of the king were so beautiful; the king's youngest daughter had no beautiful appearance；6. 怎麼樣 only the king's youngest daughter lived a happy life, and the three beautiful daughters often quarreled with their husbands

2. 抒情文

考考你的眼力 找出下面篇章中的主旨句。

No one has a smooth and care-free life. Everyone has to experience some setbacks and failures in life. What is important is that we don't lose the courage to try simply because we are afraid of failure.

Failure is not the end of the world, but sometimes it is commendable and needs to be cherished. The saying, "Failure is the mother of success," means that we can learn something from failure. Some people are devastated when they fail, and then they never have the courage to try. Some people become more determined after going through a setback, and try repeatedly or change direction, and such a person is called a winner. We have to be winners, not losers, and the experience of failure can bring us closer to success.

ANSWER What is important is that we don't lose the courage to try simply because we are afraid of failure.

解析

這篇文章是作者對失敗的感悟，並提到了作者的態度，即正面的、積極的態度，抒發了作者希望人們面對失敗不要氣餒的感情。

閱讀攻略

抒情文是作者透過直接或間接的方式抒發情感的一種文體。直接抒情文是作者直接表達出自己對人、物、事、景的感受和情感。間接抒情文是作者借助於對具體事物的描寫來表達主題。在抒情文中往往出現排比句、對比句等抒情方法來引出烘托作者的情感。抒情文的主題句往往出現在作者表達情感的句子中，並不一定是出現在開頭或結尾。在閱讀抒情文時，需要整體理解篇章，體會作者表達的情感態度。

找出下面篇章中的主旨句和抒情方法。

Before we know it, summer is over, and autumn is coming slowly with rain. If we observe carefully, we can see the signs of autumn everywhere. The annoying cicadas have stopped droning. The green leaves are turning yellow. The weather gradually becomes cooler, and rainy days start to make people sentimental. But the arrival of autumn also brings beautiful sceneries: golden crops, fruitful trees, and farmers' smiles.

Spring is the season for revitalization; summer is the season for all to work hard; autumn is the season when everything begins to come into fruition; winter is the season for all to rest. Each season has its own unique charm that is endearing to everyone, but I only love autumn. For me, autumn is the season of joy and harvest, and it is the time for people to have family reunions. I think this is the kind of life I have been longing for.

ANSWER

主旨句：Each season has its own unique charm to be loved by everyone, but I only love autumn.

抒情方法：Spring is the season for revitalization; summer is the season for all to work hard; autumn is the season when everything begins to come into fruition; winter is the season for all to rest.

3. 演講

考考你的眼力 找出下面篇章中的主旨句。

Ladies and Gentlemen,

I feel extremely honored to stand in this hall to deliver a speech. Although I spoke in many lectures, banquets, and charity events, the words I'm going to share with you carry a lot of significance to all of us. Today I want to say that it's time for us to act, to spare no efforts to save the earth.

Do you know millions of rare species on the earth have gone extinct? Do you know that our friends—animals—are in danger of constantly being shot by hunters? Do you know that every year tens of millions of people around the world are suffering from various diseases because of environmental pollution, most of whom are children? The planet we live on is now in peril; extreme weather and natural disasters are signs to warn mankind. We humans are the culprits that caused all the suffering.

Can you imagine that human beings can't survive on the earth? It is almost inconceivable, right? My friends, we should not blindly pursue industrial civilization, feeling complacent without thinking about the painful price we will have to pay.

My friends, I sincerely ask you to take action to protect the earth, even if it is about donating some money. Thank you!

ANSWER Today I want to say that it's time for us to act, to spare no efforts to save the earth.

解析

這是一篇演講稿，演講稿的最大特點是一般會在開頭直接講出演講的主要內容，也就是主旨。這篇演講的第一段的結尾處就是主旨句。

閱讀攻略

演講類篇章是演講者發表觀點、交流思想、介紹事物等的一種文體。這類文章的特點是針對性強，主旨句一般出現在第一段，全文一共分為開頭、主體和結尾三個部分。這類文章的主題句有明顯的引出特徵，比如I want to say that..., I want to say something about...而且這類文章的結尾處一般都有與主旨句相呼應的內容。演講者在主體部分多是通過道理、事實或故事等方式來進行說服或者勸告。這類文章的特殊性使得它的語言較口語化，讀者理解起來較為容易。

隨手練一練

找出下面篇章中的主旨句、總結句以及演說方式。

I'm here today to talk about dreams. Do you remember your dreams at the age of 10 and 20? What did you do in order to achieve these dreams? When we are ten years old, our dreams may be more illusionary and more distant from reality. Then what about our dreams when we are 20? In my opinion, the dreams of a 20-year-old are most likely to come true. Let me share with you a story.

When I was 20 years old, I was a college student. My biggest hobby was writing and my dream was to become a writer. I often sent papers to some newspapers and presses, but none of them has been approved by editors. I was very depressed. I thought I had no gift for writing and it was impossible to realize my dream. Even so, I did not give up writing and submitting articles to newspaper agencies. In my senior year, quite unexpectedly, I received an interview invitation of a newspaper in which I often sent my articles to. I was very pleased to participate in the interview and was successfully recruited. I think they might be moved by my insistence. I have worked in the newspaper for four years, where I follow different writers and editors and learn a lot. Then I began to try writing. When my first article was published in the newspaper, I felt close to my dream. In this way, I slowly realized my dream.

In fact, there is no shortcut to realizing dreams. Only by insisting and working hard can we make our dreams come true.

ANSWER

主旨句：I'm here today to talk about dreams.
總結句：In fact, there is no shortcut to realizing dreams.
演說方式：Let me share with you a story.

4. 論說文

考考你的眼力 找出下面篇章中的主旨句。

Nowadays, many parents allow their children to use electronic products at a very young age for school works and other reasons, which is not a good phenomenon. Children should not use electronic products too early.

First of all, the child's immunity system is weak, and the radiation of electronic products will cause certain harm to their health, especially to the eyes. Secondly, children have a strong sense of curiosity. They may dismantle the entire product because they are interested in some parts, which would be a waste of money. Third, if children contact the electronic products on a long-term basis but not with their parents, the relationship between them will become weak.

In my opinion, what children need is parents' companionship and proper guidance, not an electronic product.

ANSWER Children should not use electronic products too early.

解析

這是一篇論説文，在文章的開頭作者往往通過看法、現象等來引出自己的觀點，也就是本文的論點，也是主旨句。

閱讀攻略

論説文是透過事實、講道理、辨是非等途徑來表明作者主張的一種文體。這類文體的典型特徵包含三點：論點、論據和論證。一般在開頭引入論點，通過舉例、講道理等論據來説明論點，而論證則出現在結尾段，起到總結全文，與論點相呼應的作用。掌握這類文章的中心論點是理解文章的關鍵。這類文章中一般只有一個論點，通常出現在第一段中，結尾處的總結句並不是論點。在英文論説文中，其表示論點的句子常含有think, should, don't think, my opinion等與想法、態度相關的詞語。

隨手練一練

找出下面篇章中的論點、論據和論證。

Some people think that education does not have any influence on people's choices of occupation. I don't think that is the case. On the contrary, I think education is one of the factors for companies to consider hiring people or not.

Firstly, education is linked to a person's knowledge and learning ability. If a person has a high degree of education, it implies he/she has very strong learning abilities. So even if they work in an unfamiliar field, they can figure out how to handle their work in a short period of time. Secondly, education determines a person's choice of occupation to some extent. The higher degree a person has, the more likely he/she will get a high-level job. Thirdly, the majority of companies have definitive regulations on educational background. If you fail to meet their requirements, your resume will probably not be read, and therefore you won't get a job interview.

In a word, education does not mean everything, but education plays an important role in finding jobs.

論點：On the contrary, I think education is one of the factors for companies to consider when hiring people.

論據：Firstly, education is linked to a person's knowledge and learning ability. Secondly, education determines a person's choice of occupation to some extent. Thirdly, the majority of companies have definitive regulations on educational background.

論證：In a word, education does not mean everything, but education plays an important role in finding jobs.

5. 說明文

考考你的眼力 找出下面篇章中的主旨句。

Rose is a common flower we often see in daily life. As is known to all, rose is the symbol of love, especially red roses. On Valentine's Day every year, roses and chocolate are the essential things that people use to express love to their lovers.

In addition to expressing love, roses are popular in many ways. In fact, roses are edible and rich in vitamin C, but they don't contain sugar. Many foods, such as cakes, juice, jam, etc. can be added with roses as additional ingredients. Some fragrances are also made from roses because of their aromatic smell. This kind of perfume is very popular among women.

Surprisingly, many countries regard roses as their national flowers, such as the United States, Britain, Bulgaria, Spain, and Luxemburg. In addition, roses are also used by some cities as their city flowers.

ANSWER Rose is a common flower we often see in daily life.

解析

這篇文章是對玫瑰花的詳細介紹，玫瑰花屬於一種常見植物，該篇文章的目的是向人們介紹玫瑰花的一些知識。

閱讀攻略

與其它文體不同，說明文是一種透過對事物的特徵、功能、成因等方面進行說明來告訴人們知識的文體。說明文的目的是介紹事物，因此說明文表達的知識是直接的、集中的，語言更加簡明。閱讀這類文章時，首先要了解說明對象。說明文的說明對象一般出現在第一段中，也是該篇章的主旨句。而且說明文的段落結構主要有：並列式、遞進式、連貫式、總分式和對照式。這些段落結構常常混合出現在一篇完整的說明文中。其次，根據說明對象來理解該事物的特徵是什麼，原因是什麼，該事物是怎麼樣的。

隨手練一練

找出下面篇章中的主旨句，並說明第二段的段落類型。

Whether it's a public university or a private one, the school either sets up an internship course or a community activity. Why is that?

The school sets up the curriculum or community activity firstly to cultivate students' practical ability. The internship experience is an important stepping stone for people looking for a job. Without internship experience, people will have limited choices in their career. Secondly, these courses or community activities provide practice in all aspects and enrich the students' campus life. Third, participating in community activities can help the students learn about how to work in a team.

In summary, college students should make full use of these internship courses or community activities to enhance their abilities.

ANSWER

主旨句：Whether it's a public university or a private one, the school either sets up an internship course or a community activity. Why is that?
第二段的段落類型：並列式段落。
解析：第二段中有明顯的表示次序的詞 firstly, Secondly, Third，這些是判斷段落類型的關鍵訊息。

6. 應用文

解析

這篇文章是一封信件，信件屬於應用文的一種。

閱讀攻略

應用文是一種較為正式的包含各類體裁的文體。應用文主要包含書信、公告、通知、日記、啟事、建議、規則等各類體裁。書信是最常見的應用文體裁，包含各類信件，如邀請函、感謝信、致歉信、祝賀信等。在不同的信件中有不同的應用句型，如I'd like to...（我希望），Thank you very much for...（非常感謝），My advice is as follows.（我的建議如下）等。應用文的語言比較規範和簡潔，篇幅較短，一般不用完成時態。

隨手練一練

找出下面篇章中的主旨句並指出文章中使用的時態。

Dear John,

How are you doing? I want to tell you something about me.

Last month, our school held a sports meeting. I signed up for the 100 meter race. On the day of the match, I performed very well and won the first prize. I not only got a prize, but was also praised by my teacher and my parents. Moreover, my father promised to take me to the Disneyland.

Next week, we will move because my father got a new job. The new house is a little far away from my school, and I'm going to ride a bike to school. It's going to take 20 minutes. I've seen the new house. My bedroom is bigger than the one I live now so I can put a desk in my room.

Reply to me soon.

Linda

ᗩᑎᔕᗯᕮᖇ

主旨句：I want to tell you something about me.
時態：一般現在時，一般過去時，一般將來時

7. 科普文

考考你的眼力 找出下面篇章中的主旨句。

With the development of science and technology, human beings have discovered many factors that cause cancer, but age actually plays the the most important role in cancer. The cells in human body are normal at birth, and they replace new cells due to their own growth cycles. Some cells undergo gene mutation during the growth cycle, and then they grow out of control, and eventually become tumors. As time goes by, gene damage increases in normal cells, increasing the risk of normal cells to become cancerous. Cancer cells lead to human death by absorbing nutrition in a human body and obstructing the normal operation of organs.

The life span of people nowadays is much longer than that of people in the past. That is because science and technology have helped people overcome a lot of diseases caused by malnutrition, infectious diseases and so on. Although there are more cases of cancer in the modern society, scientists continue to make major breakthroughs in medicine, and some medical technologies can accurately diagnose cancer.

ANSWER With the development of science and technology, human beings have discovered many factors that cause cancer, but age actually plays the most important role in cancer.

解析

這篇文章在介紹人體細胞與癌症之間的關系，屬於生物科學，這是科普文的一種。

閱讀攻略

科普文與說明文有相似之處，但科普文旨在介紹科學技術和自然科學等方面的事物，針對性更強，科學性和知識性比說明文更集中。科普文一般通過描述類文字來說明事物，其段落結構有破題、概括、結尾主旨、並列和轉折等幾類。科普文的主旨句有時並不明顯，有時是對說明對象下的定義，需要整 體瀏覽篇章後再理解。這類文章的主旨句的位置比較靈活，可在開頭、文中和結尾。鑒於科普文的科學性較強，句子較難理解，讀者可結合「Pass掉不必要的成分」來把握文章，但是很多細節問題是體現在那些附加成分中的。

 **隨手練一練**

找出下面篇章中的主旨句，並pass掉主旨句中不必要的成分。

GPS is a kind of technology which measures time and position with navigation satellites combined with satellite and communication equipment. The main function of GPS is about navigation and positioning. This technology has been applied in aerospace, agriculture, manufacturing, transportation and other industries, and it has greatly increased the safety of public transportation. GPS can work full time; any change in the weather can't affect it. The accuracy of GPS is the reason why it is widely used. GPS provides accurate data to help people in terms of positioning and timing, which not only saves time but also improves efficiency. In addition, GPS covers a global area of up to 98%, which means that GPS can navigate and locate most areas around the world, even small villages.

GPS currently uses three-dimensional data, that is, longitude, latitude and elevation, and it is possible to include the fourth dimensions, namely, time in the future.

ANSWER

主旨句：GPS is a kind of technology which measures time and position with navigation satellites combined with satellite and communication equipment.

Pass掉不必要的成分：is a kind of technology which.

篇章的練習

分析下面的文章屬於哪種類型的篇章。

1.

One day in that summer, it was so hot that there were few people on the street. Several classmates and I planned to swim in the river. When we walked towards the river, there were suddenly many clouds in the sky. The thunder rumbled in the sky. Soon, it rained cats and dogs.

I remembered it clearly that before it began to rain, my classmates and I returned home quickly. The rain kept pouring down, and I saw from the window that the yard was full of water. The newly-planted trees were swaying in the wind. In the evening, the rain slowed down. My parents came back home from work, and they were all wet. After dinner, the rain stopped completely. I stood in the yard and took a deep breath. It was really cool.

2.

Quality is more important than speed. It's true when it comes to running businesses and learning skills.

Nobody likes products with poor quality. Then how can a company make speedy production while neglecting consumers' need? The products with poor quality might be sold out quickly due to their low prices, but once the consumers find out the truth, how could they possibly continue to support this product? In this case, fast production is meaningless. Similarly, if you want to acquire knowledge quickly without fully understanding it, you can only learn a little, and you can't grasp the essence of it.

In a nutshell, we should focus on quality instead of speed.

3.

Dear Mr. Bill,

We learned that you came to our city yesterday to attend the fair, so we would like to invite you to come to our company for business dinner next Monday.

The dinner will be held to thank our partners, and we will show you our new products. You have always been our biggest customer. We would like to cooperate with you continuously. Of course, you can take a look at our new products during the dinner.

In view that our dinner will be held in the evening, which is expected to end at 10, you may need a driver. Do you need us to arrange one for you or will you settle it by yourself?

Please reply soon.

Yours,

Mark

4.
Catherine Hepburn was born in the early twentieth century. Because of her family background, Hepburn was very independent. With her father's support, she participated in a variety of sports activities. She majored in drama at the university, and she often participated in drama activities.

Hepburn went to Hollywood at the age of 24. A year later, Hepburn won the Oscar Award for best actress for her outstanding performance in Morning Glory. However, the movies she starred in after the award all failed, and her film career was in crisis. A few years later, Hepburn acted in a play, and it was a great success.

In 1966, the film Hepburn played in helped her win the Oscar Award again for best actress. Then Hepburn won the third and fourth Oscar Award for best actress because of the film The Lion in Winter and On Golden Pond respectively.

5.
According to a survey, the unemployment rate rose sharply in recent years. The main reasons are as follows:

One, a lot of college students can't find a suitable job for a number of reasons after graduation while employers can't find the talent they need. College students would give up a job because of low salary, or the nature of the work; employers may not hire a college student because they lack any experience.

Two, many occupations are affected by seasons, such as agriculture and tourism. Those who are engaged in tourism face a high rate of unemployment during the off-season.

Third, wages in some cities are quite low, so most people are reluctant to pursue such occupations.

6.
Dear Leaders,

Thank you very much for providing me with the chance to compete for the position as the sales manager. As the sales department manager, I have been in office for two years.

Since I came to the sales department, I have enjoyed the job. Before I worked as a vice manager, I had been a salesman for two years. Two years ago, I began to lead an independent sales team, and we were the team with the best performance. As a team manager, I believe I have the ability to be a good leader.

I know clearly that a department manager has more responsibilities and obligations when managing a company's department. If I can be promoted as a sales manager, my team and I will work together to create greater interests for the company and employees as a whole.

Jack

7.

Flies, bees, and mosquitoes buzz when they fly, and the sound is not made by their mouths, but by the vibration of their wings when they fly.

If you fold a piece of paper into a trumpet, and speak with your mouth close to the narrow part. You'll find that the sound is louder. This is because the shape of the objects will bring the sound forward instead of allowing it to spread out evenly. That's one of the principles that people use the horn to amplify the sound.

The more intensely an object is vibrating, the louder it sounds. This is because all sounds are produced by vibration, and Baer invented the telephone using the principle that electricity transmits vibrations.

8.

Phillips created a miracle in swimming; he is the champion of many swimming events. Bolter is the "flying man on the track and field", and he is the champion of 100-meter race. However, even though many athletes did not win the championship, they did their best in the field, showing the fighting spirit and good sportsmanship, and they were the champions in our hearts.

Chusovitina is a female gymnast from Uzbekistan. What makes her respected is not that she won the gold medal in the Olympic Games, but the time and efforts she spent in pursuing her Olympic dream. Chusovitina's son was diagnosed with leukemia one year after his birth, and they needed a lot of money to pay for medical expenses. Retired Chusovitina decided to return to participate in the Olympic Games for her son and won the gold medal later. In order to be able to afford her son's huge medical expenses, Chusovitina has always insisted on participating in the Olympic Games. Even though she didn't win the game later, she won all respect because of her love for her son. Who could say she wasn't the champion?

9.

Contributions Wanted

The Children's Newspaper will publish a report related to children's life. In order to publish excellent works, we would like to collect materials from parents. We welcome moms, dads, grandpas and grandmas to provide the materials. The requirements of the materials:

1. Children's stories in kindergarten level;

2. No more than 150 words;

3. Illustrations can be attached with the materials.

4. The deadline is September 23rd.

Please send the materials to: No. 10, University Road, Children's Newspaper

Email address: Kids@cc.public.com

10.

Tarsiers get its name because their eyes are like a pair of glasses. The first species of tarsiers appeared about 60 million years ago. Tarsiers are known to the world as the smallest monkeys.

A tarsier's body shapes like a big mouse, but it has the biggest ears among primate animals. Big ears provide them with the advantage of a sensitive hearing. As a result, they can sense even the slightest movement. During the day, tarsiers cling to branches or rests in the trunk; at night, they become very active, and start looking for food in the woods. They furl their ears when they sleep so as not to be disturbed by the outside world.

Tarsiers are endangered species; they only exist in the southeast Philippines. Female tarsiers only give birth to a cub every year because they are endangered due to deforestation.

ANSWER

1. 記敘文

解析 這篇文章具備了記敘文的六要素,即何時one day in that summer, In the evening, After dinner;何地on the street, river, home, yard;何人I, classmates, parents;何因the thunder, rain;何事my classmates and I returned home, The newly-planted trees are swaying in the wind, the rain slowed down, My parents came back home, I stood in the yard and took a deep breath;怎麼樣It was really cool。

2. 論說文

解析 這篇文章的論點是Quality is more important than speed. 論據是In this case, fast production is meaningless. you can only learn a little, and you can't grasp the essence of it. 論證是In a nutshell, we should focus on quality instead of speed.

3. 應用文

解析 根據這篇文章的形式和內容可知這篇文章是一封邀請信,也可稱為邀請函,是應用文的一種。

4. 記敘文

解析 這篇文章介紹的是美國電影明星凱瑟琳‧赫本，記敘了她的生平，包括出生日期、成長經歷、人生輝煌、人生挫敗以及影視地位。

5. 說明文

解析 這是一篇原因說理型說明文。文章開頭從失業率上升引出原因，二、三、四段都是在從客觀的角度說明具體的原因。

6. 演講

解析 很多讀者可能因為這篇文章的開頭形式而判斷它為應用文，實際上根據開頭段落的主要內容可得知這是一篇求職演講稿，所以這是演講而不是應用文。

7. 科普文

解析 這篇文章是從幾種不同的發聲事物引出聲音的產生原理，屬於物理學範疇，是在介紹物理科學知識，所以是科普文。

8. 論說文

解析 雖然這篇文章沒有明顯論說文的典型特點：結論主旨的結構，但是文章第一段透過得到冠軍和沒有得到冠軍的運動員作對比，來引出論點，即 However, even though many athletes did not win the championship, they did their best in the field, showing the fighting spirit and good sportsmanship, and they were the champions in our hearts. 第二段是通過具體的人物示例來對論點進行論證。

9. 應用文

解析 這篇文章是一篇徵稿訊息，屬於公告一類的正式體裁，是應用文的一種。

10. 說明文

解析 這篇文章介紹的是一種自然界動物，眼鏡猴。介紹了眼鏡猴的名字來源、外部特徵、種族數量、生活習性以及現存狀況等方面。因此，這是一篇說明文。

Part

2

閱讀提升——
化繁為簡

少年維特的煩惱

①In other respects I am very well off here. ②Solitude in this terrestrial paradise is a genial balm to my mind, and the young spring cheers with its bounteous promises my oftentimes misgiving heart. ③Every tree, every bush, is full of flowers; and one might wish himself transformed into a butterfly, to float about in this ocean of perfume, and find his whole existence in it.

④The town itself is disagreeable; but then, all around, you find an inexpressible beauty of nature. ⑤This induced the late Count M to lay out a garden on one of the sloping hills which here intersect each other with the most charming variety, and form the most lovely valleys. ⑥The garden is simple; and it is easy to perceive, even upon your first entrance, that the plan was not designed by a scientific gardener, but by a man who wished to give himself up here to the enjoyment of his own sensitive heart. ⑦Many a tear have I already shed to the memory of its departed master in a summer-house which is now reduced to ruins, but was his favorite resort, and now is mine. ⑧I shall soon be master of the place. ⑨The gardener has become attached to me within the last few days, and he will lose nothing thereby.

補充單字片語

- solitude [ˈsɒlɪtjuːd] /n./ 單獨，孤獨，幽靜
- bounteous [ˈbaʊntɪəs] /adj./ 大方的，慷慨的

句構分析

① ~~In other respects~~ I am ~~very~~ well off ~~here~~.

　　介系詞+名詞　　主詞 be動詞 副詞 形容詞　副詞

譯 另外，我在這裡非常愉快。

結構分析 這句話是該段的主旨句，後面的幾個句子都是在具體描述感覺愉快的原因。

② Solitude ~~in this terrestrial paradise~~ is a genial balm ~~to my mind~~, and the young
　　主詞　　　介系詞+名詞　　　　be動詞　述語　　　介系詞+名詞　　　主詞
spring cheers ~~with its bounteous~~ promises my ~~oftentimes~~ misgiving heart.
　　　　　　　介系詞+名詞　　　　動詞　　　　副詞　　　　受詞

譯 這片樂園的岑寂是醫治我心的靈丹妙藥，園裡的溫暖春光充滿了我這顆時常寒慄的心。

③ Every tree, every bush, is full ~~of flowers~~; and one might wish himself
　　　　　主詞　　　　　　動詞　述詞　　　　　　　　主詞 動詞　　　受詞
transformed ~~into a butterfly~~, to float about ~~in this ocean of perfume~~, and find his
受詞補語　　　介系詞+名詞　　　　　　　　　　　介系詞+名詞　　　　　　　動詞
whole existence ~~in it~~.
受詞　　　　　介系詞+代名詞

譯 每一棵樹，每一片灌木叢都開滿了鮮花。讓人想變成一只蝴蝶，飛翔在花的海洋中，去盡情地吸露吮蜜。

結構分析 該長句是由and連接的兩個並列句。Every tree, every bush, is full of flowers是一個主詞+動詞+述詞結構的簡單句。第一個and後面的句子，主詞是one，其後有兩個並列的動詞，其中一個是 wish，另外一個是find。

④ The town itself is disagreeable; but ~~then~~, all around, you find an inexpressible
　　　主詞　　　動詞　述詞　　　　　副詞　　　　　　　主詞 動詞　　　受詞
beauty ~~of nature~~.
受詞　　介系詞+名詞

譯 城市本身是不舒服的，但是，周圍的一切，你會發現一種無法形容的自然美。

⑤ This induced the late Count M to lay out a garden ~~on one of the sloping hills~~
主詞　動詞　　　受詞　　　　　受詞補語　　　　　　介系詞+名詞
~~which here intersect each other~~ ~~with the most charming variety~~, and form the most
　　　形容詞子句　　　　　　　　介系詞+名詞
~~lovely~~ valleys.
副詞

譯 這促使後來的伯爵在一座斜坡上布置了一座花園，這裡的景色與最迷人的景色相交叉，形成了最美麗的山谷。

⑥ The garden is simple; and it is easy to perceive, even ~~upon your first entrance~~,
　　主詞　　動詞 述語　　主詞 動詞　不定詞　　　　　　介系詞+名詞
that the plan was not designed ~~by a scientific gardener~~, but by a man ~~who wished~~
　　　　　　　　　　　　　　　介系詞+名詞　　　　　　介系詞+名詞　形容詞子句
~~to give himself up here to the enjoyment of his own sensitive heart~~.
　　　　　　　　　　　　　介系詞+名詞　　　介系詞+名詞

譯 花園很簡單，即使在你第一次進來的時候，也很容易察覺到這個平面圖不是由一個科學園丁設計的，而是一個想在這裡享受自己敏感內心的人。

⑦ Many a tear have I ~~already~~ shed ~~to the memory of its departed master in a~~
　　受詞　　　　　主詞 副詞　動詞　介系詞+名詞 介系詞+名詞 介系詞+名詞

<s>summer-house</s> <s>which is now reduced to ruins</s>, but was his favorite resort, and

形容詞子句

now is mine.

譯 我已經流了許多眼淚來紀念這個避暑別墅裡過去的主人，如今它變成了廢墟，但卻是他最喜歡的度假勝地，現在這是我的了。

⑧ I shall <s>soon</s> be master <s>of the place</s>.

主詞　　副詞 動詞 述詞 介系詞+名詞

譯 我很快就會成為花園的主人。

⑨ The gardener has become attached to me <s>within the last few days</s>, and he will

主詞　　　　連綴動詞　　　述詞　　　介系詞+名詞　　　　　　主詞 動詞

lose nothing <s>thereby</s>.

受詞　　副詞

譯 幾天之後，園丁就已對我頗有好感，而他也將會得到好處。

小王子

①I jumped to my feet, completely thunderstruck. ②I blinked my eyes hard. ③I looked carefully all around me. ④And I saw a most extraordinary small person, who stood there examining me with great seriousness. ⑤Here you may see the best potrait that, later, I was able to make of him. ⑥But my drawing is certainly very much less charming than its model.

⑦That, however, is not my fault. ⑧The grown-ups discouraged me in my painter's career when I was six years old, and I never learned to draw anything, except boas from the outside and boas from the inside.

⑨Now I stared at this sudden apparition with my eyes fairly starting out of my head in astonishment. ⑩Remember, I had crashed in the desert a thousand miles from any inhabited region. ⑪And yet my little man seemed neither to be straying uncertainly among the sands, nor to be fainting from fatigue or hunger or thirst or fear. ⑫Nothing about him gave any suggestion of a child lost in the middle of the desert, a thousand miles from any human habitation. ⑬When at last I was able to speak, I said to him:

⑭"But-- what are you doing here?"

⑮And in answer he repeated, very slowly, as if he were speaking of a matter of great consequence: "If you please-- draw me a sheep..."

補充單字片語

- thunderstruck [ˈθʌndəstrʌk] /adj./ 大吃一驚的
- extraordinary [ɪkˈstrɔːdnrɪ] /adj./ 非凡的，特 的
- apparition [ˌæpəˈrɪʃn] /n./ 特異景象，幽靈

句構分析

① I jumped to my feet, completely thunderstruck.

主詞 動詞　受詞　　副詞
🔖 我宛如受到驚雷轟擊一般，一下子就跳了起來。

② I blinked my eyes hard.

主詞 動詞　受詞　副詞
🔖 我使勁地揉了揉眼睛。

③ I looked carefully all around me.

主詞 動詞　副詞 受詞 介系詞+代名詞
🔖 我仔細地看了看我的周圍。

④ And I saw a most extraordinary small person, who stood there examining me

主詞 動詞　　　　受詞　　　　　　形容詞子句

with great seriousness.

介系詞+名詞
🔖 我看見一個十分奇怪的小傢伙嚴肅地朝我凝眸望著。

⑤ Here you may see the best portrait that, later, I was able to make of him.

副詞 主詞　　動詞　　受詞　　　　副詞 主詞 動詞　　不定詞結構 介系詞+代名詞
🔖 這是後來我給他畫出來的最好的一副畫像。

⑥ But my drawing is certainly very much less charming than its model.

主詞　動詞　副詞　　副詞　　比較級形容詞 介系詞+名詞
🔖 可是，我的畫當然要比他本人的模樣遜色得多。

⑦ That, however, is not my fault.

主詞　　　　　動詞　述詞
🔖 這不是我的過錯。

⑧ The grown-ups discouraged me in my painter's career when I was six years old,

主詞　　　　　動詞　　受詞　介系詞+名詞　　時間副詞子句

and I never learned to draw anything, except boas from the outside and boas from

主詞　　動詞　　動詞　受詞　　　介系詞+名詞

the inside.

 六歲時，大人們使我對我的畫家生涯失去了勇氣，除了畫過開著肚皮和閉著肚皮的蟒蛇，後來再沒有學過畫。

⑨ Now I stared at this sudden apparition with my eyes fairly starting out of my

副詞 主詞 動詞　　　　受詞　　　　　介系詞+名詞　　副詞　　動名詞片語

head in astonishment.

 我驚奇地睜大著眼睛看著這突然出現的小傢伙。

⑩ Remember, I had crashed in the desert a thousand miles from any inhabited

　　　　　　　主詞　　動詞　　受詞　　　　　　　　　介系詞+名詞

region.

 你們不要忘記，我當時處在遠離人煙千里之外的地方。

⑪ And yet my little man seemed neither to be straying uncertainly among the

　　　　副詞　　主詞　　動詞　　　述語

sands, nor to be fainting from fatigue or hunger or thirst or fear.

　　　　述語　　　　　介系詞+名詞

 而這個小家夥給我的印象是，他既不像迷了路的樣子，也沒有半點疲乏、饑渴、懼怕的神情。

⑫ Nothing about him gave any suggestion of a child lost in the middle of the desert,

主詞 介系詞+代名詞 動詞　　受詞　　介系詞+名詞　　介系詞+名詞　　介系詞+名詞

a thousand miles from any human habitation.

　　　　　　　介系詞+名詞

 他絲毫不像是一個迷失在荒無人煙的大沙漠中的孩子。

⑬ When at last I was able to speak, I said to him:

　　　　時間副詞子句　　　　　主詞 動詞 受詞

 當我在驚訝之中終於能説出話來的時候，對他説道：

⑭ "But—what are you doing here?"

　　　　　　　　　　　　　副詞

 「但是一你在這兒幹什麼？」

⑮ And in answer he repeated, very slowly, as if he were speaking of a matter of

　　　　　　　主詞 動詞　　　副詞　　狀態副詞子句　　介系詞+名詞

great consequence: "If you please—draw me a sheep..."

介系詞+名詞

 可是他卻不慌不忙地好像在説一件重要的事一般，對我重複了一次：「請……給我畫一隻羊……」

老人與海

① He was an old man who fished alone in a skiff in the Gulf Stream and he had gone eighty-four days now without taking a fish. ②In the first forty days a boy had been with him. ③But after forty days without a fish the boy's parents had told him that the old man was now definitely and finally salao, which is the worst form of unlucky, and the boy had gone at their orders in another boat which caught three good fish the first week. ④It made the boy sad to see the old man come in each day with his skiff empty and he always went down to help him carry either the coiled lines or the gaff and harpoon and the sail that was furled around the mast. ⑤The sail was patched with flour sacks and, furled, it looked like the flag of permanent defeat.

⑥The old man was thin and gaunt with deep wrinkles in the back of his neck. ⑦The brown blotches of the benevolent skin cancer the sun brings from its reflection on the tropic sea were on his cheeks. ⑧The blotches ran well down the sides of his face and his hands had the deep-creased scars from handling heavy fish on the cords. ⑨ But none of these scars were fresh. ⑩They were as old as erosions in a fishless desert.

補充單字片語

- skiff [skɪf] /n./ 小艇
- definitely [ˈdefɪnətlɪ] /adv./ 明確地，確切地
- permanent [ˈpɜ:mənənt] /adj./ 永久的，永恒的
- benevolent [bəˈnevələnt] /adj./ 好心腸的，與人為善

句構分析

① He was <u>an old man</u> ~~who fished alone~~ <u>in a skiff</u> <u>in the Gulf Stream</u> and he <u>had</u>

主詞 動詞　　述詞　　　　形容詞子句　　　介系詞+名詞　介系詞+名詞　　主詞 動詞

<u>gone</u> <u>eighty-four days</u> ~~now~~ ~~without taking a fish~~.

受詞　　　　副詞　　介系詞+名詞

譯 他是在墨西哥灣流中的一條小船上獨自釣魚的老人，如今已經過去了八十四天，但他一條魚也沒釣到。

結構分析 本句話是本段的主旨句，後面又具體描述了這八十四天裡老人釣魚的故事。

② In the first forty days a boy had been with him.

介系詞+名詞　　　主詞　　動詞　　受詞

譯 在頭四十天裡，有個男孩和他在一起。

③ But after forty days without a fish the boy's parents had told him that the old man was now

介系詞+名詞　介系詞+名詞　　　主詞　　　動詞　受詞　　受詞子句

definitely and finally salao, which is the worst form of unlucky, and the boy had

副詞　　　　　　　形容詞子句　　　　　　　主詞　動詞

gone at their orders in another boat which caught three good fish the first week.

介系詞+名詞　　介系詞+名詞　　形容詞子句

譯 但過了四十天一條魚也沒有捉到，孩子的父母就對他說，老人如今準是十足地「倒了大霉」，也就是說，倒霉到了極點，於是孩子聽從了他們的吩咐，上了另外一條船，在第一週就捕到了三條好魚。

④ It made the boy sad to see the old man come in each day with his skiff empty and

主詞 動詞　受詞 受詞補語　不定詞　　　　　　介系詞+名詞　介系詞+名詞

he always went down to help him carry either the coiled lines or the gaff and

主詞 副詞　　　動詞　　受詞 受詞補語　介系詞+名詞　　介系詞+名詞

harpoon and the sail that was furled around the mast.

形容詞子句

譯 老人每天回來時船總是空的，孩子看見感到很難受，他總是走下岸去幫老人拿卷起的釣索，或者魚鉤和魚叉，還有繞在桅桿上的帆。

文法分析 該長句是由and 連接的兩個並列句，第一個句子It made the boy sad to see the old man come中，it是虛主詞，真正的主詞是to see the old man come；第二個句子中either...or...表示「或者……或者……」，that was furled around the mast是一個形容詞子句，用來修飾the sail。

⑤ The sail was patched with flour sacks and, furled, it looked like the flag of

主詞　　動詞　　述詞　　介系詞+名詞　　　　　　主詞 動詞　　述詞

permanent defeat.

介系詞+名詞

譯 帆上用麵粉袋打了些補丁，收攏後看起來像是一面標誌著永遠失敗的旗子。

⑥ The old man was thin and gaunt with deep wrinkles in the back of his neck.

主詞　　　動詞　　述詞　　介系詞+名詞　　介系詞+名詞

譯 老人消瘦而憔悴，脖頸上有些很深的皺紋。

⑦ The brown blotches of the benevolent skin cancer the sun brings from its

主詞　　　　介系詞+名詞　　　　　　形容詞子句

reflection on the tropic sea were on his cheeks.

動詞　　述詞

譯 在他的臉頰上有些褐斑，那是太陽在熱帶海面上反射的光線所引起的良性皮膚癌變。

文法分析 在該句中，the sun brings from its reflection on the tropic sea是形容詞子句，修飾先行詞 the benevolent skin cancer，此處的形容詞子句省略了關係代名詞which，因為關係代名詞which在句中作受詞，可省略。

⑧ The blotches ran well down the sides of his face and his hands had the deep-

主詞　　動詞 副詞　　受詞　介系詞+名詞　　主詞　動詞　受詞

<u>creased scars</u> ~~from handling heavy fish on the cords~~.

　　　　介系詞+名詞　　　　　介系詞+名詞

🈁 褐斑從他臉的兩側一直蔓延下去，他的雙手因常用繩索拉大魚，而留下了刻得很深的傷疤。

⑨ But none ~~of these scars~~ were fresh.

　　主詞　介系詞+名詞　動詞　述詞

🈁 但是這些傷疤中沒有一塊是新的。

⑩ They were ~~as old as erosions in a fishless desert~~.

主詞 動詞 副詞 述詞 介系詞+名詞 介系詞+名詞

🈁 它們像無魚可打的沙漠中被侵蝕的地方一般古老。

 飄

①A balmy, soft warmth poured into the room, heavy with velvety smells, redolent of many blossoms, of newly fledged trees and of the moist, freshly turned red earth. ②Through the window Scarlett could see the bright riot of the twin lanes of daffodils bordering the graveled driveway and the golden masses of yellow jessamine spreading flowery sprangles modestly to the earth like crinolines. ③The mockingbirds and the jays, engaged in their old feud for possession of the magnolia tree beneath her window, were bickering, the jays strident, acrimonious, the mockers sweet voiced and plaintive.

④Such a glowing morning usually called Scarlett to the window, to lean arms on the broad sill and drink in the scents and sounds of Tara. ⑤But, today she had no eye for sun or azure sky beyond a hasty thought, "Thank God, it isn't raining." ⑥On the bed lay the apple-green, watered-silk ball dress with its festoons of ecru lace, neatly packed in a large cardboard box. ⑦It was ready to be carried to Twelve Oaks to be donned before the dancing began, but Scarlett shrugged at the sight of it. ⑧ If her plans were successful, she would not wear that dress tonight. ⑨Long before the ball began, she and Ashley would be on their way to Jonesboro to be married.

- velvety [ˈvelvətɪ] /adj./ 天鵝絨般柔軟的
- mockingbird [ˈmɒkɪŋbɜːd] /n./ 仿聲鳥
- engage in... 忙於……

句構分析

① A balmy, soft warmth poured into the room, heavy with velvety smells, redolent
主詞　　　動詞　　受詞　　　　　　　　介系詞+名詞
of many blossoms, of newly fledged trees and of the moist, freshly turned red earth.
介系詞+名詞　　　　介系詞+名詞　　　　　　介系詞+名詞

譯 芬芳柔和的暖意已撒滿房間，它飽含著種種花卉、剛抽枝葉的樹木和潤溫的新翻紅土的香味。

② Through the window Scarlett could see the bright riot of the twin lanes of
介系詞+名詞　　　主詞　　動詞　　受詞　　介系詞+名詞
daffodils bordering the graveled driveway and the golden masses of yellow
介系詞+名詞　　　　　　　　　　　　　　受詞　　　介系詞+名詞
jessamine spreading flowery sprangles modestly to the earth like crinolines.
　　　　　　　　　　　　　副詞　　　介系詞+名詞

譯 史嘉麗從窗口能看到沿著石子車道的兩行水仙花和一叢叢像花裙子般紛披滿地的黃茉莉在那裡競相怒放，爭奇鬥豔。

③ The mockingbirds and the jays, engaged in their old feud for possession of the
主詞　　　　　　　　　　　　插入語
magnolia tree beneath her window, were bickering, the jays strident, acrimonious,
　　　　　　　　　　　　　動詞
the mockers sweet voiced and plaintive.

譯 仿聲鳥和松鳥正在為爭奪她窗下的一棵山茱萸又打了起來，在那裡鬥嘴，松鳥的聲音尖銳而昂揚，仿聲鳥則嬌柔而淒婉。

④ Such a glowing morning usually called Scarlett to the window, to lean arms on
主詞　　　　　　　副詞　動詞　受詞　介系詞+名詞　　不定詞
the broad sill and drink in the scents and sounds of Tara.
介系詞+名詞　　　　介系詞+名詞

譯 如此明朗的早晨常常會把史嘉麗引到窗口，倚在窗檯上領略塔拉農場的鳥語花香。

⑤ But, today she had no eye for sun or azure sky beyond a hasty thought, "Thank
副詞 主詞 動詞 受詞　介系詞+名詞　　　介系詞+名詞
God, it isn't raining."
主詞 動詞 述詞

譯 但是，今天清晨她無暇欣賞旭日和藍天，心中只有一個想法匆匆掠過：「謝謝老天爺，總算沒有下雨。」

⑥ <u>On the bed</u> lay <u>the apple-green, watered-silk ball dress</u> ~~with its festoons of~~
　主詞　　動詞　　　受詞　　　　　　　　　　　　　　　　介系詞+名詞

~~ecru lace,~~ ~~neatly~~ packed ~~in a large cardboard box~~.
介系詞+名詞　副詞　　　　介系詞+名詞
　　譯 在她床上的一個盒子裡放著一件蘋果綠的鑲著淡褐色邊的波紋綢舞衣，折疊得整整齊齊。

⑦ It was ready ~~to be carried to Twelve Oaks to be donned before the dancing began,~~
虛主詞 動詞 述詞　不定詞結構　介系詞+名詞　不定詞結構　　時間副詞子句

but Scarlett shrugged ~~at the sight of it~~.
　　主詞　　　動詞　　介系詞+名詞 介系詞+代名詞
　　譯 這是準備帶到「十二橡樹」村去，等舞會開場前穿的，但是斯嘉麗一見它便不由得聳了聳肩膀。

⑧ ~~If her plans were successful~~, she <u>would not wear</u> <u>that dress</u> ~~tonight~~.
　　條件副詞子句　　　　主詞　　動詞　　　　受詞　　　副詞
　　譯 如果她的計劃成功，今晚她就用不著穿這件衣裳了。

⑨ Long before the ball began, <u>she and Ashley</u> <u>would be</u> ~~on their way~~ to Jonesboro
　　　　　　　　　　　　　　　主詞　　　動詞　　介系詞+名詞　　　述詞

~~to be married~~.
不定詞結構
　　譯 等不到舞會開始，她和艾希禮早就啟程到瓊斯博羅結婚去了。

 ## 傲慢與偏見

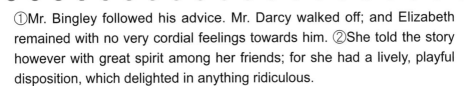

①Mr. Bingley followed his advice. Mr. Darcy walked off; and Elizabeth remained with no very cordial feelings towards him. ②She told the story however with great spirit among her friends; for she had a lively, playful disposition, which delighted in anything ridiculous.

③The evening altogether passed off pleasantly to the whole family. ④Mrs. Bennet had seen her eldest daughter much admired by the Netherfield party. ⑤Mr. Bingley had danced with her twice, and she had been distinguished by his sisters. ⑥Jane was as much gratified by this as her mother could be, though in a quieter way. ⑦ Elizabeth felt Jane's pleasure. ⑧Mary had heard herself mentioned to Miss Bingley as the most accomplished girl in the neighbourhood; and Catherine and Lydia had been fortunate enough to be never without partners, which was all that they had yet learnt to care for at a ball. ⑨They returned therefore, in good spirits to Longbourn, the village where they lived, and of which they were the principal inhabitants. ⑩They found Mr. Bennet still up. With a book, he was regardless of time; and on the present occasion he had a good deal of curiosity as to the event of an evening which had raised such splendid expectations.

補充單字片語

- cordial [ˈkɔ:dɪəl] /adj./ 熱誠的
- disposition [ˌdɪspəˈzɪʃn] /n./ 性格
- distinguish [dɪˈstɪŋgwɪʃ] /v./ 區分，辨別
- gratify [ˈgrætɪfaɪ] /v./ 使高興，使滿意
- a good deal of 很多的，好些

句構分析

① Mr. Bingley followed his advice. Mr. Darcy walked off; and Elizabeth
　　主詞　　　　動詞　　受詞　　　主詞　　　動詞　　　　　主詞
remained with no very cordial feelings towards him.
　動詞　　　　介系詞+名詞　　　　　　介系詞+代名詞
譯 彬格萊先生採納了達西先生的話，達西自己也走開了；伊麗莎白依舊坐在那裡，對達西先生仍然沒有好感。

② She told the story however with great spirit among her friends; for she had a
主詞 動詞　受詞　　　介系詞+名詞　　　　介系詞+名詞　　　原因副詞子句
lively, playful disposition, which delighted in anything ridiculous.
　　　　　　　　　　　　　　　形容詞子句
譯 然而她卻滿有興致地把這段偷聽到的話去講給她的朋友，因為她性格活潑調皮，遇到任何可笑的事情都會感到興趣。

③ The evening altogether passed off pleasantly to the whole family.
　　主詞　　　　副詞　　　動詞　　　副詞　　　介系詞+名詞
譯 總之全家人在這一個晚上都過得很高興。

④ Mrs. Bennet had seen her eldest daughter much admired by the Netherfield
　　主詞　　　　動詞　　　　受詞　　　　　　副詞　被動詞　介系詞+名詞
party.
譯 班太太看到尼日斐花園的一家人都這麼喜愛她的大女兒，覺得非常得意。

⑤ Mr. Bingley had danced with her twice, and she had been distinguished by his
　　主詞　　　動詞　　　介系詞+代名詞 副詞　主詞　　　動詞　　　　　　　介系詞+名詞

sisters.

譯 彬格萊先生邀她跳了兩次舞，而且他的姐妹們都對她另眼相看。

⑥ Jane was ~~as much~~ gratified ~~by this as her mother could be~~, though ~~in a quieter~~
主詞 動詞 副詞 　　述詞 　介系詞+代名詞 介系詞+名詞 　　　　介系詞+名詞
~~way~~.

譯 珍跟她母親一樣滿意，只不過沒有像她母親那樣聲張。

⑦ Elizabeth felt Jane's pleasure.
　主詞 　　動詞 　述詞
譯 伊麗莎白也為珍開心。

⑧ Mary had heard herself mentioned ~~to Miss Bingley as the most accomplished~~
主詞 　動詞 　　受詞 受詞補語 　　介系詞+名詞 　　　介系詞+名詞
~~girl in the neighbourhood;~~ and Catherine and Lydia had been fortunate ~~enough~~ to
　介系詞+名詞 　　　　　　　主詞 　　　　　動詞 　　　　述詞 　副詞
be never ~~without partners, which was all that they had yet learnt to care for at a ball~~.
　介系詞+名詞 　　　　　形容詞子句

譯 瑪麗曾聽到人們在彬格萊小姐面前提到她自己，說她是附近一帶最有才華的姑
娘；凱瑟琳和麗迪雅足夠的幸運，沒有哪一場舞會缺少舞伴，這是她們每逢開舞
會時唯一關心的事。

文法分析 本句是由and連接的兩個並列句，第一個句子是主詞+動詞+受詞結構，後一
個句子是主詞+動詞+述詞結構。

⑨ They returned ~~therefore, in good spirits~~ to Longbourn, the ~~village where they~~
主詞 動詞 　　副詞 　　　介系詞+名詞 　　受詞 　　　　　插入語
~~lived~~, and ~~of which they were the principal inhabitants~~.
　　　　　形容詞子句
譯 她們開開心心地回到她們所居住的浪搏恩村，她們算是這一村落的旺族。

⑩ They found Mr. Bennet still up.
　主詞 動詞 　　受語子句
譯 她們發現班納特先生還沒有睡覺。

⑪ ~~With a book~~, he was regardless ~~of time;~~ and ~~on the present occasion~~ he had ~~a~~
介系詞+名詞 主詞 動詞 述詞 　介系詞+名詞 　　介系詞+名詞 　　　　主詞 動詞
~~good deal of curiosity~~ as to the event of an evening ~~which had raised such splendid~~
　　受詞 　　　　　介系詞+名詞 　　介系詞+名詞 　形容詞子句
~~expectations~~.
譯 這位先生平常只要捧上一本書，就忘了時間；可是這次他沒有睡覺，因為他極想
知道大家朝思暮想 的這一盛會，經過情形究竟如何。

木偶奇遇記

①Pinocchio is hungry and looks for an egg to cook himself an omelet; but, to his surprise, the omelet flies out of the window. ②If the Cricket's death scared Pinocchio at all, it was only for a very few moments. ③For, as night came on, a queer, empty feeling at the pit of his stomach reminded the Marionette that he had eaten nothing as yet.

④A boy's appetite grows very fast, and in a few moments the queer, empty feeling had become hunger, and the hunger grew bigger and bigger, until soon he was as ravenous as a bear.

⑤Poor Pinocchio ran to the fireplace where the pot was boiling and stretched out his hand to take the cover off, but to his amazement the pot was only painted! ⑥ Think how he felt! ⑦His long nose became at least two inches longer.

⑧He ran about the room, dug in all the boxes and drawers, and even looked under the bed in search of a piece of bread, hard though it might be, or a cookie, or perhaps a bit of fish.

⑨A bone left by a dog would have tasted good to him!

⑩But he found nothing.
And meanwhile his hunger grew and grew. The only relief poor Pinocchio had was to yawn; and he certainly did yawn, such a big yawn that his mouth stretched out to the tips of his ears. Soon he became dizzy and faint.

補充單字片語

- omelet ['ɒmlɪt] /n./ 歐姆蛋
- ravenous ['rævənəs] /adj./ 極餓的

句構分析

① Pinocchio is hungry and looks for an egg to cook himself an omelet; but, to his
主詞　動詞　述詞　動詞　　受詞　　不定詞結構　　　　　　插入語
surprise, the omelet flies out of the window.
　　　　主詞　　動詞　介系詞+名詞
譯 皮諾丘餓了，準備找個雞蛋給自己做個歐姆蛋；但令他吃驚的是，歐姆蛋飛出了窗外。

結構分析 該句子在文章開頭給讀者介紹皮諾丘餓了，但歐姆蛋又飛出了窗外，留下了懸念，為後文故事的發展埋下伏筆。

② If the Cricket's death scared Pinocchio at all, it was only for a very few moments.
　　條件副詞子句　　　　　　　　　　　　　主詞 動詞 副詞　時間副詞片語
　圞 如果蟋蟀的死嚇到了皮諾丘，那也只是一小會兒。

③ For, as night came on, a queer, empty feeling at the pit of his stomach reminded
　　　插入語　　　　主詞　　　　介系詞+名詞 介系詞+名詞　　動詞
the Marionette that he had eaten nothing as yet.
　　受詞　　　　同位語子句
　圞 這時候天漸漸黑了，皮諾丘突然想起來自己自己還沒有吃東西，覺得肚子咕嚕咕
　　嚕叫。

④ A boy's appetite grows very fast, and in a few moments the queer, empty feeling
　　主詞　　　　動詞 副詞 述詞　　　插入語　　　　　　主詞
had become hunger, and the hunger grew bigger and bigger, until soon he was as
　動詞　　述詞　　　主詞　　動詞　　述詞
ravenous as a bear.
　圞 孩子總是這樣，一想吃就越來越想吃，幾分鐘工夫，想吃就變成了肚子饑餓，肚
　　子越來越餓，餓得他像隻饑餓的熊。

⑤ Poor Pinocchio ran to the fireplace where the pot was boiling and stretched out
　　主詞　　　動詞　　受詞　　　　形容詞子句　　　　　　動詞
his hand to take the cover off, but to his amazement the pot was only painted!
　受詞　　不定詞結構　　　　介系詞+名詞　主詞 動詞 副詞　述詞
　圞 可憐的皮諾丘馬上向壁爐撲過去，那兒有個鍋子正在冒熱氣，他伸手打算揭開鍋
　　蓋，但讓他感到意外的是那鍋子只是畫在牆上的！

⑥ Think how he felt!
　圞 諸位想像一下吧，他該是多麼失望啊！
　文法分析 該句子是how引導的感嘆句，how意為「多麼」，修飾形容詞或副詞。

⑦ His long nose became at least two inches longer.
　　主詞　　　動詞　介系詞片語　　述詞
　圞 他那個本來已經很長的鼻子，馬上又至少長了兩英寸。

⑧ He ran about the room, dug in all the boxes and drawers, and even looked under
主詞 動詞 介系詞+名詞　動詞　　介系詞+名詞　　　　副詞 動詞 介系詞+名詞
the bed in search of a piece of bread, hard though it might be, or a cookie, or perhaps
介系詞+名詞 介系詞+名詞 介系詞+名詞　　　　　　　　　　　　　　副詞
a bit of fish.
　介系詞+名詞
　圞 於是他滿屋子亂跑，搜遍了所有的箱子和抽屜，甚至想在床底下找哪怕是一丁點
　　兒乾麵包，或者一小塊餅乾，或是一小塊魚肉。

⑨ A bone left by a dog would have tasted good to him!
　主詞　　形容詞片語　　　動詞　　　述詞 介系詞+代名詞

譯 一塊狗啃過的骨頭對他來說也是美味！

⑩But he found nothing.
　　主詞 動詞 受詞
譯 可他什麼也沒找到。

⑪ And ~~meanwhile~~ his hunger grew and grew.
　　　　副詞　　　　主詞　　　　動詞
譯 這時他肚子越來越餓，越來越餓。

⑫ The only relief poor Pinocchio ~~had~~ was to yawn; and he ~~certainly~~ did yawn,
　　主詞　　　　　　　　　　　　　　　動詞 述詞　主詞 副詞　　　動詞

such a big yawn ~~that his mouth stretched out to the tips of his ears~~.
　　　　　　　　　　　形容詞子句
譯 可憐的皮諾丘，他除了打哈欠毫無辦法；他確實這麼做了，他的哈欠打得那麼
　 長，以至於嘴巴都一直咧到耳朵邊。

⑬ ~~Soon~~ he became dizzy and faint.
　副詞 主詞 動詞　　　述詞
譯 很快地，他開始頭暈目眩，變得虛弱起來。

大亨小傳

①There was music from my neighbor's house through the summer nights. ②In his blue gardens men and girls came and went like moths among the whisperings and the champagne and the stars. ③At high tide in the afternoon I watched his guests diving from the tower of his raft or taking the sun on the hot sand of his beach while his two motor-boats slit the waters of the sound, drawing aquaplanes over cataracts of foam. ④On week-ends his Rolls-Royce became an omnibus, bearing parties to and from the city, between nine in the morning and long past midnight, while his station wagon scampered like a brisk yellow bug to meet all trains. ⑤And on Mondays eight servants including an extra gardener toiled all day with mops and scrubbing-brushes and hammers and garden-shears, repairing the ravages of the night before.

⑥ Every Friday five crates of oranges and lemons arrived from a fruiterer in New York-every Monday these same oranges and lemons left his back door in a pyramid of pulpless halves. ⑦There was a machine in the kitchen which could extract the juice of two hundred oranges in half an hour, if a little button was pressed two hundred times by a butler's thumb.

補充單字片語

- champagne [ʃæmˈpeɪn] /n./ 香檳酒
- scamper [ˈskæmpə] /v./ 蹦蹦跳跳地跑，驚惶奔跑
- fruiterer [ˈfruːtərə] /n./ 水果商

句構分析

① There was music <del>from my neighbor's house through the summer nights</del>.
　　There be 句型　　　　介系詞+名詞　　　　　介系詞+名詞
　譯 在整個夏天的夜晚，都有音樂聲從我鄰居家傳過來。
　結構分析 該句是本段的主旨句，後面又圍繞為什麼會有音樂聲從鄰居家傳過來展開進行。

② <del>In his blue gardens</del> men and girls came and went <del>like moths among the</del>
　　介系詞+名詞　　　　主詞　　　動詞　　介系詞+名詞 介系詞+名詞
<del>whisperings and the champagne and the stars</del>.
　譯 在他藍色的花園裡，男男女女像飛蛾一般在笑語、香檳和繁星之間來來往往。

③ <del>At high tide in the afternoon</del> I watched his guests <del>diving from the tower of his</del>
　介系詞+名詞　介系詞+名詞　主詞 動詞　受詞　　動名詞作形容詞片語 介系詞+名詞
<del>raft or taking the sun on the hot sand of his beach</del> while his two motor-boats slit
　　動名詞作形容詞片語 介系詞+名詞　介系詞+名詞　　　　主詞　　　動詞
the waters <del>of the Sound, drawing aquaplanes over cataracts of foam</del>.
　受詞　　介系詞+名詞　　動名詞作形容詞片語　　介系詞+名詞 介系詞+名詞
　譯 下午漲潮的時候，我看著他的客人從他木筏的跳台上跳水，或是躺在他海灘的熱沙上曬太陽，同時他的兩艘小汽艇破浪前進，拖著滑水板駛過翻騰的浪花。
　文法補充 該長句是由while連接的兩個並列句子，表示「對比的關係」，另外while作連接詞還有兩種用法，其一意為「當……的時候」，引導時間副詞子句，其二意為「雖然，盡管」，引導讓步副詞子句。

④ <del>On week-ends</del> his Rolls-Royce became an omnibus, <del>bearing parties to and from</del>
　介系詞+名詞　　　主詞　　　動詞　　述詞　　動名詞作形容詞片語
<del>the city, between nine in the morning and long past midnight</del>, while his station
　　　　　　　　插入語　　　　　　　　　　　　　　　主詞
wagon scampered <del>like a brisk yellow bug</del> to meet all trains.
　　動詞　　介系詞+名詞　　　不定詞+受詞

🔤 每逢周末，他的勞斯萊斯轎車就成了公共汽車，從早晨九點到深更半夜往來城裡接送客人，同時他的旅行車也像一只輕捷的黃硬殼蟲那樣去火車站接所有的班車。

⑤ And ~~on Mondays~~ eight servants ~~including an extra gardener~~ toiled all day ~~with~~
　　　介系詞+名詞　　主詞　　　介系詞片語　　　　　　　動詞　時間副詞
~~mops and scrubbing-brushes and hammers and garden-shears, repairing the~~
　　　　介系詞+名詞　　　　　　　　　　　　　　　　　動名詞作形容詞片語
~~ravages of the night before.~~
　　　　介系詞+名詞　副詞

🔤 每周一，八個僕人，包括一個臨時園丁，辛苦整理一天，用許多拖把、板刷、榔頭、修技剪來收拾前一晚的殘局。

⑥ ~~Every Friday~~ five crates ~~of oranges and lemons~~ arrived ~~from a fruiterer in New~~
　　副詞　　　主詞　　　介系詞+名詞　　　動詞　介系詞+名詞 介系詞+名詞
~~York—every Monday~~ these same oranges and lemons left his back door ~~in a~~
　　　　　　　　　　　主詞　　　　　　　　　　動詞　　受詞
~~pyramid of pulpless halves.~~
介系詞+名詞　介系詞+名詞

🔤 每周五，五箱橙子和檸檬從紐約一家水果行送來；每周一，這些橙子和檸檬變成一座半拉半拉的果皮堆成的小金字塔從他的後門運出去。

⑦ There was a machine ~~in the kitchen which could extract the juice of two hundred~~
　　There be句型　　　介系詞+名詞　　　形容詞子句
~~oranges in half an hour, if a little button was pressed two hundred times by a butler's~~
　　　　　　　　　　　　　條件副詞子句
~~thumb.~~

🔤 在他廚房裡有一台榨果汁機，半小時之內可以榨兩百個橙子，只要男管家用大拇指把一個按鈕按兩百次就行了。

簡·愛

①No severe or prolonged bodily illness followed this incident of the red-room; it only gave my nerves a shock of which I feel the reverberation to this day. ②Yes, Mrs. Reed, to you I owe some fearful pangs of mental suffering, but I ought to forgive you, for you knew not what you did: while rending my heart-strings, you thought you were only uprooting my bad propensities.

③Next day, by noon, I was up and dressed, and sat wrapped in a shawl by the nursery hearth. ④I felt physically weak and broken down: but my worse ailment was an unutterable wretchedness of mind: a wretchedness which kept drawing from me silent tears; no sooner had I wiped one salt drop from my cheek than another followed. ⑤Yet, I thought, I ought to have been happy, for none of the Reeds were there, they were all gone out in the carriage with their mama. ⑥Abbot, too, was sewing in another room, and Bessie, as she moved hither and thither, putting away toys and arranging drawers, addressed to me every now and then a word of unwonted kindness. ⑦This state of things should have been to me a paradise of peace, accustomed as I was to a life of ceaseless reprimand and thankless fagging; but, in fact, my racked nerves were now in such a state that no calm could soothe, and no pleasure excite them agreeably.

補充單字片語

- incident [ˈɪnsɪdənt] /n./ 事件
- physically [ˈfɪzɪklɪ] /adv./ 身體上地，完全地
- unutterable [ʌnˈʌtərəbl] /adj./ 説不出的，難以形容的

句構分析

① No severe or prolonged bodily illness followed this incident of the red-room; it
副詞　主詞　動詞　受詞　介系詞+名詞　主詞
only gave my nerves a shock of which I feel the reverberation to this day.
副詞 動詞　受詞　受詞　形容詞子句
譯 紅房子事件沒有給我留下嚴重或長期的身體後遺症，它僅僅使我的神經受到了驚嚇，對此我至今記憶猶新。

② Yes, Mrs. Reed, to you I owe some fearful pangs of mental suffering, but I ought
介系詞+代名詞 主詞 動詞　受詞　介系詞+名詞　主詞
to forgive you, for you knew not what you did: while rending my heart-strings, you
動詞　受詞　原因副詞子句　主詞
thought you were only uprooting my bad propensities.
動詞　受詞子句 副詞
譯 是的，里德太太，你讓我受到了可怕的精神創傷，但我應該原諒你，因為你並不知道自己做了些什麼，明明是在割斷我的心弦，你卻自以為無非是要根除我的惡習。

③ Next day, by noon, I was up and dressed, and sat wrapped in a shawl by the
介系詞+名詞 主詞 動詞 述詞　介系詞+代名詞

095

nursery hearth.

譯 第二天中午，我起床穿好衣服，裹了塊浴巾，坐在保育室的壁爐旁邊。

④ I felt physically weak and broken down: but my worse ailment was an
主詞 動詞 副詞　　述詞　　　　　　　　　　　主詞　　　　　動詞 述詞
unutterable wretchedness of mind: a wretchedness which kept drawing from me
　　　　　　　　　　　　　介系詞+名詞　　　　　　　形容詞子句
silent tears; no sooner had I wiped one salt drop from my cheek than another
　　　　　　　　　　　　　　　　　　　　　　　介系詞+名詞
followed.

譯 我身體虛弱，幾乎要垮下來：但最大的痛楚卻是內心難以言傳的苦惱：這不幸遭
遇弄得我不斷暗暗落淚；才從臉頰上抹去一滴帶鹹味的淚水，另一滴又滾落下
來。

⑤ Yet, I thought, I ought to have been happy, for none of the Reeds were there,
副詞 主詞 動詞 主詞　　　動詞　　　述詞　　　原因副詞子句
they were all gone out in the carriage with their mama.
主詞　　　副詞 動詞　　介系詞+名詞　　　介系詞+名詞
譯 然而，我想我應該高興，因為里德一家人都不在，他們都坐了車隨媽媽出去了。

⑥ Abbot, too, was sewing in another room, and Bessie, as she moved hither and
主詞 插入語 動詞　　介系詞+名詞　　　　主詞　　　插入語
thither, putting away toys and arranging drawers, addressed to me every now and
　　　　　動詞　　　受詞　　　動詞　　　受詞　　　動詞　　　受詞 副詞
then a word of unwonted kindness.
　　　　　　介系詞+名詞
譯 艾博特也在另一個房間裡做針線活，而貝茜呢，來回忙碌著，一面把玩具收拾起
來，將抽屜整理好，一面還不時地同我說兩句少有的體貼話。

⑦ This state of things should have been to me a paradise of peace, accustomed as I was to a
主詞　　介系詞+名詞　　　　動詞　　介系詞+名詞 述詞 介系詞+名詞　　形容詞子句
life of ceaseless reprimand and thankless fagging; but, in fact, my racked nerves were now
　　　　　介系詞+名詞　　　　　　　　　　　　　介系詞+名詞　　　主詞　　　動詞 副詞
in such a state that no calm could soothe, and no pleasure excite them agreeably.
　述詞　　　　　　　　　　　同位語子句
譯 對我來說，過慣了那種成天挨罵、辛辛苦苦吃力不討好的日子後，這光景好比是
平靜的樂園，然而，我的神經己被折磨得痛苦不堪，終於連平靜也撫慰不了我，
歡樂也難以使我興奮了。

茶花女

①I was at that time recently returned from my travels. ②It was quite natural that no one had told me about Marguerite's death, for it was hardly one of those momentous news-items which friends always rush to tell anybody who has just got back to the capital city of News. ③ Marguerite had been pretty, but the greater the commotion that attends the sensational lives of these women, the smaller the stir once they are dead. ④They are like those dull suns which set as they have risen: they are unremarkable. ⑤News of their death, when they die young, reaches all their lovers at the same instant, for in Paris the lovers of any celebrated courtesan see each other every day. ⑥A few reminiscences are exchanged about her, and the lives of all and sundry continue as before without so much as a tear.

⑦For a young man of twenty-five nowadays, tears have become so rare a thing that they are not to be wasted on the first girl who comes along. ⑧The most that may be expected is that the parents and relatives who pay for the privilege of being wept for are indeed mourned to the extent of their investment.

補充單字片語

- commotion [kəˈməʊʃn] /n./ 混亂，喧鬧
- unremarkable [ˌʌnrɪˈmɑːkəbl] /adj./ 尋常的，平凡的
- reminiscence [ˌremɪˈnɪsns] /n./ 舊事，回憶
- privilege [ˈprɪvəlɪdʒ] /n./ 特權

句構分析

① I was ~~at that time recently~~ returned ~~from my travels~~.
　主詞　介系詞+名詞 副詞　 動詞　 介系詞+名詞
　譯 那個時候，我剛從外地旅遊歸來。

② It was ~~quite natural~~ that no one had told me ~~about Marguerite's death~~, for it was ~~hardly~~
虛主詞 動詞 副詞　述詞　　　　 主詞子句　　　　　 介系詞+名詞　　　　　　　　　 副詞
~~one of those momentous news-items which friends always rush to tell anybody~~
　　　 介系詞+名詞　　　　　　　　　　 形容詞子句
~~who has just got back to the capital city of News~~.
　　形容詞子句　　　　　　 介系詞+名詞　 介系詞+名詞

🈐 當一個人剛回到消息靈通的首都時，朋友們總是要告訴他一些重要新聞的，但是沒有人把瑪格麗特的去世當作什麼大事情來告訴我，這也是很自然的。

　　語法分析 在該句中，為了避免頭重腳輕，it作虛主語，放在句首，真正的主詞是that no one had told me。

③ Marguerite had been pretty, but the greater the commotion that attends the sensational
　　　　主詞　　　動詞　　　述詞　　　　　　　　　　　　　　同位語子句

lives of these women, the smaller the stir once they are dead.
　　　介系詞+名詞　　　　　　　時間副詞子句

　　🈐 瑪格麗特一直很漂亮，但是，這些女人生前考究的生活越是鬧得滿城風雨，她們死後也就越是無聲無息。

　　語法分析 該句中採用了「the+比較級+...，the+比較級+...」的句式結構，表示「越……，越……」。

④ They are like those dull suns which set as they have risen: they are unremarkable.
　　　　　介系詞+名詞　　　　　形容詞子句　　　　　　　主詞 動詞　述詞

　　🈐 她們就像某些星辰，隕落時和初升時一樣黯淡無光。

⑤ News of their death, when they die young, reaches all their lovers at the same instant,
　主詞　介系詞+名詞　　　插入語　　　　動詞　　受詞　　介系詞+名詞

for in Paris the lovers of any celebrated courtesan see each other every day.
　　　　　原因副詞子句

　　🈐 如果她們年紀輕輕就死了，那麼她們所有的情人都會同時得到消息，因為在巴黎，一位名妓的所有情人彼此幾乎都是密友。

⑥ A few reminiscences are exchanged about her, and the lives of all and sundry
　　　　主詞　　　　動詞　述詞　介系詞+名詞　　主詞　　介系詞+名詞

continue as before without so much as a tear.
　動詞　介系詞+名詞　介系詞+名詞

　　🈐 大家會相互回憶幾件有關她過去的事，然後各人將依然故我，絲毫不受這事的影響，甚至誰也不會因此而掉一滴眼淚。

⑦ For a young man of twenty-five nowadays, tears have become so rare a thing
　　介系詞+名詞　　　　介系詞+名詞　　　主詞　　動詞　　　述詞

that they are not to be wasted on the first girl who comes along.
　　形容詞子句　　　　　　　　介系詞+名詞　　形容詞子句

　　🈐 如今，人們到了二十五歲的年紀，眼淚就變得非常珍貴，決不能輕易亂流。

⑧ The most that may be expected is that the parents and relatives who pay for the
　主詞　　形容詞子句　　動詞　　述詞子句　　　　　形容詞子句

privilege of being wept for are indeed mourned to the extent of their investment.
　　　　　　　　　　　　　　　　　　　介系詞+名詞　　介系詞+名詞

　　🈐 充其量只對為他們花費過金錢的雙親才哭上幾聲，作為對過去他們破費的報答。

湯姆歷險記

①Saturday morning was come, and all the summer world was bright and fresh, and brimming with life. ②There was a song in every heart; and if the heart was young the music issued at the lips. ③There was cheer in every face and a spring in every step. ④The locusttrees were in bloom and the fragrance of the blossoms filled the air. ⑤Cardiff Hill, beyond the village and above it, was green with vegetation and it lay just far enough away to seem a Delectable Land, dreamy, reposeful, and inviting.

⑥Tom appeared on the sidewalk with a bucket of whitewash and a long-handled brush. ⑦He surveyed the fence, and all gladness left him and a deep melancholy settled down upon his spirit. ⑧Thirty yards of board fence nine feet high. ⑨Life to him seemed hollow, and existence but a burden. ⑩Sighing, he dipped his brush and passed it along the topmost plank; repeated the operation; did it again; compared the insignificant whitewashed streak with the far-reaching continent of unwhitewashed fence, and sat down on a tree-box discouraged. Jim came skipping out at the gate with a tin pail, and singing Buffalo Gals.

補充單字片語

- fragrance [ˈfreɪgrəns] /n./ 芳香，芬芳
- vegetation [ˌvedʒəˈteɪʃn] /n./ 植物，草木
- reposeful [rɪˈpəʊzfəl] /adj./ 寧靜的，安詳的
- melancholy [ˈmelənkəlɪ] /n./ 憂鬱，惆悵
- insignificant [ˌɪnsɪgˈnɪfɪkənt] /adj./ 不重要的

句構分析

① Saturday morning was coming, and all the summer world was bright and fresh, and
　　　主詞　　　　動詞 現在進行式　　　　主詞　　　　動詞　　述詞
brimming with life.
　　介系詞+名詞
譯 星期六的早晨來了，整個夏天的世界，陽光明媚，空氣新鮮，充滿了生機。
結構分析 本句是整段的主旨句，後面幾個句子又具體描述了夏天的世界是怎麼樣的。

② There was a song in every heart; and if the heart was young the music issued at the lips.
　　there be句型　　　介系詞+名詞　　　條件副詞子句　　　主詞　　動詞　　　受詞

譯 每個人的心中都蕩漾著一首歌，有些年輕人情不自禁地唱出了這首歌。

③ There was cheer ~~in every face~~ and a spring ~~in every step~~.
    there be句型　　介系詞+名詞　　　　　　　介系詞+名詞
譯 每個人臉上都洋溢著快樂，每個人的腳步都是那麼輕盈。

④ The locust-trees were in bloom and the fragrance ~~of the blossoms~~ filled the air.
    主詞　　　　動詞　　述詞　　　　　主詞　　　介系詞+名詞　動詞　受詞
譯 槐樹開花了，空氣中瀰漫著花香。

⑤ Cardiff Hill, ~~beyond the village and above it~~, was green ~~with vegetation~~ and it lay
    主詞　　　　　　插入語　　　　　　　　動詞 述詞　介系詞+名詞　　主詞 動詞
just far enough away to ~~seem a Delectable Land, dreamy, reposeful, and inviting~~.
副詞 述詞 副詞　　　　　不定詞結構
譯 村莊外面高高的卡第夫山上覆蓋著綠色的植被，這山離村子不遠不近，就像一塊
「樂土」，寧靜安詳，充滿夢幻，令人嚮往。

⑥ Tom appeared on the sidewalk ~~with a bucket of whitewash and a long-handled brush~~.
    主詞　動詞　　　受詞　　　　介系詞+名詞　介系詞+名詞
譯 湯姆一只手拎著一桶灰漿，另一只手拿著一把長柄刷子，出現在人行道上。

⑦ He surveyed the fence, and all gladness left him and a deep melancholy settled down
  主詞　動詞　　受詞　　　　　主詞　　動詞 受詞　　　　主詞　　　　　動詞
upon his spirit.
    受詞
譯 他環顧柵欄，所有的快樂，立刻煙消雲散，心中充滿了惆悵。

⑧ Thirty yards ~~of board~~ fence nine feet high.
       介系詞+名詞
譯 三十碼長九英尺高的木柵欄。

⑨ Life ~~to him~~ seemed hollow, and existence but a burden.
主詞 介系詞+代名詞 動詞　　述詞
譯 對他來說生活似乎很空虛，活著只是一種負擔。

⑩ ~~Sighing~~, he dipped his brush and passed it ~~along the topmost plank~~; repeated the
    主詞 動詞　　受詞　　　　動詞 受詞 介系詞+名詞　　　　　動詞
operation; did it ~~again~~; compared the insignificant whitewashed streak ~~with the far-reaching~~
受詞　動詞 受詞 副詞　　動詞　　　　　　受詞　　　　　　　　介系詞 +名詞
~~continent of unwhitewashed fence~~, and sat down ~~on a tree-box~~ discouraged.
    介系詞 +名詞　　　　　　　動詞　　介系詞 +代名詞　被動分詞
譯 他嘆了一口氣，用刷子蘸上灰漿，沿著最頂上一層木板刷起來；接著又刷了一
下，兩下；看看剛刷過的不起眼的那塊，再和那遠不著邊際的柵欄相比，湯姆灰
心喪氣地在一塊木箱子上坐下來。

⑪ Jim came skipping out ~~at the gate with a tin pail~~, and singing Buffalo Gals.
主詞　動詞　　　　　介系詞 +名詞　介系詞 +名詞　動詞
譯 這時，吉姆手裡提著一個錫皮桶，嘴中唱著「布法羅的女娃們」蹦蹦跳跳地從大
門口跑出來。

安娜·卡列妮娜

①Stepan Arkadyevitch was a truthful man in his relations with himself. ②He was incapable of deceiving himself and persuading himself that he repented of his conduct. ③He could not at this date repent of the fact that he, a handsome, susceptible man of thirty-four, was not in love with his wife, the mother of five living and two dead children, and only a year younger than himself. ④All he repented of was that he had not succeeded better in hiding it from his wife. ⑤But he felt all the difficulty of his position and was sorry for his wife, his children, and himself. ⑥Possibly he might have managed to conceal his sins better from his wife if he had anticipated that the knowledge of them would have had such an effect on her. ⑦ He had never clearly thought out the subject, but he had vaguely conceived that his wife must long ago have suspected him of being unfaithful to her, and shut her eyes to the fact. ⑧He had even supposed that she, a worn-out woman no longer young or good-looking, and in no way remarkable or interesting, merely a good mother, ought from a sense of fairness to take an indulgent view. ⑨It had turned out quite the other way.

補充單字片語

- repent [rɪˈpent] /v./ 後悔，懺悔（對自己）
- susceptible [səˈseptəbl] /adj./ 易被影響的，多情的
- conceal [kənˈsi:l] /v./ 隱瞞，隱藏
- vaguely [ˈveɪglɪ] /adv./ 模糊地，含糊地
- turn out 結果是，關掉

句構分析

① <u>Stepan Arkadyevitch</u> was a truthful man ~~in his relations with himself~~.

　　　主詞　　　　　　動詞　　述詞　　介系詞+名詞　　介系詞+名詞

譯 與他自己的關係來說，斯特潘·阿爾卡季奇是一個忠於自己的人。

句構分析 該句子是該段落的主旨句。

② He was incapable ~~of deceiving himself and persuading himself that he repented of his conduct~~.

主詞 動詞 述詞　　　介系詞+現在分詞　　　　　　　　　　　受詞子句

譯 他不能欺騙和說服自己他後悔自己的行為。

③ He could not ~~at this date~~ repent of the fact ~~that he, a handsome, susceptible man~~

主詞　　　　　介系詞+名詞　　動詞　　受詞　　　　同位語子句

~~of thirty four, was not in love with his wife, the mother of five living and two dead~~
~~children, and only a year younger than himself.~~

譯 他現在並不後悔這個事實，即他這位英俊多情的三十四歲的男子並不愛自己的妻子，而他的妻子是五個活著的和兩個死去的孩子的母親，而且只比他小一歲。

句構分析 該句子是由一個主句和一個同位語子句構成的複合句，同位語子句中的主幹是he was not in love with his wife，repent與介詞of連用，是固定搭配，不可被分開。

④ All he repented of was that he had not succeeded ~~better in hiding it from his wife.~~

　　主詞　　　　動詞　　　　述詞子句　　　　　　　副詞　介系詞+動名詞　介系詞+名詞

譯 他後悔的是沒有在妻子面前成功地把自己隱藏起來。

⑤ But he felt all the difficulty ~~of his position~~ and was sorry ~~for his wife, his children,~~

　　主詞 動詞 受詞　　　介系詞+名詞　　　　動詞　述詞　　　介系詞+名詞

~~and himself.~~

譯 但是他感到了自己處境的所有困難，他為妻子、孩子和自己感到難過。

⑥ ~~Possibly~~ he might have managed to conceal his sins ~~better from his wife if he had~~

　　副詞　主詞　　　動詞　　　　受詞　　　　副詞　介系詞+名詞

~~anticipated that the knowledge of them would have had such an effect on her.~~

條件副詞子句

譯 如果他早知道自己的罪行會如此影響妻子，也許他會更好地把它們隱藏起來。

⑦ He had never ~~clearly~~ thought out the subject, but he had ~~vaguely~~ conceived that his wife

主詞　　　　副詞　動詞　　受詞　　　主詞　　副詞　　動詞　　受詞子句

must ~~long ago~~ have suspected him ~~of being unfaithful to her~~, and shut her eyes ~~to the fact.~~

　　副詞　　　　　　　　　　　　介系詞+動名詞　　　　動詞 受詞　　不定詞結構

譯 他從來沒有清楚地想過這個問題，但他有一種模糊的想法，就是他的妻子很久以前就懷疑他的不忠，並且裝作不知道。

句構分析 該句是由主句和一個受詞子句構成的複合句，受詞子句中and連接兩個小分句，這都屬於受詞子句的一部分。

⑧ He had ~~even~~ supposed that she, ~~a worn-out woman no longer young or good-looking,~~

主詞　　副詞　　動詞　　受詞子句

~~and in no way remarkable or interesting, merely a good mother,~~ ought ~~from a sense of fairness~~

插入語　　　　　　　　　　　　　　　　　　　　　　　　介系詞+名詞　　介系詞+名詞

to takean indulgent view.

譯 他甚至認為她是一個不再年輕，不再漂亮的老婦人，毫不惹人矚目，十分無趣，僅僅是一個好母親，她應該從公平的角度來給予他寬容。

句構分析 該句子中有較長的插入語，是對子句的主詞做的說明，化繁為簡時，可一併去掉。

⑨ It had turned out quite the other way.

主詞　　動詞　　　副詞　　述詞

譯 結果恰是相反的。

動物農莊

①The singing of this song threw the animals into the wildest excitement. ②Almost before Major had reached the end, they had begun singing it for themselves. ③Even the stupidest of them had already picked up the tune and a few of the words, and as for the clever ones, such as the pigs and dogs, they had the entire song by heart within a few minutes. ④And then, after a few preliminary tries, the whole farm burst out into Beasts of England in tremendous unison. ⑤The cows lowed it, the dogs whined it, the sheep bleated it, the horses whinnied it, the ducks quacked it. ⑥They were so delighted with the song that they sang it right through five times in succession, and might have continued singing it all night if they had not been interrupted.

⑦Unfortunately, the uproar awoke Mr. Jones, who sprang out of bed, making sure that there was a fox in the yard. ⑧He seized the gun which always stood in a corner of his bedroom, and let fly a charge of number 6 shot into the darkness. ⑨ The pellets buried themselves in the wall of the barn and the meeting broke up hurriedly. ⑩Everyone fled to his own sleeping-place. The birds jumped on to their perches, the animals settled down in the straw, and the whole farm was asleep in a moment.

補充單字片語

- unison ['juːnɪsn] /n./ 和諧，一致
- whine [waɪn] /v./ 嗚嗚，哀叫
- bleat [bliːt] /v./ 羊叫，咩咩
- whinny ['wɪnɪ] /v./ 嘶叫
- quack [kwæk] /v./ 鴨叫，嘎嘎聲
- as for 至於，關於

句構分析

① The singing ~~of this song~~ threw the animals into the wildest excitement.
　　主詞　　　介系詞+名詞 動詞　　受詞　　　　　　受詞補語
　圞 唱著這首歌讓動物們陷入了狂野的興奮中。

② ~~Almost before Major had reached the end~~, they had begun singing it ~~for themselves~~.
　　副詞　　　時間副詞子句　　　　　　　　主詞　　　動詞　　　受詞 介系詞+代名詞

103

譯 幾乎在梅傑唱完之前，他們已經自己唱了起來。

句構分析 該句是由一個時間副詞子句和主句構成的複合句，在化繁為簡時，可把副詞子句去掉。

③ ~~Even~~ the stupidest ~~of them~~ had ~~already~~ picked up the tune and a few of the words,
　　副詞　　　主詞　　介系詞+名詞　副詞　　動詞　　　　　　受詞

and ~~as for the clever ones, such as the pigs and dogs,~~ they had the entire song
　　　介系詞+名詞　　　　　　　插入語　　　　　　　主詞 動詞　　受詞

~~by heart within a few minutes.~~
　　介系詞+名詞

譯 甚至他們中最愚笨的也學會了曲調和一些歌詞，而那些聰明的動物，比如豬和狗，在幾分鐘內就記住了整首歌。

④ And ~~then, after a few preliminary tries,~~ the whole farm burst out ~~into Beasts of~~
　　　　副詞　　　　時間副詞子句　　　　　　主詞　　　　動詞　　介系詞+名詞

~~England in tremendous unison.~~
　　　介系詞+名詞

譯 然後，在幾次初步嘗試之後，整個農場爆發出震動的《英格蘭獸》齊聲合唱。

⑤ The cows lowed it, the dogs whined it, the sheep bleated it, the horses whinnied it,
　　主詞　　動詞 受詞　主詞　　動詞 受詞　主詞　　動詞 受詞　主詞　　　動詞　受詞

the ducks quacked it.
　　主詞　　動詞　受詞

譯 牛哞哞地叫，狗汪汪地叫，羊咩咩地叫，馬嘶嘶地叫，鴨子嘎嘎地叫。

句構分析 該句子是由五個並列的小分句構成的，五個小分句都是主詞+動詞+受詞結構。

⑥ They were ~~so~~ delighted ~~with the song that they sang it right through five times in succession,~~
　　主詞 動詞 副詞　述詞　　介系詞+名詞　　結果副詞子句　　副詞 介系詞+名詞　　介系詞+名詞

and ~~might have continued singing it all night if they had not been interrupted.~~
　　　結果副詞子句　　　　　　　　　副詞　　條件副詞子句

譯 唱著這首歌他們太高興了，連續唱了整整五次，如果他們沒有被打斷的話，可能會唱個通宵。

句構分析 該句子是由主句和結果副詞子句構成的複合句，而if條件副詞子句是結果副詞子句的條件子句。

⑦ ~~Unfortunately,~~ the uproar awoke Mr. Jones, ~~who sprang out of bed, making sure~~
　　　副詞　　　　　主詞　　動詞　　受詞　　　形容詞子句　　　動名詞作形容詞片語

~~that there was a fox in the yard.~~
　　受詞子句　　　　介系詞+名詞

譯 不幸的是，喧鬧聲吵醒了瓊斯先生，他從床上跳起來，他以為院子裡有一隻狐狸。

⑧ He seized the gun ~~which always stood in a corner of his bedroom,~~ and let fly
　　主詞　動詞　受詞　　形容詞子句　　　　介系詞+名詞　　介系詞+名詞　　　　動詞

a charge of number 6 shot ~~into the darkness.~~
　　受詞補語　　　　　　　　介系詞+名詞

圞 他抓著那把一直立在臥室角落裡的槍，用槍膛裡的6號子彈向黑暗處開了一槍。

句構分析 and前是一個由主句和形容詞子句構成的複合句，and後是一個簡單句。

⑨ The pellets buried themselves ~~in the wall of the barn~~ and the meeting broke up ~~hurriedly~~.
    主詞   動詞   受詞   介系詞+名詞 介系詞+名詞   主詞   動詞   副詞

圞 子彈射進谷倉的牆壁裡，聚會匆匆解散了。

⑩ Everyone fled to his own sleeping-place.
    主詞   動詞   受詞

圞 動物們都溜回自己睡覺的地方去了。

⑪ The birds jumped ~~on~~ to their perches, the animals settled ~~down in the straw~~, and
    主詞   動詞   副詞   受詞   主詞   動詞   副詞   介系詞+名詞

the whole farm was asleep ~~in a moment~~.
    主詞   動詞   述詞 介系詞+名詞

圞 鳥兒們跳到了架子上，動物們在稻草上安歇了下來，整個農場瞬間沈寂了下來。

句構分析 該句子是由and連接的三個並列分句構成的簡單句。

名校勵志演講：
一切皆有可能

①One of the things I've learned about myself is that I tend to be impatient in solving problems. ②Instead of listening to the opinions of others, I try right away to find solutions. ③I have had to learn that other people can give me valuable input and that listening makes me a better leader.

④To be a better listener, I now bring employees from all over the world—including China—to New York City four times a year to hear their suggestions for how to improve our business. ⑤I meet with them for a full day and spend most of my time listening. ⑥This is one of the most important things I do.

⑦ Balance is another essential leadership quality in today's complex world, and it's a quality that is especially critical for women who are juggling many and sometimes competing roles. ⑧As a working mother with two children—my daughter Lauren is 14 and my some Jamie is 6—I constantly struggle with the issue of balance.⑨People always ask me how I do it, and my answer is....it's never easy to balance work and family.

補充單字片語

- impatient [ɪmˈpeɪʃnt] /adj./ 不耐煩的
- input [ˈɪmpʊt] /n./ 輸入，投入
- essential [ɪˈsenʃl] /adj./ 基本的，必要的
- constantly [ˈkɒnstəntlɪ] /adv./ 不斷地，時常地

句構分析

① One of the things I've learned about myself is that I tend to be impatient in solving problems

主詞 介系詞+名詞 形容詞子句 介系詞+反身代名詞 動詞　　述語子句　　　　介系詞+名詞

譯 就我對自己的了解，其中有一點就是，我在解決問題時會很不耐煩。

② Instead of listening to the opinions of others, I try right away to find solutions.
　　副詞　　介系詞+動名詞　　介系詞+名詞　介系詞+名詞 主詞 動詞　副詞　　　　受詞
譯 我直接去尋找解決方案而不是先聽別人的意見。

③ I have had to learn that other people can give me valuable input and that listening
　主詞　　　動詞　　　　形容詞子句

makes me a better leader.
　　受詞子句
譯 我必須要懂得其他人能給我有價值的建議，而傾聽會使我成為更好的領導者。
語法分析 此長句的主詞是I，後面的句子是由and連接兩個句子，這兩個句子都是
　　　　　learn的受詞，故 and連接的是兩個受詞子句。

④ To be a better listener, I now bring employees from all over the world-including China-to
　　動詞不定詞　　　　　主詞 副詞 動詞　受詞　　　介系詞+名詞　　　介系詞+名詞

New York City four times a year to hear their suggestions for how to improve our business.
　介系詞+名詞　　　　副詞　　　　　不定詞結構　　　　　介系詞+名詞子句
譯 為了成為一個好的傾聽者，我現在每年4次把世界各地的員工（包括中國）集合到
　　紐約，以便聽取他們對改進業務的建議。

⑤ I meet with them for a full day and spend most of my time listening.
　主詞 動詞　　受詞　介系詞+名詞　　動詞　　受詞　　　受詞補語
譯 我會花費一整天的時間與他們見面，而我大多數時間主要是傾聽。

⑥ This is one of the most important things I do.
　主詞 動詞 述詞　　介系詞+名詞
譯 這是我做的最重要的事情之一。

⑦ Balance is another essential leadership quality in today's complex world, and it's a quality
　主詞 動詞　　　述詞　　　　　　介系詞+名詞　　　虛主詞 動詞 述詞

that is especially critical for women who are juggling many and sometimes competing roles.
　　　　主詞子句　　　　　　　　　　形容詞子句
譯 在當今複雜的世界中，獲取平衡是另一個重要的領導能力，尤其對於女性這個掙
　　扎於各種角色中的群體，有時這些角色還是相互矛盾的。
語法分析 該長句是由and連接的兩個並列句，前一個句子是一個簡單的主詞+動詞+述
　　　　　詞結構，後一個句子是 一個複合句，句中不僅有that引導的主詞子句 而且
　　　　　還有who引導的形容詞子句來修飾women。

⑧ As a working mother with two children-my daughter Lauren is 14 and my son Jamie is 6-
　介系詞+名詞　　　介系詞+名詞　　　　主詞　　　動詞 述詞　　主詞　　動詞 述詞

I constantly struggle with the issue of balance.
　主詞　副詞　　動詞　　　　受詞　介系詞+名詞
譯 我是一個有著兩個孩子的職業母親，我的女兒勞倫今年14歲，兒子傑米今年6歲，
　　我經常在如何求得平衡中摸索。

⑨ People always ask me how I do it, and my answer is... .it's never easy to balance work and
　主詞　副詞 動詞 受詞 受詞補語　　　主詞　　動詞　　　述詞子句

family.

譯 別人總問我是怎麼做的，我的回答是——在工作和家庭之間取得平衡絕非一件容易的事情。

 提姆・庫克於喬治華盛頓大學演講

①The idea that great progress is possible, whatever line of work you choose.

②There will always be cynics and critics on the sidelines tearing people down, and just as harmful are those people with good intentions who make no contribution at all.

③In his letter from the Birmingham jail, Dr. King wrote that our society needed to repent, not merely for the hateful words of the bad people, but for the appalling silence of the good people.

④The sidelines are not where you want to live your life.

⑤The world needs you in the arena. ⑥There are problems that need to be solved.

⑦Injustices that need to be ended. ⑧People that are still being persecuted, diseases still in need of cure.

⑨No matter what you do next, the world needs your energy, your passion, your impatience with progress.

⑩Don't shrink from risk. And tune out those critics and cynics.

⑪History rarely yields to one person, but think, and never forget, what happens when it does.

⑫That can be you. That should be you. That must be you.

⑬Congratulations Class of 2015. I'd like to take one photo of you, because this is the best view in the world. And it's a great one.

補充單字片語

- contribution [ˌkɒntrɪˈbjuːʃn] /n./ 貢獻
- persecute [ˈpɜːsɪkjuːt] /v./ 迫害
- congratulation [kənˌɡrætʃʊˈleɪʃn] /n./ 祝賀

句構分析

① The idea that great progress is possible, whatever line of work you choose.
　　　　　　同位語子句　　　　　　　　　讓步副詞子句
譯 這個信念：無論你從事哪個行業，都有可能取得巨大進步。

② There will always be cynics and critics on the sidelines tearing people down, and just as
there be句型 副詞　　　　　　　　　　介系詞+名詞　　　動名詞作形容詞片語
harmful are those people with good intentions who make no contribution at all.
　　方式副詞子句　　　　　　　　　　　　　　　形容詞子句
譯 總會有憤世嫉俗和好批評的局外人在一旁挑撥離間，他們對社會的毒害與那些心
懷善意但並無任何貢獻的人一樣。

③ In his letter from the Birmingham jail, Dr. King wrote that our society needed to repent, not
介系詞+名詞　　介系詞+名詞　　　　主詞　　動詞　　　受詞子句
merely for the hateful words of the bad people, but for the appalling silence of the good people.
副詞　　介系詞+名詞　　　介系詞+名詞　　　介系詞+名詞　　　介系詞+名詞
譯 金博士在伯明翰監獄的來信中寫道，我們的社會需要懺悔，不僅僅是那些可惡的
壞人，還有那些可怕的沈默的好人。

④ The sidelines are not where you want to live your life.
　　主詞　　　動詞　　　　述詞子句
譯 置身事外不是你想要的生活。

⑤ The world needs you in the arena.
　　主詞　　動詞 受詞 介系詞+名詞
譯 世界需要你在這個舞台上。

⑥ There are problems that need to be solved.
　　there be句型　　　　形容詞子句
譯 那裡有需要解決的問題。

⑦ Injustices that need to be ended.
　　　　　　形容詞子句
譯 不公需要結束。

⑧ People that are still being persecuted, diseases still in need of cure.
　　　　　　形容詞子句　　　　　　　　　副詞　介系詞+名詞
譯 人們仍在遭受迫害，疾病仍需要治癒。

⑨ No matter what you do next, the world needs your energy, your passion, your impatience
　　讓步副詞子句　　　　　主詞　　動詞　　　　受詞
with progress.
介系詞+名詞
譯 不管你下一步要做什麼，世界都需要你的能量，你的激情，你對進步的渴望。

⑩ Don't shrink from risk. And tune out those critics and cynics.
　　　　　　介系詞+名詞
譯 不要回避風險，無視那些憤世嫉俗者和吹毛求疵的人。

⑪ History ~~rarely~~ yields to one person, but think, and never forget, what happens when it does.

　　主詞　副詞　動詞　　受詞

📖 歷史很少屈服於個人，但試想當它實現的時候會是什麼樣子，不要忘記這種感受。

⑫ That can be you. That should be you. That must be you.

　　主詞 動詞 述詞　主詞　　動詞　　述詞 主詞 動詞　　述詞

📖 歷史屈服的對象可能是你。應該是你。必須是你。

⑬ Congratulations Class ~~of 2015~~. I'd like to take one photo ~~of you~~, ~~because this is the~~

　　　　　　　介系詞+名詞 主詞　　動詞　　　受詞　　介系詞+名詞 原因副詞子句

~~best view in the world~~. And it's a great one.

　　介系詞+名詞　　　　　主詞 動詞 述詞

📖 祝賀2015屆。我想拍一張你們的照片，因為這是世界上最好的風景。它很偉大。

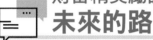

財富精英勵誌演講：
未來的路

①The range of currencies included in the SDRs would have to be widened and some of the newly added currencies, which would include the renminbi, may not be fully convertible. ②Therefore the dollar could still reestablish itself as the preferred reserve currency, provided it is prudently managed.

③One of the great advantages of SDRs is that they allow the international creation of money. ④That would be particularly useful at times like the present. ⑤The money could be directed to it is most needed. ⑥That would be a great improvement over what is happening currently. ⑦A mechanism which allows rich countries that don't need additional reserves to transfer their allocations to those who need them is readily available, and has already been used on a small scale.

⑧The reorganization of the prevailing world order may have to extend beyond the financial system if we are to make progress in resolving issues like global warming and nuclear proliferation. ⑨ It may have to involve the United Nations, especially membership of the Security Council.

⑩ The profound process needs to be initiated by the United States, but China and other developing countries ought to participate in it as equals. ⑪They are reluctant members of the Bretton Woods institutions which are dominated by countries that are no longer dominant. ⑫The rising powers need to be present at the creation of the new order to ensile that they will be active supporters of it.

Part
1

Part
2

閱讀提升──化繁為簡

Part
3

補充單字片語

- convertible [kənˈvɜːtəbl] /adj./ 可改變的
- mechanism [ˈmekənɪzəm] /n./ 機制
- dominant [ˈdɒmɪnənt] /adj./ 占優勢的

句構分析

① The range ~~of currencies included in the SDRs~~ would have to be widened and some ~~of the~~
主詞　　介系詞+名詞　被動分詞　介系詞+名詞　　　　動詞　　　　　　　主詞
~~newly added currencies, which would include the renminbi,~~ may not be ~~fully~~ convertible.
介系詞+名詞　　　　　　插入語　　　　　　助動詞　副詞　述詞

📖 貨幣納入「特別提款權」的範圍也必須擴大，包括人民幣在內的一些新增的貨幣或許不能完全自由兌換。

② ~~Therefore~~ the dollar could ~~still~~ reestablish itself ~~as the preferred reserve currency,~~
副詞　　主詞　　　副詞　動詞　受詞　　介系詞+名詞
~~provided it is prudently managed.~~
條件副詞子句

📖 因此，如果美元是被審慎管理，它就仍可能成為首選的儲備貨幣。

③ One ~~of the great advantages of SDRs~~ is that they allow the international creation ~~of money.~~
主詞　介系詞+名詞　　介系詞+名詞　　　述詞子句　　　　　介系詞+名詞

📖 「特別提款權」所具有的重大優勢之一是：它們允許貨幣的國際性創造。

④ That would be ~~particularly~~ useful ~~at times like the present.~~
主詞　　動詞　副詞　述詞　介系詞+名詞 介系詞+名詞

📖 這在目前的情況下尤其有用。

⑤ The money could be directed to it is most needed.
主詞　　　動詞　　　受詞

📖 貨幣就可以流向最需要它的地方。

⑥ That would be a great improvement ~~over what is happening currently.~~
主詞　　動詞　　述詞　　　　副詞+名詞子句　　副詞

📖 這將是對目前狀況一個很大的改善。

⑦ A mechanism ~~which allows rich countries that don't need additional reserves to transfer their~~
主詞　　　形容詞子句　　　　　　形容詞子句
~~allocations to those who need them is readily available,~~ and has ~~already~~ been
形容詞子句　　　　　　　副詞　動詞
used on a small scale.
受詞

📖 目前已經形成了這樣一種在小規模範圍內正在應用的機制，即如果富國不需要額外儲備，就可以將它們的份額讓給需要的國家了。

111

⑧ The reorganization ~~of the prevailing world order~~ may have to extend
　　　主詞　　　　　　　介系詞+名詞　　　　　　　　動詞
~~beyond the financial system if we are to make progress in resolving issues like~~
　　介系詞+名詞　　　　　　　　　條件副詞子句
~~global warming and nuclear proliferation.~~

> 譯 如果我們想在解決諸如全球變暖和核擴散等問題上取得進展，那麼對於當前的世界秩序重組問題可能就會超出金融體系的範疇。

⑨ It may have to involve the United Nations, ~~especially~~ membership ~~of~~
主詞　　　動詞　　　　　　受詞　　　　　　副詞
~~the Security Council.~~
　介系詞+名詞

> 譯 這可能得有聯合國，特別是安理會成員國的參與。

⑩ The profound process needs to be initiated ~~by the United States~~, but
　　　　主詞　　　　　　　動詞　　　受詞　　　介系詞+名詞
China and other developing countries ought to participate in it ~~as equals~~.
　　　　　　主詞　　　　　　　　　　　　　動詞　　　受詞 介系詞+名詞

> 譯 這個過程需要由美國發起，但中國和其他發展中國家也應該以平等的地位參與。

⑪ They are reluctant members ~~of the Bretton Woods institutions which are~~
主詞 動詞　　述詞　　　　　介系詞+名詞　　　　　形容詞子句+名詞
~~dominated by countries that are no longer dominant.~~
　　　　　形容詞子句

> 譯 他們是布雷頓森林體系機構中的非積極成員，而該機構被一些已經不再占主導地位的國家所主導。

⑫ The rising powers need to be present ~~at the creation of the new order to~~
　　　主詞　　　　　　動詞　　　　介系詞+名詞　　　介系詞+名詞
~~ensile~~ that they will be active supporters of it.
不定詞結構　　　　受詞子句　　　　　介系詞+代名詞

> 譯 新興國家需要參與構建新秩序，以確保它們成為積極支持者。

默斯·希尼在諾貝爾宴會上的演講：
榮耀的時刻

①Today's ceremonies and tonight's banquet have been mighty and memorable events.

②Nobody who has shared in them will ever forget them, but for the laureates these celebrations have had a unique importance. ③Each of us has participated in a ritual, a rite of passage, a public drama which has been commensurate with the inner experience of winning a Nobel Prize. ④The slightly incredible condition we have lived in since the news of the prizes was announced a couple of weeks ago has now been rendered credible. ⑤The mysterious powers represented by the words Nobel Foundation and Swedish Academy have manifested themselves in friendly human form.

⑥For me, it has been a great joy and a great reassurance to come to Stockholm and to meet at every turn people of such grace, such intelligence and such good will. ⑦Which is another way of saying that the whole week has not only been ceremonially impressive: it has also felt emotionally true, and it is that sense of something personally trustworthy at the centre of the great event that I finally value most, and cherish and give you thanks for. ⑧It has helped more than anything else to bring home to me the reality of the great honor I have received.

- memorable [ˈmemərəbl] /adj./ 難忘的
- participate in 參加
- commensurate [kəˈmenʃərət] /adj./ 相等的
- reassurance [ˌriːəˈʃʊərəns] /n./ 使安心

① Today's ceremonies and tonight's banquet have been mighty and memorable
　　　　主詞　　　　　　　　　　　助動詞　　　　述詞
events.
譯 今天的典禮和宴會舉辦得都很隆重，令人難以忘懷。
結構分析 本句話是為了引出下文，為下文作鋪路。

② Nobody who has shared in them will ever forget them, but for the
主詞　　　形容詞子句　　　　　助動詞 副詞 動詞 受詞　介系詞 + 名詞
laureates these celebrations have had a unique importance.
　　　　　主詞　　　　助動詞 動詞　　　受詞
譯 不管是誰，只要是參加了，誰也不會忘記，但對於獲獎者來説，這些慶典有著特殊的意義。

③ Each <s>of us</s> has participated in a ritual, <s>a rite of passage</s>, a public drama <s>which</s>
　　主詞 介系詞+代名詞　　動詞　　　受詞　　　　插入語
<s>has been commensurate with the inner experience of winning a Nobel Prize.</s>
　　　　　　形容詞子句
譯 我們每個人都參加過儀式慶典，其內心體驗與獲得諾貝爾獎的心情差不多。

④ The <s>slightly</s> incredible condition <s>we have lived in since the news of the prizes</s>
　　　　　副詞　　　主詞　　　　　　　形容詞子句　　　　　時間副詞子句
<s>was announced a couple of weeks ago</s> has <s>now</s> been rendered credible.
　　　　　　　　　　　　　　　　　　　　副詞　　　動詞　　　　受詞補語
譯 自從幾周前宣布獲獎消息以來，我們從感覺些許不可思議轉變為相信。

⑤ The mysterious powers <s>represented by the words Nobel Foundation and</s>
　　　　主詞　　　　　　過去分詞　　　　介系詞+名詞
<s>Swedish Academy</s> have manifested themselves <s>in friendly human form.</s>
　　　　　　　　　動詞　　　　　受詞　　　介系詞+名詞
譯 因為諾貝爾基金會和瑞典學院字裡行間所代表的神秘力量，以友好的形式表現出
　來。

⑥ <s>For me</s>, it has been a great joy and a great reassurance <s>to come to Stockholm</s>
介系詞+代名詞 主詞　動詞　　述詞　　　　　　　　述詞　　　　　　不定詞結構
and <s>to meet at every turn people of such grace, such intelligence and such good will.</s>
　　　　　　不定詞結構　　　　　　　　　　　　　　　　　介系詞+名詞
譯 對我來說，來到斯德哥爾摩，能夠到處遇見到優雅、智慧、善良的人們，我感到
　極大的喜悅和安慰。

⑦ Which is another way <s>of saying</s> that the whole week has not <s>only</s> been <s>ceremonially</s>
　　　　　　　　　　　介系詞+動名詞　　　　　　　　　　　　　副詞
impressive: it has <s>also</s> felt <s>emotionally</s> true, and it is that sense <s>of something</s>
　　　　　　主詞 副詞 動詞 副詞　　述詞　主詞 動詞 述詞　介系詞+名詞
<s>personally</s> trustworthy <s>at the centre of the great event that I finally value most, and</s>
　　副詞　　　　　　介系詞+名詞　　　介系詞+名詞　　　形容詞子句
<s>cherish and give you thanks for.</s>
譯 這同時也說明，整個一周不僅典禮令人印象深刻，而且感覺也很真實，最讓人珍
　視的是，處在如此盛大典禮的中央，我感受到的是信任，對此我很珍惜，在此向
　各位表示感謝。

⑧ It has helped <s>more than anything else</s> to bring home <s>to me</s> the <s>reality of the</s>
　主詞 動詞　　　副詞　　　介系詞+名詞　副詞　　　受詞　　介系詞+代名詞　介系詞+名詞
<s>great honor</s> I have received.
　　　　　　　　形容詞子句
譯 能夠把這項巨大的榮譽帶回家，讓我感到萬分榮幸。

賈伯斯史丹佛大學演講

①I am honored to be with you today at your commencement from one of the finest universities in the world.

②Truth be told, I never graduated from college.

③And this is the closest I've ever gotten to a college graduation.

④Today I want to tell you three stories from my life.

⑤That's it. No big deal. Just three stories.

⑥The first story is about connecting the dots.

⑦I dropped out of Reed College after the first 6 months.

⑧But then stayed around as a drop-in for another 18 months or so before I really quit.

⑨So why did I drop out? It started before I was born.

⑩My biological mother was a young, unwed college graduate student.

⑪And she decided to put me up for adoption.

⑫She felt very strongly that I should be adopted by college graduates, so everything was all set for me to be adopted at birth by a lawyer and his wife.

⑬Except that when I popped out they decided at the last minute that they really wanted a girl.

⑭So my parents, who were on a waiting list, got a call in the middle of the night asking.

補充單字片語

- commencement [kəˈmensmənt] /n./ 畢業典禮
- drop out of 不參與，退出
- biological [ˌbaɪəˈlɒdʒɪkl] /adj./ 有血親關係的
- adoption [əˈdɒpʃn] /n./ 收養

① I am honored ~~to be with you~~ today ~~at your commencement from one of the finest~~
主詞 動詞 述詞　　不定詞結構　　副詞　　介系詞+名詞　　　　介系詞+名詞
~~universities in the world.~~
　　　　介系詞+名詞
譯 今天，我很榮幸能與諸位，來自世界上最好大學之一的畢業生們，一起參加畢業典禮。

② Truth be told, I never graduated ~~from college.~~
　　　　　　　主詞　　　動詞　　介系詞+名詞
譯 老實說，我從未大學畢業。

③ And this is the closest ~~I've ever gotten to a college graduation.~~
　　　　主詞 動詞 述詞　　　　形容詞子句
譯 這應該算是我離大學畢業最近的一次。

④ ~~Today~~ I want to tell you three stories ~~from my life.~~
　　副詞 主詞 動詞　　　　受詞　　　　介系詞+名詞
譯 今天我想告訴你們我生活中的三個故事。
語法分析 該句中want是動詞，to tell you three stories是動詞不定式作受詞，tell後加雙受詞，tell three stories是直接受詞，you是間接受詞。

⑤ That's it. No big deal. Just three stories.
　　主詞 動詞 述詞
譯 不是什麼大不了的事情，僅僅是三個故事而已。

⑥ The first story is ~~about connecting~~ the dots.
　　　　主詞　　　動詞 介系詞+動名詞　述詞
譯 第一個故事是關於如何把生活中的點點滴滴連接起來。

⑦ I dropped out of Reed College ~~after the first 6 months.~~
主詞　　　動詞　　　受詞　　　介系詞+名詞
譯 我在里德大學學習了六個月之後就退學了。

⑧ But ~~then~~ stayed around as a drop-in ~~for another 18 months~~ or so before I ~~really~~
　　副詞　　　　　　　　　　　　介系詞+名詞　　　　　副詞
quit.
譯 但是在十八個月以後——我真正的作出退學決定之前，我還是經常去學校。

⑨ So why did I drop out? It started ~~before I was born.~~
　　　　　　　　　　主詞 動詞　　時間副詞子句
譯 那我為什麼退學呢？那要從我出生的時候講起。

⑩ My biological mother was a young, unwed college graduate student.
　　　　　主詞　　　　動詞　　　述詞
譯 我的親生母親是一個年輕的、未婚的大學畢業生。

⑪ And she decided to put me up ~~for adoption.~~
　　　主詞　　動詞　　受詞　　介系詞+名詞

譯 她決定讓我被別人領養。

⑫ She felt ~~very strongly~~ that I should be adopted ~~by college graduates~~, so
　　主詞 動詞 副詞 　　　　　述語子句 　　　　　介系詞+名詞

everything was ~~all~~ set ~~for me~~ to be adopted ~~at birth by a lawyer and his wife~~.
　主詞 　　　副詞 動詞 介系詞+名詞 受詞 　　　介系詞+名詞 介系詞+名詞

譯 她十分想讓我被大學畢業生收養，所以她為我準備好了一切，我一出生就被一個律師一家收養。

⑬ ~~Except that when I popped out~~ they decided ~~at the last minute~~ that they really
　介系詞+代名詞 時間副詞子句 　主詞 動詞 　介系詞+名詞 　　受詞子句 副詞

wanted a girl.

譯 但出乎意料的是，當我出生之後，律師夫婦突然想要一個女孩。

⑭ So my parents, ~~who were on a waiting list~~, got a call ~~in the middle of the night~~
　　主詞 　　　　插入語 　　　　　　動詞 受詞 介系詞+名詞 　介系詞+名詞

~~asking~~.

譯 所以我（在待選名單上的）養父母突然在半夜接到了一個電話。

 ## 臉書首席執行長桑德伯格演講

①We need to start talking about how women underestimate their abilities compared to men and for women, but not men, success and likeability are negatively correlated.

②That means that as a woman is more successful in your workplaces, she will be less liked.

③This means that women need a different form of management and mentorship, a different form of sponsorship and encouragement and some protection, in some ways, more than men.

④And there aren't enough senior women out there to do it, so it falls upon the men who are graduating today just as much or more as the women, not just to talk about gender but to help these women succeed.

⑤When they hear a woman is really great at her job but not liked, take a deep breath and ask why.

⑥We need to start talking openly about the flexibility all of us need to have both a job and a life.

⑦A couple of weeks ago in an interview I said that I leave the office at 5:30 p. m. to have dinner with my children.

⑧And I was shocked at the press coverage.

⑨One of my friends said she wasn't sure I couldn't get more headlines if I had murdered someone with an ax.

⑩I told her I wasn't really interested in trying that.

補充單字片語

- underestimate [ˌʌndərˈɛstɪmeɪt] /v./ 低估
- sponsorship [ˈspɒnsəʃɪp] /n./ 贊助，發起
- take a deep breath 深呼吸

句構分析

① We need to start talking ~~about how women underestimate their abilities~~
主詞　動詞　　受詞　　　　　介系詞+名詞子句
~~compared to men and for women,~~ but not men, success and likeability are
　　　　　　　　　　　　　　　　　插入語　　　　主詞　　　動詞
negatively correlated.
　　述詞
📖 我們需要開始討論相比於男性，女性為什麼會低估自己的能力。而且和男性不同，對於女性，成功和受歡迎程度是成反比的。

② That means that as a woman is more successful ~~in your workplaces~~, she will
主詞　動詞　　　　受詞子句　　　　　　　　　介系詞+名詞　　主詞
be less liked.
動詞　述詞
📖 這就意味著一個女性在事業上越成功，她就越不受歡迎。

③ This means that women need a different form ~~of management and mentorship,~~
主詞　動詞　　　受詞子句　　　　　　　　介系詞+名詞
a different form ~~of sponsorship and encouragement and some protection,~~ in some
　　　　　　　　介系詞+名詞　　　　　　　　　　　　　　　　　插入語
~~ways,~~ more than men.
📖 這就意味著女性需要另一種形式的管理和輔導，另一種形式的支持和鼓勵，以及一些保護，在某些方面，要比男性需要更多的保護。

④ And there aren't enough senior women ~~out there to do it~~, so it falls upon the
　　there be句型　　　　　　　　　　　副詞 不定詞結構 主詞 動詞　受詞
men ~~who are graduating today just as much or more as the women,~~ not ~~just to talk~~
　　形容詞子句　　　　　　　　　　　　　　　　　　　　副詞 不定詞結構

about gender but ~~to help these women succeed.~~
　　　　　　　　　　不定詞結構
　📖 而且有資歷做這些的女性還太少，所以今天在座的男性畢業生們要和女性畢業生們一起肩負起這個責任，甚至更多，不僅僅討論性別，而且要幫助女性取得成功。

⑤ ~~When they hear a woman is really great at her job but not liked,~~ take a deep
　　　　　　　時間副詞子句
breath and ask why.
　📖 當聽到一個工作上很優秀的女性不受人歡迎時，深呼吸一下，問問這是為什麼。

⑥ We need to start talking ~~openly about the flexibility all of us need to have both a~~
主詞　動詞　　受詞　　副詞　　介系詞+名詞
~~job and a life.~~
介系詞+名詞
　📖 我們需要開始公開討論我們都需要的靈活機制來平衡工作和生活。

⑦ ~~A couple of weeks~~ ago ~~in an interview~~ I said that I leave the office ~~at 5:30 p.m.~~
　介系詞+名詞　　　介系詞+名詞　主詞 動詞　　受詞子句　　　介系詞+名詞
to have dinner ~~with my children~~.
不定詞結構　　　介系詞+名詞
　📖 幾週之前，我在一次採訪中說我會在五點半離開公司去和我的小孩吃晚飯。

⑧ And I was shocked ~~at the press coverage~~.
　　主詞 動詞　述詞　　介系詞+名詞
　📖 我對由此帶來的媒體報導感到震驚。

⑨ One ~~of my friends~~ said she wasn't sure I couldn't get more headlines ~~if I had~~
主詞　介系詞+名詞　動詞　　　　受詞子句　　　　　條件副詞子句
~~murdered someone with an ax~~.
　　　　　　　介系詞+名詞
　📖 一個我的朋友說她不確定如果我用斧頭砍人，是否能上一樣多的頭條。

⑩ I told her I wasn't ~~really~~ interested ~~in trying~~ that.
主詞 動詞 受詞 受詞子句 副詞　　　介系詞+動名詞
　📖 我告訴她我對嘗試那件事並不感興趣。

TED 演講：
個體 DNA 檢測的時代來了

①This ability to make copies of DNA, as simple as it sounds, has transformed our world.

②Scientists use it every day to detect and address disease, to create innovative medicines, to modify foods, to assess whether our food is safe to eat or whether it's contaminated with deadly bacteria.③Even judges use the output of these machines in court to decide whether someone is innocent or guilty based on DNA evidence.

④The inventor of this DNA-copying technique was awarded the Nobel Prize in Chemistry in 1993. ⑤But for 30 years, the power of genetic analysis has been confined to the ivory tower, or bigwig PhD scientist work.⑥Well, several companies around the world are working on making this same technology accessible to everyday people like the pig farmer, like you.

⑦I cofounded one of these companies. ⑧Three years ago, together with a fellow biologist and friend of mine, Zeke Alvarez Saavedra, we decided to make personal DNA machines that anyone could use.⑨Our goal was to bring DNA science to more people in new places.

⑩We started working in our basements. We had a simple question: What could the world look like if everyone could analyze DNA? ⑫We were curious, as curious as you would have been if I had shown you this picture in 1980.

補充單字片語

- detect [dɪˈtɛkt] /v./ 查明，發現
- innocent [ˈɪnəsnt] /adj./ 無辜的
- accessible [əkˈsɛsəbl] /adj./ 易接近的，易理解的

句構分析

① This ability to make copies of DNA, as simple as it sounds, has transformed
　　主詞　　　　不定詞結構　介系詞+名詞　　插入語　　　　　　　　　動詞
our world.
受詞
譯 DNA的這種複製能力聽起來很簡單，卻改變了我們的世界。
結構分析 本句總領全文，為後文設置懸念，埋下伏筆。

② Scientists use it every day to detect and address disease, to create innovative
　　主詞　　動詞 受詞　　副詞　　　不定詞結構　　　　　　　不定詞結構
medicines, to modify foods, to assess whether our food is safe to eat or whether
　　　　　不定詞結構　不定詞結構　　　　　形容詞子句

120

it's contaminated with ~~deadly~~ bacteria.
　　　　　　　　　　　　副詞

🈡 科學家們每天都用它來檢測和治療疾病，創造新藥物，改進食品，評估我們的食物是否安全，或者 是否被致命的細菌污染。

③ ~~Even~~ judges use the output ~~of these machines in court to decide~~ whether
副詞　主詞　動詞　　受詞　　　介系詞+名詞　　　介系詞+名詞　　　受詞子句
someone is innocent or guilty ~~based on DNA evidence~~.
　　　　　　　　　　　　　　　過去分詞　介系詞+名詞

🈡 即使法官在法庭上也使用這些機器輸出的結果，可以根據DNA證據來判定某人是無罪或有罪。

④ The inventor ~~of this DNA-copying technique~~ was awarded the Nobel Prize ~~in~~
主詞　　　　介系詞+名詞　　　　　　　　　動詞　　　　　受詞
~~Chemistry in 1993~~.
介系詞+名詞 介系詞+名詞

🈡 這種DNA複製技術的發明者在1993年被授予諾貝爾化學獎。

⑤ ~~But for 30 years~~, the power ~~of genetic analysis~~ has been confined to the ivory
介系詞+名詞　　　主詞　　　介系詞+名詞　　　　動詞　　　　　受詞
tower, or bigwig PhD scientist work.

🈡 但是30年來，遺傳分析的力量一直局限於象牙塔，或是有重大影響力的博士科學家的工作之中。

⑥ Well, several companies ~~around the world~~ are working on making this same
　　　　主詞　　　　介系詞+名詞　動詞　　　　受詞
technology accessible ~~to everyday people like the pig farmer, like you~~.
　　　　　受詞補語　　　　介系詞+名詞　　　　　介系詞+名詞

🈡 世界上有數家公司正致力於把同樣的技術簡易化，方便人們在日常生活中使用，例如養豬農戶以及我們大家。

⑦ I cofounded one ~~of these companies~~.
主詞　動詞　受詞　介系詞+名詞

🈡 我成立了其中一家這樣的公司。

⑧ Three years ago, ~~together with a fellow biologist and friend of mine, Zeke~~
　　　　　　　　　　插入語　　　　　　　　　　　　　　插入語
~~Alvarez Saavedra~~, we decided to make personal DNA machines ~~that anyone could~~
　　　　　　　主詞　動詞　　　　受詞　　　　　　　形容詞子句
~~use~~.

🈡 三年前，和我的一位生物學家朋友齊克‧阿爾瓦雷斯‧薩維德拉一起，我們決定讓個人化DNA檢測器能被任何人所使用。

⑨ Our goal was to bring DNA science ~~to more people in new places~~.
主詞　　動詞　　　受詞　　　介系詞+名詞　　　介系詞+名詞

🈡 我們的目標是在新的地方將DNA科學帶給更多的人。

⑩ We started working ~~in our basements~~.
主詞　動詞　動名詞　介系詞+名詞
📖 我們在地下室開始工作。

⑪ We had a simple question: What could the world look like ~~if everyone could~~
主詞 動詞　　受詞　　　　　　　　　　　　　　　　　　條件副詞子句
~~analyze DNA?~~
📖 我們有一個簡單的問題：如果每個人都能分析DNA，世界將會是什麼樣子的呢？

⑫ We were curious, as curious as you would have been ~~if I had shown you this~~
主詞 動詞　述詞　　　　　　　　　　　　　　　　　　　條件副詞子句
~~picture in 1980~~.
　　　介系詞+名詞
📖 我們很好奇，如果我在1980年向你們展示這張照片你們也會這樣好奇。

善良女孩的一道陽光

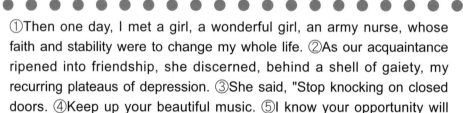

①Then one day, I met a girl, a wonderful girl, an army nurse, whose faith and stability were to change my whole life. ②As our acquaintance ripened into friendship, she discerned, behind a shell of gaiety, my recurring plateaus of depression. ③She said, "Stop knocking on closed doors. ④Keep up your beautiful music. ⑤I know your opportunity will come. ⑥You're trying too hard. ⑦Why don't you relax, and have you ever tried praying?"

⑧The idea was strange to me. ⑨It sounded too simple. ⑩Somehow, I had always operated on the premise that, if you wanted something in this world, you had to go out and get it for yourself. ⑪Yet, sincerity and hard work had yielded only meager returns, and I was willing to try anything. ⑫Experimentally, self-consciously, I cultivated the daily practice of prayer. ⑬I said: God, show me the purpose for which you sent me to this world. ⑭Help me to be of use to myself and to humanity.

⑮In the years to follow, the answers began to arrive, clear and satisfying beyond my most optimistic anticipation. ⑯One of the answers was Enchanted Hills, where my nurse friend and I have the privilege of seeing blind children come alive in God's out-of-doors.

補充單字片語

- stability [stəˈbɪlətɪ] /n./ 穩定性
- acquaintance [əˈkweɪntəns] /n./ 熟人
- experimentally [ɪkˌsperɪˈmentəlɪ] /adv./ 實際上，實驗地
- optimistic [ˌɒptɪˈmɪstɪk] /adj./ 樂觀的

句構分析

① Then one day, I met a girl, a wonderful girl, an army nurse, whose faith and
　　　　　　　主詞 動詞 受詞　　插入語　　　　插入語　　　　　形容詞子句

stability were to change my whole life.

譯 直到有一天，我遇見一個女孩，一個了不起的女孩，這名隨軍護士的信念和執著
　 將改變我的一生。

結構分析 本句是整段的中心句，後面又詳細介紹了作者與女孩之間發生的故事。

② As our acquaintance ripened into friendship, she discerned, behind a shell of gaiety,
　　　　時間副詞子句　　　　　　　　主詞　動詞　　　介系詞+名詞

my recurring plateaus of depression.
　　受詞　　　　　介系詞+名詞

譯 我們相識發展成友誼，她也慢慢察覺出在我快樂的外表之下，內心卻時常愁雲密
　 布。

③ She said, "Stop knocking on closed doors.
主詞 動詞　　　　　　　　介系詞+名詞

譯 她對我說，「停止敲已經鎖緊的門」。

④ Keep up your beautiful music.

譯 堅持你的美好的音樂夢想。

⑤ I know your opportunity will come.
主詞 動詞　　　受詞子句

譯 我相信機會終將來臨。

⑥ You're trying too hard.
主詞　　動詞　　副詞

譯 你太辛苦了。

⑦ Why don't you relax, and have you ever tried praying?
　　　　　　　　　　　　　　　　　　副詞

譯 為何你不放鬆一下，你有沒有試過祈禱？

⑧ The idea was strange to me.
　主詞　　動詞　述詞　介系詞+代名詞

譯 我從未想到過祈禱。

⑨ It sounded ~~too~~ simple.

主詞 動詞　副詞　述詞
📖 聽起來太天真了。

⑩ ~~Somehow,~~ I had ~~always~~ operated on the premise that, ~~if you wanted something~~

副詞　主詞　　副詞　　動詞　　　　受詞　　　　　　　　條件副詞子句

~~in this world,~~ you had to go out and get it ~~for yourself.~~

受詞子句　　　　　　　介系詞+代名詞

📖 不知怎的，我的行事準則都是，如果你想得到世界上的某樣東西，你就必須靠自己去努力爭取。

⑪ ~~Yet,~~ sincerity and hard work had yielded ~~only~~ meager returns, and I was

副詞　　　　主詞　　　　　動詞　　副詞　　受詞　　　主詞 動詞

willing ~~to try anything.~~

述詞　　不定詞結構

📖 然而，從前的熱誠和辛勞回報甚微，我什麼都願意嘗試。

⑫ ~~Experimentally, self-consciously,~~ I cultivated the daily practice ~~of prayer.~~

副詞　　　　　副詞　　主詞 動詞　　　受詞　　　介系詞+名詞

📖 雖然有些不自在，我嘗試著每天都禱告。

⑬ I said: God, show me the purpose ~~for which you sent me to this world.~~

主詞 動詞　　　　　　　　　　　　形容詞子句

📖 我說：上帝啊，你派我來到世上，請告訴我你賜予我的使命。

⑭ Help me to be of use ~~to myself~~ and ~~to humanity.~~

介系詞+反身代名詞　介系詞+名詞

📖 幫幫我，讓我於人於己都有用處。

⑮ ~~In the years to follow,~~ the answers began to arrive, clear and satisfying ~~beyond~~

主詞　　　動詞　　受詞

~~my most optimistic anticipation.~~

介系詞+名詞

📖 在接下來的幾年裡，我得到了清晰而令人滿意的回答，超出了我最樂觀的預期。

⑯ One of the answers was Enchanted Hills, ~~where my nurse friend and I have the~~

主詞　　　　動詞　　受詞　　　　地方副詞子句

~~privilege of seeing blind children come alive in God's out-of-doors.~~

📖 其中一個回答就是魔山盲人休閒營地，在那裡，我和我的護士朋友每年都有幸看到失明的孩子們在大自然的懷抱中是多麼生氣勃勃。

 **匆匆**

①If swallows go away, they will come back again. ②If willows wither, they will turn green again.③If peaches shade their blossoms, they will flower again.④But, tell me, you the wise, why should our days go by never to return?⑤Perhaps they have been stolen by someone. ⑥But who could it be and where could he hide them?⑦Perhaps they have just run away by themselves. ⑧But where could they be at the present moment?

⑨I don't know how many days I am entitled to altogether, but my quota of them is

undoubtedly wearing away. ⑩Counting up silently, I find that more than 8,000 days have already slipped away through my fingers. ⑪Like a drop of water falling off a needle point into the ocean, my days are quietly dripping into the stream of time without leaving a trace. ⑫At the thought of this, sweat oozes from my forehead and tears trickle down my cheeks.

⑬What is gone is gone, what is to come keeps coming. ⑭How swift is the translation in between! ⑮When I get up in the morning, the slanting sun casts two or three squarish patches of light into my small room. ⑯ The sun has feet too, edging away softly and stealthily. ⑰And, without knowing it, I am already caught in its revolution.

補充單字片語

- blossom [ˈblɒsəm] /n./ 花，開花時期
- at the present moment 目前
- silently [ˈsaɪləntlɪ] /adv./ 沉默地
- trickle down 向下滴流
- slanting [ˈslɑːntɪŋ] /adv./ 傾斜的
- revolution [ˌrevəˈluːʃn] /n./ 革命

句構分析

① ~~If swallows go away~~, they will <u>come back</u> ~~again~~.

　　　條件副詞子句　　主詞　　動詞　　　副詞

譯 燕子去了，有再來的時候。

② If willows wither, they will turn green again.
　　條件副詞子句　　　主詞　　　動詞　述詞　副詞
譯 楊柳枯了，有再青的時候。

③ If peaches shade their blossoms, they will flower again.
　　　　條件副詞子句　　　　　　　主詞　　動詞　　副詞
譯 桃花謝了，有再開的時候。

④ But, tell me, you the wise, why should our days go by never to return?
譯 但是，聰明的你，告訴我，我們的日子為什麼一去不復返呢？

⑤ Perhaps they have been stolen by someone.
　　　　　主詞　　　動詞　　　　介系詞+代名詞
譯 許是有人偷了他們吧。

⑥ But who could it be and where could he hide them?
譯 那是誰？又藏在何處呢？

⑦ Perhaps they have just run away by themselves.
　副詞　　主詞 助動詞 副詞　動詞　　介系詞+名詞
譯 是他們自己逃走了。

⑧ But where could they be at the present moment?
　　　　　　　　　　　　　介系詞+名詞
譯 現在又到了哪裡呢？

⑨ I don't know how many days I am entitled to altogether, but my quota of them
　主詞　　動詞　　　　受詞子句　　　　　　　　副詞　　　　主詞　　介系詞+名詞
is undoubtedly wearing away.
　　副詞　　　　動詞
譯 我不知道他們給了我多少日子；但我的手確乎是漸漸空虛了。

⑩ Counting up silently, I find that more than 8,000 days have already slipped
　動名詞作形容詞片語 主詞 動詞　　　　受詞子句　　　　　　副詞
away through my fingers.
　　　介系詞+名詞
譯 在默默裡算著，八千多日子已經從我手中溜去；

⑪ Like a drop of water falling off a needle point into the ocean, my days are quietly
　介系詞+名詞　介系詞+名詞 動名詞 介系詞+名詞　　介系詞+名詞　　主詞　　　副詞
dripping into the stream of time without leaving a trace.
　動詞　　　受詞　　　介系詞+名詞　介系詞+動名詞
譯 像針尖上一滴水滴在大海裡，我的日子滴在時間的流裡，沒有聲音，也沒有影
　　子。
結構分析 本句運用極新奇巧妙的比喻，作者把自己過去的八千多日子比喻成極小極
　　　　小的針尖上的水滴，把時間的流比喻成浩瀚的大海。

126

⑫ At the thought of this, sweat oozes from my forehead and tears trickle down my
　　介系詞+名詞　　　　主詞　動詞　介系詞+名詞　　　　主詞　　　動詞

cheeks.
受詞

譯 想到這裡，我不禁頭涔涔而淚潸潸了。

⑬ What is gone is gone, what is to come keeps coming.

譯 去的儘管去了，來的儘管來著。

⑭ How swift is the translation in between!

譯 去來的中間，又怎樣地匆匆呢！

⑮ When I get up in the morning, the slanting sun casts two or three squarish
　　時間副詞子句　　　　　　　　主詞　　　　動詞　　　　　受詞

patches of light into my small room.
　　介系詞+名詞 介系詞+名詞

譯 早上我起來的時候，小屋裡射進兩三方斜斜的陽光。

⑯ The sun has feet too, edging away softly and stealthily.
　　主詞　　動詞 受詞 副詞 動名詞作形容詞片語 副詞　　副詞

譯 太陽他有腳啊，輕輕悄悄地挪移了。

⑰ And, without knowing it, I am already caught in its revolution.
　　　　介系詞+名詞　　主詞 動詞 副詞　　動詞　　介系詞+名詞

譯 我也茫茫然跟著旋轉。

人在旅途

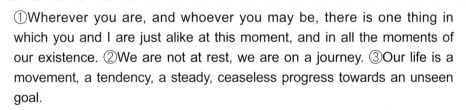

①Wherever you are, and whoever you may be, there is one thing in which you and I are just alike at this moment, and in all the moments of our existence. ②We are not at rest, we are on a journey. ③Our life is a movement, a tendency, a steady, ceaseless progress towards an unseen goal.

④We are gaining something, or losing something, everyday. ⑤Even when our position and our character seem to remain precisely the same, they are changing. ⑥For the mere advance of time is a change. ⑦It is not the same thing to have a bare field in January and in July. ⑧The season makes the difference. ⑨The limitations that are childlike in the child are childish in the man. ⑩Everything that we do is a step in one direction or another. Even the failure to do something is in itself a deed, it sets us forward or backward, the action of the negative pole of a magnetic needle is just as real as the action of the positive pole. To decline is to accept——the other alternative.

補充單字片語

- existence [ɪgˈzɪstəns] /n./ 存在
- precisely [prɪˈsaɪslɪ] /adv./ 精確地，嚴謹地
- childlike [ˈtʃaɪldlaɪk] /adj./ 孩子般的，天真的
- alternative [ɔːlˈtɜːnətɪv] /adj./ 備選的　/n./ 可供選擇的事物

句構分析

① Wherever you are, and whoever you may be, there is one thing in which you and
　讓步副詞子句　　　　　讓步副詞子句　　　　　　there be句型　　　形容詞子句
I are just alike at this moment, and in all the moments of our existence.
　　　　　　　　　　　　　　　　　　介系詞+名詞　　　介系詞+名詞
🔁 不論你在哪裡，也不論你是什麼人，不管是在此時此刻，還是在我們生命中的任何一個瞬間，有一件事對你和我來說是恰巧相同的。

② We are not at rest, we are on a journey.
　主詞 動詞　述詞　主詞 動詞　述詞
🔁 我們不是在休息，我們是在一次旅途中

③ Our life is a movement, a tendency, a steady, ceaseless progress towards an
　主詞 動詞　　　　述詞　　　　　　　　　　　介系詞+名詞
unseen goal.
🔁 我們的生活是一種運動，一種趨勢，是向一個看不見的目標穩定而不停地進步。

④ We are gaining something, or losing something, everyday.
　主詞　動詞　　受詞　　動詞　　受詞　　副詞
🔁 我們每一天都會贏得一些東西，或者會失去一些東西。

⑤ Even when our position and our character seem to remain precisely the same,
　　　　　　　　時間副詞子句
they are changing.
　主詞　動詞
🔁 即使當我們的地位和我們的性格看起來跟以前完全相似時，它們事實上仍然在變化著。

⑥ For the mere advance of time is a change.
　　　主詞　　介系詞+名詞 動詞 述詞
🔁 因為時間的前進僅僅是一種變化。

⑦ It is not the same thing ~~to have a bare field in January~~ and ~~in July~~.

　　虛主詞 動詞　　述詞　　　　　　　主詞　　　　　介系詞+名詞　　介系詞+名詞

　　譯 對於一塊荒地來說，在1月和7月是不一樣的。

　　語法分析 為了避免頭重腳輕，在此句中it是虛主詞，真正的主詞是to have a bare field。

⑧ The season makes the difference.

　　　　主詞　　　　動詞　　　受詞

　　譯 季節造就了差異。

⑨ The limitations ~~that are childlike in the child~~ are childish ~~in the man~~.

　　　　主詞　　　　　　　形容詞子句　　　　　　動詞　述詞　介系詞+名詞

　　譯 能力上的缺陷對於孩子來說是一種可愛的品質，但對於大人來說就是一種幼稚的表現。

⑩ Everything ~~that we do~~ is a step ~~in one direction or another~~.

　　　主詞　　形容詞子句 動詞 述詞　　介系詞+名詞

　　譯 我們所做的一切都是朝著一個或另一個方向前進一步。

⑪ Even the failure ~~to do something~~ is ~~in itself~~ a deed, it sets us forward or

　　　主詞　　　　動詞不定詞　　　　動詞 介系詞+名詞 述詞 主詞 動詞 受詞 受詞補語

backward, the action ~~of the negative pole of a magnetic needle~~ is just as real ~~as the~~

　　　　　　主詞　　　　介系詞+名詞　　　　　介系詞+名詞　　動詞 副詞　　述詞

~~action of the positive pole~~.

介系詞+名詞

　　譯 甚至沒有做任何事情這件事本身也是一種行為，它讓我們前進或後退，一根磁針陰極的作用和陽極的作用都是一樣真實的，

⑫ To decline is to accept——the other alternative.

　　　主詞　動詞　述語

　　譯 拒絕也是一種接受——這些都是二中擇一的選擇。

　　語法分析 在該句中，動詞不定詞to decline作主詞，動詞不定詞to accept 作述詞。

 # 那些美麗的花兒

①As the sun rose over the horizon, I went out to enjoy the beauty of the grassland scenery. ②On the way, I saw a pair of red flowers blooming. ③They had flat petals and were incredibly full of smiling beauty. ④Those independent flowers seemed very vibrant. ⑤Gazing at the flowers made me think of many things.

⑥Dew like pearls shone on the grass brightly. ⑦Rays of sun offered happiness. ⑧I stood and stared at the beautiful flowers for a long time, enjoying the bright, pleasant sunshine.

⑨Butterflies and little bees were flying about. ⑩Then some naughty children with sticks came. ⑪One child swung his stick when he saw the flowers. ⑫Many petals fell to the earth, and with them, my heart fell too.

⑬The next day, beside the road, the red flowers were brighter than the day before. ⑭The natural beauty made me gasp. ⑮It gave me an understanding of the energy of growing and youth and convinced me it couldn't be destroyed with a heartless stick. ⑯I wanted to be like the soul of a flower.

⑰Then I saw an old woman and child coming along the road. ⑱When they reached the flowers the child quickly plucked one. ⑲I felt great horror and then heard the old woman say, "What beautiful flowers. ⑳Don't pick them."

補充單字片語

- horizon [həˈraɪzn] /n./ 地平線
- incredibly [ɪnˈkrɛdəblɪ] /adv./ 難以置信地
- destroy [dɪˈstrɔɪ] /v./ 破壞，摧毀

句構分析

① As the sun rose over the horizon, I went out to enjoy the beauty of the grassland
　　　　　　　副詞片語　　　　　　　　主詞 動詞　　　受詞　　　　　　　介系詞+名詞
scenery.
圜 當太陽升過地平線時，我走到屋外去欣賞草原的美景。

② On the way, I saw a pair of red flowers blooming.
　介系詞+名詞 主詞 動詞 受詞　　介系詞+名詞　受詞補語
圜 在路上，我看見兩朵紅色的花在盛開。

③ They had flat petals and were incredibly full of smiling beauty.
　主詞 動詞　受詞　　　　動詞　副詞　　　述詞　　補語
圜 扁平的花瓣，花朵有著讓人無法抵禦的美麗。

④ Those independent flowers seemed very vibrant.
　　　　　　主詞　　　　　　　動詞　副詞　述詞
圜 這些自由的花朵看起來充滿了活力。

⑤ Gazing ~~at the flowers~~ made me think ~~of many things~~.
　主詞　　介系詞+名詞　　動詞　受詞　動詞　介系詞+名詞
　🈳 看見這些花兒我想起許多事。

⑥ Dew ~~like pearls~~ shone ~~on the grass brightly~~.
　主詞 介系詞+名詞 動詞 介系詞+名詞 副詞
　🈳 草上的露珠像晶瑩剔透的珍珠在閃爍。

⑦ Rays ~~of sun~~ offered happiness.
　主詞 介系詞+名詞 動詞 受詞
　🈳 陽光給人送來了幸福。

⑧ I stood and stared at the beautiful flowers ~~for a long time~~, enjoying the bright,
　主詞 動詞 　動詞 　受詞 　　　　　　介系詞+名詞 　　動名詞片語
　pleasant sunshine.
　受詞
　🈳 我站在那裡，凝視著這些美麗的花兒，享受著明亮而又愜意的陽光。

⑨ Butterflies and little bees were flying about.
　　　　　主詞　　　　　　　動詞
　🈳 蝴蝶和蜜蜂在花叢中飛舞。

⑩ Then some naughty children ~~with sticks~~ came.
　　　　　主詞　　　　　介系詞+名詞 動詞
　🈳 這時，有些頑皮的小男孩拿著棍子來到這裡。

⑪ One child swung his stick ~~when he saw the flowers~~.
　主詞　 動詞　 受詞　　　時間副詞子句
　🈳 一個男孩一看到這些花，馬上就揮舞著棍子。

⑫ Many petals fell to the earth, and ~~with them~~, my heart fell too.
　　主詞　 動詞　 受詞　　　介系詞+名詞　 主詞　 動詞
　🈳 許多花瓣飄落到地上，我的心也隨之跌入低谷。

⑬ The next day, ~~beside the road~~, the red flowers were brighter ~~than the day before~~.
　　　　　　介系詞+名詞　 .　 主詞　　 動詞　 述詞　 介系詞+名詞　 副詞
　🈳 接下來的一天，路邊的那兩朵紅花看起來比前一天更加嬌艷。

⑭ The natural beauty made me gasp.
　　主詞　　　　動詞 受詞 受詞補語
　🈳 自然的美景令我幾乎窒息。

⑮ It gave me an understanding ~~of the energy of growing and youth~~ and convinced
　主詞 動詞 受詞　 受詞補語　　　 介系詞+名詞　　 介系詞+名詞　　　　 動詞
　me it ~~couldn't be destroyed with a heartless stick~~.
　受詞　　受詞子句
　🈳 它讓我理解了成長和青春的力量，使我相信那是棍子所不能摧毀的。

Part 3

⑯ I wanted to be like the soul ~~of a flower~~.

主詞 動詞　　　受詞　　　　介系詞+名詞

　　譯 我也想擁有像花兒一樣的靈魂。

⑰ Then I saw an old woman and child ~~coming along the road~~.

　　主詞 動詞　　　受詞　　　　動名詞　　介系詞+名詞

　　譯 這時，我看到一位老婦人和小孩沿著馬路邊走來。

⑱ ~~When they reached the flowers~~ the child ~~quickly~~ plucked one.

　　時間副詞子詞　　　　　　主詞　　副詞　動詞　受詞

　　譯 小孩一看到花兒，馬上就摘下了一朵。

⑲ I felt great horror and then heard the old woman say, "What beautiful flowers.

主詞 動詞　　受詞　　　　　　　　動詞　　　　受詞

Don't pick them."

　　譯 我為可憐的花兒感到難過，這時聽老婦人說道：「多美的花兒啊！不要去摘。」

兩條路

①It was New Year's night. ②An aged man was standing at a window. ③He raised his mournful eyes towards the deep blue sky, where the stars were floating like white lilies on the surface of a clear calm lake. ④When he cast them on the earth where few more hopeless people than himself now moved towards their certain goal-the tomb. ⑤He had already passed sixty of the age leading to it, and he had brought from his journey nothing but errors and remorse. ⑥Now his health was poor, his mind vacant, his heart sorrowful, and his old age short of comforts.

⑦The days of his youth appeared like dream before him, and he recalled the serious moment when his father placed him at the entrances of the two roads. ⑧One leading to a peaceful, sunny place covered with flowers, fruits and resounding with soft, sweet songs; the other leading to a deep dark cave which was endless, where poison flowed instead of water and where devils and poison snakes hissed and crawled.

⑨He looked towards the sky and cried painfully," Oh youth, return! Oh, my father, place me once more at the entrance to life and I'll chose the better way! "⑩But both his father and the days of his youth had passed away.

補充單字片語

- mournful [ˈmɔːnfl] /adj./ 哀痛的，令人傷心的
- remorse [rɪˈmɔːs] /n./ 懊悔，悔恨，自責
- crawl [krɔːl] /v./ 爬行，緩慢行進
- painfully [ˈpeɪnfəlɪ] /adv./ 痛苦地，費力地

句構分析

① It was New Year's night.
　主詞 動詞　　受詞
　圜 這是新年的夜晚。

② An aged man was standing at a window.
　　　　主詞　　　　　動詞　　　　介系詞+名詞
　　圜 一個老人站在窗前。

③ He raised his mournful eyes towards the deep blue sky, where the stars were
　主詞 動詞　　受詞　　　　　介系詞+名詞　　　　　　形容詞片語
floating like white lilies on the surface of a clear calm lake.
　　　　　　　　　　介系詞+名詞　　介系詞+名詞
　圜 他悲傷的眼睛望著深藍的天空，天空中的繁星猶如漂浮在清澈如鏡的湖面上的朵
　　朵百合。

④ When he cast them on the earth where few more hopeless people than himself
　　　　　　　　　介系詞+名詞　　　　　　　　　　　　　介系詞+代名詞
now moved towards their certain goal—the tomb.
副詞　　　　　　　介系詞+名詞
　圜 他慢慢將目光投向地面，此刻，沒有比他還絕望的人，他即將邁向他最終的歸
　　宿——墳墓。

⑤ He had already passed sixty of the age leading to it, and he had brought from
　主詞 動詞 副詞　　動詞 受詞　介系詞+名詞　　　　　　主詞　　動詞　　介系詞+名詞
his journey nothing but errors and remorse.
　　　　　　受詞
　圜 他已經走過了通向墳墓的六十歲，除了錯誤和悔恨，他一無所獲。

⑥ Now his health was poor, his mind vacant, his heart sorrowful, and his old age short of comforts.
　介系詞+名詞
　圜 現在，他體弱多病，精神空虛，心哀神傷，人到晚年卻無所慰藉。

⑦ The days of his youth appeared like a dream before him, and he recalled the
　主詞　介系詞+名詞　　動詞　介系詞+名詞　受詞　　　主詞　動詞
serious moment when his father placed him at the entrances of the two roads.
　　受詞　　　　　　時間副詞子句　　　　　　　　介系詞+名詞

譯 他的年輕歲月，如夢般出現在他面前，他想起父親把他帶到岔路口的那個莊嚴時刻。

⑧ One <u>leading to</u> a peaceful, sunny place <s>covered</s> <s>with flowers, fruits and</s>
　　主詞　動名詞片語　　　受詞　　　　　被動分詞　介系詞+名詞

<s>resounding with soft, sweet songs;</s> <u>the other</u> <u>leading to</u> <u>a deep dark cave</u> <s>which was</s>
　　介系詞+名詞　　　　　　　主詞　動名詞片語　　受詞　　　形容詞片語

<s>endless,</s> <s>where poison flowed instead of water</s> and <s>where devils and poison snakes</s>
　　　　　　地方副詞片語　　　　　　　　　地方副詞片語

<s>hissed and crawled.</s>

譯 一條路通向安寧、快樂的世界，鮮花漫布，果實豐碩，甜美輕柔的歌聲在空中迴盪；另一條路則通 向幽深黑暗、沒有盡頭的洞，洞內流淌著的不是水而是毒液，群魔亂舞，毒蛇嘶嘶爬動。

⑨ He looked <u>towards the sky</u> and cried <s>painfully,</s> "oh youth, return! Oh, my father,
　主詞　動詞　　受詞　　　　　　動詞　　副詞

place me once more <s>at the entrance</s> <s>to life</s> and I'll chose the better way! "
　　　　　　　　　介系詞+名詞　　介系詞+名詞

譯 他仰望星空，痛苦地大喊：「啊，青春，回來吧！啊，我的父親，再一次把我帶到人生的岔路口吧， 我會選一條更好的道路！」

⑩ But both his father and the days of his youth had passed away.

譯 但是，他的父親和他的青春歲月都已經一去不復返了。

在自然界中探險

①A night or two later the storm had blown itself out and I took Roger again to the beach, this time to carry him along the water's edge, piercing the darkness with the yellow cone of our flashlight. ②Although there was no rain the night was again noisy with breaking waves and the insistent wind. ③It was clearly a time and place where great and elemental things prevailed.

④One adventure on this particular night had to do with life, for we were searching for ghost crabs, those sand-colored, fleet-legged beings which Roger had sometimes glimpsed briefly on the beaches in daytime. ⑤But the crabs are chiefly nocturnal, and when not roaming the night beaches they dig little pits near the surf line where they hide, seemingly watching and waiting for what the sea may bring them. ⑥For me, the sight of these small living creatures, solitary and fragile against the brute force of the sea, had moving philosophic overtones, and I do not pretend that Roger and I reacted with similar emotions. ⑦But it was good to see his infant acceptance of a world of elemental things, fearing neither the song of the wind nor the darkness nor the roaring surf, entering with baby excitement into the search for a "ghost."

補充單字片語

- prevail [prɪˈveɪl] /v./ 盛行，流行
- crab [kræb] /n./ 螃蟹
- nocturnal [nɒkˈtɜ:nl] /adj./ 夜間活動的，夜間的
- roam [rəʊm] /v./ 漫步，漫遊
- do with 處理，與……有關
- a world of 極大的，很多

句構分析

① A night or two later the storm had blown itself out and I took Roger again to the
　副詞　　　　　　　主詞　　動詞　　受詞 副詞　主詞 動詞 受詞　副詞 受詞補語
beach, this time to carry him along the water's edge, piercing the darkness with the
　　副詞　不定詞結構　介系詞+名詞　　　　動名詞作形容詞片語　　介系詞+名詞
yellow cone of our flashlight.

譯 一兩天之後，暴風雨過去了，我再次把羅傑帶到海灘上，這次我帶著他沿著海水的邊緣漫步，用手電筒黃色椎體的光芒照亮黑暗。

句構分析 and連接兩個簡單分句，後面有較多的附加訊息，在化繁為簡時可一併去掉。

② Although there was no rain the night was again noisy with breaking waves and
　　讓步副詞子句　　　　　　名詞　　動詞 副詞　述詞　介系詞+動名詞
the insistent wind.

譯 儘管沒有雨，這個夜晚還是因為海浪的巨響和持續的風聲而熱鬧了起來。句構分析 該句是由讓步副詞子句和主句構成的複合句。

③ It was clearly a time and place where great and elemental things prevailed.
名詞 動詞 副詞　　述詞　　　　　形容詞子句
譯 顯然，偉大的自然力量在此時此地顯現無疑。

④ One adventure on this particular night had to do with life, for we were searching
　　主詞　　　介系詞+動名詞　　　　動詞　　受詞　　原因副詞子句
for ghost crabs, those sand-colored, fleet-legged beings which Roger had sometimes
　　　　　　　插入語　　　　　　　　　形容詞子句
glimpsed briefly on the beaches in daytime.
　　　　副詞　介系詞+名詞　介系詞+名詞

⑤ But the crabs are chiefly nocturnal, and when not roaming the night beaches they
   主詞 動詞 副詞 述詞   地方副詞片語   主詞

dig little pits near the surf line where they hide, seemingly watching and waiting for
動詞 受詞 介系詞+名詞 形容詞子句 副詞 動名詞作形容詞片語

what the sea may bring them.
 介系詞+名詞子句

  譯 但是這些螃蟹主要是在夜間活動的，當它們不在夜晚的海灘上遊蕩時，它們會在靠近海岸線的地方挖一些小坑，它們躲在那裡，似乎在觀察和等待大海會給它們帶來些什麼。

  句構分析 and後的when not roaming the night beaches中缺少動詞，無法構成副詞子句，故為是地方副詞片語。

⑥ For me, the sight of these small living creatures, solitary and fragile against the
 介系詞+代名詞 主詞 介系詞+名詞   插入語   介系詞+名詞

brute force of the sea, had moving philosophic overtones, and I do not pretend that
  介系詞+名詞 動詞   受詞   主詞 動詞

Roger and I reacted with similar emotions.
  形容詞子句   介系詞+名詞

  譯 對我來説，看到這些小小的生物因對抗大海的蠻力而顯得孤獨和脆弱時，我察覺了一些令人感動的哲學寓意，我不認為羅傑和我有相似的情緒反應。

⑦ But it was good to see his infant acceptance of a world of elemental things,
 虛主詞 動詞 述詞 主詞   介系詞+名詞

fearing neither the song of the wind nor the darkness nor the roaring surf, entering with
  動名詞作形容詞片語   動名詞作形容詞片語

baby excitement into the search for a "ghost."
 介系詞+名詞 介系詞+名詞 介系詞+名詞

  譯 但是很高興看到嬰兒般的他接受自然界的許多事物，不懼風聲、黑暗和咆哮的海浪，帶著嬰兒般的興奮開始探索幽靈螃蟹。

  語法分析 句子的主幹是it was good to see his infant acceptance...，it是虛主詞，真正的主詞是動詞不定詞to see his infant acceptance，在化繁為簡時，要注意這一點，不能把to see his infant acceptance去掉。

熱愛生活

①However mean your life is, meet it and live it; do not shun it and call it hard names. ②It is not so bad as you are. ③It looks poorest when you are richest. ④The fault-finder will find faults in paradise.

⑤Love your life, poor as it is. ⑥You may perhaps have some pleasant, thrilling glorious hours, even in a poorhouse. ⑦The setting sun is reflected from the windows of the almshouse as brightly as from the rich man's abode; the snow melts before its door as early in the spring.

⑧I do not see but a quiet mind may live as contentedly there and have as cheering thoughts. ⑨As in a palace, the town's poor seem to me often to live the most independent lives of any.

⑩Maybe they are simply great enough to receive without misgiving. ⑪ Most think that they are above being supported by the town, but it often happens that they are not above supporting themselves by dishonest means, which should be more disreputable.

⑫Cultivate poverty like a garden herb, like sage. ⑬Do not trouble yourself much to get new things, whether clothes or friends. ⑭Turn the old, return to them. ⑮Things do not change, we change. ⑯ Sell your clothes and keep your thoughts.

補充單字片語

- shun [ʃʌn] /v./ 迴避，逃避
- glorious [ˈglɔːrɪəs] /adj./ 光輝的，輝煌的
- abode [əˈbəʊd] /n./ 公寓，住所
- contentedly [kənˈtentɪdlɪ] /adv./ 滿足地，滿意地
- not so ... as 和……不一樣

句構分析

① <del>However mean your life is</del>, meet it and live it; do not shun it and call it hard

     讓步副詞子句   動詞 受詞 動詞 受詞 動詞   受詞   動詞 受詞 受詞補語

names.

譯 不管你的生活多麼卑微，面對它生活，不要避開它，也不要咒罵它。

語法分析 該句子中除了讓步副詞子句，還有並列的主句，這些主句缺少主詞，均是祈使句。

② It is not ~~so~~ bad ~~as you are~~.

主詞 動詞　副詞 述詞　副詞子句
譯 它沒有像你一樣糟糕。

③ It looks poorest ~~when you are richest~~.

主詞 動詞　述詞　　時間副詞子句
譯 當你最富有的時候它看起來最貧窮。

④ The fault-finder will find faults ~~in paradise~~.

　　主詞　　　　　　動詞　　受詞 介系詞+名詞
譯 吹毛求疵的人在天堂也能找到缺點。

⑤ Love your life, ~~poor as it is~~.

動詞　受詞　　讓步的副詞子句
譯 雖然貧窮，你也要熱愛你的生活。

⑥ You may ~~perhaps~~ have some pleasant, thrilling glorious hours, ~~even~~ in a

主詞　　　副詞　　動詞　　　　　　受詞　　　　　　　　副詞 介系詞+名詞

poorhouse.

譯 即使是在破舊的房子裡，你可能也有一些愉快、興奮和極好的時光。

⑦ The setting sun is reflected ~~from the windows of the alms-house as brightly as~~

　　　主詞　　　　動詞　　　介系詞+名詞　　　介系詞+名詞　　　副詞

~~from the rich man's abode~~; the snow melts ~~before its door as early in the spring~~.

　　介系詞+名詞　　　　　　主詞　　動詞　介系詞+名詞　　副詞 介系詞+名詞
譯 映射在濟貧院的窗戶上的夕陽和富人家裡的窗戶上的光一樣明亮；門前的雪都能在早春融化。
語法分析 該句子是由兩個分句構成的簡單句，兩個分句都是主詞+動詞結構。

⑧ I do not see but a quiet mind ~~may live as contentedly there~~ and ~~have as cheering~~

主詞　動詞　　受詞　　　　受詞補語　　　　　副詞　　　受詞補語

~~thoughts~~.

譯 我只看到一個從容的人在哪裡都能生活得心滿意足而富有愉快的思想。句構分析 see後可接動詞原形，may live和have後的內容都是對受詞mind的補充。

⑨ ~~As in a palace~~, the town's poor seem ~~to me often~~ to live the most independent

　　副詞　　　　　　主詞　　　　介系詞+名詞 副詞 動詞　　受詞

lives ~~of any~~.

　　　介系詞+名詞
譯 對我來說，城鎮的窮人與任何人相比，就像皇宮裡的人，往往過著獨立不羈的生活。

⑩ ~~Maybe~~ they are ~~simply~~ great ~~enough to receive without misgiving~~.

副詞　主詞 動詞 副詞 述詞　副詞　　不定詞結構　　介系詞+名詞
譯 也許是因為他們足夠偉大，所以可以接受任何事。

⑪ Most think <u>that they are above being supported</u> ~~by the town~~, but it ~~often~~
　　主詞 動詞　　　　　受詞　　　　　　　　　介系詞+名詞　主詞 副詞
happens ~~that they are not above supporting themselves~~ by dishonest means, ~~which~~
　動詞　　　同位語子句　　　　　　　　　　介系詞+名詞
~~should be more disreputable~~.
　　　形容詞子句
　譯　多數人認為他們不屑接受城市的扶持，但他們常常用不誠實的手段來維持自己的
　　　生活，這是更不 體面。
　句構分析　but前的句子是主句和受詞子句構成的複合句，but後是一個主句和同位語子
　　　　　　句構成的複合句。受詞子句一般不能去掉，同位語子句則可以去掉。

⑫ Cultivate poverty ~~like a garden herb, like sage~~.
　　動詞　　受詞　　　介系詞+名詞　　介系詞+名詞
　譯　像聖人培養花園中的花草一樣來培養貧窮吧。

⑬ Do not trouble ~~yourself~~ ~~much~~ to get new things, ~~whether clothes or friends~~.
　　　動詞　　　　受詞　　副詞　　受詞補語　　　　介系詞+名詞
　譯　不要自找麻煩去得到新的事物，不論是衣服或是朋友。

⑭ Turn the old, return to them.
　　動詞 受詞　動詞 受詞
　譯　讓舊物歸新，回歸舊物。

⑮ Things do not change, we change.
　主詞　　　動詞　　　主詞 動詞
　譯　事物沒有改變，是我們在改變。

⑯ Sell your clothes and keep your thoughts.
　動詞　受詞　　　　動詞　　受詞
　譯　賣掉你的衣服，保留你的思想。

 ## 以書為伴

①A good book is often the best urn of a life enshrining the best that life could think out; for the world of a man's life is, for the most part, but the world of his thoughts. ②Thus the best books are treasuries of good words, the golden thoughts, which, remembered and cherished, become our constant companions and comforters. ③"They are never alone," said Sir Philip Sidney, "that are accompanied by noble thoughts." ④The good and true thought may in times of temptation be as an angel of mercy purifying and guarding the soul. ⑤It also enshrines the germs of action, for good words almost always inspire to good works.

⑥Books possess an essence of immortality. ⑦They are by far the most lasting products of human effort. ⑧Temples and statues decay, but books survive. ⑨Time is of no account with great thoughts, which are as fresh today as when they first passed through their author's minds, ages ago. ⑩What was then said and thought still speaks to us as vividly as ever from the printed page. The only effect of time has been to sift out the bad products; for nothing in literature can long survive but what is really good.

補充單字片語

- urn [ɜːn] /n./ 茶壺，缸
- enshrine [ɪnˈʃraɪn] /v./ 銘記，珍藏
- germ [dʒɜːm] /n./ 胚芽，幼芽
- be of no account 無足輕重

句構分析

① A good book is often the best urn of a life enshrining the best that life could think
主詞　動詞 副詞　　述詞　　　介系詞+名詞　動名詞作形容詞片語　形容詞子句
out; for the world of a man's life is, for the most part, but the world of his thoughts.
　　原因副詞子句
譯 一本好書往往就像是珍貴的寶物珍藏著人們思想的精華，因為一個人的生活境界主要在於思想的境界。
語法分析 該句子包含主句、形容詞子句和原因副詞子句，所以理解時要充分利用「pass掉不必要的成分」。

② Thus the best books are treasuries of good words, the golden thoughts, which,
副詞　　主詞　　　動詞　　述詞　　介系詞+名詞
remembered and cherished, become our constant companions and comforters.
形容詞子句
譯 因此最好的書是承載著金玉良言和崇高思想的寶庫，銘記和珍視它們會成為我們永遠的伴侶和慰藉。

③ "They are never alone," said Sir Philip Sidney, "that are accompanied by noble
主詞 動詞 副詞 述詞　　動詞　　　主詞　　　　　　形容詞子句　　　　介系詞+名詞
thoughts."
譯 菲利普‧西德尼先生說，「有崇高思想陪伴的人從不孤獨。」

④ The good and true thought may in times of temptation be as an angel of mercy
　　　主詞　　　　　　　　　介系詞+名詞 介系詞+名詞 動詞　　述詞　　介系詞+名詞

140

purifying and guarding the soul.

動名詞作形容詞片語

譯 善良和真實的思想會像仁慈的天使一樣，在受到誘惑的時候淨化和保護靈魂。

⑤ It also enshrines the germs of action, for good words almost always inspire to
主詞 副詞 動詞　　受詞　　介系詞+名詞　　原因副詞子句

good works.

譯 它也孕育著行為的胚芽，因為良言總是啟發善行。

⑥ Books possess an essence of immortality.
　主詞　　動詞　　受詞　　介系詞+名詞

譯 書籍在本質上是不朽的。

⑦ They are by far the most lasting products of human effort.
　主詞 動詞 介系詞片語　　受詞　　　介系詞+名詞

譯 迄今為止，它們是人類創造的最持久的產品。

⑧ Temples and statues decay, but books survive.
　　　　　主詞　　　　動詞　　　主詞　　動詞

譯 廟宇和雕像都衰敗了，但是書本還存在著。

句構分析 but連接兩個主詞+動詞結構的簡單句。

⑨ Time is of no account with great thoughts, which are as fresh today as when they
主詞 動詞　述詞　　介系詞+名詞　　形容詞子句　　　副詞

first passed through their author's minds, ages ago.
時間副詞子句　　　　　　　　　　　　副詞

譯 時間對於偉大的思想來說是無足輕重的，如今它們依然清晰，正如它們多年前初
　 次從作者的腦海中穿過時一樣。

⑩ What was then said and thought still speaks to us as vividly as ever from the
　　　　　主詞　　　　　　副詞 動詞 受詞 副詞　　　介系詞+名詞

printed page.

譯 他們當時的言論和思想印刷在紙張上，如今仍然像和我們對話一樣生動如初。

句構分析 該句子是一個複合句，句子的主語是what引導的名詞子句。

⑪ The only effect of time has been to sift out the bad products; for nothing in
　主詞　　介系詞+名詞 動詞　　述詞　　　　　　原因副詞子句

literature can long survive but what is really good.
　　　　　　　　　　　　　　形容詞子句

譯 時間的唯一作用是淘汰不良作品，因為只有真正好的作品才能在文學中長存。

語法分析 形容詞子句what is really good修飾的是名詞nothing。

戴森公司擬2020年前推出電動汽車

①British company Dyson is known for inventing new vacuum cleaner technology and producing other devices for the home.

②Now the company has entered new territory by announcing plans to launch an electric vehicle by 2020.

③In a recent announcement to employees, company founder James Dyson said about 400 engineers are working with other teams on the project.

④The company – based in Malmesbury, England – is known for creating innovative

product designs started by Dyson himself. ⑤Dyson is seen by many as having revolutionized the industry by engineering products that are powerful and easy to use. ⑥For example, the company makes fans and heating devices that do not use blades like most other products on the market.

⑦Dyson has been working on vehicle technology since 1990, when its engineers invented a way to trap diesel engine pollutants. ⑧ In recent years, the company has increased its research and development efforts for electric vehicles.

⑨According to Dyson, the company will invest at least $2.6 billion in the project. ⑩He said he looks forward to offering the world "a solution to the world's largest single environmental risk."

補充單字片語

- technology [tekˈnɒlədʒɪ] /n./ 科技
- electric vehicle 電動汽車
- announce [əˈnaʊns] /v./ 宣布
- be known for 因……而著名
- looks forward to... 期待……

句構分析

① <u>British company Dyson</u> <u>is known</u> ~~for inventing~~ <u>new vacuum cleaner</u>
　　　　主詞　　　　　　　動詞　　介系詞+動名詞　　　受詞

<u>technology</u> and producing other devices ~~for the home~~.
　　　　　　　　　　　　　　　　　　　　介系詞+名詞

譯 英國戴森公司因發明新型真空吸塵器和生產其它家庭設備而聞名。

② ~~Now~~ <u>the company</u> <u>has entered</u> <u>new territory</u> <u>by announcing plans</u> ~~to launch an~~
　副詞　　主詞　　　　動詞　　　　受詞　　　介系詞+名詞　　　　不定詞結構

~~electric vehicle by 2020~~.
　　　　介系詞+名詞

譯 如今該公司宣布進軍新領域——將於2020年前推出一款電動車。

結構分析 該句話是整則新聞的主題句，概括了段落大意，其它段落都是圍繞該主題句展開的。

③ ~~In a recent announcement to employees~~, <u>company founder James Dyson</u> <u>said</u>
　　　　介系詞+名詞　　　　　　　　　　　　主詞　　　　　　　　　　動詞

about 400 engineers are working ~~with other teams~~ ~~on the project~~.
　　受詞　　　　　介系詞+名詞　　　介系詞+名詞

譯 在近期發給員工的公告中，公司創始人詹姆斯‧戴森表示，約400名工程師正與其它團隊合力研發該項目。

④ <u>The company</u> ~~– based in Malmesbury, England –~~ <u>is known</u> ~~for creating~~
　　主詞　　　　　　　插入語　　　　　　　　　　動詞　　介系詞+動名詞

<u>innovative product designs</u> ~~started by Dyson himself~~.
　　　受詞　　　　　　被動分詞結構　介系詞+名詞

譯 這家總部位於英國馬爾姆斯伯裡的公司由戴森本人一手創辦，該公司以打造創新型產品設計而著稱。

⑤ <u>Dyson</u> <u>is seen</u> ~~by many~~ as having revolutionized the industry ~~by engineering~~
　主詞　　動詞　介系詞+名詞　　　　受詞　　　　　　　介系詞+名詞

~~products~~ that are powerful and easy to use.
　　　　形容詞子句

譯 很多人認為，戴森功能齊全、使用方便的產品徹底改變了整個行業。

⑥ ~~For example~~, <u>the company</u> <u>makes</u> <u>fans and heating devices</u> <u>that do not use</u>
　介系詞+名詞　　主詞　　　動詞　　　受詞　　　　　形容詞子句

<u>blades</u> ~~like most other products~~ ~~on the market~~.
　　　介系詞+名詞　　　　介系詞+名詞

譯 例如，與市場上大多數產品不同，該公司生產的風扇和加熱設備沒有使用葉片。

⑦ <u>Dyson</u> <u>has been working on</u> <u>vehicle technology</u> ~~since 1990~~, ~~when its engineers~~
　主詞　　　動詞　　　　　　受詞　　　　介系詞+名詞　時間副詞子句

~~invented a way to trap diesel engine pollutants~~.

譯 自1990年起，戴森一直致力於研究汽車技術，當時該公司的工程師們發明了一種收集柴油廢氣的辦法。

⑧ ~~In recent years~~, the company has increased its research and development
  介系詞+名詞   主詞   動詞   受詞

efforts ~~for electric vehicles~~.
    介系詞+名詞

譯 近些年來，公司加大了對電動汽車的研發力度。

⑨ ~~According to Dyson~~, the company will invest ~~at least~~ $2.6 billion ~~in the project~~.
   介系詞+名詞   主詞   動詞 介系詞+名詞   受詞   介系詞+名詞

譯 據戴森透露，公司將在電動汽車項目投資至少26億美元。

⑩ He said he looks forward to offering the world "a solution ~~to the world's largest~~
 主詞 動詞   受詞片語   介系詞+名詞

~~single environmental risk.~~"

譯 他說，他期待為世界提供一種「解決全球最大單一環境風險的方案」。

舊書巧作藝術品

①Some people are using old books to create works of art, including sculptures.

②They can change the shape of a hardcover book so it becomes three-dimensional, for example. ③The resulting sculpture has not only a length and width, but depth.

④The process can be very simple, and the result is often beautiful.

⑤There are many kinds of book folding. ⑥Artists fold, bend, and sometimes cut, a book's pages while keeping them together. ⑦The art work can be hung on a wall or placed on a table.

⑧They look impressive on the wall, says writer Candice Caldwell. ⑨A group of six of these on the wall together can look really beautiful, and they're just really simple folds.

⑩Caldwell operates a blog called the ReFab Diaries. ⑪She writes about re-purposing everyday objects like books for uses other than what they were designed for.

⑫In 2003, Caldwell was making clocks from old books when she saw plans for a simple book-folding project in a do-it-yourself magazine. ⑬ She tried it. She has since taught several friends and her mother how to create wall art from books.

⑭Clare Youngs has written a book called Folded Book Art . She says book folding is easy.

補充單字片語

• sculpture [ˈskʌlptʃə] /n./ 雕刻
• impressive [ɪmˈpresɪv] /adj./ 令人印象深刻的

句構分析

① Some people are using old books to create works of art, including sculptures.
　　主詞　　　動詞　　受詞　　　不定詞結構　　　介系詞片語
譯 有些人用舊書來創作藝術品，比如雕塑。

② They can change the shape of a hardcover book so it becomes three-
　主詞　　動詞　　受詞　　介系詞+名詞　　　主詞　動詞　述詞
dimensional, for example.
　　　　介系詞+名詞
譯 例如，他們可以改變一本精裝書的形狀，使它變得立體化。

③ The resulting sculpture has not only a length and width, but depth.
　　　主詞　　　　動詞　　　　　受詞
譯 由此做出來的雕塑不僅有長度和寬度，亦有深度。

④ The process can be very simple, and the result is often beautiful.
　　主詞　　動詞　副詞　述詞　　　　主詞　動詞副詞　述詞
譯 這個過程可能非常簡單，但作品卻十分美觀。

⑤ There are many kinds of book folding.
　　　there be句型　　　介系詞+名詞
譯 折書的方式有很多種。

⑥ Artists fold, bend, and sometimes cut, a book's pages while keeping them
　主詞 動詞 動詞　　　副詞　　動詞　　　受詞
together.
副詞
譯 藝術家們會折疊、彎曲或者裁剪書頁而同時保持書不會散架。

⑦ The art work can be hung on a wall or placed on a table.
　　主詞　　　動詞　　介系詞+名詞　　動詞　介系詞+名詞

譯 藝術品可以掛在牆上或放在桌子上。

⑧ They look impressive ~~on the wall~~, says writer Candice Caldwell.
主詞　動詞　　述詞　　　介系詞+名詞
譯 作家坎蒂絲‧考德威爾說，這些藝術品掛在牆上特別美。

⑨ A group of six ~~of these~~ ~~on the wall~~ together can look ~~really~~ beautiful, and they're
　　主詞　　　　介系詞+代名詞 介系詞+名詞　　動詞　　副詞　　述詞　　主詞 動詞
~~just~~ ~~really~~ simple folds.
副詞\副詞　　述詞
譯 這樣的作品六個一組一起掛在牆上會很好看，但他們僅僅是非常簡單的折疊品。

⑩ Caldwell operates a blog ~~called the ReFab Diaries~~.
　　主詞　　　動詞　受詞　　　過去分詞作形容詞片語
譯 考德威爾經營著一個名叫作ReFab Diaries 的部落格。

⑪ She writes ~~about re-purposing~~ everyday objects ~~like books~~ ~~for uses~~ other than
主詞 動詞　　介系詞+動名詞　　　　　受詞　　　　介系詞+名詞　介系詞+名詞
what they were designed for.
譯 部落格上的內容是有關將日常物品（比如書）用作並非其本來性能的其他用途。

⑫ ~~In 2003~~, Caldwell was making clocks ~~from old books~~ when she saw plans for a
介系詞+名詞　主詞　　動詞　　受詞　介系詞+名詞　　　時間副詞子句
~~simple bookfolding project in a do-it-yourself magazine~~.
譯 2003年，考德威爾開始用舊書製作鐘錶，因為她在一本DIY雜誌上看到了一個簡
單折書項目的計劃。

⑬ She tried it. She has ~~since~~ taught several friends and her mother how to create
主詞 動詞 受詞 主詞　　副詞　動詞　　　　　　受詞　　　　　　受詞補詞
wall art from books.
　　　介系詞+名詞
譯 於是她開始嘗試。從那以後，她已經教了幾個朋友和她的母親如何用書來製作牆
面的藝術。

⑭ Clare Youngs has written a book ~~called~~ Folded Book Art. She says book folding
　　主詞　　　　動詞　　受詞 動詞過去分詞　　　　　　主詞 動詞　　受詞子句
is easy.
譯 克萊爾‧揚斯寫了一本名為《折書的藝術》的書，在書中，她寫道，折書是件容
易事。

研究表明貧困會影響學習

①Studies have shown that children from poor families have more difficulty in school than other boys and girls. ②Children with higher socioeconomic roots seem better prepared and perform better on school tests.

③Now, American researchers may have found a biological reason for that difference. ④They found differences in the brains of students who had low standardized test scores. ⑤Their brains had less gray matter and their temporal lobes developed more slowly than the other children. ⑥The findings were reported in the journal JAMA Pediatrics.

⑦Temporal lobes and gray matter are very important brain areas, says researcher Barbara Wolfe. ⑧She is a professor of economics, population health and public affairs at the University of Wisconsin at Madison.

⑨The brain areas are "critical in the sense that they keep developing until individuals are well into their adolescence or early 20s, and critical in the sense that they are important for executive function," she said.

⑩Researchers studied brain images of nearly 400 children and young adults. ⑪The youngest subjects were four years old. The oldest were 22. ⑫Researchers looked for a connection between the person's socioeconomic status and his or her test results.

⑬On average, young people from poor families had test scores between three and four points below what is expected for their age group.

補充單字片語

- socioeconomic [ˌsəʊsɪəʊˌiːkəˈnɒmɪk] /adj./ 社會經濟學的
- temporal [ˈtempərəl] /adj./ 時間的，暫存的
- on average 平均，一般來說

句構分析

① Studies <u>have shown</u> <u>that children</u> ~~from poor families~~ have more difficulty in~

   主詞   動詞   受詞子句   介系詞+名詞

school than other boys and girls.
　　介系詞+名詞
　譯 研究表明，與其他男孩、女孩相比，來自貧困家庭的孩子在學業上會遇到更多困難。

② Children with higher socioeconomic roots seem better prepared and perform
　　主詞　　　　介系詞+名詞　　　　　　動詞　　　述詞
better on school tests.
　　　介系詞+名詞
　譯 具有較高社會經濟地位的孩子似乎準備更充分，在學校考試中表現的更好。

③ Now, American researchers may have found a biological reason for that
　　副詞　　　主詞　　　　　動詞　　　　　受詞　　　　介系詞+名詞
difference.
　譯 現在，美國研究人員可能已經發現了導致這一差異的生理原因。

④ They found differences in the brains of students who had low standardized test
　　主詞 動詞　受詞　　介系詞+名詞　介系詞+名詞　　形容詞子句
scores.
　譯 他們發現在標準化考試中分數低的學生的大腦差異。

⑤ Their brains had less gray matter and their temporal lobes developed more
　　　主詞　　動詞　受詞　　　　　　　主詞　　　　動詞
slowly than the other children.
　副詞　　　介系詞+名詞
　譯 與其他孩子相比，他們的大腦中的灰質更少，頂葉發育得更慢。

⑥ The findings were reported in the journal JAMA Pediatrics.
　　　主詞　　　動詞　　　　　介系詞+名詞
　譯 這一發現發表在期刊《兒科學》上。

⑦ Temporal lobes and gray matter are very important brain areas, says
　　　　　　主詞　　　　　　動詞　　　述詞
researcher Barbara Wolfe.
　譯 研究者芭芭拉・沃爾夫說，頂葉和灰質都是大腦中很重要的區域。

⑧ She is a professor of economics, population health and public affairs at the
主詞 動詞 述詞　　　　介系詞+名詞　　　　　　介系詞+名詞
University of Wisconsin at Madison.
　譯 她是威斯康辛大學麥迪遜分校經濟學、人口健康和公共事務學教授。

⑨ "The brain areas are critical in the sense that they keep developing until
　　　主詞　　動詞 述詞 介系詞+名詞　　形容詞子句
individuals are well into their adolescence or early 20s, and critical in the sense that
　　　　　　　　　介系詞+名詞　　　　　　　　　述詞 介系詞+名詞 形容詞子句
they are important for executive function," she said.
　　　　　　　　介系詞+名詞

　　圝 這些大腦區域很重要，它們能在個體進入青春期或20歲以前一直處於發展狀態，對於執行功能來說非常重要。

⑩ Researchers studied <u>brain images</u> ~~of nearly 400 children and young adults~~.
　　主詞　　動詞　　受詞　　　　介系詞+名詞
　　圝 研究人員對近400名兒童和年輕人的大腦圖像進行了研究。

⑪ <u>The youngest subjects</u> were <u>four years old</u>. <u>The oldest</u> were <u>22</u>.
　　　　主詞　　　　　　動詞　　述詞　　　主詞　　動詞　述詞
　　圝 最年輕的被研究者只有4歲，最大的22歲。

⑫ Researchers <u>looked for</u> <u>a connection</u> ~~between the person's socioeconomic status~~
　　主詞　　　　動詞　　　受詞　　　　　　介系詞+名詞
~~and his or her test results~~.
　　圝 研究者發現了這些人社會經濟地位與其測試結果之間的聯繫。

⑬ ~~On average,~~ <u>young people</u> ~~from poor families~~ had <u>test scores</u> ~~between three and~~
介系詞+名詞　　主詞　　　　介系詞+名詞　　動詞　受詞　　　介系詞+名詞
~~four points below what is expected for their age group~~.
　　　　　介系詞+名詞子句
　　圝 通常情況下，來自貧困家庭的年輕人其考試成績比這個年齡組的期待成績要低三到四分。

蘋果臉部辨識功能引爭議

①The brand new iPhone X has been heralded as the most groundbreaking and technologically advanced since the first iPhone was unveiled in 2007.

②But one of the key new features, the Face ID recognition software which allows users to open their phone by scanning their face, has sparked privacy fears.

③Experts warned that the new technology has the potential be abused by thieves, forcing iPhone X owners to unlock their phones to steal information and wipe them to sell, or even an abusive partner wanting to look through their spouses' messages.

④It could also potentially allow police to unlock phones of suspects to find incriminating evidence, without having to get a court to try and force them to hand over their passcode.

⑤The technology throws up many similar concerns as to when Apple launched its fingerprint technology on earlier iPhone models. ⑥But with Face ID, there is also the concern the scan can normalize facial recognition software - and unlike the iPhone which only stores information about its user's face on the phone itself - other applications could have far greater privacy concerns.

⑦The Fifth Amendment protects citizens from being forced to divulge their passwords if it will incriminate themselves.

⑧But ever since Apple introduced Touch ID, legal experts have argued that biometric evidence such as blood, DNA, and fingerprints do not count as testimony against ourselves.

補充單字片語

- groundbreaking [ˈgraʊndbreɪkɪŋ] /adj./ 開創性的
- spouse [spaʊs] /n./ 配偶
- normalize [ˈnɔ:məlaɪz] /v./ 使正常化，使標準化

句構分析

① The brand new iPhone X has been heralded as the most groundbreaking and
　　　　主詞　　　　　　　　動詞　　　　　　　受詞
technologically advanced since the first iPhone was unveiled in 2007.
　副詞　　　　　　　　　　時間副詞子句
　譯　自從2007年推出第一款iPhone以來，這款全新的iPhone X被譽為最具開創性和技術進步的產品。

② But one of the key new features, the Face ID recognition software which allows
　　　　介系詞+名詞　　　　　　　　主詞　　　　　　　　形容詞子句
users to open their phone by scanning their face, has sparked privacy fears.
　　　　　　　　　　　　　　　　　　　　　　　　動詞　　　受詞
　譯　iPhone X的主要新技能之一「臉部解鎖（Face ID）」可以讓使用者通過手機掃描面部就打開手機，但是這項面部識別系統引發了大家對隱私的顧慮。

③ Experts warned that the new technology has the potential be abused by thieves,
　主詞　動詞　　　　受詞子句　　　　　　　　　　　　　介系詞+名詞
forcing iPhone X owners to unlock their phones to steal information and wipe them
　　　　　　　　　　　　動詞不定詞　　　　　動詞不定詞
to sell, or even an
　　　　　副詞

150

abusive partner wanting ~~to look through their spouses' messages~~.

　　　　　　　　　　　　　　　　　不定詞結構

圙 專家警告説這項新技術可能會被小偷濫用，迫使用戶解鎖手機，盜取訊息然後把
　手機賣掉，或者有涉虐待的伴侶想藉此偷窺另一半的信息。

④ It could ~~also potentially~~ allow police ~~to unlock phones of suspects to find~~

　主詞　副詞　副詞　動詞　受詞　不定詞結構　介系詞+名詞　不定詞結構

~~incriminating evidence, without having to get a court to try and force them to hand~~

　　　　　　　　　　介系詞+動名詞　　不定詞結構　　　不定詞結構　　　不定詞結構

~~over their passcode~~.

圙 警方也可能通過臉部解鎖功能打開嫌犯的手機，發現犯罪證據，這樣就不需要帶
　人到法院強制他們交出手機密碼了。

⑤ The technology throws up many similar concerns as to when Apple launched its

　　主詞　　　　動詞　　　受詞

fingerprint technology ~~on earlier iPhone models~~.

　　　　　　　　　　介系詞+名詞

圙 蘋果早期在iPhone產品上推出指紋解鎖功能時，也出現過類似的擔憂。

⑥ But ~~with Face ID,~~ there is ~~also~~ the concern ~~the scan can normalize facial~~

　　介系詞+名詞　there be句型 副詞　　　　　　同位語子句

~~recognition software~~ - and ~~unlike the iPhone which only stores information about its~~

　　　　　　　　　　　　　　介系詞+名詞　　　形容詞子句

~~user's face on the phone itself~~ - other applications could have far greater privacy concerns.

圙 但是臉部解鎖功能還會引發其他問題：面部識別有可能被常規化，iPhone手機當
　然只是在機體上儲存了用戶的面部訊息，但是其他應用就不一定了，它們帶來的
　隱私問題威脅性更大。

⑦ The Fifth Amendment protects citizens ~~from being forced to divulge their~~

　　主詞　　　　　　動詞　　　受詞　　　介系詞+動名詞

~~passwords if it will incriminate themselves~~.

　　　　　　　條件副詞子句

圙 第五修正案保護公民在強權中仍無需透漏密碼的權利，即使密碼將會證明他們的
　罪行。

⑧ But ~~ever since Apple introduced Touch ID,~~ legal experts have argued that

　　副詞　時間副詞子句　　　　　　主詞　　　動詞

biometric evidence such as blood, DNA, and fingerprints do not count ~~as testimony~~

　　　受詞子句　　　　　　　　　　　　　　　　　　介系詞+名詞

~~against ourselves~~.

圙 但是，蘋果推出指紋解鎖功能時，也有法律人士稱，諸如血液、DNA、指紋這樣
　的生理證據並不能 作為呈堂證供用來揭發自己。

每天一分鐘運動有益健康

①There is good news for people who think they do not have time to exercise.

②A group of researchers from a university in Canada recently published a study that says short bursts of high-intensity exercise are good for you.

③In fact, this kind of exercise is just as good as spending up to an hour riding a bike or running steadily.

④The research team followed 27 men who were not very active for 12 weeks. ⑤They divided the men into three groups. ⑥One group did short, intense workouts on a bicycle three times a week. ⑦Another group rode a bicycle for about 50 minutes, three times a week. ⑧A third group did nothing.

⑨The researchers found something they did not expect. ⑩The group that exercised for only 10 minutes each session was just as healthy after 12 weeks as the group that exercised for 50 minutes each session.

⑪That is because of the way the researchers organized the workouts.

⑫Each group started with a two-minute warm-up and finished with a three-minute cooldown. But in-between, the high-intensity group sprinted for 20 seconds, followed by a two-minute recovery period. ⑬They did three sprints for a total of 10 minutes of exercise. This kind of exercise is known as interval training.

補充單字片語

- university [ˌjuːnɪˈvɜːsətɪ] /n./ 大學
- intense [ɪnˈtens] /adj./ 熱情的，熱烈的
- because of 因為，由於

句構分析

① There is good news ~~for people~~ ~~who think they do not have time~~ ~~to exercise~~.
there be句型　　　　　介系詞+名詞　形容詞子句　　　　　　動詞不定詞
譯 對那些認為自己沒有時間鍛煉的人來說，這是個好消息。

結構分析 本句在整篇報道開頭處設置懸念，為下文的書寫埋下伏筆。

② A group of researchers from a university in Canada recently published a study
　　主詞　　介系詞+名詞　　　介系詞+名詞　　　介系詞+名詞　　副詞　　　動詞　　　受詞
that says short bursts of high-intensity exercise are good for you.
　　　　　　　　　　　　形容詞子句
📖 加拿大一所大學的一組研究人員最近發表了一項研究，稱短時間的高強度運動對健康有益。

③ In fact, this kind of exercise is just as good as spending up to an hour riding a
介系詞+名詞　　　主詞　　　　動詞 副詞 述詞　介系詞+動名詞　　介系詞+名詞　受詞
bike or running steadily.
　　　　　　　　　副詞
📖 事實上，這種運動和花費一小時時間持續地騎自行車或跑步的效果相當。

④ The research team followed 27 men who were not very active for 12 weeks.
　　　　主詞　　　　　　動詞　　受詞　　　形容詞子句　　　　　　　介系詞+名詞
📖 連續12周，該研究團隊追蹤記錄了27名不太愛運動的男子。

⑤ They divided the men into three groups.
　主詞　動詞　　受詞　　介系詞+名詞
📖 他們把這些人分成三組。

⑥ One group did short, intense workouts on a bicycle three times a week.
　　主詞　　動詞　　　　受詞　　　　介系詞+名詞
📖 其中一組每週三次騎自行車進行短暫的高強度訓練。

⑦ Another group rode a bicycle for about 50 minutes, three times a week.
　　主詞　　　動詞　受詞　　介系詞+名詞
📖 另外一組每周騎三次自行車，每次50分鐘。

⑧ A third group did nothing.
　　主詞　　　動詞　受詞
📖 第三組什麼也不做。

⑨ The researchers found something they did not expect.
　　　主詞　　　　動詞　　受詞　　　形容詞子句
📖 研究人員發現了一些他們沒有想到的結果。

⑩ The group that exercised for only 10 minutes each session was just as healthy
　　主詞　　　　　　形容詞子句　　　　　　　　　　　　動詞　副詞　　述詞
after 12 weeks as the group that exercised for 50 minutes each session.
介系詞+名詞　　　　　　　　形容詞子句
📖 12週之後，每次只鍛鍊10分鐘的一組和每次運動50分鐘的一組健康狀況相同。

⑪ That is because of the way the researchers organized the workouts.
主詞 動詞 述詞子句 介系詞+名詞
📖 這是因為研究人員安排鍛鍊的方式。

153

⑫ Each group started ~~with a two-minute warm-up~~ and finished ~~with a three-minute~~
　　主詞　　　動詞　　　介系詞+名詞　　　　　　　　　　　　　　　　介系詞+名詞
~~cool-down~~.
📖 每個小組都以兩分鐘的熱身運動開始，以三分鐘的放鬆活動結束。

⑬ But in-between, the high-intensity group sprinted ~~for 20 seconds~~, followed ~~by a~~
　　　　　　　　　主詞　　　　　　　動詞　　介系詞+名詞　　　動詞
~~two-minute recovery period~~.
介系詞+名詞
📖 但是在此期間，高強度運動的一組衝刺了20秒鐘，隨後進行兩分鐘的恢復。

⑭ They did three sprints ~~for a total of 10 minutes of exercise~~.
主詞 動詞　受詞　　　介系詞+名詞 介系詞+名詞 介系詞+名詞
📖 他們在十分鐘的運動時間內進行了三次衝刺。

⑮ This kind of exercise is known as interval training.
　　主詞　　　　　　　動詞　　　　受詞
📖 這種運動叫做間歇訓練。

 馬鈴薯短缺造成洋芋片末日

①Potato lovers in New Zealand could be in for a big shock. ②New Zealand is facing a possible potato shortage in the next few months. ③This means there could be a lack of potato chips (crisps in British English) until next year. ④Newspapers are calling this situation the "chipocalypse". ⑤They combined the words "chip" and "apocalypse" to make this new word. ⑥ A possible chipocalypse is because of a very wet winter in New Zealand. ⑦This has hit potato growers. ⑧In some areas, a third of the potato crop has been lost. ⑨The wet weather has particularly hit the potatoes that are used to make potato chips. ⑩This means makers will make fewer potato chips and prices for potato chips will be higher.

⑪A spokesman for New Zealand potato farmers told the Radio Live NZ news station about the problem. ⑫Chris Claridge, head of Potatoes New Zealand, said: " ⑬It started raining in March, and it just simply hasn't stopped. ⑭We've had the entire year's worth of rainfall already, so the rainfall is 25 per cent above average and while that might not sound like a lot what it means is it's continuous, so the soils never get a chance to dry out."

補充單字片語

- shortage [ˈʃɔːtɪdʒ] /n./ 不足，缺少
- grower [ˈɡrəʊə] /n./ 種植者
- entire [ɪnˈtaɪə(r)] /adj./ 整個的
- continuous [kənˈtɪnjʊəs] /adj./ 連續的

句構分析

① Potot lovers ~~in New Zealand~~ could be in for a big shock.
     主詞   介系詞+名詞   連綴動詞   述詞
  譯 紐西蘭的馬鈴薯愛好者將遭受巨大衝擊。
  結構分析 本句是主題句，在開頭設置懸念，為下文詳細介紹「洋芋片末日」埋下伏筆。

② New Zealand is facing a possible potato shortage ~~in the next few months~~.
     主詞   動詞   受詞   介系詞+名詞
  譯 在未來幾個月，紐西蘭可能面臨馬鈴薯短缺。

③ This means there could be a lack ~~of potato chips~~ (crisps in British English) ~~until~~
  主詞 動詞   there be 句型   介系詞+名詞
  ~~next year~~.
  介系詞+名詞
  譯 這就意味著洋芋片（在英國英語中叫作crisps）在明年之前都會短缺。

④ Newspapers are calling this situation the "chipocalypse".
     主詞   動詞   受詞   受詞補語
  譯 報紙稱這種情況為「洋芋片末日」。

⑤ They combined the words "chip" and "apocalypse" ~~to make this new word~~.
  主詞 動詞   受詞   不定詞結構
  譯 他們把「洋芋片」和「末日」兩個詞組合起來，組成了新詞。

⑥ A possible chipocalypse is because of a very wet winter ~~in New Zealand~~.
     主詞   動詞   述詞子句   介系詞+名詞
  譯 可能出現洋芋片末日是因為紐西蘭目前正處於非常潮濕多雨的的冬天。

⑦ This has hit potato growers.
  主詞 動詞   受詞
  譯 這對馬鈴薯的種植者造成了衝擊。

⑧ ~~In some areas~~, a third ~~of the potato crop~~ has been lost.
  介系詞+名詞   主詞   介系詞+名詞   動詞
  譯 在一些地區，馬鈴薯損失達三分之一。

⑨ The wet weather has ~~particularly~~ hit the potatoes ~~that are used to make potato~~
     主詞   副詞 動詞 受詞   形容詞子句

chips.

譯 潮濕的天氣使專門用來製作洋芋片的馬鈴薯遭遇的損失最大。

⑩ This means <u>makers</u> <u>will make</u> <u>fewer potato chips and prices</u> <s>for potato chips</s>
　　　　 主詞　動詞　　　　　　　受詞子句　　　　　　　　　介系詞+名詞
<u>will be</u> higher.

譯 這就意味著商家製作的洋芋片數量減少，價格會提高。

⑪ <u>A spokesman</u> <s>for New Zealand potato farmers</s> <u>told</u> <u>the Radio Live NZ news</u>
　　主詞　　　　　介系詞+名詞　　　　　　　　　動詞　　　　　受詞
<u>station</u> <s>about the problem</s>.
　　　　　　介系詞+名詞

譯 紐西蘭馬鈴薯種植者的一名發言人向紐西蘭無線直播新聞臺反映了這個問題。

⑫ <u>Chris Claridge</u>, <s>head of Potatoes New Zealand</s>, <u>said</u>:
　　主詞　　　　　　　　　　插入語　　　　　　　　動詞

譯 紐西蘭馬鈴薯聯盟負責人克里斯·克拉里奇表示：

⑬ <u>It</u> <u>started</u> <u>raining</u> <s>in March</s>, and <u>it</u> <s>just</s> <u>simply</u> <u>hasn't stopped</u>.
　主詞　動詞　　動名詞　介系詞+名詞　主詞　　副詞　　　　動詞

譯 從三月份就開始下雨，一直都沒有停。

⑭ <u>We've</u> <u>had</u> <u>the entire year's worth</u> <s>of rainfall already</s>, so <u>the rainfall</u> <u>is</u> <u>25 per</u>
　主詞　動詞　　　　受詞　　　　　　　介系詞+名詞　　　主詞　　　動詞　述詞
<u>cent</u> <s>above average</s> and while that might not sound like a lot what it means is it's
　　　介系詞+名詞
continuous, so <u>the soils</u> <u>never</u> <u>get</u> <u>a chance</u> <s>to dry out</s>."
　　　　　　　　主詞　　　副詞　動詞　述詞　　　不定詞結構

譯 目前的降雨量已經達到以前的全年降雨量了，今年的降雨量比以前的平均降雨量
多了25%，聽上去也許不是很多，但是關鍵是一直在降雨，所以土壤很難變乾。

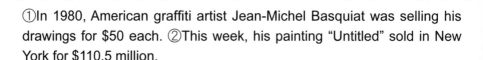

巴斯奎特畫作拍出1.1億美元高價

①In 1980, American graffiti artist Jean-Michel Basquiat was selling his drawings for $50 each. ②This week, his painting "Untitled" sold in New York for $110.5 million.

③Only 10 works of art have sold at auction for more than $100 million.

④Basquiat's painting sets a new record for price of a work by an American artist. ⑤An Andy Warhol painting called "Silver Car Crash" was sold in 2013 for $105 million.

⑥The painting "Untitled" is of a skull-like head against a blue background. ⑦It last sold more than 30 years ago for $19,000.

⑧Japanese billionaire Yosaku Maezawa bought "Untitled" at Sotheby's auction house on Thursday night.

⑨Basquiat was a street artist who became famous in the early 1980s. ⑩He died of a drug overdose in 1987 at the age of 27.

⑪He was known for using bright colors, words and mixed materials in his work. ⑫His art captured the imagination of many artists, gallery owners and musicians in New York City.

⑬Fans and supporters included Andy Warhol, David Bowie and gallery owner Larry Gagosian. ⑭At one time, Basquiat's girlfriend was music star Madonna.

⑮Maezawa is a big fan of Basquiat. ⑯He bought another Basquiat painting for more than $57 million last year.

⑰Maezawa said he will loan the painting to museums around the world before displaying it in his hometown of Chiba, Japan.

補充單字片語

- graffiti [grəˈfiːtɪ] /n./ 亂塗亂寫
- billionaire [ˌbɪljəˈneə(r)] /n./ 億萬富翁
- overdose [ˈəʊvədəʊs] /n./ 過量用藥 /v./ 用藥過量
- set a new record 創造新紀錄

句構分析

① ~~In 1980,~~ American graffiti artist Jean-Michel Basquiat was selling his drawings
　介系詞+名詞　　　　　　　　　主詞　　　　　　　　動詞　　受詞
~~for $50 each.~~
　介系詞+名詞
🔤 1980年，美國塗鴉藝術家讓·米切爾·巴斯奎特以每幅50美元的價格售賣畫作。

② ~~This week,~~ his painting "Untitled" was sold ~~in New York for $110.5 million.~~
　副詞　　　　　主詞　　　　動詞　介系詞+名詞　介系詞+名詞

157

譯 本週，他的畫作《無題》在紐約以1億1050萬美元出售。

句構分析 該句是本篇新聞的主題句，後面的內容均是圍繞這個話題展開。該句所在的段落屬於轉折型段落。

③ Only 10 works ~~of art~~ have sold ~~at auction for more than $100 million~~.
　　主詞　　介系詞+名詞　述詞　　介系詞+名詞　介系詞+名詞

譯 只有10幅作品在拍賣會上以1億美元的價格成交。

④ Basquiat's painting sets a new record ~~for price of a work by an American artist~~.
　　　主詞　　　　　動詞　　受詞　　介系詞+名詞　介系詞+名詞　介系詞+名詞

譯 巴斯奎特的畫作創造了美國藝術家作品價格的新記錄。

⑤ An Andy Warhol painting ~~called "Silver Car Crash"~~ was sold ~~in 2013 for $105~~
　　　　　主詞　　　　　　被動詞作形容詞片語　　　　　動詞 介系詞+名詞 介系詞+名詞

~~million~~.

譯 安迪‧沃霍爾的一幅稱為「銀色車禍」的畫作在2013年賣了1億500萬美元。

⑥ The painting "Untitled" is of a skull-like head ~~against a blue background~~.
　　　　主詞　　　　　　動詞　　述詞　　　　　介系詞+名詞

譯 這幅名為《無題》的畫是在藍色背景下的一個骷髏頭。

⑦ It ~~last~~ sold ~~more than 30 years ago for $19,000~~.
主詞 副詞 動詞　　　副詞　　　　介系詞+名詞

譯 它上次在30年前賣了1萬9000美元。

句構分析 該句子與本文的主題句構成了對比，起烘托作用。

⑧ Japanese billionaire Yosaku Maezawa bought "Untitled" ~~at Sotheby's auction~~
　　　　　　　　主詞　　　　　　　　　　　動詞　　受詞　　介系詞+名詞

~~house on Thursday night~~.
　介系詞+名詞

譯 星期四晚上，日本的億萬富翁前澤友作在蘇富比拍賣會上買下了《無題》。

⑨ Basquiat was a street artist ~~who became famous in the early 1980s~~.
　　主詞　　動詞　　述詞　　　　形容詞子句　　　　介系詞+名詞

譯 巴斯奎特是一位街頭藝術家，他在20世紀80年代初期成名。

⑩ He died ~~of a drug overdose in 1987 at the age of 27~~.
主詞 動詞　　介系詞+名詞　　介系詞+名詞 介系詞+名詞

譯 1987年，他27歲的時候死於服藥過量。

⑪ He was known ~~for using bright colors, words and mixed materials in his work~~.
主詞 動詞 述詞　　　介系詞+動名詞　　　　　　　　介系詞+名詞

譯 他以在作品中使用明亮的色彩、語言和混合材料而聞名。

語法分析 be + 過去分詞一般表示被動結構，主詞和動詞有動詞和受詞關係，也可構成動詞+述詞結構，此時表示的是主句的狀態。

⑫ His art captured the imagination ~~of many artists, gallery owners and musicians~~
　主詞　　動詞　　受詞　　介系詞+名詞　　　介系詞+名詞

~~in New York City~~.

譯 他的藝術吸引了眾多紐約藝術家、美術館老闆和音樂家的注意。

⑬ Fans and supporters included Andy Warhol, David Bowie and gallery owner
　　　主詞　　　　　　　　　動詞　　　　　　　　受詞
Larry Gagosian.
　圞 他的粉絲和支持者有安迪‧沃霍爾、大衛‧鮑伊和畫廊老闆拉里‧高古軒。

⑭ ~~At one time,~~ Basquiat's girlfriend was music star Madonna.
　介系詞+名詞　　　　　主詞　　　　　動詞　　述詞
　圞 那時,巴斯奎特的女朋友是歌星瑪丹娜。

⑮ Maezawa is a big fan ~~of Basquiat~~.
　　主詞　　動詞　述詞
　圞 前澤友作是巴斯奎特的忠實粉絲。

⑯ He bought another Basquiat painting ~~for more than $57 million last year~~.
　主詞　動詞　　　　　受詞　　　　　　　介系詞+名詞　　　　　　副詞
　圞 去年,他以5700多萬美元的價格買下了巴斯奎特的另一幅畫作。

⑰ Maezawa said he will loan the painting to museums ~~around the world before~~
　主詞　　動詞　　　　受詞子句　　　　　　　　介系詞+名詞　　介系詞+名詞
~~displaying it in his hometown of Chiba, Japan.~~
　　　　　介系詞+名詞
　圞 前澤友作表示,在將畫作陳列在家鄉日本千葉之前,他願意將這幅畫借給世界各地的博物館來展示。

2017年全球失業人口超過2億

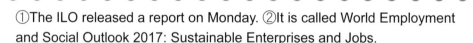

①The ILO released a report on Monday. ②It is called World Employment and Social Outlook 2017: Sustainable Enterprises and Jobs.

③The report states that more than 200 million people worldwide are jobless.④It said that number represents an increase of 3.4 million people compared to 2016.

⑤The ILO says private companies, especially small- and medium-sized ones, can help to create good jobs around the world.

⑥The ILO study found that such companies employ almost 3 billion workers, or 87 percent of total employment worldwide. ⑦And it says a strong public sector can serve as the base for economic growth, job creation and poverty reduction.

⑧Deborah Greenfield is the ILO's deputy director-general for policy. ⑨She says investing in workers is important for continued growth. ⑩Greenfield notes that providing training for permanent workers results in higher wages, higher productivity and lower unit labor costs. But she said many part-time and temporary workers are losing out.

⑪"But intensified use of temporary employment is associated with lower wages and lower productivity without achieving any gains in unit labor costs. ⑫The report also finds that on-the-job training is an important driver of innovation. ⑬Since temporary workers are rarely offered training, this might also affect innovation in firms in a negative way."

補充單字片語

- poverty [ˈpɒvətɪ] /n./ 貧窮，不足
- innovation [ˌɪnəˈveɪʃn] /n./ 創新，改革
- negative [ˈnegətɪv] /adj./ 消極的，負面的
- serve as 擔任

句構分析

① The ILO released a report on Monday.
　　主詞　　動詞　　受詞　　介系詞+名詞
　譯 國際勞工組織在週一發布了一份報告。

②It is called World Employment and Social Outlook 2017: Sustainable
　主詞 動詞　　　　　　　　　　受詞
Enterprises and Jobs.
　譯 報告名為《2017世界就業和社會展望：可持續企業和工作》。

③ The report states that more than 200 million people worldwide are jobless.
　　主詞　　動詞　　　　　　　　受詞子句
　譯 報告稱全世界超過2億人 有工作。

④ It said that number represents an increase of 3.4 million people compared to
主詞 動詞　　　受詞子句　　　　　　介系詞+名詞　　　過去分詞片語
2016.
　譯 報告稱這個數字代表了與2016年相比，失業人數增加了340萬人。
　語法分析 compared to 2016是過去分詞片語，在句中作副詞，在進行化繁為簡時，可被pass掉。

⑤ The ILO says private companies, especially small- and medium-sized ones, can
　　主詞 動詞　　受詞子句　　　　　　　　　　插入語

help to create good jobs ~~around the world~~.

介系詞+名詞

譯 國際勞工組織稱私人企業,特別是中小型企業,有助於在世界範圍內制造好的就業機會。

⑥ The ILO study found that such companies employ ~~almost~~ 3 billion workers, or

主詞　　　　動詞　　　受詞子句　　　　　　　　副詞

87 percent ~~of total employment worldwide~~.

介系詞+名詞　　　　副詞

譯 國際勞工組織研究發現這些企業雇傭了約30億員工,占全球總就業人數的87%。

⑦ And it says a strong public sector can serve as the base ~~for economic growth, job~~

主詞 動詞　　　　受詞子句　　　　　　　　　　　　介系詞+名詞

~~creation and poverty reduction~~.

譯 報告還指出強大的公共部門是經濟增長、創造就業機會和縮減貧困的基礎。

⑧ Deborah Greenfield is the ILO's deputy director-general ~~for policy~~.

主詞　　　　動詞　　　述詞　　　　　　　　介系詞+名詞

譯 黛博拉‧格林菲爾德是國際勞工組織的政策副總幹事。

⑨ She says investing in workers is important ~~for continued growth~~.

主詞 動詞　　受詞子句　　　　　　介系詞+名詞

譯 她説在工作人員身上的投資對於持續增長很重要。

⑩ Greenfield notes that providing training for permanent workers results in

主詞　　　動詞　　　受詞子句

higher wages, higher productivity and lower unit labor costs.

譯 格林菲爾德指出,為長期員工提供培訓可以帶來更高的工資、提高生產率和降低單位勞動力成本。

語法分析 result是不及物動詞,要和介系詞in連用才能接受詞

⑪ But she said many part-time and temporary workers are losing out.

主詞 動詞　　　受詞子句

譯 但是,她説很多兼職和臨時工人在逐漸失業。

⑫ "But intensified use ~~of temporary employment~~ is associated ~~with lower wages and~~

主詞　　　介系詞+名詞　　　動詞　　　介系詞+名詞

~~lower productivity~~ ~~without achieving any gains~~ ~~in unit labor costs~~.

介系詞+動名詞　　　介系詞+名詞

譯 但是過度雇用臨時工與低工資和低生產率相關,而單位勞動力成本並沒有增加。

語法分析 介詞+動名詞時,其後常接其它名詞,在化繁為簡時,要一併去掉。

⑬ The report ~~also~~ finds that on-the-job training is an important driver ~~of~~

主詞　　　副詞 動詞　　　形容詞子句　　　　　　　　介系詞+名詞

~~innovation~~.

譯 報告還指出在職培訓是創新的重要驅動力。

⑭ ~~Since temporary workers are rarely offered training~~, this might ~~also~~ affect

原因副詞子句　　　　　　　　　　主詞　　　副詞 動詞

innovation ~~in firms in a negative way.~~"

受詞　　介系詞+名詞　介系詞+名詞
譯 因為臨時工人很少有機會接受培訓，這可能也對企業的創新產生負面影響。

美式足球會嚴重損傷大腦

①The number of young people who play American football decreased from 2008 to 2016 according to the Aspen Institute, a research center.

②There are many reasons for this decrease. ③But some parents, such as businessman Mark Cuban, will not let their children play the sport because of concern about brain injuries.

④A recent study seems to support some of these concerns. ⑤It gives more evidence that too much American football is seriously damaging the brains of players.

⑥Scientists at the Brain Bank are studying a kind of brain injury known as Chronic Traumatic Encephalopathy.

⑦The Brain Bank is a center at Boston University in Massachusetts where brains and other tissue are stored and studied.

⑧Chronic Traumatic Encephalopathy, or CTE, is caused by collisions that push the brain around inside the skull.

⑨In a recent study, the scientists at the Brain Bank found high levels of CTE in dead football players.

⑩The scientists studied the brains of 202 former players. ⑪These athletes, who had donated their brains for research, played at high school, college or professional levels.

⑫The scientists found CTE in 177 of the 202 brains. ⑬The scientists found especially high rates of CTE in the brains of former National Football League, or NFL, players. Out of the 111 former NFL players studied, 110 showed signs of CTE.

補充單字片語

• evidence [ˈɛvɪdəns] /n./ 證據，明顯
• collision [kəˈlɪʒn] /n./ 衝突，碰撞

句構分析

① The number ~~of young people who play American football~~ decreased ~~from 2008~~
　　主詞　　　介系詞+名詞　　　形容詞子句　　　　　　　動詞　　介系詞+名詞
~~to 2016 according to the Aspen Institute, a research center~~.
　　介系詞+名詞
譯 阿斯本研究所（一家研究中心）發現玩美式橄欖球的年輕人的數量從2008年到2016年有所下降。

② There are many reasons ~~for this decrease~~.
　there be句型　　　　　　　介系詞+名詞
譯 造成人數下降的原因有很多。
句構分析 該句子是本文的主旨句。本文屬於原因說明文。

③ But some parents, ~~such as businessman Mark Cuban,~~ will not let their children
　　　　主詞　　　　　　　　插入語　　　　　　　動詞　　受詞
play the sport ~~because of concern about brain injuries~~.
　　受詞補語　　　　介系詞+名詞
譯 但是有些家長，如商人馬克·庫班，因為擔心對大腦造成的損害而不願意自己的孩子玩這種運動。
結構分析 插入語在句中的明顯特徵是用後是否與前後的內容隔開，在進行化繁為簡時，可以去掉。

④ A recent study seems to support some ~~of these concerns~~.
　　主詞　　　　　動詞　　　受詞　介系詞+名詞
譯 最近一份的報告似乎證實了這些擔憂。

⑤ It gives more evidence that too much American football is ~~seriously~~ damaging
主詞 動詞　受詞　　　　同位語子句　　　　　　副詞
the brains ~~of players~~.
　　　介系詞+名詞
譯 報告提供了更多證據，證明了頻繁的美式足球活動在嚴重損傷球員的大腦。
語法分析 同位語子句的that一般不省略，子句是對前面內容的展開。

⑥ Scientists ~~at the Brain Bank~~ are studying a kind of brain injury ~~known as~~
　　主詞　　介系詞+名詞　　　　動詞　　　受詞　　　過去分詞結構
~~Chronic Traumatic Encephalopathy~~.
譯 大腦銀行的科學家們正在研究一種大腦損傷，名為「慢性創傷性腦病」。

⑦ The Brain Bank is a center ~~at Boston University in Massachusetts where brains~~
　　主詞　　動詞 述詞　　介系詞+名詞　　　介系詞+名詞　　　形容詞子句

163

and other tissue are stored and studied.

譯 大腦銀行位於馬薩諸塞州波士頓大學，是一家研究儲存的大腦和其它組織的研究中心。

⑧ Chronic Traumatic Encephalopathy, or CTE, is caused by collisions that push
　　　　　　受詞　　　　　　　　插入語　　　動詞　　主詞　　形容詞片語
the brain around inside the skull.
　副詞　　　介系詞+名詞

譯 慢性創傷性腦病（CTE），是由碰撞所引起的，這種碰撞導致大腦在顱骨內震盪。

⑨ In a recent study, the scientists at the Brain Bank found high levels of CTE in
　介系詞+名詞　　　　主詞　　介系詞+名詞　　動詞　　受詞　　介系詞+名詞
dead football players.
　介系詞+名詞

譯 在最近的一次研究中，大腦銀行的科學家發現已經去世的美式足球球員患有嚴重的CTE。

⑩ The scientists studied the brains of 202 former players.
　　主詞　　　　動詞　　受詞　　介系詞+名詞
譯 科學家們對202名退役球員的大腦進行了研究。

⑪ These athletes, who had donated their brains for research, played at high school,
　　主詞　　　　　　　　　　形容詞子句　　　　　　　　動詞　介系詞+名詞
college or professional levels.
譯 這些貢獻了大腦作研究的運動員們曾在高中、大學或專業球隊裡玩美式足球。

⑫ The scientists found CTE in 177 of the 202 brains.
　　主詞　　　動詞 受詞 介系詞+名詞 介系詞+名詞
譯 科學家們發現202個大腦中的177個患有CTE。

⑬ The scientists found especially high rates of CTE in the brains of former
　　主詞　　　動詞　　副詞　　　　受詞　　　介系詞+名詞　介系詞+名詞
National Football League, or NFL, players.
譯 科學家們發現，國家足球聯盟的退役球員患有CTE的風險特別高。

⑭ Out of the 111 former NFL players studied, 110 showed signs of CTE.
　　介系詞+名詞　　　　　　被動分詞 主詞　動詞　受詞　介系詞+名詞
譯 在被研究的111個國家足球聯盟退役球員中，110個患有CTE。

阿布達比羅浮宮博物館成立

①On November 11, the Louvre Abu Dhabi museum will open in the capital of the United Arab Emirates.

②The museum is part of a project designed to appeal to millions of visitors every year.

③The waterfront museum will hold hundreds of pieces of art representing ancient and modern times around the world. ④It will include Middle Eastern objects and paintings, as well as works by Western artists.

⑤The Louvre in Paris, France is one of the most famous museums in the world. ⑥In 2007, France agreed to take part in a joint project to open an art museum in Abu Dhabi. ⑦French officials say the collection does not face any restrictions.

⑧Jean-Francois Charnier is the scientific director of Agence France-Museums. ⑨He said the museum organizers had complete freedom in making decisions about the art to present.

⑩"You have nude statues in the museum, contemporary paintings. You also have religious images from all religions," he said. ⑪The works will represent major periods of human development and will show connections between different cultures, Charnier said.

⑫"The objective," he said, "is to show that in history there are more links and bridges than walls."

⑬The museum has major pieces of art including a 15th century painting by Giovanni Bellini and a 19th century painting by Osama Hamdy Bey.

補充單字片語

- restriction [rɪˈstrɪkʃn] /n./ 限制，約束
- contemporary [kənˈtemprərɪ] /adj./ 同代的，當代的
- take part in 參加，參與

句構分析

① On November 11, the Louvre Abu Dhabi museum will open in the capital of the

　　介系詞+名詞　　　　　　　　　　主詞　　　　　　　　　動詞　　介系詞+名詞

United Arab Emirates.

　介系詞+名詞

譯 在11月11日，阿布達比羅浮宮博物館將在阿拉伯聯合大公國的首都開幕。

結構分析 該句子是本文的主旨句，本文是記敘文。該句子是五大簡單句中的主詞+動詞結構。

② The museum is part of a project designed to appeal to millions of visitors every

　　主詞　　動詞 述詞　　　　　　　不定詞結構　　　　　　　　　　副詞

year.

譯 這個博物館是一個項目的一部分，這個項目設計的目的是每年吸引數百萬遊客。

句構分析 該句子是五大簡單句中的主詞+be動詞+述詞結構，所以與該結構沒有關系的成分可被去掉。

③ The waterfront museum will hold hundreds of pieces of art representing

　　　　主詞　　　　　　　動詞　　　　受詞　　　　動名詞作形容詞片語

ancient and modern times around the world.

譯 這個水邊的博物館將容納上千件代表世界各地的古代和現代的藝術品。

語法分析 該句子是五大簡單句中的主詞+動詞+受詞結構，切記pieces of後的art才是受詞，而pieces of只是修飾art的數量詞，不能代表art。

④ It will include Middle Eastern objects and paintings, as well as works by

主詞　動詞　　　受詞　　　　　　　　　　　　　　　　介系詞+名詞

Western artists.

譯 它將包含中東的物品和畫作，還有西方藝術家的作品。

⑤ The Louvre in Paris, France is one of the most famous museums in the world.

　　主詞　　　介系詞+名詞　動詞　　　述詞　　　　　　　介系詞+名詞

譯 法國巴黎的羅浮宮是世界上最著名的博物館之一。

語法分析 one of +最高級修飾的名詞作述詞時，名詞的修飾詞不能被去掉。

⑥ In 2007, France agreed to take part in a joint project to open an art museum in

介系詞+名詞　主詞　動詞　　　　受詞　　　　　不定詞結構

Abu Dhabi.

介系詞+名詞

譯 2007年，法國同意參加一個聯合計畫，目的是在阿布達比開一家藝術博物館。

⑦ French officials say the collection does not face any restrictions.

　　主詞　　　動詞　　　　受詞子句

譯 法國官員説，這些要展覽的藏品沒有任何限制。

語法分析 該句子是一個包含主句和受詞子句的複合句。

⑧ Jean-Francois Charnier is the scientific director of Agence France-Museums.

　　　　主詞　　　　　動詞　　　述詞　　　　介系詞+名詞

譯 尚・富朗索瓦・沙爾尼耶是國博物館管理會的科學主任。

⑨ He said the museum organizers had complete freedom in making decisions

主詞 動詞　　　　受詞子句　　　　　　　　　介系詞+動名詞

about the art to present.

介系詞+名詞　　　不定詞結構

譯 他說該博物館的組織者可以完全自主地決定要展示的藝術品。

⑩ "You have nude statues in the museum, contemporary paintings. You also

主詞　動詞　　受詞　　　　介系詞+名詞　　　　受詞　　　　　主詞　副詞

have religious images from all religions," he said.

動詞　　　受詞　　　　介系詞+名詞　　主詞 動詞

譯 他說，「你們在博物館裡可以看到裸體的雕塑和當代的畫作。你也可以看到各個
宗教的聖像。」

⑪ The works will represent major periods of human development and will show

主詞　　　　動詞　　　受詞　　　　　介系詞+名詞　　　　　動詞

connections between different cultures, Charnier said.

受詞　　　介系詞+名詞　　　　　　主詞　　動詞

譯 沙爾尼耶說，這些作品代表了人類發展的重要時期，也顯示了不同文化之間的聯
系。

⑫ "The objective," he said, "is to show that in history there are more links and

主詞　　　插入語 動詞　述詞　介系詞+名詞　　　受詞子句

bridges than walls."

介系詞+名詞

譯 他說，「目的是為了顯示在歷史上聯繫和橋樑比阻隔多。」

⑬ The museum has major pieces of art including a 15th century painting by

主詞　　　動詞　　受詞　　　介系詞片語　　　　　　介系詞+名詞

Giovanni Bellini and a 19th century painting by Osama Hamdy Bey.

介系詞+名詞

譯 該博物館有很多重要的藝術品，包括一件15世紀喬凡尼‧貝里尼的畫作和一件19
世紀烏薩馬‧哈 姆迪‧貝伊的畫作。

劍橋大學考慮取消書面考試

①The world-renowned Cambridge University is considering abolishing handwritten exams after 800 years. ②University officials may ask students to type their exam answers on a computer rather than use a pen. ③The move follows complaints from examination markers who say they are finding test papers increasingly illegible due to poor handwriting. ④Academics say today's students primarily use laptops in lectures and tutorials instead of pens. ⑤Students are losing the ability to write by hand. ⑥One academic said asking students to hand-write exams actually causes them physical difficulties. ⑦The muscles in their hand are not used to writing extensively for prolonged periods of two to three hours.

⑧A Cambridge University lecturer, Dr Sarah Pearsall, told Britain's ' Daily Telegraph ' newspaper that handwriting was becoming a "lost art". ⑨She said: "Twenty years ago, students routinely wrote by hand several hours a day, but now they write virtually nothing by hand, except exams." ⑩She added: "We have been concerned for years about the declining handwriting problem. There has definitely been a downward trend. ⑪It is difficult for both the students and the examiners as it is harder and harder to read these exam scripts."

⑫Dr Pearsall says some students' handwriting is so illegible that they had to return to the university over the summer to read their answers out loud to examiners who could not read their writing.

補充單字片語

- abolish [əˈbɒlɪʃ] /v./ 癈除，取消
- illegible [ɪˈledʒəbl] /adj./ 難辨認的，潦草的
- routinely [ruːˈtiːnlɪ] /adv./ 常規地，慣常地

句構分析

①The world-renowned Cambridge University is considering abolishing
　　　　　　　主詞　　　　　　　　　　　　　　動詞　　　　受詞
handwritten exams after 800 years.
　　　　　　介系詞+名詞
　世界著名的劍橋大學正在考慮廢除持續了800年的書面考試。 結構分析 該句是整
　篇文章的主旨句，後面的內容都是圍繞廢除書面考試的內容展開進行的。

② University officials may ask students to type their exam answers on a computer
　　　主詞　　　　　動詞　受詞　　不定詞結構　　　　　　　　　介系詞+名詞
rather than use a pen.
　學校官方可能會要求學生在電腦上輸入出考試答案，而不再是手寫。

③ The move follows complaints from examination markers who say they are finding
　　主詞　　動詞　　受詞　　　介系詞+名詞　　　　　　形容詞片語
test papers increasingly illegible due to poor handwriting.
　這是因為閱卷老師抱怨到，由於書寫潦草，越來越難以辨認試卷。

④ Academics say today's students ~~primarily~~ use laptops ~~in lectures and tutorials~~

主詞　　動詞　　受詞子句　　　　副詞　　　　　　介系詞+名詞

instead ~~of pens~~.

介系詞+名詞

譯 專家學者表示，現在的學生在講座和輔導課上主要使用筆記本電腦，而不是鋼筆。

⑤ Students are losing the ability ~~to write by hand~~.

主詞　　　動詞　　　受詞　不定詞結構 介系詞+名詞

譯 學生們正在失去用手寫字的能力。

⑥ One academic said asking students ~~to hand-write exams actually~~ causes them

主詞　　　　動詞　　受詞子句　　　　不定詞結構　　　　副詞

physical difficulties.

譯 一位學者表示，要求學生們參加書面考試給他們帶來身體困難。

⑦ The muscles ~~in their hand~~ are not used to writing ~~extensively for prolonged~~

主詞　　　介系詞+名詞　　　動詞　　　受詞　　副詞　　　介系詞+名詞

~~periods of two to three hours~~.

介系詞+名詞

譯 他們手部肌肉不適合連續兩三個小時高強度書寫。

⑧ A Cambridge University lecturer, ~~Dr Sarah Pearsall~~, told Britain's *Daily*

主詞　　　　　　　　插入語　　　　動詞　受詞

Telegraph newspaper that handwriting was becoming a "lost art".

受詞補語

譯 劍橋大學講師薩拉·皮爾索爾博士告訴英國《每日電訊報》，手寫正在變成「失去的藝術」。

⑨ She said: "Twenty years ago, students ~~routinely~~ wrote ~~by hand~~ several hours a day,

主詞 動詞　　　　　　　　　　　　副詞　　　介系詞+名詞

but now they write ~~virtually~~ nothing ~~by hand~~, ~~except exams~~."

副詞　　　　介系詞+名詞 介系詞+名詞

譯 她說：「20年前，學生們經常一天手寫幾個小時，但是現在除了考試的時候他們幾乎每天都不動手寫。」

⑩ She added: "We have been concerned ~~for years about the declining handwriting~~

主詞 動詞　　　　　　　　　介系詞+名詞　　介系詞+名詞

~~problem~~.

譯 她補充說：「多年來，我們一直關注不斷退化的手寫問題。

⑪ There has definitely been a downward trend.

譯 這絕對是一個下降的趨勢。

⑫ It is difficult ~~for both the students and the examiners~~ as it is harder and harder to

主詞 動詞 述詞　　介系詞+名詞

read these exam scripts.

譯 對學生和考官來說，這種考試形式越來越困難。

⑬ Dr Pearsall says some students' handwriting is so illegible ~~that they had to~~

   主詞   動詞   受詞子句

~~return to the university over the summer to read their answers out loud to examiners~~

                  目的副詞子句

~~who could not read their writing.~~

         形容詞子句

譯 皮爾索爾博士表示，一些學生的書寫簡直太潦草了，根本認不出來，暑假期間必須重返學校大聲向主考官讀出他們的答案。

語法分析 該句中運用了「so...that...」表示「如此……以致於……」，常引導結果副詞子句。

芝麻街和IBM聯合開發詞彙app

①Sesame Workshop (the company behind the hugely successful children's TV show Sesame Street) and IBM have teamed up to create a revolutionary new app for kids to learn vocabulary. ②The joint venture has created the first vocabulary learning app powered by IBM's artificial intelligence software. ③The app discovers for itself a child's current reading level and vocabulary range, and then uses its algorithms to challenge the child with appropriate, new vocabulary to improve the child's skills. ④It personalizes the learning experience for children. ⑤As the child continues to use the app, it will ensure he or she has learned and understood the new words before introducing additional, tailored vocabulary items.

⑥IBM says it has just completed a pilot program testing the app. ⑦It collected 18,000 multiple-choice assessments given to kindergarteners over a two-week period. ⑧The researchers said the results were very promising. ⑨They said the kids learned words like "arachnid," "amplify," "camouflage," and "applause," which are typically learned at a much later age. ⑩The children could also use these words in context. ⑪Sesame Workshop CEO Jeffrey Dunn said: "We expect to develop the next generation of tailored learning tools...

⑫Educational technology like the platform we've created...is a promising new channel for learning opportunities inside and outside the classroom, and we're excited to explore it further."

補充單字片語

- revolutionary [ˌrevəˈluːʃənərɪ] /adj./ 革命的，革命性的
- joint venture 合資企業
- platform [ˈplætfɔːm] /n./ 台，站台，平台

句構分析

① Sesame Workshop (the company behind the hugely successful children's TV show
　　　主詞

Sesame Street) and IBM have teamed up to create a revolutionary new app ~~for kids~~
　　　　　　　　　　　　　動詞　　　　　受詞　　　　　　　　　介系詞+名詞

~~to learn vocabulary~~.
　不定詞結構

譯 芝麻街工作室（該公司打造的兒童電視節目芝麻街是非常成功的）和IBM聯手開發
　了一款新的革命性app，讓兒童學習詞彙。

② The joint venture has created the first vocabulary learning app ~~powered by~~
　　　主詞　　　　動詞　　　　受詞　　　　　　　　動詞過去分詞

~~IBM's artificial intelligence software~~.
介系詞+名詞

譯 這項聯合項目創造了首款由IBM人工智慧軟體驅動的詞彙學習app。

③ The app discovers ~~for itself~~ a child's current reading level and vocabulary
　主詞　　動詞　　介系詞+名詞　　　　受詞

range, and then uses its algorithms to challenge the child ~~with appropriate, new~~
　　　　　　　　動詞　　受詞　　　受詞補語　　　　介系詞+名詞

~~vocabulary to improve the child's skills~~.
　　　　　　不定詞結構

譯 這款app自行檢測兒童當前的閱讀水平和詞彙範圍，然後使用其運算法則，用合適
　的新詞彙來挑戰孩子，提高他的技能。

④ It personalizes the learning experience for children.

譯 這款app使兒童的學習經驗個性化。

⑤ As the child continues to use the app, it will ensure he or she has learned and
　　　　　　　　　　　　　　　　　　主詞　動詞　　受詞子句

understood the new words ~~before introducing additional, tailored vocabulary items~~.
　　　　　　　　　　　　介系詞+名詞

譯 隨著兒童持續使用這款app，它將確保引入新的量身訂製的字彙之前兒童已經學習
　並理解了新單詞。

⑥ IBM says it has ~~just~~ completed a pilot program testing the app.
主詞 動詞 受詞子句 副詞

171

譯 IBM表示，他們已經完成了一個試點項目的測試程序。

⑦ It collected 18,000 multiple-choice assessments ~~given to kindergarteners over a~~
　主詞　動詞　　　　　受詞　　　　　　　　　　　動詞過去分詞　介系詞+名詞　介系詞+名詞
~~two-week period~~.
譯 他們對幼兒園的小朋友進行了為期兩週的1.8萬份多項選擇評估。

⑧ The researchers said the results were very promising.
　　　主詞　　　　動詞　　　受詞子句
譯 研究人員表示，結果非常令人滿意。

⑨ They said the kids learned words ~~like "arachnid," "amplify," "camouflage," and~~
　主詞 動詞　　受詞子句　　　　　介系詞+名詞
~~"applause,"~~ ~~which are typically learned at a much later age~~.
　　　　　　　形容詞子句
譯 他們表示，孩子們學會了「arachnid」、「amplify」、「camouflage」和
　「applause」等詞彙，這些詞彙基本上是年齡比較大的時候才學習的。

⑩ The children could ~~also~~ use these words ~~in context~~.
　　主詞　　　　副詞 動詞　　受詞　　　介系詞+名詞
譯 孩子們能夠根據語境使用這些詞彙。

⑪ Sesame Workshop CEO Jeffrey Dunn said: "We expect to develop the next
　　　　　　　　　　　　　　　　　　　　　　主詞 動詞　　　受詞
generation ~~of tailored learning tools~~...
　　　　　介系詞+名詞
譯 芝麻街工作室首席執行官傑弗里·鄧恩表示：「我們希望開發出下一代量身打造
　的學習工具。

⑫ Educational technology ~~like the platform~~ we've created... is a promising new
　　　　主詞　　　　　　　介系詞+名詞　　　　　　　動詞　　述詞
channel ~~for learning opportunities inside and outside the classroom~~, and we're excited
　　　介系詞+名詞　　　　　　　　　介系詞+名詞　　　　　　　　主詞 動詞 述詞
to explore it ~~further~~."
　　　　　　　副詞
譯 類似我們開發的平台的教育技術是教室內外學習機會非常有前景的新途徑，我們
　希望能夠進一步探索。

睡眠不足會給健康帶來致命影響

①New research shows that many people are not sleeping enough and that this is having a serious impact on health. ②Professor Matthew

Walker from the Center for Human Sleep Science at the University of California warned that a "catastrophic sleep-misfortune plague" was putting people in danger of ill health. ③He said a continued lack of sleep was putting people at risk from a large number of possibly fatal diseases. ④Professor Walker said people need eight hours sleep a night to stay healthy. ⑤He continued that people who don't sleep enough will have a shorter life. ⑥Walker said the effect of not sleeping enough negatively impacts every single aspect of our health and every part of our body.

⑦Professor Walker warned that a lack of sleep is linked to debilitating diseases such as Alzheimer's, cancer, heart disease, obesity and diabetes. ⑧He warned that we are in a dangerous situation whereby we do not fully understand the very serious, "catastrophic" consequences of not getting eight hours a night. ⑨He gave several reasons why we are sleeping less. ⑩He said: "First, we electrified the night. Light is a profound degrader of our sleep." He also blamed longer working hours and longer commuting times, a desire to be with friends more rather than sleep, mobile devices, and the increased availability of alcohol and caffeine.

補充單字片語

- impact on 影響
- plague [pleɪg] /n./ 瘟疫,災害,折磨
- fatal ['feɪtl] /adj./ 致命的,嚴重的
- negatively ['nɛgətɪvlɪ] /adv./ 否定的,消極的
- debilitate [dɪ'bɪlɪteɪt] /v./ 使虛弱,使衰弱

句構分析

① New research shows that many people are not sleeping enough and that this is
　　主詞　　　動詞　　受詞子句　　　　　　　　　　受詞子句
having a serious impact on health.
　　　　　　　介系詞+名詞
譯 新的研究表明,許多人睡眠不足,這對健康有嚴重影響。
結構分析 該句是本文的主旨句,開宗名義介紹了睡眠不足給健康會帶來嚴重影響,後面又具體圍繞這一主題展開進行。

② Professor Matthew Walker from the Center for Human Sleep Science at the University of
　　　主詞　　　　　　　介系詞+名詞　　　　介系詞+名詞　　　　　介系詞+名詞

173

~~California~~ warned that a "catastrophic sleep-misfortune plague" was putting
介系詞+名詞　　動詞　　　　受詞子句
people in danger ~~of ill health~~.
　　　　　　　　介系詞+名詞
譯 來自加利福尼亞大學人類睡眠科學中心的馬修‧沃克教授警告説，「災難性睡眠不足症」會使人們處於健康狀況不佳的危險之中。

③ He said a continued lack ~~of sleep~~ was putting people ~~at risk from a large number~~
主詞 動詞　受詞子句　　　介系詞+名詞　　　　　　　介系詞+名詞 介系詞+名詞
~~of possibly fatal diseases~~.
介系詞+名詞
譯 他表示，持續睡眠不足會使人們處於大量的可能致命的疾病風險之中。
語法分析 在該句中，省略了受詞子句中的that，因為受詞子句中如果that只起引導作用，在句中不做任何成分，沒有實際意義，通常可以將其省略。

④ Professor Walker said people need eight hours sleep a night ~~to stay healthy~~.
　　主詞　　　　動詞　　　受詞子句　　　　　　　　　　不定詞結構
譯 沃克教授稱，人們每晚需要八小時的睡眠來保持健康。

⑤ He continued that people ~~who don't sleep enough~~ will have a shorter life.
主詞　　動詞　　受詞子句　　　形容詞子句
譯 他繼續説，睡眠不足的人壽命會縮短。

⑥ Walker said the effect ~~of not sleeping enough~~ negatively impacts every single
主詞　　動詞　受詞　　介系詞+名詞
aspect ~~of our health~~ and every part ~~of our body~~.
　　　介系詞+名詞　　　　　　　介系詞+名詞
譯 沃克教授表示，睡眠不足會造成我們健康各方面和身體的每一部位都有負面影響。

⑦ Professor Walker warned that a lack ~~of sleep~~ is linked to debilitating diseases
　　　主詞　　　　動詞　受詞子句　介系詞+名詞
~~such as Alzheimer's, cancer, heart disease, obesity and diabetes~~.
介系詞+名詞
譯 Walker教授警告説，睡眠不足與許多衰弱的疾病有關聯，比如老年癡呆症、癌症、心臟病、肥胖和糖尿病。

⑧ He warned that we are in a dangerous situation ~~whereby we do not fully~~
主詞 動詞　　　受詞子句　　　　　　　　形容詞子句
~~understand the very serious, "catastrophic" consequences of not getting eight~~
　　　　　　　　　　　　　　　　　　　　　介系詞+名詞
~~hours a night~~.
譯 他警告説，若我們不能完全理解每晚睡眠不足八小時的所帶來的悲慘後果，我們將處於危險的境地。

⑨ He gave several reasons ~~why we are sleeping less~~.
主詞 動詞　　受詞　　　　形容詞子句

譯 他給出了我們睡眠越來越少的幾個原因。

⑩ He said: "First, we electrified the night. Light is a profound degrader ~~of our sleep~~."
　主詞 動詞　　　　　　　　　　　　　　　　　　　　　　　　　　　　　　介系詞+名詞
　譯 他說：「首先，我們晚上會開燈。光線會嚴重影響睡眠」。

⑪ He ~~also~~ blamed longer working hours and longer commuting times, a desire
　主詞 副詞　動詞　　　　　　　　受詞
　to be ~~with friends~~ more rather than sleep, mobile devices, and the increased
　　　　　介系詞+名詞
　availability ~~of alcohol and caffeine~~.
　　　　　　　　介系詞+名詞
　譯 他還指責工作時長和通勤時間長，比起睡覺更願意和朋友一起玩，行動裝置、越來越多的飲酒和咖啡等的機會。

動物愛好者慶祝世界動物日

①World Animal Day has been celebrated on October 4 for many years.

②The World Animal Day website says it was first celebrated in 1925 in Berlin, Germany on a different date. ③It moved to October 4 in 1929.

④October 4 is the day Roman Catholics honor Saint Francis of Assisi, who was the patron saint of animals.

⑤What happens on World Animal Day? ⑥Aside from Twitter getting filled up with lots of cute photos of animals, the day is designed to promote the rights of animals.

⑦The group that organizes the day wants to make sure animals are treated well around the world.

⑧In honor of the day, many organizations held special events. ⑨ For example, some shelters held adoption events. ⑩Other organizations held workshops to make sure owners learned the best way to take care of their animals.

⑪One Twitter account called The Dodo has almost 500,000 followers. ⑫ The account owners made a video showing people treating animals "with love."

⑬The video showed a man taking a beached dolphin back to the water, a police officer helping free a deer from a backyard volleyball net and a driver stopping to move a kitten off a busy roadway.

⑭The television channel Nat Geo WILD posted a video of a baby elephant taking its first steps.

補充單字片語

- patron [ˈpeɪtrən] /n./ 資助人，贊助人
- channel [ˈtʃænl] /n./ 渠道，頻道
- in honor of 為了紀念

句構分析

① World Animal Day has been celebrated on October 4 for many years.
　　主詞　　　　　　動詞　　　　　介系詞+名詞　　介系詞+名詞
　譯 世界動物日已經在10月4日慶祝了很多年了。

② The World Animal Day website says it was first celebrated in 1925 in Berlin,
　　主詞　　　　　　　動詞　　受詞子句　　　　介系詞+名詞 介系詞+名詞
Germany on a different date.
　　　介系詞+名詞
　譯 世界動物日官網稱第一次慶祝於1925年在德國柏林舉辦的，但不是10月4日。

③ It moved to October 4 in 1929.
主詞 動詞　　受詞　　介系詞+名詞
　譯 1929年，它改為了10月4日。

④ October 4 is the day Roman Catholics honor Saint Francis of Assisi, who was the
　　主詞　動詞 述詞　　　　形容詞子句　　　　　　　　　　　形容詞子句
patron saint of animals.
　　　介系詞+名詞
　譯 10月4日是羅馬天主教紀念阿西西的聖‧弗朗西斯的日子，聖‧弗朗西斯是動物的
　　守護神。
　句構分析 該句子是由主句和定語從句構成的複合句。

⑤ What happens on World Animal Day?
主詞　　動詞　　介系詞+名詞
　譯 在世界動物日那天會發生什麼事？

⑥ Aside from Twitter getting filled up with lots of cute photos of animals, the day is
副詞　介系詞+名詞　動名詞作形容詞片語　介系詞+名詞　　　　介系詞+名詞　　主詞 動詞
designed to promote the rights of animals.
　　　不定詞結構　　　介系詞+名詞

176

Part 2

譯 除了推特上充滿很多可愛的動物照片，設立這個日子是為了提升動物們的權益。

⑦ The group that organizes the day wants to make sure animals are treated well
　　　主詞　　　　形容詞子句　　　　　　動詞　　　　　　受詞子句　　　　　　副詞
around the world.
　　介系詞+名詞
譯 設立這個日子的組織希望確保世界各地的動物們受到良好的對待。

⑧ In honor of the day, many organizations held special events.
　　介系詞+名詞　　　　主詞　　　　動詞　　受詞
譯 為了紀念這個日子，很多機構舉辦了特別的活動。
句構分析 該句子可視為本文的主題句。

⑨ For example, some shelters held adoption events.
　　插入語　　　主詞　　動詞　　受詞
譯 比如，一些收容所舉辦了收養活動。

⑩ Other organizations held workshops to make sure owners learned the best way
　　　主詞　　　　　　動詞　　受詞　　　不定詞結構　　　受詞子句
to take care of their animals.
不定詞結構
譯 其它的組織舉辦研討會，確保動物的主人了解照顧動物們的最好方式。

⑪ One Twitter account called The Dodo has almost 500,000 followers.
　　　主詞　　　　　被動分詞　　動詞　副詞　　　受詞
譯 一個叫做「渡渡鳥」的推特帳戶差不多有50萬個關注者。

⑫ The account owners made a video showing people that we should treat animals
　　　主詞　　　　動詞　受詞　動名詞作形容詞片語　名詞子句
"with love."
譯 帳戶的所有者製作了一段影片，教人們用「愛」善待動物。

⑬ The video showed a man taking a beached dolphin back to the water, a police
　　主詞　　動詞　受詞　　動名詞作形容詞片語　　　　介系詞+名詞　受詞
officer helping free a deer from a backyard volleyball net and a driver stopping to
　　動名詞作形容詞片語　　　介系詞+名詞　　　　　　受詞　動名詞作形容詞片語
move a kitten off a busy roadway.
　　　　介系詞+名詞
譯 影片顯示，一位男士將一條擱淺的海豚放回到水裡；一位警官幫助一隻鹿從後院
　　排球網裡掙脫開；一位司機停車，然後將一隻小貓帶離繁忙的交通道路。
句構分析 該句子是簡單句，由主幹和三個並列的動名詞作形容詞片語所構成。

⑭ The TV channel National Geographic posted a video of a baby elephant taking
　　　　　主詞　　　　　　　　　動詞　　受詞　　介系詞+名詞　　動名詞作
its first steps.
形容詞片語
譯 國家地理電視頻道發布了一段有關一頭小象正在開始學步的影片。

Part 3

新發現的基因或有助於孕婦足月生產

①The study found six genes that seemed to control how long a baby would stay in the mother's womb.

②Dr. Louis Muglia is the co-director of the Perinatal Institute at Cincinnati Children's Hospital Medical Center in Ohio. ③He helped organize the study, and explains what the researchers found.

④"For the first time, we have the clues that are going to lead us to rational ways of understanding a woman's risk for preterm birth."

⑤Dr. Muglia says scientists have known for a long time that preterm birth involves a combination of genetic and environmental causes.

⑥One of the newly identified genes is involved in how the body uses the mineral selenium.

⑦Selenium is found in soil, seafood and meat. ⑧It is also sold in some stores, but not currently included in vitamin supplements women usually take while pregnant.

⑨Selenium supplements are low-cost. ⑩If the results of the study are confirmed, this could save millions of lives.

⑪Supplements such as folic acid have been shown to greatly reduce birth defects. ⑫Folic acid, a B vitamin, is added to food in many countries to help prevent health problems.

⑬Another finding is that the cells lining a woman's uterus have a larger-than-expected influence on the length of pregnancy.

⑭This study showed that the genes thought to be responsible for the timing of the birth were from the mother.

補充單字片語

- womb [wu:m] /n./ 子宮，搖籃
- preterm [ˌpriːˈtɜːm] /adj./ 早產的
- selenium [səˈliːnɪəm] /n./ 硒
- defect [ˈdiːfekt] /n./ 缺陷，缺點
- uterus [ˈjuːtərəs] /n./ 子宮
- add to 添加，增加
- be responsible for 對……負責

句構分析

① The study found six genes that seemed to control how long a baby would stay in
  主詞　　動詞　　受詞　　　　形容詞子句　　　　　　　受詞子句
the mother's womb.
介系詞+名詞
譯 研究發現6個基因似乎能控制嬰兒在母體子宮內停留的時間。
句構分析 該句子是本篇科普文的主旨句。

② Dr. Louis Muglia is the co-director of the Perinatal Institute at Cincinnati
  主詞　　　　動詞　　述詞　　　　介系詞+名詞　　　　介系詞+名詞
Children's Hospital Medical Center in Ohio.
　　　　　　　　　　　　　介系詞+名詞
譯 路易・穆格里亞博士是俄亥俄州辛辛那提兒童醫院醫學中心周產期研究所的主任。

③ He helped organize the study, and explains what the researchers found.
  主詞　　動詞　　　受詞　　　　　動詞　　　受詞子句
譯 他幫助組織了這次研究，並解釋了研究人員發現了什麼。

④ "For the first time, we have the clues that are going to lead us to rational ways of
  介系詞+名詞　　主詞 動詞　受詞　　　形容詞子句　　　　不定詞結構
understanding a woman's risk for preterm birth."
介系詞+名詞　　　　　介系詞+名詞
譯 「這是我們第一次有了線索幫助我們更加理性地理解女性早產的風險。」

⑤ Dr. Muglia says scientists have known for a long time that preterm birth
  主詞　　動詞　　　受詞子句　　　　介系詞+名詞　　　受詞子句
involves a combination of genetic and environmental causes.
　　　　　　　　　介系詞+名詞
譯 穆格里亞博士說科學家們很早就知道了早產受基因和環境因素的共同影響。
句構分析 該句子是一個複合句，包含一個主句和兩個受詞子句，但是兩個受詞子句不是並列關係。

179

⑥ One of the newly identified genes is involved in how the body uses the mineral
　主詞　　　　　介系詞+名詞　　　　　動詞　　　介系詞+名詞子句
selenium.
　　翻 新發現的基因之一涉及人體如何利用礦物質硒。

⑦ Selenium is found in soil, seafood and meat.
　　主詞　　動詞　　　介系詞+名詞
　　翻 土壤、海產品和肉類中都有硒。

⑧ It is also sold in some stores, but not currently included in vitamin supplements
　主詞 副詞 動詞　介系詞+名詞　　　　　　　副詞　　　動詞　　　介系詞+名詞
women usually take while pregnant.
　形容詞子句　　　　　　介系詞+名詞
　　翻 有些商店也在出售含硒的食物，但是目前女性在懷孕期間服用的維生素補充劑並
　　　 不包含在內。

⑨ Selenium supplements are low-cost.
　　　　　主詞　　　　　動詞 述詞
　　翻 硒補充劑的價格不貴。

⑩ If the results of the study are confirmed, this could save millions of lives.
　　　　　　　條件副詞子句　　　　　　　　　主詞　　動詞　　　受詞
　　翻 如果研究結果被證實，這會拯救數百萬的生命。
　　語法分析 millions of + 名詞時不能被去掉。

⑪ Supplements such as folic acid have been shown to greatly reduce birth defects.
　　　主詞　　　　插入語　　　　動詞　　　　　不定詞結構
　　翻 如葉酸之類的補充劑已經被證實可以大大減少出生缺陷。

⑫ Folic acid, a B vitamin, is added to food in many countries to help prevent health
　　主詞　　插入語　　動詞 受詞　介系詞+名詞　　不定詞結構
problems.
　　翻 葉酸是一種B族維生素，在很多國家被添加到食物中來幫助預防健康問題。

⑬ Another finding is that the cells lining a woman's uterus have a larger-than-
　　　主詞　　動詞　述詞子句　動名詞作形容詞片語
expected influence on the length of pregnancy.
　　　　　　　　　介系詞+名詞　介系詞+名詞
　　翻 另外一個發現是女性子宮內的細胞對孕期長短的影響大於預期。

⑭ This study showed that the genes thought to be responsible for the timing of the
　　主詞　　動詞　　受詞子句　　形容詞子句　　　　　介系詞+名詞 介系詞+名詞
birth were from the mother.
　　翻 這項研究表明，影響出生時間的基因來自於母親。

Chapter 4　公告信件

 祖克伯寫給女兒的一封信

Dear Max,

①Your mother and I don't yet have the words to describe the hope you give us for the future. ②Your new life is full of promise, and we hope you will be happy and healthy so you can explore it fully. ③You've already given us a reason to reflect on the world we hope you live in.

④Like all parents, we want you to grow up in a world better than ours today.

⑤While headlines often focus on what's wrong, in many ways the world is getting better.

⑥Health is improving. Poverty is shrinking. Knowledge is growing. People are connecting. ⑦ Technological progress in every field means your life should be dramatically better than ours today.

⑧We will do our part to make this happen, not only because we love you, but also because we have a moral responsibility to all children in the next generation.

⑨Max, we love you and feel a great responsibility to leave the world a better place for you and all children. ⑩We wish you a life filled with the same love, hope and joy you give us.

⑪We can't wait to see what you bring to this world.

Love, Mom and Dad

補充單字片語

- promise ['prɒmɪs] /n./ 許諾希望
- headline ['hedlaɪn] /n./ 大字標題，新聞提要
- focus on... 致力於……
- dramatically [drə'mætɪklɪ] /adv./ 戲劇化地

句構分析

① Your mother and I don't ~~yet~~ have the words to describe the hope you give us
　　　　主詞　　　　　　　 副詞 動詞　　 受詞

~~for the future~~.
介系詞+名詞
📖 我和你的媽媽還找不到詞彙來描述你給我們帶來的對未來的期望。

② Your new life is full of promise, and we hope you will be happy and healthy so
　　主詞　　動詞 述詞 介系詞+名詞　　 主詞 動詞　　　受詞子句

you can explore it ~~fully~~.
　　　　　　　　　副詞
📖 你的新生活充滿了希望，我們願你能健康快樂，以讓你充分地去探索研究。

③ You've ~~already~~ given us a reason to reflect ~~on the world we hope you live in~~.
　主詞　　副詞　 動詞 受詞　受詞補語　　 介系詞+名詞　　 形容詞子句
📖 你已經給了我們一個理由去反思我們希望你生活的那個世界。

④ ~~Like all parents~~, we want you to grow up ~~in a world~~ better ~~than ours~~ today.
　介系詞+名詞　　 主詞 動詞 受詞 受詞補語　 介系詞+名詞　 介系詞+代名詞 副詞
📖 像所有的父母一樣，我們想要你長大後的世界比我們今天更好。

⑤ ~~While headlines often focus on what's wrong~~, ~~in many ways~~ the world is getting
　　　　　　時間副詞子句　　　　　　　　　 介系詞+名詞　 主詞　　 動詞

better.
述詞
📖 新聞總是會報導哪裡出了問題，但在好多方面這個世界正變得越來越好。

⑥ Health is improving. Poverty is shrinking. Knowledge is growing. People are
　主詞　 動詞　　　 主詞　　 動詞　　　　 主詞　　　 動詞　　　 主詞　 動詞

connecting.
📖 健康狀況在改善、貧困人群在減少、大家的知識水準在提升，人們彼此的聯繫越
　 來越緊密。

⑦ Technological progress ~~in every field~~ means your life should be ~~dramatically~~
　　　主詞　　　　　 介系詞+名詞　 動詞　　 受詞子句　　　 副詞

better than ours ~~today~~.
　　　　　　　　副詞
📖 技術在各個領域的進步意味著你們的生活與我們現在的相比有巨大的變化。

⑧ We will do our part to make this happen, not only because we love you, but
　主詞 動詞　 受詞　 受詞補語

also because we have a moral responsibility ~~to all children~~ ~~in the next generation~~.
　　　　　　　　　　　　　　　　　　　 介系詞+名詞　　 介系詞+名詞
📖 我們會盡全力讓這種變化發生，不僅僅是因為我們愛你，更是因為我們有責任去
　 愛護下一代所有的孩子。

⑨ Max, we love you and feel a great responsibility to leave the world a better
　　　 主詞 動詞 受詞　 動詞　　 受詞　　　　　　 受詞補語

place ~~for you and all children~~.
　　　　介系詞+名詞
🔤 麥柯斯，我們愛你，我們覺得為你和所有的孩子們建立一個更好的世界是我們的責任。

⑩ We wish you a life ~~filled~~ ~~with the same love, hope and joy~~ you give us.
　主詞 動詞 受詞　受詞補語 被動語態　　介系詞+名詞
🔤 我們祝願你的一生都充滿了愛、希望、歡樂，就像你帶給我們的那樣。

⑪ We can't wait to see what you bring ~~to this world~~.
　主詞　　動詞 受詞　　受詞子句　　　介系詞+名詞
🔤 我們已等不及想要看到你會給世界帶來什麼。

班傑明‧富蘭克林給年輕朋友的一封信

My dear friend,

①I know of no medicine fit to diminish the violent natural inclination you mention; and if I did, I think I should not communicate it to you. ②Marriage is the proper remedy. ③It is the most natural State of man, and therefore the state in which you will find solid Happiness.

④Your reason against entering into it at present appears to be not well founded. ⑤The circumstantial advantages you have in view by postponing it, are not only uncertain, but they are small in comparison with the thing itself, the being married and settled. ⑥It is the man and woman united that makes the complete human Being, Separate she wants his force of body and strength of reason; he her softness, sensibility and acute discernment.

⑦Together they are most likely to succeed in the world. ⑧A single man has not nearly the value he would have in that state of union. ⑨He is an incomplete animal. ⑩He resembles the odd half of a pair of scissors.

⑪If you get a prudent, healthy wife, your industry in your profession, with her good economy, will be a fortune sufficient.

Your affectionate Friend

句構分析

① I know of no medicine fit to diminish the violent natural inclination you mention;
　主詞 動詞　介系詞+名詞

　and if I did, I think I should not communicate it to you.
　　　插入語　　　主詞　　　動詞　　　　　　受詞 介系詞+代名詞

　譯 我知道沒有什麼藥物可以減少你們所提到的瘋狂的自然傾向，即使我知道，我想
　　 我也不應該把它傳達給你們。

② Marriage is the proper remedy.
　主詞 動詞　　述詞

　譯 婚姻是正確的補救辦法。

③ It is the most natural State of man, and therefore the state in which you will find
　主詞 動詞　述詞　　　　　介系詞+名詞　　　副詞　　　　　形容詞子句

　solid Happiness.

　譯 它是人類最自然的狀態，因此也是你找到幸福的狀態。

④ Your reason against entering into it at present appears to be not well founded.
　　　主詞　　　　系詞+代名詞 介系詞+名詞 動詞　　　　受詞

　譯 你目前反對進入婚姻的理由似乎沒有充分的根據。

⑤ The circumstantial advantages you have in view by postponing it, are not only
　　　　主詞　　　　　　　形容詞子句　　　　　　動詞

　uncertain, but they are small in comparison with the thing itself, the being married
　　述詞　　　主詞 動詞 述詞　介系詞+名詞　　介系詞+名詞

　and settled.

　譯 你認為推遲婚姻可能會存在一定的優勢，但是不確定能實現，而且那些好處跟婚
　　 姻本身以及婚後安定相比就顯得微不足道了。

⑥ It is the man and woman united that makes the complete human Being, Separate
　主詞 動詞　　述詞　　　　　　副詞子句

　she wants his force of body and strength of reason; he her softness, sensibility and
　　　　　　　　　介系詞+名詞　　介系詞+名詞

　acute discernment.

184

譯 男人和女人只有聯合起來才能自稱一個完整的人類，女人相比男人缺乏力量和周密的推理，男人缺乏女人的溫柔、感性和敏銳的洞察力。

⑦ ~~Together~~ they are most likely to succeed ~~in the world~~.
　副詞　主詞　　　動詞　　　　　　　介系詞+名詞
譯 他們在一起最有可能在世界上取得成功。

⑧ A single man has not nearly the value ~~he would have in that state of union~~.
　主詞　　　動詞　　副詞　受詞　　　形容詞子句
譯 單身和男男女女不可能具有婚姻生活中的價值。

⑨ He is an incomplete animal.
　主詞 動詞　　述詞
譯 是一種不完整的動物。

⑩ He resembles the odd half ~~of a pair of scissors~~.
　主詞　動詞　　受詞　　介系詞+名詞 介系詞+名詞
譯 他好像半把剪刀孤掌難鳴。

⑪ ~~If you get a prudent, healthy wife,~~ your industry ~~in your profession,~~ ~~with her~~
　條件副詞子句　　　　　　　主詞　　　介系詞+名詞　　　介系詞+名詞
~~good economy,~~ will be a fortune sufficient.
　　　　　助動詞　　　　述詞
譯 如果你有一個謹慎又健康的妻子，你的辛勤工作，加上她的勤儉節約，必定會創造足夠的財富。

戰士的最後一封信

My very dear Sarah,

①Indications are very strong that we shall move in a few days, perhaps tomorrow. ②Lest I should not be able to write you again, I feel impelled to write a few lines that may fall under your eye when I shall be no more.

③I have no misgivings about or lack of confidence in the cause in which I am engaged, and my courage does not halt or falter. ④I know how strongly American civilization now leans on the triumph of the government, and how great a debt we owe to those who went before us through the blood and suffering of the Revolution. ⑤And I am willing, perfectly willing, to lay down all my joys in this life to help maintain this government and to pay that debt.

⑥Sarah, my love for you is deathless. ⑦It seems to bind me with mighty cables that nothing but Omnipotence could break. ⑧And yet my love of country comes over me like a strong wind and bears me irresistibly, with all these chains, to the battlefield.

⑨The memory of all the blissful moments I have enjoyed with you come crowding over me, and I feel most deeply grateful to God and you that I have enjoyed them so long. July 14,1861 Washington, D.C.

補充單字片語

- indication [ˌɪndɪˈkeɪʃn] /n./ 指示，象徵
- triumph [ˈtraɪʌmf] /n./ 勝利
- irresistibly [ˌɪrɪˈzɪstəblɪ] /adv./ 無法抵抗地

句構分析

① Indications are very strong that we shall move in a few days, perhaps tomorrow.
　　主詞　　動詞 副詞 述詞　　　　　　　　介系詞+名詞　　　副詞
　譯 任務十分緊迫，部隊將在數天內出發，也許就在明天。

② Lest I should not be able to write you again, I feel impelled to write a few lines
　　　　　　　　　　　　　　　　　　　　　　主詞 動詞 述詞　　　不定詞結構
that may fall under your eye when I shall be no more.
形容詞子句　　　介系詞+名詞　　　時間副詞子句
　譯 恐怕我再也不能給你寫信了，我覺得有必要寫給你幾句話，這樣，在我離開的時候，信就會出現在你眼前。

③ I have no misgivings about or lack of confidence in the cause in which I am
主詞 動詞　　受詞　　　　　　介系詞+名詞　介系詞+名詞　形容詞子句
engaged, and my courage does not halt or falter.
　　　　　　主詞　　　　　　　動詞
　譯 我對於我所投身的事業毫無擔憂和害怕，我的勇氣也絲毫沒有減弱和動搖。

④ I know how strongly American civilization now leans on the triumph of the
主詞 動詞　　副詞　　　受詞子句　　　　副詞　　介系詞+名詞　　介系詞+名詞
government, and how great a debt we owe to those who went before us through the
　　　　　　　　　　受詞子句　　　　　　　　形容詞子句
blood and suffering of the Revolution.
　譯 我知道美國文明現在就完全依賴於政府的勝利，而比起我們之前為革命拋頭顱、灑熱血的先烈們，我們虧欠太多。

⑤ And I am willing, perfectly willing, to lay down all my joys in this life to help
主詞 動詞 述詞　　　插入語　　　不定詞結構　　　介系詞+名詞 不定詞結構

maintain this government and to pay that debt.
　　　　　　　　　　　不定詞結構
🔄 我願意，非常願意，以此生我拋卻的所有歡樂，來維護政府和償還債務。

⑥ Sarah, my love for you is deathless.
　　　　　主詞　　　　動詞 述詞
🔄 莎拉，我對你的愛是永恆的。

⑦ It seems to bind me with mighty cables that nothing but Omnipotence could
主詞　　動詞　　受詞　　介系詞+名詞　　　　形容詞子句
break.
🔄 它似乎是有一種結實的鎖鏈將我牢牢繫住，只有萬能的主才能打破它。

⑧ And yet my love of country comes over me like a strong wind and bears me
　　副詞 主詞　介系詞+名詞　動詞　　受詞　介系詞+名詞
irresistibly, with all these chains, to the battlefield.
　副詞　　　插入語　　　　介系詞+名詞
🔄 但對祖國的熱愛似一陣強風，將我和所有這些鐵鏈一起吹向戰場。

⑨ The memory of all the blissful moments I have enjoyed with you come crowding
　主詞　　　介系詞+名詞　　　　形容詞子句　　　　　動詞
over me, and I feel most deeply grateful to God and you that I have enjoyed them so
受詞　　主詞 動詞　　副詞　　述詞
long.
🔄 和你一起度過的所有歡樂時光的記憶如潮水般湧上心頭，我為擁有許多那樣的日子而感激上帝，感激你。

英語文化週公告

①With the careful preparation by the English-lovers' Association, the annual English Culture Week is ready to meet you at the beginning of next month.

②The programs in this year's Culture Week will be more diverting and colorful. ③There will be a variety of activities such as English Drama Contest, English Songs Contest and English Speech Contest. ④There will be music, dancing, singing, games and exchanging of gifts. ⑤Everybody may bring a small gift for this purpose. ⑥ Remember to wrap it up, sign your name and write a few words of good wishes.

⑦The English Culture Exhibition will give a vivid introduction to the western customs. ⑧The highlight will be the famous British music band ABC's performance of Beatles' classical songs at the closing ceremony.

⑨The Week will start on Nov. 1st and last seven days in the Students Club Center. ⑩All the competitions will be held at night, from 7: 00 p. m. to 9: 00 p. m., while the exhibition will be open from 8:00 a. m. to 9:00 p.m. for the whole week. ⑪You can find more details of the schedule on the bulletin board in front of the Center.

⑫Welcome all of you to join us!

補充單字片語

- preparation [ˌprepəˈreɪʃn] /n./ 準備，預備
- annual [ˈænjʊəl] /adj./ 每年的
- a variety of... 各式各樣的……
- highlight [ˈhaɪlaɪt] /n./ 最重要的事情

句構分析

① With the careful preparation by the English-lovers' Association, the annual
　　介系詞 + 名詞　　　　　　　　介系詞 + 名詞　　　　　　主詞
English Culture Week is ready to meet you at the beginning of next month.
　　　　　　　　　動詞 述詞　　不定詞結構　介系詞 + 名詞
譯 在英語愛好者協會精心準備下，一年一度的英語文化週即將在下個月初與你們見面。
結構分析 本句是整篇公告的主旨句，後面又詳細介紹了英語文化周的時間、地點以及具體的內容。

② The programs in this year's Culture Week will be more diverting and colorful.
　　主詞　　　　　介系詞 + 名詞　　　　助動詞　　　述詞
譯 今年文化周的節目將更加豐富多彩。

③ There will be a variety of activities such as English Drama Contest, English
there be 句型　　　　　　　　　　　　介系詞 + 名詞
Songs Contest and English Speech Contest.
譯 會有各種各樣的活動，如英語戲劇比賽、英語歌曲比賽和英語演講比賽。

④ There will be music, dancing, singing, games and exchanging of gifts.
　　there be 句型　　　　　　　　　　　　　　介系詞 + 名詞
譯 會有音樂、舞蹈、唱歌、遊戲以及交換禮物的活動。

⑤ Everybody may bring a small gift for this purpose.
　　主詞　　　動詞　受詞　　介系詞 + 名詞

譯 每個人可以帶一個小禮物來。

⑥ Remember to wrap it up, sign your name and write a few words ~~of good wishes~~.

介系詞 + 名詞

譯 記住把它包起來，簽上你的名字，並寫上幾句祝福語。

⑦ The English Culture Exhibition will give a vivid introduction ~~to the western~~

主詞　　　　　　　　　動詞　　　　受詞　　　　介系詞 + 名詞

~~customs~~.

譯 英國文化展將生動地介紹西方的風俗習慣。

⑧ The highlight will be the famous British music band ABC's performance ~~of~~

主詞　　　助動詞　　　　　　述詞

~~Beatles' classical songs at the closing ceremony~~.

介系詞+名詞　　　　　　介系詞+名詞

譯 最精彩的是英國著名樂團ABC將在閉幕式上演唱匹頭四樂團的經典歌曲。

⑨ The Week will start ~~on Nov. 1st~~ and last seven days ~~in the Students Club Center~~.

主詞　　　　　動詞　介系詞+名詞　　　動詞　　受詞　　　介系詞+名詞

譯 本周將於11月1日開始，持續七天在學生俱樂部中心舉行。

⑩ All the competitions will be held ~~at night, from 7: 00 p. m. to 9: 00 p. m.~~, while

主詞　　　　　　　　動詞　介系詞+名詞 介系詞+名詞

the exhibition will be open ~~from 8:00 a. m. to 9:00 p.m. for the whole week~~.

介系詞+名詞　　　　　　　介系詞+名詞

譯 所有比賽將在晚上舉行，從晚上的七點到九點，而展覽是在上午八點到晚上九點整週開放。

⑪ You can find more details ~~of the schedule on the bulletin board in front of the~~

主詞　　動詞　　受詞　　介系詞+名詞　　　介系詞+名詞　　　　介系詞+名詞

~~Center~~.

譯 你可以在俱樂部中心前面的公告牌上找到更多的時間表。

⑫ Welcome all ~~of you~~ to join us!

介系詞+名詞

譯 歡迎各位加入我們！

甘道夫讀信：讓靈魂成長

Dear Xavier High School, and Ms. Lockwood, and Messrs Perin, McFeely, Batten, Maurer and Congiusta:

①I thank you for your friendly letters. ②You sure know how to cheer up a really old geezer (84) in his sunset years.

③I don't make public appearances any more because I now resemble nothing so much as an iguana.

④What I had to say to you, moreover, would not take long, to wit: Practice any art, music, singing, dancing, acting, drawing, painting, sculpture, poetry, fiction, essays, reportage, no matter how well or badly, not to get money and fame, but to experience becoming, to find out what's inside you, to make your soul grow.

⑤Seriously! I mean starting right now, do art and do it for the rest of your lives.

⑥Draw a funny or nice picture of Ms. Lockwood, and give it to her.

⑦Dance home after school, and sing in the shower and on and on.

⑧Make a face in your mashed potatoes.

⑨Pretend you're Count Dracula.

⑩Here's an assignment for tonight, and I hope Ms. Lockwood will flunk you if you don't do it: Write a six-line poem, about anything, but rhymed.

⑪You have experienced becoming, learned a lot more about what's inside you, and you have made your soul grow.

God bless you all!

補充單字片語

- cheer up 振作起來
- resemble [rɪˈzɛmbl] /v./ 類似於
- no matter how 不論如何
- seriously [ˈsɪərɪəslɪ] /adv./ 嚴肅地

句構分析

① I thank you ~~for your friendly letters~~.
　主詞 動詞 受詞　　介系詞+名詞
　　譯 我很感謝你們的友好來信。

② You sure know how to cheer up a ~~really~~ old geezer (84) ~~in his sunset years~~.
　主詞　　　動詞　　受詞子句　　　　副詞　　　　　　介系詞+名詞

譯 你們一定很懂得如何去讓一位垂暮之年（84歲）的老人獲得莫大的鼓舞。

③ I don't make <u>public appearances</u> any more ~~because I now resemble nothing so~~

主詞　　動詞　　　受詞　　　　　　　　　　　原因副詞子句

~~much as an iguana.~~

譯 我不再公開露面，因為我知道我現在老得像一隻蜥蜴。

④ <u>What I had to say to you</u>, moreover, <u>would not take long</u>, to wit: Practice any art,

　　　主詞子句　　　　　　　　　　　　動詞

music, singing, dancing, acting, drawing, painting, sculpture, poetry, fiction, essays,

reportage, ~~no matter how well or badly~~, not ~~to get money and fame~~, but ~~to experience~~

　　　　　讓步副詞子句　　　　　　　　不定詞結構　　　　　　　不定詞結構

~~becoming, to find out what's inside you, to make your soul grow.~~

　　　不定詞結構　　　　　　　不定詞結構

譯 同時我要告訴你們的話並不太長，即：進行任何藝術活動，音樂、唱歌、舞蹈、表演、繪畫、油彩、雕塑、詩歌、小說、散文、報告文學，無論做的好與壞，也不是為了收獲金錢和名利，而是為了利用這 些經歷去了解你內心真正的樣子，讓你的靈魂成長。

⑤ Seriously! I mean starting right now, do art and do it ~~for the rest of your lives~~.

　　　主詞 動詞　　　　　　　　　　　　　　介系詞+名詞　　介系詞+名詞

譯 我是認真的！我的意思是從現在就開始，從事藝術活動，並且在你的一生中堅持下去。

⑥ Draw a funny or nice picture ~~of Ms. Lockwood~~, and give it ~~to her~~.

　　　　　　　　　　　　　　介系詞+名詞　　　　　　　　介系詞+受詞

譯 畫一張有趣的或者美麗的洛克伍德女士照片，然後送給她。

⑦ Dance home ~~after school~~, and sing ~~in the shower~~ and on and on.

　　　　　介系詞+名詞　　　　　　　介系詞+名詞

譯 放學之後跳著舞回家，淋浴的時候放聲歌唱，諸如此類的事情。

⑧ Make a face ~~in your mashed potatoes~~.

　　　　　　介系詞+名詞

譯 在你的馬鈴薯泥裡畫個鬼臉。

⑨ Pretend you're Count Dracula.

譯 假裝你是德古拉爵士。

⑩ Here's <u>an assignment</u> ~~for tonight~~, and I hope <u>Ms. Lockwood will flunk you</u> if

主詞 動詞　　述詞　　　介系詞+名詞　　主詞 動詞　　受詞子句

~~you don't do it~~: Write a six-line poem, ~~about anything~~, but rhymed.

條件副詞子句　　　　　　　　　　　　介系詞+名詞

譯 這是今天晚上的任務，如果你們不做的話，我希望洛克伍德女士會讓你們不及格：寫一首六行的詩，關於什麼都行，但一定要押韻。

⑪ You <u>have experienced</u> becoming, ~~learned a lot more about what's inside you~~, and

主詞　　動詞　　　　受詞　　　插入語

you have made your soul grow.
主詞　　動詞　　受詞　受詞補語
譯 你體會了這種經歷，已經對你的靈魂了解更多，也使它得到了成長。

 國家旅遊度假區公告

① National tourist vacation areas refer to comprehensive tourist areas established in conformity with international requirements for vacation tours and mainly open to overseas tourists. ②The areas shall be bounded clearly and shall be located in the places which are suitable for concentrating complete sets of tourist facilities, abundant with tourist vacation resources and source of tourists, convenient for communications and have relatively firm foundations of foreign relations.

③ The state encourages the development of tourism and treats it as a key industry for earning foreign exchange. ④ National tourist vacation areas shall be granted the following preferential policies：

⑤The income tax on the enterprises with foreign investment established within the areas shall be levied at a reduced rate of twenty-four percent.

⑥ Machinery, equipment and other materials for capital construction required by the construction of infrastructure within vacation areas shall be exempted from customs duties and product taxes (or value-added taxes).

⑦ Foreign exchange payment shops may be established within the areas. ⑧ The examination and approval of these shops shall be handled according to the relevant state provisions.

⑨Tourist agencies of category 1 in co-operation with foreign investors may be established within the areas for overseas tourist services. ⑩The national tourism administration shall be in charge of the examination and administration of the tourist agencies.

補充單字片語

- comprehensive [ˌkɒmprɪˈhensɪv] /adj./ 廣泛的，有理解力的
- conformity [kənˈfɔ:mətɪ] /n./ 符合，一致
- foreign exchange 外滙
- preferential [ˌprefəˈrenʃl] /adj./ 優先的，優惠的
- in charge of 負責

句構分析

① National tourist vacation areas refer to comprehensive tourist areas
主詞　　　　　　　　動詞　　　　　受詞
established in conformity with international requirements for vacation tours and
被動分詞　介系詞+名詞　　介系詞+名詞　　　　　介系詞+名詞
mainly open to overseas tourists.
副詞　動詞　　受詞
譯 國家旅遊度假區是指按照國際要求建立的綜合旅遊區，主要面向海外遊客開放。

② The areas shall be bounded clearly and shall be located in the places which are
主詞　　　　　動詞　　　副詞　　　　　　動詞　　　地方副詞片語
suitable for concentrating complete sets of tourist facilities, abundant with tourist
形容詞子句
vacation resources and source of tourists, convenient for communications and have
relatively firm foundations of foreign relations.
譯 各個度假區應明確界定，應位於適合集中配套旅遊設施、旅遊資源和客源豐富、
交通便利、國外關係相對牢固的地方。

③ The state encourages the development of tourism and treats it as a key industry
主詞　　　動詞　　　　受詞　　　介系詞+名詞　動詞 受詞 介系詞+名詞
for earning foreign exchange.
副詞
譯 國家鼓勵發展旅遊業，把旅遊業作為賺取外匯的重點產業。

④ National tourist vacation areas shall be granted the following preferential
主詞　　　　　　　　　　　　動詞　　　受詞
policies:
譯 國家旅遊度假區實行以下優惠政策：

⑤ The income tax on the enterprises with foreign investment established within the
主詞　　　　介系詞+名詞　　介系詞+名詞　　　　動詞過去分詞 介系詞+名詞
areas shall be levied at a reduced rate of twenty-four percent.
動詞　　　　　　　　受詞
譯 在本區域內設立的外商投資企業，按24%的稅率徵收企業所得稅。

⑥ Machinery, equipment and other materials for capital construction required by
主詞　　　　　　　　　　　　　介系詞+名詞
the construction of infrastructure within vacation areas shall be exempted from
介系詞+名詞　　　介系詞+名詞　　介系詞+名詞　　　　　　動詞
customs duties and product taxes or value-added taxes.
受詞
譯 度假區基礎設施建設所需的機械、設備和其他基本建設物資，免徵關稅和產品稅
（增值稅）。

⑦ Foreign exchange payment shops may be established within the areas.
主詞　　　　　　　　　　　　　動詞　　　　　　受詞

該區域內可開辦外匯支付的商店。

⑧ <u>The examination and approval</u> <s>of these shops</s> shall be <u>handled</u> <s>according to the</s>
      主詞   介系詞+名詞   動詞   介系詞+名詞
<s>relevant state provisions.</s>

這些商店的審批應按照國家有關規定辦理。

⑨ <u>Tourist agencies</u> <s>of category 1</s> <s>in co-operation</s> <s>with foreign investors</s> may be
   主詞   介系詞+名詞   介系詞+名詞   介系詞+名詞
established within the areas <s>for overseas tourist services.</s>
  動詞   受詞

與外國投資者合作的第1類旅行社可以在境外旅遊服務領域內設立。

⑩ <u>The national tourism administration</u> shall be <u>in charge</u> <u>of the examination</u>
        主詞   述詞   受詞
and administration <s>of the tourist agencies.</s>
         介系詞+名詞

國家旅遊局負責審核和管理旅遊機構。

艾伯特・施韋策致父母

①The worst is behind us! ②That was last night's organ concert and the lecture preceding it. ③ Quite frankly I was somewhat worried about this lecture. ④ Since I am not used to giving long talks in French and the hall is enormous: three thousand people. ⑤ But to my amazement I discovered that I felt as much at home in French as I do in German, and that it was easier for me to speak loudly and clearly in French than in German! ⑥I stood there without a manuscript, and within three minutes. ⑦I sensed that I had captured my audience more surely than I had ever done before. ⑧ I spoke for fifty-five minutes, and next came an organ recital that lasted for one hour. ⑨ I have never been so successful. ⑩ When the program ended, they all remained in their seats: I had to go back to my organ and play for another half hour; the audience was sorry to leave it was half-past midnight!

⑪ Here, the concerts are announced for 9:15, but at that time there's not a soul in the auditorium; toward 9: 30 the first few people arrive, strolling about in the hall and the lobby, and toward ten o'clock, after three rings of a bell, the people deign to finally take their scats!

⑫ On Saturday, a grand concert with organ and orchestra is scheduled in the morning, and I have long rehearsals in the evening, for the organ is very difficult to play since the sound is always delayed. ⑬ Luckily, I am well rested, and I am managing to overcome the difficulties. ⑭ Absolutely everyone addresses me as "cher ma re"; the art critics settle down in the auditorium during rehearsals; my portrait is displayed in the music stores. It's such fun.

補充單字片語

- preceding [prɪˈsi:dɪŋ] /adj./ 在先的，在前的
- manuscript [ˈmænjʊskrɪpt] /n./ 手稿，原件
- recital [rɪˈsaɪtl] /n./ 小型音樂會，獨奏會
- orchestra [ˈɔ:kɪstrə] /n./ 管弦樂，管弦樂隊
- be used to 習慣，適應
- stroll about 閒逛，遊玩

句構分析

① The worst is behind us!
　　主詞　　動詞　述詞
譯 最糟糕的事情過去了！
語法分析 定冠詞the與最高級形式連用可用作名詞，除了表示一類人之外，還可表示事物。

② That was last night's organ concert and the lecture preceding it.
主詞 動詞　　述詞　　　　　　　　　　述詞　　形容詞片語
譯 我說的是昨晚的風琴音樂會和之前的講座。
句構分析 該句是一個承上啟下的句子，既對應前文提到的「糟糕的事情」，又引起下文對這兩件事的 詳細記敘。

③ Quite frankly I was somewhat worried about this lecture.
　　　副詞　主詞 動詞　副詞　　述詞　　介系詞+名詞
譯 坦白地說，我有點擔心這次演講。

④ Since I am not used to giving long talks in French and the hall is enormous:
連接詞 主詞　　動詞　　　　受詞　　　介系詞+名詞　　主詞 動詞 述詞
three thousand people.
　　解釋說明
譯 因為我不習慣用法語做長篇演講，而且音樂廳很大，可容納三千人。

⑤ But to my amazement I discovered that I felt as much at home in French as I do
　　介系詞片語　主詞 動詞　　受詞子句　副詞　介系詞+名詞 方式副詞子句

in German, that it was easier for me to speak loudly and clearly in French than in

介系詞+名詞　　虛主詞 動詞 述詞 介系詞+代名詞 主句　　副詞　　　副詞　介系詞+名詞 介系詞+名詞

German!

譯 但是令我驚訝的是，我發現用法語演講就像我用德語演講一樣自在，而且對我來說用法語比用德語更容易洪亮清楚地演講。

⑥ I stood there without a manuscript, and within three minutes.

主詞 動詞　副詞　介系詞+名詞　　　　介系詞+名詞

譯 在三分鐘裡，我站在那裡，並沒有拿演講稿。

⑦ I sensed that I had captured my audience more surely than I had ever done

主詞　動詞　　　形容詞子句　　　　副詞　　介系詞+名詞子句

before.

副詞

譯 我感覺到我比以前任何一次都成功地深深地吸引了觀眾。

⑧ I spoke for fifty-five minutes, and next came an organ recital that lasted for one

主詞 動詞　介系詞+名詞　　　副詞 動詞　　主詞　　　形容詞子句 介系詞+名詞

hour.

譯 我講了五十五分鐘，接下來是風琴獨奏音樂會，持續了一個小時。

語法分析 and後的句子是主詞、動詞倒裝結構，起強調的作用。

⑨ I have never been so successful.

主詞　　動詞　　　副詞　述詞

譯 我從來沒有如此成功過。

⑩ When the program ended, they all remained in their seats: I had to go back to

　時間副詞子句　　　主詞 副詞 動詞　　述詞　　主詞　動詞

my organ and play for another half hour; the audience was sorry to leave it was

受詞　　　動詞 介系詞+名詞　　　　主詞　　動詞 述詞 不定詞結構 時間副詞子句

half-past midnight!

譯 曲目演奏結束時，觀眾們不願離席，我不得不返回到風琴前，又演奏了半個小時。觀眾不捨地離開時，已經是深夜了。

⑪ Here, the concerts are announced for 9:15, but at that time there's not a soul in

副詞　主詞　　動詞　　　介系詞+名詞　介系詞+名詞　述詞動詞　主詞

the auditorium; toward 9: 30 the first few people arrive, strolling about in the hall

介系詞+名詞　介系詞+名詞　　主詞　　　　動詞　動名詞作形容詞片語 介系詞+名詞

and the lobby, and toward ten o'clock, after three rings of a bell, the people deign to

介系詞+名詞　　介系詞+名詞　　　主詞　　動詞

finally take their seats.

動詞　受詞

譯 在這裡，雖然音樂會被通知是從9:15開始，但是時間到了禮堂裡並沒有人；快到9:30的時候，來了很少的幾個人在大廳和走廊閒逛；快到10點的時候，在鈴聲響了三次後，人們才最終坐下。

⑫ ~~On Saturday,~~ a grand concert ~~with organ and orchestra~~ is scheduled ~~in the~~

   介系詞+名詞   主詞   介系詞+名詞   動詞   介系詞+名詞

~~morning,~~ and I have long rehearsals ~~in the evening, for the organ is very difficult to~~

     主詞 動詞   受詞   介系詞+名詞   原因副詞子句

~~play since the sound is always delayed.~~

不定詞結構   原因副詞子句

譯 星期六上午安排了一場風琴和管弦樂隊的大型音樂會，晚上我排練了很長時間，因為風琴的聲音總 是延遲從而很難演奏。

⑬ ~~Luckily,~~ I am ~~well~~ rested, and I am managing to overcome the difficulties.

  副詞 主詞 動詞 副詞 述詞   主詞   動詞   受詞

譯 幸運的是，我停頓地很好，想方設法克服了這些難題。

⑭ ~~Absolutely~~ everyone addresses me ~~as "cher ma re"~~; the art critics settle down ~~in~~

   副詞   主詞   動詞 受詞   受詞補語   主詞   動詞

~~the auditorium during rehearsals;~~ my portrait is displayed ~~in the music stores.~~

  介系詞+名詞   介系詞+名詞   主詞   動詞   介系詞+名詞

譯 每一個人都稱呼我為「尊敬的藝術家」；在彩排期間，藝術評論家們都認真地坐在座位上；我的肖像在很多樂器店裡展示著。

⑮ It's ~~such~~ fun.

主詞 動詞 副詞 述詞

譯 這很有趣。

約翰・亞當斯致妻

① Your account of the rain refreshed me. ② I hope our husbandry is prudently and industriously managed. ③Frugality must be our support. ④Our expenses, in this journey, will be very great — our only reward will be the consolatory reflection that we toil, spend our time, and tempt dangers for the public good — happy indeed, if we do any good! ⑤The education of our children is never out of my mind. ⑥Train them to virtue, habituate them to industry, activity, and spirit. ⑦ Make them consider every vice, as shameful and unmanly: fire them with ambition to be useful — make them disdain to be destitute of any useful, or ornamental knowledge or accomplishment. ⑧ Fix their ambition upon great and solid objects, and their contempt upon little, frivolous, and useless ones.

⑨ It is time, my dear, for you to begin to teach them French. ⑩Every decency, grace, and honesty should be inculcated upon them. I have kept a few minutes by way of journal, which shall be your entertainment when I come home, but we have had so many persons and so various characters to converse with, and so many objects to view, that I have not been able to be so particular as I could wish — I am, with the tenderest affection and concern, your wandering.

補充單字片語

- husbandry [ˈhʌzbəndrɪ] /n./ 農業
- prudently [ˈpruːdntlɪ] /adv./ 謹慎地，慎重地
- frugality [frʊˈɡælətɪ] /n./ 節儉，簡約
- consolatory [kənˈsɒlətərɪ] /adj./ 慰藉的，安慰的
- inculcate [ˈɪnkʌlkeɪt] /v./ 反覆灌輸，主張

句構分析

① Your account of the rain refreshed me.
　　主詞　　　介系詞+名詞　動詞　受詞
譯 你提到了下雨，這讓我很振奮。

② I hope our husbandry is prudently and industriously managed.
　主詞 動詞 受詞子句　　　　副詞　　　副詞
譯 我希望慎重管理我們的農業並苦心經營。

③ Frugality must be our support.
　　主詞　　　助動詞　述詞
譯 我們必須要堅持節儉。

④ Our expenses, in this journey, will be very great — our only reward will be
　　主詞　　　介系詞+名詞 助動詞 副詞 述詞　　主詞　　　助動詞
the consolatory reflection that we toil, spend our time, and tempt dangers for the
　　　述詞　　　　　形容詞子句　　　　　　　　　介系詞+名詞
public good — happy indeed, if we do any good!
　　述詞 副詞　條件副詞子句
譯 我們在這段旅程中的開支會非常大——我們為了公益事業辛苦工作、花費時間、甘冒風險，這給予我們備受安慰的唯一回報——如果我們做了任何好事，的確是很快樂的！

⑤ The education of our children is never out of my mind.
　　主詞　　　介系詞+名詞 動詞 副詞　述詞
譯 我一直惦記著孩子們的教育問題。

語法分析 never雖然是副詞，但是它本身帶有否定的含義，所以在去繁化簡時不能被去掉。

⑥ Train them to virtue, habituate them to industry, activity, and spirit.
　　動詞　受詞　受詞補語　　動詞　　　　受詞　　　　受詞補語

譯 培養他們的美德，讓他們養成勤勞、活潑和勇敢的習慣。

句構分析 該句子是由兩個簡單分句構成的簡單句。

⑦ Make them consider every vice, ~~as shameful and unmanly~~: fire them ~~with~~
　　動詞　受詞　　受詞補語　　　　介系詞+名詞　　　　　　動詞 受詞　介系詞+名詞

~~ambition~~ to be useful — make them disdain to be destitute ~~of any useful, or~~
　　　　　受詞補語　　　動詞 受詞　　受詞補語　　　　介系詞+名詞

~~ornamental knowledge or accomplishment~~.

譯 讓他們知道每一個缺點是可恥的和懦弱的：激勵他們成為有用之人的雄心──讓他們不屑於任何沒有學問的、沒有造詣的和沒有成就的人。

⑧ Fix their ambition ~~upon great and solid objects~~, and their contempt ~~upon little,~~
　　動詞　　受詞　　　介系詞+名詞　　　　　　　　　受詞　　　介系詞+名詞

~~frivolous, and useless ones~~.

譯 把他們的雄心建立在偉大而堅實的目標上，讓他們無視那些細小的、無意義的和無用的事情。

⑨ It is time, ~~my dear,~~ ~~for you~~ to begin to teach them French.
虛主詞 動詞 述詞 插入語 介系詞+名詞　　　　主句

譯 親愛的，你是時候開始教他們法語了。

⑩ Every decency, grace, and honesty should be inculcated ~~upon them~~.
　　　　　　主詞　　　　　　　　　　　動詞　　　介系詞+名詞

譯 應該把禮貌、優雅和誠實牢牢地灌輸給他們。

⑪ I have kept a few minutes ~~by way of journal~~, ~~which shall be your entertainment~~
主詞 動詞　　受詞　　　介系詞+名詞　　　　形容詞子句

~~when I come home~~, but we have had ~~so~~ many persons and ~~so~~ various characters ~~to~~
時間副詞子句　　　　主詞 動詞 副詞　受詞　　副詞　受詞

~~converse with~~, and ~~so~~ many objects ~~to view~~, ~~that I have not been able to be so~~
不定詞結構　　　　副詞 受詞　　不定詞結構　結果副詞子句

~~particular as I could wish~~ — I am, ~~with the tenderest affection and concern,~~ your
方式副詞子句　　　　　主詞 動詞　介系詞+名詞　　　　　述詞

wandering.

譯 我以日記的形式保存了一些備忘錄，等我回家的時候，你可以用來消遣。然而，我們有那麼多不同的人來交流和那麼多的事物來觀察，以致於我不能像我希望的那樣來詳細描述這一切──請接受我最溫柔的情意和關懷，你的流浪者。

句構分析 該句子是由主句和多個子句構成的複合句。

蘇珊・奧格登・納什致女兒

①There are many, many interesting things to see here. ②Paris is a very old city, and today Mummy and I saw a beautiful building, that was started by the Romans more than 1600 years ago. ③It is called Cluny. ④We have also been to the Louvre, a museum now full of the most beautiful paintings and statues; but years ago the kings and queens of France used to live there, until the French people got angry with them and chopped off their heads.

⑤This afternoon we went to a beautiful cathedral on an island in the middle of the river. ⑥It is called the Cathedral of tre Dame, which means the cathedral of Our Lady the Virgin. ⑦It is more than 900 years old, and so high that you can hardly see the top. ⑧The windows are of gorgeous stained glass, red and blue and yellow and green and purple, so that they cast light like a rainbow on the walls. ⑨A very good king of France who lived 700 years ago and later became Saint Louis was buried there. ⑩Tell Delia that we offered a candle to the Virgin Mary for each of you there, and that we are bringing her back a rosary from there also. Mummy and I climbed the tower later. We were very tired when we got to the top, but it was interesting. Some hideous stone gargoyles were looking right into our faces, so we looked down at Paris lying at our feet, and it was beautiful. We could see miles of river, at the bridges and the lovely old buildings.

補充單字片語

- chop off 砍掉
- cathedral [kəˈθiːdrəl] /n./ 大教堂
- gorgeous [ˈgɔːdʒəs] /adj./ 華麗的，美麗的
- rosary [ˈrəʊzərɪ] /n./ 玫瑰經，念珠
- gargoyle [ˈgɑːgɔɪl] /n./ 怪獸狀滴水嘴
- used to 過去常常

句構分析

① There are many, many interesting things to see here.

　　there be句型　　　　　　　　不定詞結構 副詞
　🗝 這裡有很多很多有趣的事情可以看。

② Paris is a very old city, and ~~today~~ Mummy and I saw a beautiful building, ~~that~~

主詞 動詞　述詞　　　　　　副詞　主詞　動詞　　　受詞　　　形容詞子句

~~was started by the Romans more than 1600 years ago.~~

　　　　介系詞+名詞　　時間副詞

🔲 巴黎是一個非常古老的城市，媽媽和我今天看到了一座漂亮的建築，那是羅馬人在1600多年前建造的。

句構分析 該句子是由and連接的兩個主句和that引導的一個形容詞子句構成的複合句。

③ It is called Cluny.

主詞 動詞　受詞

🔲 它被稱為克盧尼。

④ We have ~~also~~ been to the Louvre, ~~a museum now full of the most beautiful~~

主詞　　副詞 動詞　述詞　　　　插入語副詞

~~paintings and statues;~~ but years ago the kings and queens ~~of France~~ used to live

　　　　　　　　　　　　　　　　主詞　　　　　　介系詞+名詞　動詞

~~there, until the French people got angry with them and chopped off their heads.~~

副詞　　　時間副詞子句

🔲 我們還去了羅浮宮，一個充滿了最漂亮的畫作和雕像的博物館；但是多年前法國的國王和王后在這裡居住，後來法國人民起義了，把他們的頭砍掉了。

句構分析 該句子是由but連接的兩個主句和until引導的時間副詞子句構成的複合句。

⑤ ~~This afternoon~~ we went to a beautiful cathedral ~~on an island in the middle of the~~

　　　副詞　　主詞 動詞　　　受詞　　　　介系詞+名詞　　介系詞+名詞

~~river.~~

🔲 今天下午我們去了一個漂亮的大教堂，教堂在河中央的一個小島上。

⑥ It is called the Cathedral of the Dame, ~~which means the cathedral of Our Lady~~

主詞 動詞　　受詞　　　　　　　　形容詞子句

~~the Virgin.~~

🔲 它被稱為聖母院大教堂，意思是「我們的聖母大教堂」。

句構分析 該句子是由主句和非限制性形容詞子句構成的複合句，非限制性形容詞子句去掉後對句子的影響不大。

⑦ It is more than 900 years old, and ~~so~~ high ~~that you can hardly see the top.~~

主詞 動詞　　述詞　　　　　　副詞 述詞　結果副詞子句

🔲 它已經900多年了，而且很高，你幾乎看不到頂端。

句構分析 該句子是由主句和so ... that引導的結果副詞子句構成的複合句。

⑧ The windows are of gorgeous stained glass, ~~red and blue and yellow and green~~

主詞　　　動詞　　　述詞　　　　　　插入語

~~and purple, so that they cast light like a rainbow on the walls.~~

　　　結果副詞子句　　　　　介系詞+名詞　介系詞+名詞

🔲 窗戶上裝飾著華麗的彩色玻璃，紅色的、藍色的、黃色的、綠色的和紫色的，使它們像彩虹一樣投射在牆上。

⑨ A very good king ~~of France who lived 700 years ago and later became Saint~~
　　　主詞　　　　介系詞+名詞　形容詞子句

~~Louis~~ was buried ~~there~~.
　　　　動詞　　　副詞
🔤 法國的一位非常好的國王葬在那裡，他生活在700年前，後世稱他為聖路易士。

⑩ Tell Delia that we offered a candle to the Virgin Mary ~~for each of you there,~~
　動詞 受詞　　　形容詞子句　　　　　　　　　介系詞+名詞

and that we are bringing her back a rosary ~~from there~~ also.
　　　形容詞子句　　　　　　　　　　介系詞+副詞　副詞
🔤 告訴迪莉亞，我們為你們每個人在聖母瑪麗亞像那裡獻了一支蠟燭，我們還會從那裡為她帶回一串念珠。

⑪ Mummy and I climbed the tower ~~later~~.
　　主詞　　　動詞　　述詞　　副詞
🔤 後來，媽媽和我去爬高塔了。

⑫ We were ~~very~~ tired ~~when we got to the top~~, but it was interesting.
　主詞 動詞 副詞 述詞　　　時間副詞子句　　　　主詞 動詞 述詞
🔤 當我們到達塔頂的時候，我們非常累，但是很有意思。

⑬ Some hideous stone gargoyles were looking right ~~into our faces, so we looked~~
　　　　　主詞　　　　　　　動詞　　述詞　介系詞+名詞　結果副詞子句

~~down at Paris lying at our feet~~, and it was beautiful.
　　　　　動名詞作形容詞片語　主詞 動詞　述詞
🔤 一些醜陋的石頭怪獸狀滴水嘴正對著我們，我們看著巴黎在我們腳下，很漂亮。

⑭ We could see miles of river, ~~at the bridges~~ and the lovely old buildings.
　主詞　動詞　　　受詞　　介系詞+名詞　　　　受詞
🔤 我們可以看見數英里長的河流，河上的橋，和可愛的古老建築

 ## 切斯特菲爾德勛爵致兒子

London
March 6, 1747
Dear boy,

① I have often said, and do think, that a Frenchman, who, with a fund of virtue, learning and good-sense, has the manners and good-breeding of his country, is the perfection of human nature. ②This perfection you may, if you please, and I hope you will, arrive at.

③ You know what virtue is: you may have it if you will; it is in every man's power, and miserable is the man who has not it. ④ Good sense God has given you. ⑤ Learning you already possess enough of, to have, in a reasonable time, all that a man need have. ⑥With this, you are thrown out early into the world, where it will be your own fault, if you do not acquire all the other accomplishments necessary to complete and adorn your character.

⑦ You will do well to make your compliments to Madame St. Germain and Monsieur Pampigny; and tell them how sensible you are of their partiality to you, in the advantageous testimonies which, you are informed, they have given of you here.

⑧ Adieu! Continue to deserve such testimonies; and then you will not only deserve, but enjoy my truest affection.

Affectionately
Love, Dad

補充單字片語

- virtue [ˈvɜːtʃuː] /n./ 美德，德行
- human nature 人性，人情
- miserable [ˈmɪzrəbl] /adj./ 悲慘的，令人痛苦的
- reasonable [ˈriːznəbl] /adj./ 合理的，有理性的
- throw out 扔掉，不受理
- deserve [dɪˈzɜːv] /v./ 應受，應得報酬，值得
- accomplishment [əˈkʌmplɪʃmənt] /n./ 成就，完成

句構分析

① I have ~~often~~ said, and do think, that a Frenchman, ~~who, with a fund of virtue,~~
主詞　　副詞　　動詞　　　　受語子句　　　　　形容詞子句
learning and good ~~sense, has the manners and good-breeding of his country,~~ is the
perfection ~~of human nature.~~
　　　　　介系詞+名詞
譯 我常常這樣説，也這樣認為，一個品德高尚、學識淵博、理性健全的法國人，擁有來自國家代代相傳的禮儀和教養，造就了完美的人格。

② This perfection you may, ~~if you please,~~ and I hope you will, arrive at.
　　　　　　　　　　　插入語　　　　　主詞 動詞　受詞子句
譯 如果你願意的話，你一樣也能達到這種境界，我也期望你達到。

③ You know <u>what virtue is</u>: you may have it ~~if you will~~; it is ~~in every man's power~~,
主詞 動詞　受詞子句　　　　　　　　　條件副詞子句　　　介系詞+名詞
and miserable is the man ~~who has not it~~.
　　　　　　　　　　　　　形容詞子句

📖 你懂得什麼是美德：如果你願意，你就能擁有它；而且人人都有能力得到，不具備美德的人是不幸的。

④ Good sense God has given you.

📖 上帝已經賦予你遠見卓識。

⑤ Learning you ~~already~~ possess enough of, ~~to have~~, ~~in a reasonable time~~, all ~~that a~~
　　　　　　　　　副詞　　　　　　　　插入語　　　介系詞+名詞　　　　形容詞子句
~~man need have~~.

📖 你在合理的時間裡，已經學了身而為人所需要的一切足夠學問。

⑥ ~~With this~~, you <u>are thrown out</u> ~~early~~ into the world, ~~where it will be your own~~
介系詞+代名詞 主詞　　動詞　　副詞　　受詞　　形容詞子句
~~fault, if you do not acquire all the other accomplishments necessary to complete and~~
　　　　條件副詞子句
~~adorn your character~~.

📖 你在擁有這些之後，很早就被送到大千世界中去增長見識，你在外面如果吸取不到其他能使你的品格變得盡善盡美的修養，那就是你自己的過失了。

⑦ You will <u>do well</u> to make <u>your compliments</u> ~~to Madame St. Germain and~~
主詞　　　動詞　　　　受詞　　　　　　介系詞+名詞
~~Monsieur Pampigny~~; and tell them how sensible you are ~~of their partiality to you~~, in
　　　　　　　　　　　　動詞 受詞　　　　　　　　介系詞+名詞　　介系詞+名詞
the advantageous testimonies which, you are informed, they have given ~~of you here~~.
　　　　　　　　　　　　　　　　　　　　　　　　　　　　　　　　介系詞+名詞

📖 你應該再去拜訪聖・日耳曼夫人和龐比尼先生，告訴他們你從我這裡了解到他們對你的偏愛和讚美，並向他們表示感謝。

⑧ Adieu! Continue to deserve such testimonies; and ~~then~~ you will not only deserve,
　　　　　　　　　　　　　　　　　　　　　　　　　副詞 主詞　　　　　動詞
but enjoy <u>my truest affection</u>.
　動詞　　　受詞

📖 再見！繼續努力吧，孩子！你要讓自己配得上這些溢美之詞，這樣的話，你將不僅值得享有，而且會真正享有我最真摯的愛。

Part

3

閱讀實踐──
整體掌握文章

Passage 1

Twenty-three states have announced plans to fund primary and secondary education on a ___1___ tax basis instead of per county, following the lead of a ___2___ decision in Ohio.

Ohio's S.B. 320 follows the Ohio Supreme Court ruling that funding schools from local property taxes and private initiatives does not ___3___ with the Ohio Constitution's guarantee of a "thorough and efficient" public education system. The new statewide system ___4___ that resources are more ___5___ distributed, with inner city schools receiving the same amount as suburban ones.

The Ohio decision began with Governor Ted Strickland's 2006 campaign promise to assure that" where you grow up in Ohio should not ___6___ where you end up in life." Hundreds of grassroots campaigns throughout the state, including The Ohio Coalition for Equity and Adequacy of School Funding, took the cue from Mr. Strickland's statement and spent the last two years working hard to hold him to it.

"Finally, this is a real step towards the equality our Constitution recommends," says Amanda Fullerton, of Columbus. Ms. Fullerton, a mother of two, voted for Mr. Strickland because of his long history of support for educational reform, but was soon ___7___ by the governor's inaction in office. When she first heard about the proposed bill in the Ohio Senate, Ms. Fullerton decided to occupy the Governor's office to demonstrate how ___8___ she felt the bill was. Over two hundred mothers soon ___9___ her, camping out for six days. Many observers feel that actions like the mothers' played a key role in convincing Governor Strickland to push hard for the bill.

Following the announcements of twenty-three states that they would be voting on similar bills, the U.S. Department of Education said it would be ___10___ a plan for a national tax base for schools, to finally assure that as in most other developed countries, a child's opportunities to learn will not depend on his or her birthplace.

From *The New York Times*

[A] equitably	[B] developing	[C] statewide
[D] joined	[E] comply	[F] amusing

[G] landmark   [H] determine   [I] directed

[J] means   [K] complained   [L] important

[M] disappointed   [N] adopts   [O] particularly

ANSWER

1答案：[C]

解析 根據空格後的內容instead of per county（而不是每個縣）可知前面的內容與後面的county是 同類型，選項[C]項的statewide指的是「遍及全州的」，與per county相呼應，根據下文第二段第三句的The new statewide system也可看出，因此選[C]。

2答案：[G]

解析 根據內容空格處需要一個形容詞，選項中的developing、amusing、landmark、directed、important、disappointed都是形容詞，而第一句話的內容是説二十三個州計劃在全州範圍內徵税，amusing 作「有趣的」，只有landmark 和 important 符合其句意，因下文第八題只能選擇 important，因此該處選擇[G]，意為「具有里程碑意義的」。

3答案：[E]

解析 該空後的with是解題的關鍵，空格後出現public education system（公共教育體制），因此應 選擇[E]的comply，構成comply with，意為「遵循，遵守」。

4答案：[J]

解析 空格前的內容是The new statewide system（新的全州系統），而該空處需要是第三人稱單數形式，根據句子意思可知[J]項「意味著」符合。

5答案：[A]

解析 根據空格處的內容可知需要選用副詞，只有[A] 和[O] 適合，而[O] 的particularly 搭配 distributed不合適，因此選[A]equitably「公正地」。

6答案：[H]

解析 空格所在句的意思是：「無論你在俄亥俄的哪裡長大都不能_____你的人生走向」，根據句意，determine放在此處合適，意為「決定」。

7答案：[M]

解析 空格前的內容是voted for Mr. Strickland because of his long history of support for educational reform（投票支持斯特里克蘭先生因其長期以來對教育改革的支持），以及空格後的內容是「很快對州長的不作為_____」，中間有一個but作轉折，根據選項，[M] disappointed（失望的） 符合題意，構成be disappointed by，意為「對……失望」。

8答案：[L]

解析 該空前的內容是「她決定占據州長辦公室來證明法案是多麼_____」，該空處應選擇形容詞，而從該段的最後一句Many observers feel that actions like the mothers' played a key role in convincing Governor Strickland to push hard for the bill，可推出她們是為了推動法案，因此應是為了證明法案的重要性，故選[L]。

9答案：[D]

解析 該空格處的內容是「兩百多名母親很快_____了她」，後面的內容是露營了六天，這個指的是她們共同的行動，該空應用過去分詞，[K]項意為「抱怨，舉報」，與句子意思不符，只有[D]項的「加入」表明了她們的決心。

10答案：[B]

解析 該空前的would be 和空格後的a plan表明空格處應為動詞，而用選項[B] developing在此意為「發展」，be developing則是表明將要出現的事情。

Passage 2

Fatal wildfires ___11___ eight Northern California counties have dealt a devastating blow to the important wine and tourism industries, destroying more than 1,500 buildings, including ___12___ wineries.

Although the seasonal harvest is nearly ___13___, the conflagration threatens to disrupt tens of thousands of jobs and destroy valuable stores of grapes waiting in bins, barrels and bottles to be fermented or aged. The extent of the damage will be unclear for days because the fires are blocking many winery owners from reaching their facilities.

Tourism in the region — a multibillion-dollar economic machine that ___14___ high-end hotels, wine-tasting tours and upscale cuisine — is suffering as the flames claimed many establishments and forced many others to shutter for the rest of the week.

"It has been a ___15___ fire," the Sonoma County Winegrowers group said in a Facebook post. "Reports of fire damage to wineries, businesses and homes continue to grow."

The blazes — which have left at least 11 people dead — continued to rage on Tuesday. Seventeen separate fires, across 94,000 acres, have forced more than 20,000 people to evacuate.

The fires also destroyed several Santa Rosa establishments, including the Fountaingrove Inn, the Hilton Sonoma Wine Country hotel, Willi's Wine Bar, the Cricklewood steakhouse and more.

The rebuilding effort will help buoy the local economy as it ___16___, but wineries that lost vineyards will have to wait three or five years to ___17___ the soil back to health and coax out a viable crop of grapes, said Karissa Kruse, president of the Sonoma County Winegrowers.

Surviving grapes may suffer smoke taint — a smoky flavor that makes them __18__ for fine wine, she said. Wineries damaged or destroyed by the fire could lose vast reserves of wines aging in barrels and bottles. The repercussions of the fire on wine stored in barrels and tanks are unclear.

Still, Ms. Kruse pointed to some silver linings. In most cases, the flames destroyed the brush planted between the rows of grapes, and not the resilient vines themselves. And record-breaking temperatures in September __19__ that fewer grapes were left exposed to the fires.

"For the most part, the vintage is in, and we should still have a viable wine community as we move forward," Ms. Kruse said. "We all __20__ that the Labor Day heat was going to define the 2017 vintage, but it expedited the harvest, which we now look at as such a blessing."

From *The New York Times*

[A] strict	[B] scorching	[C] grumbled
[D] recovers	[E] unusable	[F] barbecuing
[G] historic	[H] controls	[I] nurse
[J] complete	[K] devastating	[L] promotes
[M] includes	[N] meant	[O] interrupt

ANSWER

11答案：[B]

解析 該句中出現了動詞have dealt，因此該空處應用v-ing形式，選項中scorching、barbecuing 和devastating都符合這一要求，但整篇文章是在講述大火的危害，排除barbecuing，而devastating 除了作v-ing形式外還可作形容詞，該詞只能用在下文第15題的空格裡，故要選擇scorching，本意是「燒焦，烤焦」，此處可翻譯為「波及」。

12答案：[G]

解析 根據該句子可知該空是一個形容詞，用來修飾wineries（葡萄酒廠），根據選項，[A] strict、[E] unusable、[G] historic以及[J] complete都是形容詞，可排除[A]和[J]，其不能用來修飾葡萄酒廠，而[E] unusable（不能用的）與後文中的酒廠內的葡萄酒矛盾，故選[G]historic「歷史上著名的」。

13答案：[J]

解析 該空格需要一個形容詞，空前的seasonal harvest指的是葡萄的季節性收獲，即「雖然葡萄的季節性收獲幾近_____」，空格後的意思是：但是大火可能導致數萬人失去工作。[A] strict放在這裡沒有關聯，[E] unusable不能用來修飾葡萄採收，因此只有[J] complete符合，意為「雖然葡萄的採摘工作基本完工」。

14答案：[M]

解析 根據該空的位置可知該詞需要是第三人稱單數形式，空格前後的意思是：該區的旅遊業——一個價值數十億美元的產業，_____高檔酒店、葡萄酒品嘗之旅等，因此選擇[M]「包括」。

15答案：[K]

解析 該空處需要一個形容詞修飾fire，[K]合適，意為「毀滅性的」。

16答案：[D]

解析 該空前面的意思是：「重建工作能幫助經濟_____」，且需要是第三人稱單數形式，這句話放在文章中指的是大火摧毀了很多東西，重建工作能幫助恢復經濟，[D]recovers「恢復」符合該句意思。

17答案：[I]

解析 空格前後的意思是：「需要花費三到五年的時間將葡萄園_____至健康狀態」，根據選項，[I] 的nurse可用來修飾土地，表示「將土壤養至健康狀態」。

18答案：[E]

解析 空格前後的意思是：「幸存的葡萄酒遭到了煙燻，那種味道使它們_____制成葡萄酒」，因此這裡應是表示否定的詞彙，選[E]「不能用的」。

19答案：[N]

解析 空格前後的意思是：「九月份打破記錄的高溫_____留下被大火摧毀的葡萄更少」。根據選項[N] meant符合這句話的意思，意為「意味著」。

20答案：[C]

解析 根據該空後的這句話but it expedited the harvest, which we now look at as such a blessing（但大火加快了葡萄的收獲，現在看來是一件幸運的事），可知前面講的是過去的事情，故該空用過去時態，選[C]，意為「抱怨」。

Passage 3

In long-awaited guidelines for the booming industry of automated vehicles, the Obama administration promised strong safety ___21___, but sent a clear signal to automakers that the door was wide open for ___22___ cars.

"We ___23___ in the future, you can take your hands off the wheel, and your commute becomes restful or productive instead of frustrating and exhausting, "said Jeffrey Zients, director of the National Economic Council, adding that highly automated vehicles will save time, money and lives.

The statements were the most ___24___ signal yet by federal regulators that they see automated car technology as a win for auto safety. Yet having officially ___25___ the fast-evolving technology, regulators must now balance the commercial interests of companies including Tesla, Google and Uber with concerns over public safety, especially in light of recent crashes involving semiautonomous cars.

Driverless and semiautonomous cars have already hit the open roads, forcing regulators to keep up. "We are in this weird transition," Mr Brauer said, "It's a tough balance for the regulators. You want to __26__ this technology out, but you don't want to move too quickly." The new guidelines on Monday targeted four main areas. The Department of Transportation announced a 15-point safety standard for the design and development of autonomous vehicles; __27__ for states to come up with uniform policies applying to driverless cars; clarified how current regulations can be applied to driverless cars; and opened the door for new regulations on the technology.

Currently, driverless cars face a patchwork of state regulations. In the last three years, about a dozen states have __28__ laws that specifically address testing of driverless vehicles. Most laws require a licensed driver to be in the car.

Mr Foxx said states would continue to __29__ the licensing of drivers and insurance. But Mr Foxx affirmed the agency's oversight over the software technology used in driverless cars. "What we are trying to do is avoid a patchwork of state laws," Mr Foxx said.

The federal guidelines were welcomed by auto manufacturers. Ford, which is targeting fully autonomous vehicles by 2021 for ride-sharing, said in a statement that the guidance "will help establish the basis for a national framework that enables the safe deployment of autonomous vehicles. We also look forward to __30__ with states on areas that complement this national framework."

The government's endorsement will speed up the rollout of autonomous cars, experts said, potentially within the next five years.

From *The New York Times*

[A] experience   [B] called   [C] envision
[D] expect   [E] driverless   [F] passed
[G] collaborating   [H] oversight   [I] pick
[J] endorsed   [K] negative   [L] aggressive
[M] regulate   [N] get   [O] applying

ANSWER

21答案：[H]

解析 空格前的意思是「歐巴馬政府承諾要進行強有力的安全_____（自動汽車行業）」，且該空需要的是一個名詞，根據選項可知只有[H]適合，oversight意為「監管」。

22答案：[E]

解析 該空是用來修飾car的，根據文章的整體意思可知是在講述無人駕駛汽車，因此選項中[E] driverless正確。

23答案：[C]

解析 該空前後的意思是：「我們_____，在未來，大家可以把雙手從方向盤上拿開」，可知這是在將來發生的事情，只是在假想，且需要是動詞，選項[C] envision符合，意為「想像」。

24答案：[L]

解析 該空格後的they see automated car technology as a win for auto safety（他們認為自動汽車技術有利於駕車安全）因此這是聯邦監管機構發出的積極的訊號，而非消極的，故選[L]。

25答案：[J]

解析 該空前的having officially可推斷出空格處應為過去分詞形式，[B] called, [F] passed和[J] endorsed都符合這一點，但是空格後指的是technology，就只能選擇[J] endorsed（採用）。

26答案：[N]

解析 該空前後的意思是：「你既希望讓技術_____，又不想將步子邁得太快」，根據選項以及空後的out可知構成get out，意為「（使）出現」，符合題意。

27答案：[B]

解析 該空前的分號可知與後面的句子是並列的關係，因此要與clarified和opened時態一致，根據選項，[B]called和[F]passed符合這一點，但pass for意為「被誤認為是」，不符合句意，因此選[B] call for，意為「呼籲」。

28答案：[F]

解析 根據空格前的have可知該空應為過去分詞，且後面是跟law搭配。因此只有[F] passed正確，意為「通過法律」。

29答案：[M]

解析 該空前後的意思是：「政府將繼續_____駕照和保險事宜」，因此選項[M] regulate（監管）符合句意。

30答案：[G]

解析 根據該空前的look forward to可知需要用動名詞形式，且跟with搭配，故選[G] collaborating，collaborate with意為「與……合作」，正好與後面的名詞states（各州）相搭配。

Passage 4

Deceiving others __31__ its advantages. Camouflage in nature is useful to the hunter and the __32__. The smarter the animal, the more likely it is to use (and detect) deception to its benefit. Humans are particularly good at exploiting trickery to get ahead—for more money, more power or a desired mate. Yet deception is difficult, __33__ of intelligence. Lying often __34__ us nervous and twitchy, and complicated fictions can __35__ to depression and poor immune function. And then there are the ethical implications.

The book "The Folly of Fools" explains that the most effectively devious __36__ are often unaware of their deceit. Self-deception makes it easier to manipulate others to get ahead. Particularly intelligent people can be especially good at deceiving themselves.

There are also links between deception and evolutionary progress. Some of it is intuitive. The grey squirrel, for example, cleverly builds false caches to discourage others __37__ raiding its acorns. Placebos are sometimes as effective as medication without the nasty side effects. Other illustrations require more head-scratching. Competition between our maternal and paternal genes can create "split selves", which try to fool each other on a biological level. Human memory often involves an unconscious __38__ of selection and distortion, which prompts us to believe the stories we tell others.

All of this deceit comes at a price. The most cunning people (whether conscious fibbers or not) tend to benefit at the __39__ of everyone else. The way of overconfident Wall Street traders may hurt investors and taxpayers at __40__ personal risk. Then there are politicians who spin stories of national greatness to bolster support for costly wars in which they will not be fighting.

From *The Economist*

[A] lead	[B] price	[C] leaves
[D] regardless	[E] from	[F] brings
[G] expense	[H] hunted	[I] progress
[J] exists	[K] seldom	[L] has
[M] people	[N] program	[O] little

ANSWER

31答案：[L]

解析 該句主詞是動名詞片語Deceiving others，動詞要用單數形式。空格後直接跟受詞，該動詞應是及物動詞，選項[L]為正確答案。

32答案：[H]

解析 and是連接詞，連接前後兩個並列結構，「the + 形容詞」可以表示一個群體。the hunted 表示「被捕獵者」，即「獵物」，正好與the hunter對應，答案為[H]。

33答案：[D]

(解析) 此題考查的是固定片語的用法。regardless of 表示「不管，不顧」的意思。spit和disregard 之前都要加介系詞in，組成片語in spite of 和 in disregard of，也表示「不管，不顧」的意思。neglectful是形容詞，後加of時，表示「疏忽的，對……不註意的」，主詞多是人。答案為[D]。

34答案：[C]

(解析) 此處應填動詞，根據空缺後的受詞以及受詞後的形容詞可知，此動詞應是連綴動詞，只有選項[C] leave是連綴動詞。

35答案：[A]

(解析) to作介系詞，此處考查動詞詞組用法。lead to 表示「導致」的意思，refer to表示「參考，指的是」的意思。根據語境，應選擇[A] lead，該句意為「複雜的謊言還會導致憂鬱及免疫力下降」。

36答案：[M]

(解析) 根據be動詞are可推斷，此處名詞應是複數名詞，或集體名詞。people是集合名詞，動詞用複數。答案為[M]。

37答案：[E]

(解析) discourage sb from doing sth 表示「使某人洩氣」，是固定用法。

38答案：[I]

(解析) 根據不定冠詞an可以判斷此處的名詞應是單數名詞，根據詞義，選項[I]為正確答案。

39答案：[G]

(解析) at the expense of表示「以……為代價」，其他三項均沒有此用法，答案為[G]。

40答案：[O]

(解析) risk是不可數名詞，此處應用形容詞little修飾，表示「幾乎沒有個人風險」，答案為[O]。

Passage 5

Chances are, you ___41___ in your phone before you go to bed at night, thinking it's best to greet the morning with a fully charged device.

Is this a good idea?

That depends.

Here's the thing. Many people don't expect to keep their phones for much longer than two years.

For the most part, experts say, those people are not going to __42__ much damage to their phone batteries before they start hankering for a new device. If that sounds like you, feel free to charge every night, and as often as you like in between.

But __43__ charging takes a toll on the lithium-ion batteries in our phones. And it's not because they can be overcharged, said Edo Campos, a spokesman for Anker, which produces phone chargers.

"Smart phones are, in fact, smart," Mr. Campos said. "they know when to stop charging." So in theory, any damage from charging your phone overnight with an official charger, or a trustworthy off-brand charger, should be __44__. But the act of charging is itself bad for your phone's battery.

Here's why.

Most phones make use of a technology that __45__ their batteries to accept more current faster. Hatem Zeine, the founder, chief scientist and chief technical officer of the wireless charging company Ossia, says the __46__ enables phones to adjust to the amount of charge that a charger is capable of supplying.

The technology allows power to pulse into the battery in specific modulations, increasing the speed at which the lithium ions in the battery travel from one side to the other and __47__ the battery to charge more quickly. But this process also leads lithium-ion (and lithium-polymer) batteries to corrode faster than they otherwise would. "When you charge fast all the time, you __48__ the life span of the battery," Mr. Zeine said.

Is there a solution?

If you're intent on __49__ a lithium-ion battery beyond the lifetime of the typical phone or tablet, Mr. Zeine suggested using a charger meant for a less powerful device, though he couldn't __50__ that it would work. People looking to preserve their batteries should make sure their phones don't become overheated, Mr. Campos advised, because high temperatures further excite the lithium-ion in batteries, leading to even quicker deterioration.

From *The New York Times*

[A] damaging	[B] allows	[C] made
[D] negligible	[E] advocate	[F] plug
[G] preserving	[H] limit	[I] frequent
[J] emphasizes	[K] causing	[L] notice
[M] technology	[N] guarantee	[O] suggest

ANSWER

215

41答案：[F]

解析 文章的整篇內容是在講述給手機徹夜充電是否會影響電池的壽命，因此該空處的意思作「充電」使用，又根據選項和空格後的in可選擇plug，構成plug in，意為「插上，充電」，故選[F]。

42答案：[L]

解析 該空前後的意思是：「這些人在對一個新的設備心生向往之前不會_____這個對他們舊手機的電池有多大傷害，」因為Many people don't expect to keep their phones for much longer than two years（很多人不期待他們用手機的時間能超過兩年）因此選項[L] notice放在這裡符合句意。

43答案：[I]

解析 在選擇該空的單詞之前要先了解take a toll的意思，即「產生不良的影響，傷害」，這句話指的是什麼情況下會對手機的鋰離子電池造成傷害，根據選項，[I] frequent符合意思，意為「頻繁的」。

44答案：[D]

解析 該空前的句子Smart phones are, in fact, smart，they know when to stop charging以及an official charger, or a trustworthy off-brand charger（原廠充電器或者信得過的其他廠牌的充電器）指的是積極的方面，damage from charging your phone overnight（整夜充電的傷害）應該是「小的」傷害，根據選項，[D] negligible符合，意為「忽略不計的」。

45答案：[B]

解析 該空所在的句子是用來解釋technology，因此要用第三人稱單數形式，選項[B] allows和 [J] emphasizes符合這一點，而根據句意，allow（允許）可用於該空構成allows their batteries to accept more current faster（允許他們的電池接受更快的電流），故選[B]。

46答案：[M]

解析 該空所在的整段話都是在講述這種技術所帶來的好處，還可根據這段話第一句中的technology判斷該空選擇[M] technology。

47答案：[K]

解析 根據該空前的and可知，該詞彙與increasing並列，故只能用現在分詞形式，根據選項，[A] damaging，[G] preserving和[K] causing符合這一點，而空格後的意思是：「（技術）_____這種 電池更快地充好電」，因此只有[K] causing「使得，導致」符合句意。

48答案：[H]

解析 該空前後的意思是：「總是快速充電會_____電池的壽命」，可知該空的詞是類似「損壞、限制」的詞，選項[H] limit符合，意為「限制」。

49答案：[G]

解析 根據該空前的on可知該詞是動名詞形式，前後句的意思是：「如果你想
_____鋰離子電池使 其壽命更長」，根據選項只有[G] preserving適合，意為
「保護、保存」。

50答案：[N]

解析 由該空前的couldn't可判斷該詞是動詞原形，前面的意思是「澤恩建議用
小功率設備配備的充電器（來延長電池壽命），但是不能_____（這種方法）有
效」，根據選項，只有[N] guarantee符合句意，意為「保證」。

Passage 6

Women have been rapidly ___51___ the employment and wage ladders in recent decades. But only a small ___52___ have made it to the top rungs — and their progress may be slowing.

New research shows that after making big strides in the 1980s and 1990s, the number of women ___53___ into the top 1 percent of earners has stalled. Women account for only 16 percent of the 1 percent, a number that has remained essentially flat over the past decade, according to a paper by three economists. And they ___54___ for only 11 percent of the top 0.1 percent of earners.

"The higher up you move in the income distribution, the lower the ___55___ of women," said Gabriel Zucman, an economics professor at the University of California, Berkeley, and an author of the paper, which analyzes gender in the 1 percent." It shows that there is a fundamental form of inequality at the top related to gender."

The world of billionaires and millionaires, ___56___ by wealth, also remains a predominantly male club. Of the nearly 2,500 billionaires in the world, only 294 (around 12 percent) are women, according to Wealth-X, a research firm.

The number of female billionaires is growing only half as fast as the male billionaire population, Wealth-X says. And women may even be losing ___57___ in the millionaire population: Worldwide, the number of women worth $30 million or more declined in 2015, even as the ___58___ male population grew.

Of course, women are making inroads among the rich. By some ___59___, there are more wealthy or high-earning women than ever, in the United States and around the world. In 2000, there were 11 female billionaires on the planet, according to Forbes; by 2016, there were 190. (Forbes and Wealth-X have different ___60___ for the female billionaire population.)

From *The New York Times*

[A] ingredient　　　　　[B] measured　　　　　[C] prejudiced

[D] equivalent	[E] climbing	[F] tallies
[G] measures	[H] breaking	[I] pay
[J] fraction	[K] estimates	[L] proportion
[M] account	[N] ground	[O] plunging

ANSWER

51答案：[E]

解析 由該空前的have been 可知該空需要的是現在分詞形式，又結合空後的 wage ladders可知應 選擇[E] climbing，引申為「在就業和工資階梯上快速上升」。

52答案：[J]

解析 該空的前一句指的是女性在薪水道路上上升得很快，空格所處的這一句是：「但是只有小的 _____達到了頂層」，選項[J] fraction符合，a small fraction意為「一小部分」指的是一小部分女性。

53答案：[H]

解析 該空後的into the top 可作解題的關鍵，選項中可與into 搭配的有[H] breaking 和[O] plunging，而plunge into意為「投入，跳入」，break into可作「進入」使用，符合句意。

54答案：[M]

解析 根據該空後的11 percent（11%）且前有一個for，根據選項可知要用[M] account，構成 account for，意為「（在數量、比例上）占」。

55答案：[L]

解析 該空前後的意思是：「收入階梯上越往上走，女性的_____越低」，根據選項，[L] proportion 作「比例」符合句意，而ingredient是作「成分」使用，故選[L]。

56答案：[B]

解析 該空要選擇的詞彙是要來證明billionaires and millionaires（億萬富翁和百萬富翁）與by wealth（通過財富）之間的關系，根據選項[B] measured符合題意，意為「衡量」。

57答案：[N]

解析 由and可知空格前的The number of female billionaires is growing only half as fast as the male billionaire population（女性億萬富翁的增長速度僅為男性的一半）與空格後的內容應是相似的，都是指的女性所占的比例不高，根據選項，[N] ground可用於此，構成lose ground，意為「下跌、縮小」。

58答案：[D]

解析 由句子結構可知該詞是一個形容詞來修飾male，選項中[C] prejudiced和

[D] equivalent符合 這一點，空格前的是the number of women worth $30 million or more declined（資產超過3000萬 美元的女性人數減少了），空格處的是「即使＿＿＿男性人數上升」，由此可知選項[D] equivalent 符合句意，減少和上升的依據是在同等數量的基礎上比較。

59答案：[G]

解析 該空前的By some（按照一些）可知此處應用名詞，根據句意選項[G] measures可用於此，意為「按照一些衡量標準」。

60答案：[F]

解析 該空處的意思是：《富比士》和Wealth-X有著不同的「測量標準」，選項[F] tallies可作為「統計方式」使用，與其意思最接近。

Passage 7

Global warming ___61___ by human emissions of greenhouse gases is having clear effects in the physical world: more heat waves, heavier rainstorms and higher sea levels, to cite a few.

In recent years, though, social scientists have been ___62___ with a murkier question: What will climate change mean for human welfare?

Forecasts in this ___63___ are tricky, necessarily based on a long chain of assumptions. Scientific papers have predicted effects as varied as a greater spread of tropical diseases, fewer deaths from cold weather and more from hot weather, and even bumpier rides on airplanes.

Now comes another entry in this literature: a prediction that in a hotter world, people will get less sleep.

In a paper published online Friday by the journal Science Advances, Nick Obradovich and colleagues predicted more restless nights, especially in the summer, as global temperatures rise. They found that the poor, who are less likely to have air-conditioning or be able to run it, as well as the elderly, who have more difficulty ___64___ their body temperature, would be hit hard.

If global emissions are allowed to continue at a high level, the ___65___ found, then additional nights of sleeplessness can be expected beyond what people normally experience. By 2050, for every 100 Americans, an extra six nights of sleeplessness can be ___66___ every month, the researchers calculated. By 2099, that would more than double, to 14 additional nights of tossing and turning each month for every 100 people, in their estimation.

Researchers have long known that being too hot or too cold at night can disturb anyone's sleep, but nobody had ___67___ to ask how that might affect people in a world grown hotter because of climate change.

Dr. Obradovich is a political scientist who researches both the politics of climate change and its likely human impacts, holding ___68___ at Harvard

219

and the Massachusetts Institute of Technology. He started the research while completing a doctoral degree at the University of California, San Diego.

He got the idea for the study while enduring a 2015 heat wave in an apartment in San Diego with no air-conditioner in the bedroom.

To calculate the effect of warmer temperatures in the future, he turned to data collected by the Centers for Disease Control and Prevention, which asks people in a survey to recall their sleep patterns in the previous month. Sure enough, he found a ___69___ between higher temperatures in particular cities and disturbed sleep as reported by their residents. To make forecasts, he drew on computer estimates of how hot particular places will get if greenhouse emissions continue at a high level.

A bigger ___70___ in the study, perhaps, is that it is impossible to know what human society will look like 100 years from now. How many people will be without air-conditioning in that world?

From *The New York Times*

[A] dealing	[B] measuring	[C] paper
[D] thought	[E] caused	[F] weakness
[G] expected	[H] realm	[I] report
[J] correlation	[K] wrestling	[L] district
[M] regulating	[N] appointments	[O] projects

ANSWER

61答案：[E]

解析 這裡是要用一個動詞來表明全球變暖與人類排放的溫室氣體之間的關係，且這句話中有謂語動詞is，故選項[E] caused正確，構成caused by，意為「由……造成」。

62答案：[K]

解析 根據句子結構可知該空格需要的是現在分詞形式，空格前後的意思是：「社會學家一直在_____更為複雜的問題」，故選項[K] wrestling正確，可構成wrestle with，意為「設法解決，全力對付」。

63答案：[H]

解析 由該句可知該詞是一個名詞，句子前後的意思是：「在這個_____預測很難」，所以選項[H] realm適合，意為「領域」。

64答案：[M]

解析 根據空格前的have more difficulty可知該詞需要是動名詞形式，該詞前後的句意是：「老人很難_____其身體溫度」，選項[M] regulating，意為「調節」，這段話的意思指的是老人很難調節自身的溫度使其會受到高溫的傷害。

65答案：[C]

（解析）根據句意，該詞所在的一小句話是作插入語使用，即：「_____發現」，後面跟的是發現的內容，空格處的主詞需要從上一段得知，與選項相結合可知要選[C] paper，指的是上一段落中發表的論文發現的內容。

66答案：[G]

（解析）該詞前後的意思是：「到2050年，每一百個美國人一個月_____會增加六個不眠之夜。」到2050年的事只能是估算，根據選項只能選擇[G] expected，作「預估」使用。

67答案：[D]

（解析）該空需要是過去分詞形式，根據選項thought適合，意為「沒有人想著去問……」。

68答案：[N]

（解析）該空後的內容是哈佛和麻省理工，故選項[N] appointment適合，可構成hold appointments，意為「任職於」。

69答案：[J]

（解析）該詞所處的這段話前面所指的是在作一項研究，即全球氣溫對睡眠的影響，根據Sure enough（果然）可知higher temperatures（高溫）和disturbed sleep（睡眠困擾）之間存在著「聯繫」，選項[J] correlation，表示「關聯，相互關係」正確。

70答案：[F]

（解析）該詞後的句子it is impossible to know what human society will look like 100 years from now（我們不可能知道人類社會一百年後的樣子），因此這是對研究結果的質疑，根據選項，[F] weakness 可用於此，意為「這項研究的缺陷」。

Passage 8

Emotional viewers were left in tears as they watched a little boy help a girl with Down's syndrome overcome her fear of rabbits in a heart-warming episode of The Secret Life Of 4-Year Olds.

Fans tweeted that they were 'bawling their eyes out' after Tomas helped his 'best friend' Ada find the ___71___ to stroke the pet rabbit after she ___72___ ran away scared.

Clutching a soft toy, he told her 'rabbits don't eat humans... only carrots' before standing by her side as she gingerly ___73___ the pet.

Child development experts, who are on hand to watch the children as they get to know each other at the school in Epping, Essex, commented that Tomas displayed huge amounts of empathy when he went to ___74___ the little girl.

The scene also ___75___ dozens of viewers, who took to Twitter to praise Tomas and his newfound friendship.

Parents Matt Dixon, 37, and Laura, 38, who live with Ada and six-year-old daughter Sophie, previously told how they decided to apply for the show as a way of raising awareness of what it means to be a young child with Down's — but also because they thought it would suit their daughter's big personality.

Ada initially struggled to find someone to play with at the nursery but by the end of the week had made firm friends with Tomas, who firmly ___76___ she was his 'best friend'.

In a bid to help his friend, Tomas brought a soft toy bunny to Ada and ___77___: "Rabbits don't eat humans, they only eat carrots and carrot cake," before asking her encouragingly: "Are we going to stroke the bunny? Are you going to stroke that?"

The episode also saw best friends Vinnie and Harper, gobbling up nine delicious chocolate-covered strawberry snacks, just moments after their teacher Katie had explained that they were for the entire class to ___78___ together.

Within minutes of Katie leaving the room, Vinnie ___79___ Harper that they should split the sprinkle-covered lolly between them and tucked into the snacks together.

But while it might at first appear to be a ___80___ of naughty behaviour, a child psychologist explained that there was a scientific reason behind it as the boys hadn't yet developed the executive functioning skills which control good decision making.

Dr Shona Goodall, a clinical psychologist at Sheffield Children's NHS Trust, said: "Executive functioning is the ability to make decisions, it's the control center of the brain."

From *The Daily Mail*

[A] frequently	[B] sign	[C] comfort
[D] convinced	[E] enjoy	[F] courage
[G] steal	[H] moved	[I] initially
[J] explained	[K] understood	[L] touched
[M] speaking	[N] declared	[O] gesture

ANSWER

71答案：[F]

解析 這篇文章的第一段中指出help a girl with Down's syndrome overcome her fear of rabbits（幫助一個患有唐氏症的女孩克服了對兔子的恐懼），因此是讓阿達在摸寵物兔這件事上找到了「勇氣，信心」，根據選項[F]正確。

72答案：[I]

解析 該空缺少的是一個副詞，根據選項[A] frequently和[I] initially都是副詞，但是用initially「開始，最初」來修飾ran away scared符合句意。

73答案：[L]

解析 空格前的gingerly意為「小心翼翼地」，這個空格缺少的是一個動詞，且根據時態需要是過去式，故選項[L] touched正確。

74答案：[C]

解析 空格前的he指的是那個小男孩，空格後的she指的是那個小女孩，這個文章通篇都是在講述男孩安慰小女孩的事，故[C] comfort正確。

75答案：[H]

解析 這裡的主語是the views（觀眾），這裡用also，是因為前面粉絲們看到這個場景時大哭，因此這裡的應該也是被這個場景所「感動」，根據選項，選[H] moved符合句意。

76答案：[N]

解析 這個空格前後的意思是：「男孩堅定地＿＿＿女孩是他的好朋友」。選項[N] declared 符合句意，意為「宣稱」。

77答案：[J]

解析 空格前的內容是托馬斯為了幫助阿達克服恐懼，給了她一個玩具兔子，那麼空格後的內容就是在解釋讓她接受的原因，根據選項，[J] explained正確。

78答案：[E]

解析 由空格前的to可知，這裡要用動詞原形。選項[G] steal和[E] enjoy符合這一點，但是這裡的內容是巧克力，因此[E] enjoy更合適。

79答案：[D]

解析 空格的前後是Vinnie ＿＿＿ Harper that they should，這個空格處應該是類似「建議」之類的詞，選項[D] convinced，意為「說服」，符合題意。

80答案：[B]

解析 空格處的內容是心理學家對於維尼和哈柏表現的描述，該空格處應是一個名詞，[B] sign適合，意為「表現，跡象」。

Passage 9

Baby eels are one of Spain's most ___81___ foods, but when you see them for the first time you might wonder why.

They're not, to put it ___82___, something that cries out to be eaten. When alive, they're ___83___ and slimy, slithering and squirming like tiny snakes. Cooked, they turn opaque and resemble limp, dead worms, except they're

223

white with two ___84___ black dots for eyes. Hungry yet?

But lots of delicious things are not particularly good looking; what's important is the ___85___. Here's where it gets strange. It's not that angulas, as they're called in Spain, taste good or bad. They don't taste of much at all - which is strange because they're astronomically expensive, up to 1,000 euros a kilo. Even ___86___ still, legend has it they were once so unappreciated they were used as fodder for chickens and pigs. But then again, when it comes to eels, everything is strange.

Many ___87___ find it difficult to understand why some people are willing to ___88___ so much for angulas, including me. As a writer and podcaster about Spanish food and culture, I've always found it mystifying. Especially because the traditional recipe (a la bilbaína) calls for frying garlic and hot peppers in lots of olive oil and then adding angulas -a sure way to overpower their mild flavour.

Of course, mystery surrounds eels, not least when it comes to their life cycle, which sounds like something out of a dark fairy tale. They live in freshwater, but can breathe through their ___89___ and travel over land for long distances. They eat just about anything, living or ___90___. Then at the age of 10 or so, they swim downstream in rivers across Europe to the Atlantic Ocean and somehow (it's still unknown to science) they find their way to the Sargasso Sea, some 5,000km away. At depths of more than 500m - quite a feat for a creature that lives most of its life in shallow freshwater -they spawn and die, and their hatchlings drift on the Gulf Stream currents towards Europe, a journey that takes at least two years.

From *The New York Times*

[A] non-transparent	[B] taste	[C] gill
[D] expensive	[E] sublime	[F] skin
[G] stranger	[H] mildly	[I] transparent
[J] dead	[K] pay	[L] tiny
[M] colour	[N] Spaniards	[O] European

ANSWER

81答案：[D]

解析 由空格後的foods可知前面空格處是一個形容詞，此外這篇短文講述的是西班牙的幼鰻，在短文的第三段提到（which is strange because they're astronomically expensive（但這對幼鰻來說就很奇怪了，因為它們尤其昂貴），可知該空應選擇expensive，來講述為什麼幼鰻在西班牙這麼昂貴卻還很受歡迎。故選[D]。

82答案：[H]

解析 由該空的位置可知，該空與to put it構成了插入語，是固定搭配，所以選項中的mildly正確，構成to put it mildly，意為「說得委婉些」，故選[H]。

83答案：[I]

解析 由該空格的位置可知，該詞是一個形容詞，與slimy, slithering and squirming構成並列詞，來形容西班牙幼鰻的外表，顯然選項中[A] non-transparent和[I] transparent符合這一點，但由於空後的 Cooked, they turn opaque（不透明的），所以該空選擇[I] transparent。

84答案：[L]

解析 由空格前後的內容可知：眼睛上有兩個_____黑點，符合這個意思的形容詞通常是「大的，小的」，根據選項[L] tiny正確，意為「極小的，微小的」。

85答案：[B]

解析 空格前的意思是：很多美味可口的東西都沒有很漂亮的外表，重要的是_____。我們知道食物除了描述外表外就是其的味道，所以該空根據選項選擇[B] taste，意為「滋味，味道」。

86答案：[G]

解析 空格前的even（甚至，更加）可知是對前一個內容程度的加深，空格前的那句話講述的是令作者感到奇怪的是幼鰻嘗起來不怎麼樣，卻售價甚高。空格後的內容也表述出了作者奇怪的觀點，故根據選項答案是[G] stranger，用比較級來表示對奇怪程度的加深。

87答案：[N]

解析 由空格前後可知：許多_____ 發現，所以空格處應是表示「人」的單詞，根據選項[N] Spaniards和[O] European表示出了這個意思，但全短文都是在講西班牙和幼鰻的故事，與歐洲人無關，故選[N]。

88答案：[K]

解析 由空格前的be willing to可知該空是一個動詞，且是動詞原形，還需與for構成固定詞組，根據選項[K]pay正確。

89答案：[F]

解析 空格前講述了幼鰻生活在淡水裡，但它們可以通過_____呼吸，顯然不能選擇[C] gill（魚鰓），而應選[F] skin（皮膚）。

90答案：[J]

解析 空格處的詞彙顯然與living構成並列詞彙，所以其也是一個形容詞，又因空格前的「它們幾乎什麼都吃」，所以該空應選dead來表示它們死的活的都吃。故選[J]。

Many of New York's most __91__ new Asian restaurants in recent years have been imports — spinoffs of established places in Japan and China, often with a distinct innovation or specialty. This season's __92__ follow suit.

At Wokuni, the first American outpost for Tokyo Ichiban Foods, which __93__ 50 restaurants in Japan, bluefin tuna and king yellow tail will arrive by air from the company's own aquaculture farm in Japan. Those fish and others will be prepared in __94__ fashion — sushi, sashimi, tempura or grilled — and sold at a retail counter.

Ramen has become commonplace in New York, but, at Tonchin New York in Midtown Manhattan, a Tokyo-based restaurant group will shine the spotlight on Tokyo-style ramen: broth seasoned with soy sauce. The curly noodles are made in-house.

Tonchin will also serve teppanyaki dishes, seared on vintage-style iron griddles, and fried chicken. Toru Okuda, who __95__ many Michelin stars in Tokyo and runs a restaurant in Paris, has secured a tiny niche in New York, where he will join the recent parade of chefs serving finely wrought kaiseki dinners. His Chelsea restaurant, Okuda, will offer two seatings each night at a counter with just seven seats. A private room __96__ another six.

But there will be no __97__ of tables at DaDong New York, a vast addition to Midtown by way of Beijing, Shanghai and Chengdu, with about 300 seats __98__ and nearly 200 on outdoor terraces on two floors. Here the pièce de résistance is Peking duck, cooked in special ovens to produce skin with a glassy crispness and sheen. The menu promises to deliver "the artistic conception of Chinese cuisine," in beautifully rendered preparations by the chef, Dong Zhenxiang, better known as DaDong, and his executive chef, Andy Xu.

Other distinctive imports are on the __99__. Zauo, a multistory restaurant from Tokyo where customers can reel in their own fish from pools in the dining room, is set to open early next year at 152 West 24th Street. Marugame Udon, which __100__ noodles that are kneaded, cut and cooked to order and has nearly 1,000 locations in Japan and elsewhere, is about to open in Los Angeles and has plans to expand, with New York in its sights.

From *The New York Times*

[A] captured   [B] unwelcome   [C] holds
[D] features   [E] traditional   [F] inside
[G] intriguing   [H] horizon   [I] earned
[J] lacking   [K] newcomers   [L] schlepped
[M] shortage   [N] runs   [O] conveys

ANSWER

91答案：[G]

解析 由句子結構可知該空格是一個形容詞，來形容新出現的亞洲餐廳，根據空格後的with a distinct innovation or specialty（有著獨特的創新和鮮明的特色）可知對於這些亞洲餐廳的態度是積極的，[E] traditional放進這裡意思是「最傳統的」與innovation相違背，因此只有選項中的[G] intriguing符合題意，意為「吸引人的」。

92答案：[K]

解析 該空位於段落的最後，表示「本季的_____也是如此」，該句話中的This season（本季）對應的是前面的in recent years（近幾年），該空格的名詞要指代的是前面提到的亞洲餐廳，根據選項可用[K] newcomers。

93答案：[N]

解析 該空後指的是50 restaurants（50家餐廳），主詞是Wokuni公司，其之間的關係在文章的第四段有提示的線索，runs a restaurant in Paris，因此選[N] runs。

94答案：[E]

解析 由句子結構可知該空格應該是一個形容詞，用來修飾fashion（方式），破折號後的內容是對這個詞的解釋，根據sushi, sashimi, tempura or grilled（壽司、生魚片、天婦羅或燒烤）以及選項可知應是選項[E] traditional，指的是「用傳統的方式烹製」。

95答案：[I]

解析 該詞前後的意思是Toru Okuda _____ Michelin stars（米其林之星），他們之間的關係是「獲得」，且需要是過去時態，選項[I] earned符合句意。

96答案：[C]

解析 這裡的private room指的是「包間」，與another six（另外六個人）的關係是「容納」，且該詞應該是第三人稱單數形式，根據選項，[C] holds正確。

97答案：[M]

解析 該空前的but是對前一段內容的轉折，即對一個餐廳餐桌數量很少的轉折，又因空格後的餐桌的數量300 seats和nearly 200明顯高於前一段落中的餐桌數量，因此這裡指的是不會缺乏餐桌，故選項[M] shortage正確。

98答案：[F]

解析 該詞位於with about 300 seats _____ and nearly 200 on outdoor terraces on two floors這句話中，該詞的線索在於後面的outdoor（戶外的），介紹餐桌的數量當然要室內和戶外的，故選項[F] inside正確。

99答案：[H]

解析 選擇該詞的關鍵在於後面的is set to open early next year at 152 West 24th Street，可知這個餐廳是計劃明年初開業，因此首句指出的distinctive imports（獨特的外國餐廳）是「即將到來」，根據選項構成on the horizon，意為「即將落戶」，故選[H]。

100答案：[D]

解析 該空的內容是對這個即將到來的新餐廳的介紹，故該空需要是第三人稱單數形式，空格後的是 _____noodles that are kneaded, cut and cooked to order，所以選項[D] features正確，意為「以……麵條為特色」。

Passage 11

The tech industry, ___101___ we are often told, is fond of disrupting things, and lately the automakers have been a big target. Cars that use artificial intelligence to ___102___ themselves, for example, have been in development for a few years and can be spotted on roads in a number of cities. And now, coming onto the radar screen, are flying machines that do not ___103___ look like your father's Buick with wings.

More than a dozen start-ups backed by deep-pocketed industry figures like Larry Page, a Google founder — along with big aerospace firms like Airbus, the ride-hailing company Uber and even the government of Dubai — are taking on the ___104___ of the flying car.

The approaches by the different companies vary and the realization of their competing visions seems far in the future, but they have one thing in ___105___: a belief that one day regular people should be able to fly their own vehicles around town.

There are ___106___, no doubt, with both the technology and government regulations. Perhaps the biggest hurdle will be ___107___ the public that the whole idea isn't crazy.

"I love the idea of being able to go out into my backyard and hop into my flying car," said Brad Templeton, a Silicon Valley entrepreneur who has served as a consultant on Google's self-driving project. "I hate the idea of my next-door neighbor having one."

Kitty Hawk, the company backed by Mr. Page, is trying to be one of the first out of the gate and plans to start selling its vehicle by the end of the year.

The company has attracted intense interest because of Mr. Page and its chief executive, Sebastian Thrun, an influential technologist and self-driving car pioneer who is the founding director of Google's X lab.

In 2013, Zee Aero, a Kitty Hawk division, became the object of Silicon Valley rumors when reports of a small air taxi-like vehicle first ___108___. During his recent test flight, Cameron Robertson, the aerospace engineer, used two joystick like controls to ___109___ the vehicle back and forth above Clear Lake, sliding on the air as a Formula One car might shimmy through a racecourse. The flight, just 15 feet above the water, circled ___110___ the lake about 20 or 30 yards from shore, and after about five minutes Mr. Robertson steered back to a floating landing pad at the end of a dock.

From *The New York Times*

[A] surfaced   [B] over   [C] common
[D] wing   [E] swing   [F] convincing
[G] which   [H] experiment   [I] seemed
[J] challenges   [K] as   [L] convince
[M] dream   [N] drive   [O] exactly

ANSWER

101答案：[K]

解析 空格處應為一個連接詞，空格處所在的句子是一個非限制性形容詞子句，如果非限制性形容詞子句與句子前後都隔開，那麼連接詞只能用as，而不能用which。所以選[K]。

102答案：[N]

解析 空格處應為一個動詞而且是原形，符合該條件的是[E] swing 搖擺，[L] convince 使信服，[N] drive 駕駛。該句子的主語是car，句意：使用人工智能自動_____的汽車，由此可知，swing和 convince填入其中，均不符合語義，只有drive可構成通順的邏輯關系，因此選[N] drive。

103答案：[O]

解析 分析句子結構可知，該句子是一個形容詞子句，而且並不缺少主要的成分，所以空格處應填入副詞來修飾感官動詞look，符合該條件的只有[O] exactly，故為答案。

104答案：[M]

解析 根據空格後的介系詞片語和前面的介系詞on和定冠詞the可知，空格處應為一個名詞，符合該條件 的有[C] common 相同，[D] wing 翅膀，[H] experiment 實驗，[J] challenges 挑戰，[M] dream 夢想。根據句意：「十幾家初創企業都在追求飛行汽車的_____」。只有「追求夢想」符合語境，因此選[M] dream。

105答案：[C]

解析 空格前的介系詞in可判斷，空格處為名詞，且與in連用，選項中只有common最符合，in common表示有共同之處，與前文構成邏輯關系：但是他們有一個共同點。

106答案：[J]

(解析) 根據句意，空格處應為名詞，而且是複數形式，所以選[J]。該句子的意思是：在技術和政府法規的雙重壓力下，毫無疑問，這很有挑戰。

107答案：[F]

(解析) 空格處所在的句子缺少的是引導述詞的動詞，此處只能用不定詞或現在分詞，所以選[F] convincing。該句子的意思是：也許最大的挑戰是讓人們相信這整個想法並不瘋狂。

108答案：[A]

(解析) 空格處所在的句子是一個時間副詞子句，該子句缺少的是一個動詞，而且根據前面的時間和became可知，該子句的動詞應為過去時，只有[A] surfaced符合。該句子的意思是：2013年，當小型出租車式的交通工具開始出現的時候，基蒂霍克的分公司Zee Aero成為了矽谷傳聞的話題。

109答案：[E]

(解析) 該句子的意思是：卡梅隆·羅伯遜使用兩個像遊戲操縱桿一樣的控制器，駕駛著飛行器在克利爾湖上空來回_____。該空格處應為一個動詞原形，符合條件的是swing 搖擺，[L] convince 使信服，convince是及物動詞，其後必須要接受詞，而且不符合語義。因此選[E] swing。

110答案：[B]

(解析) 空格前後是動詞和名詞，只有介系詞才能把二者連接起來，所以[B] over是正確答案。該句子的意思是：飛行器在離水面15英尺的地方盤旋在湖上繞行，離湖岸約20碼或30碼。

Passage 12

Social scientists have been trying to ___111___ the conditions most likely to promote satisfying human lives. Their findings give some important clues about choosing a career: Money matters, but as the economist Richard Easterlin and others have demonstrated, not always in the ways you may think. Consider this thought experiment. ___112___ you had to choose between two parallel worlds that were alike except that people in one had significantly higher incomes. If you occupied the same position in the income distribution in both — say, as a median earner — there would be compelling reasons for ___113___ the richer world. After all, societies with ___114___ incomes tend also to enjoy cleaner air and water, better schools, less noisy environments, safer working conditions, longer life expectancy and many other obvious benefits. But context also ___115___. If you faced a choice between being a relatively low earner in a high-income society or being near the top in a society in which your income was lower in absolute terms, the answer would be less clear.

If the income difference was very small, being a top earner in the poorer world would probably be more satisfying. Your house would be smaller in absolute terms, but because it would be bigger than most other people's, you would be more likely to regard it as ___116___.

It's not just that more money doesn't provide a straightforward increase in happiness. Social science research also underscores the ___117___ of focusing carefully on the many ways in which jobs differ along dimensions other than pay. As economists have long known, jobs that offer more attractive working conditions — greater autonomy, for example, or better opportunities for learning, or enhanced workplace safety — also ___118___ to pay less.

One of the most important dimensions of job satisfaction is ___119___ you feel about your employer's mission. Suppose you're weighing two offers for jobs writing advertising copy: One is for an American Cancer Society campaign to discourage teenage smoking, the other for a tobacco industry campaign to ___120___ it.

From *The New York Times*

[A] choosing	[B] how	[C] important
[D] identify	[E] signify	[F] higher
[G] less	[H] Suppose	[I] abandoning
[J] shortage	[K] adequate	[L] encourage
[M] tend	[N] matters	[O] importance

ANSWER

111答案：[D]

解析 不定詞to後接動詞原形，符合條件的有[D] identify 確認，[E] signify 意味，[M] tend 傾向於，tend後要接動詞不定式，不能直接接名詞，故排除；signify在此處與語義不符，故排除；只有[D] identify是正確答案，句意是：科學家們一直試圖找出提高人們對生活滿意度的情況。

112答案：[H]

解析 該題答案很明顯，空格處位於句子的開頭，因此所缺的詞的首字母應為大寫，選[H] Suppose 假設，在此處引導一個條件副詞子句。子句的意思是：假設你必須在兩個相似的世界做出選擇。

113答案：[A]

解析 空格前是介詞for，介系詞後跟名詞或動詞的現在分詞形式，分析句子結構可知，此處應為現在分詞形式，符合條件的只有[A] choosing 和[I] abandoning，根據前文提到的假設在兩個相似的世界裡選擇可知，此處應為choosing（選擇），與上文保持一致。

231

114答案：[F]

解析 首先，空格處應為修飾incomes的形容詞，其次，根據空格後出現的一系列並列的比較級形 式可知，此處應為比較級，符合條件的有[F] higher 和[G] less，根據後文的cleaner air and water, better schools, less noisy environments, safer working conditions, longer life expectancy and many other obvious benefits可知，只有高收入才能享受這些，因此選[F] higher。

115答案：[N]

解析 空格處是一個表示轉折的句子，應該聯系上文來理解。上文提到了高收入的重要性，那麼該句提到的「背景也很_____」可選擇與「重要，要緊」相關的動詞，而且是單數形式，matters是正確答案。

116答案：[K]

解析 首先，空格處應為一個形容詞作述詞，[G] less後要接修飾詞，可排除；其次，該句子的意思是：「但是因為它比大多數人的房子都大，所以你可能會認為它已經_____了」，important和adequate 相比，顯然adequate「足夠的」更符合語義，所以選[K]。

117答案：[O]

解析 空格處應為一個名詞，符合條件的只有[J] shortage 不足和[O] importance 重要性，根據句意「社會科學研究也強調了關注工作的差異，強調了薪資外的其它方面的_____」可知，importance在此處 更符合語義。

118答案：[M]

解析 該句子的主幹是jobs .... _____ to pay less，空格處應為動詞，且該動詞後接不定式，只有[M] tend符合該條件。

119答案：[B]

解析 空格後是一個完整的句子，空格前是系動詞，由此可知，空格處應為一個連接詞，引導一個述語子句，故選[B] how是正確答案。

120答案：[L]

解析 空格處應為動詞原形，而且應該與前面的discourage構成反義關係，因此[L] encourage 鼓勵是正確答案。

Chapter 2 匹配段落大意

Passage 1

1. The hardcore barbecue travelers sometimes try things you've never seen before.
2. I can almost see barbecues around the world, and there are a lot of unusual foods.
3. Customers can see what's going on in a completely open kitchen.
4. We can see many kinds of food on the menu.
5. People's obsession with Southern-style smoked meats has led to a boom in barbecue restaurants across the country.

[A] The scene: Central Connecticut is not famous for barbecue. But in recent years, America's obsession with Southern-style smoked meats has led to an explosion of barbecue eateries in every corner of the country, some good, some great, but most subpar. It sometimes seems like anyone who has visited Memphis or Texas or watched an episode of Project Smoke decided to run out and open a barbecue joint, but in some cases, there have been great successes in surprising places, and this column has found top-notch smokers in rural New Jersey (Hot Rods BBQ), Boston (Sweet Cheeks), Ann Arbor, Mich. (Zingerman's Roadhouse), and even the star-studded heart of Los Angeles (La Barbecue).

[B] Bear's Smokehouse is one of the bigger and more ambitious undertakings, and has quickly proven to be immensely popular in a rib and brisket-starved region. Chef/owner Jamie "The Bear" McDonald is a Kansas City native who opened the original Bear's in Hartford, Conn., the state capital, in 2015 and immediately won awards, such as the Connecticut Restaurant Association's Casual Restaurant of the Year, and the Best of Hartford Readers' Polls for both Best New Restaurant and Best Ribs / BBQ. There is now a second equally large location in Windsor, Conn., about 15 minutes away, directly next to Hartford's Bradley International Airport (BDL).

[C] Bear's is big and always busy, and has a roadhouse feel with high ceilings, a huge menu board on the wall, and a very efficient order at the counter system that quickly serves the loyal customers. It also lets customers see what is going on in a fully open kitchen. You order your meat(s) and get them hand-cut on a metal tray, then move along and add sides, drinks and sweets, settle up, then grab a table. Staff is friendly and efficient, and each table is fully equipped with the chief necessities of enjoying real barbecue: a roll of paper towels, plastic cutlery and bottles of Bear's four distinct homemade sauces.

[D] Reason to visit: Brisket, ribs, burnt ends, collard greens, Moink balls

[E] The food: While many barbecue places specialize in one or two meats or particular dishes, especially on a regional basis (no brisket in the South, little pulled pork in Texas), Kansas City is an amalgam of regional dishes and has it all, and as such, is arguably (I firmly believe this) the best place in the entire country to eat great barbecue. Bear's claims to be a KC-style eatery, and takes it even further with a menu that is actually too big with too many choices and variants. The results are a bit hit or miss, but fortunately, mostly hits, with a few home runs. The highlight is the mastery of smoking itself — while some taste better than others, every meat I try is perfectly cooked, which is not common.

[F] The meat selection is staggering, with just about every kind you will see across the world of barbecue: beef brisket, baby back ribs, pulled pork, pulled chicken, half or whole chicken, turkey breast, kielbasa, Texas sausage (with cheddar and jalapeño), burnt ends, and "chopped," a cleavered combo of the pulled pork and brisket, which is a brilliant idea. On weekends they even offer giant beef spareribs as a recurring special, one of my favorites and a rarity in barbecue. About the only barbecue proteins I've seen in my many smoky travels that are missing here are lamb and Prime rib, both uncommon.

[G] As if that is not enough, meats are offered by the pound, as plates with two sides, in family combos, and in a variety of sandwiches, salads and most confusingly, Bear's Favorites. This is an entire section of the menu with options like mac and cheese, cornbread, both combined, fries (Paw Paw's Poutine) or baked potato, all topped with your choice of meats. Then there are the inventive appetizers, which include the addictive "Moink" (a combination of moo and oink) balls: beef meatballs wrapped in bacon, skewered and smoked, and optionally tossed in a sauce of your choice. They are very good and worth starting with.

[H] There are crispy ribs, a half rack breaded and deep fried, which are more interesting than good. The ribs are not separated, it comes out sitting in a pool of grease, is one of the least user-friendly things you can try to eat — especially with plastic cutlery — and at the end of the day, the frying dries out the otherwise excellent ribs and overwhelms them with too much corndog-like coating that obscures the meat. It's sort of an experimental stare fair spectacle that adds nothing to the ribs and which I would skip, unless you're a hardcore barbecue traveler who just wants to try something you haven't seen before.

From *USA Today*

ANSWER

1. 答案：[H]

解析 這句話的關鍵點在hardcore barbecue travelers，出現在段落[H]中。

2. 答案：[F]

解析 這句話中有almost see barbecues around the world（見到幾乎世界各地的烤肉），這個出現在段落[F]中的with just about every kind you will see across the world of barbecue，因此 [F]正確。

3. 答案：[C]

解析 這句話中的關鍵是in a completely open kitchen，與文章[C]段的in a fully open kitchen是一個意思，故選[C]。

4. 答案：[G]

解析 這句話中的關鍵是many kinds of food on the menu（菜單上有很多種食物），體現在段落[G] 中的This is an entire section of the menu with options like，所以兩者吻合。

5. 答案：[A]

解析 這句話中出現了obsession with Southern-style smoked meats（對南方風味的烤肉的迷戀）出現在段落[A]中。

Passage 2

6. The image of private insurance companies in America is getting worse, because they are for profit.

7. Although per capita medical expenditure in the United States is higher than in other countries, it is relatively backward in some categories.

8. Welfare can be provided for people without insurance through change.

9. Many doctors are very dissatisfied with the private insurance companies, and they agreed with the new bill from the bottom of their hearts.

10. The new plan is not approved by everyone, and they have their own opinions.

[A] H.R. 676, the United States National Health Insurance Act, also known as "expanded and improved Medicare for all," has moved through Congress, and is expected to be signed into law shortly. The legislation provides publicly funded health insurance, with a free choice of health care providers, for every United States citizen and permanent resident.

[B] Prior to the bill's passage, the U.S. health care system was widely regarded to be in a state of severe crisis. Over 46 million Americans have been without health insurance and another 50 million have been under-insured. Despite spending more money per capita on health care than any other nation, the U.S. has lagged behind many countries in such key health-related categories as life expectancy, infant mortality, and preventable deaths. The Institute of Medicine estimates that in recent years approximately 22,000 people have died annually in the U.S. due to a lack of health insurance. Furthermore, nearly one million Americans, many who have private health insurance plans, have filed for bankruptcy each year because they have been unable to pay medical bills. In recent polls, a clear majority of Americans have said they believe government should guarantee health care for all U.S. residents.

[C] Under the private insurance system that has been in place until now, 30 percent of health insurance premiums have gone toward administrative costs, including advertising, profits, and executive salaries. This compares with a 3 percent cost for administering Medicare. Moving from the private health insurance system to single payer is expected to save $350 billion dollars each year, enough to fund health care for those who are currently uninsured or underinsured.

[D] According to the Congressional Budget Office, most U.S. residents — including those who previously received employer-based coverage–will pay less for this new public health insurance than they did for their private insurance, since there will no longer be any premium, copay, or deductible charges.

[E] Many Republicans in Congress remain opposed to the new plan, arguing that quality care is best provided by private industry and free markets. Former Speaker of the House Newt Gingrich released a statement saying: "Only market competition can bring choice and lower prices. To see the opposite trend is to be obtuse and shortsighted." During the House floor debate, some cited claims about long waits for treatment under a similar single-payer system of medical care in Canada; these claims have been discredited by most independent researchers.

[F] The medical services industry is promising to challenge the new bill. In an e-mail to investors, Kaiser Chief George Halvorson wrote: "I remain exclusively committed as always to our investors and we plan on using every resource to protect our interests, against which this measure is obviously aimed." Cigna C.E.O. H. Edward Han way issued a similar statement: "HMOs have been in business for decades. Now Washington insiders want to take away our profits, our investments, and our property. That is unacceptable, and we will fight tooth and nail to insure our rights under our nation's Constitution."

[G] "There has been a long-accepted myth, which is now thankfully receding, that if it's private, it must be more efficient," said Secretary of Health and Human Services, former Oregon Governor Dr. John Kitzhaber. "Yet our private, largely for-profit system was bloated, redundant, inefficient, and much more expensive than the better performing national health care models of many other countries. Plus, many Americans were growing increasingly frustrated with private insurers acting as gatekeepers interfering in doctor-patient decisions, and with receiving denial letters from insurance bureaucrats sitting in cubicles far removed from their medical diagnoses. The single-payer system we will be implementing under H.R. 676 will be a vast improvement over the previous, dysfunctional health care model. And it will pay for itself by eliminating the waste and duplication of the private health insurance industry."

[H] "Health care should be like water — a right for everyone. Anything less is barbaric," said a spokesperson for Physicians for a National Health Program, an organization that has advocated for health care reform since 1987.

[I] In recent years, a majority of physicians had grown tired of the growing, confusing, and sometimes disruptive role of the private insurance companies, with a 2008 poll showing 59 percent of doctors supporting a single-payer system. At an American Medical Association banquet last night, a spontaneous standing ovation occurred when doctors learned of the bill's success. A.M.A. President Nancy Nielsen, M.D. said in her speech: "We're trained to save lives. We're trained to practice medicine. Finally, we can do what we entered this field to do — practice with the interest of patients at heart."

From *The New York Times*

ANSWER

6. 答案：[G]

解析 該句中的The image of private insurance companies in America is getting worse 與 [G] 段裡的Plus, many Americans were growing increasingly frustrated with private insurers acting as gatekeepers interfering in doctor-patient decisions 相匹配，都是指的私人保險公司，private insurers意為「私人保險公司」。

7. 答案：[B]

解析 該句中的per capita出現在[B]段裡，以及段落[B]的spending more money than any other nation 與該句中的higher than in other countries意思一致，故選 [B]。

8. 答案：[C]

解析 該句的內容與文章中[C]段的Moving from the private health insurance system to single payer is expected to save \$350 billion dollars each year, enough to fund health care for those who are currently uninsured or underinsured相匹配，可知是將私人醫療保險體系轉換就可每年節省3500億美元以及為沒有保險或保險不足的人提供醫療保險，故選[C]。

9. 答案：[I]

解析 該句指的是醫生對新法案的認同感，與段落[I]中的a spontaneous standing ovation occurred when doctors learned of the bill's success（當醫生聽到這項法案成功的消息時自發起立鼓掌）相匹配，選[I]。

10. 答案：[E]

解析 該句的意思是：這項新的計劃並不被所有人認可，他們有自己的見解，與[E]項中的Many Republicans in Congress remain opposed to the new plan, arguing that quality care is best provided by private industry and free markets相匹配，後者指出的是很多共和黨人不支持這個計劃，故選[E]。

Passage 3

11. Choi's diploma was questioned because he can't fully prove the authenticity of his resume.

12. In addition to fraud, many people working in start-up companies have experienced most of the problems that arise at WrkRiot.

13. Choi's company began to show its failure in an open way for some reason.

14. Some employees are willing to work at WrkRiot, but their ideas are in conflict with reality.

15. There are a lot of examples like Choi, but we usually just learn about the success stories, not the failures of those small companies.

[A] Like so many bright, young entrepreneurs these days, Isaac Choi arrived here last year, set up shop and promised employees that he would lead them to the Silicon Valley dream.

[B] That dream is turning out mostly to be a mirage.

[C] This week, Choi's company, WrkRiot, began unraveling in a highly public fashion. Its former head of marketing revealed that the startup had been mired in chaos and had sometimes paid employees in cashier's checks before delaying payment altogether. She also alleged that Choi had forged wire transfer documents to make it look as if compensation were on the way. By late Tuesday, WrkRiot had taken itself offline. The veracity of Choi's credentials is also in question.

[D] While WrkRiot is not widely known, the startup's collapse has gripped Silicon Valley. Choi's situation may be extreme, but the company's implosion has a familiar ring to many who came west to be the next Mark Zuckerberg — but ended up instead at the next WrkRiot. Silicon Valley is eager to celebrate its success stories, but the reality is that numerous tiny startups that few ever hear about form the tech industry's dysfunctional underbelly.

[E] "With the exception of the alleged fraud, almost anyone who has worked at a startup has experienced most everything that went wrong at WrkRiot," said Semil Shah, a startup investor based in Menlo Park, California. "People don't realize the word startup is a broad concept that includes everything from a proven entrepreneur raising $15 million to a guy with money from friends and family." To an outsider, he said, "they're both the same."

[F] On Hacker News, an online forum for techies, WrkRiot's tale has exploded into one of the most popular threads, attracting more than 500 comments, including one from a poster who said that the startup's experience was "pretty much a rite of passage here." Tech blogs have also seized upon the tale; one called it "one of the ugliest startup stories we've ever heard."

[G] Choi's credibility is on the line. As he built WrkRiot, the entrepreneur said that he had graduated from the Stern School of Business at New York University and that he had worked at JPMorgan for nearly four years as an analyst. NYU and JPMorgan both said they had no record of Choi. At least one company listed on his LinkedIn profile could not be found.

[H] At WrkRiot, a handful of the startup's remaining 10 or so employees gathered Tuesday night to discuss their situation. And a few were hopeful that Choi could save the company. But by then, WrkRiot had shut down its website, its Facebook page and its Twitter account. Many of the employees are hunting for other Silicon Valley startup jobs.

From *The New York Times*

ANSWER

11. 答案：[G]

解析 這句話中出現了Choi's diploma was questioned（崔的學歷遭到了質疑），與段落[G]中的 Choi's credibility is on the line（崔的個人信譽也面臨危機）意思相近，故選[G]。

12. 答案：[E]

解析 該句話中的In addition to fraud（除了詐騙）與段落 [E] 中的With the exception of the alleged fraud（除涉嫌欺詐外）意思相近，選[E]。

13. 答案：[C]

解析 該句中出現了Choi's company began to show its failure in an open way（崔的公司開始以一種公開的方式展現它的失敗）在[C] 段中有展現，例如

had been mired in chaos（陷入混亂）and had sometimes paid employees in cashier's checks before delaying payment altogether（有時用銀行本票給員工支付工資，後來開始拖欠工資），以及began unraveling in a highly public fashion（以一種極其公開的方式），故選[C]。

14. 答案：[H]

解析 該句話指的是某些員工還是願意在WrkRiot工作，這種想法體現在了[H]段中的a handful of the startup's remaining 10，但是該句中的but their ideas are in conflict with reality（但是他們的想法與現實有相衝突）體現在了[H]段中的WrkRiot had shut down its website, its Facebook page and its Twitter account（WrkRiot關掉了網站、臉書主頁和推特帳戶），因此選[H]。

15. 答案：[D]

解析 這句話中的we usually just learn about the success stories, not the failures of those small companies（通常只是了解到那些成功的案例而不是那些小公司的失敗案例）可以在段落[D] 中的 Silicon Valley is eager to celebrate its success stories, but the reality is that numerous tiny startups that few ever hear about form the tech industry's dysfunctional underbelly（矽谷熱衷於宣揚自己的成功故事，但現實是無數默默無名的小型創業公司構成了科技行業那有些病態的現象）看出，選[D]。

Passage 4

16. Although economic growth can bring people higher income, it also causes a lot of air pollution, and air pollution is the main factor affecting mortality.

17. We can see through some examples that although small economic growth increases mortality, greater economic growth can decrease it.

18. Through the analysis, we can find that mortality is closely related to economic development, that is to say, economic recession reduces mortality to some extent.

19. Through a lot of research data, we can find that there is a relationship between unemployment and mortality.

20. There are many factors that also affect mortality during booms.

[A] The health of a nation's economy and the health of its people are connected, but in some surprising ways. At times like these, when the economy is strong and unemployment is low, research has found that death rates rise.

[B] At least, in the short term. In the long term, economic growth is good for health. What's going on?

[C] One study of European countries just before and during the Great Recession found that a one-percentage-point increase in the unemployment rate is associated with a 0.5 percent decline in the overall mortality rate. Other studies of Europe during different periods, as well as those of the United States, found a similar relationship between joblessness and mortality.

[D] This is counterintuitive, since economic growth is a major factor in higher living standards. When the economy is more productive, we have more resources to promote health and wellbeing.

[E] But a surging economy does more than generate greater income. An industrial economy also pumps out more air pollution as more goods are produced. Polluted air, it turns out, is a major contributor to the mortality-increasing effect of an economic boom. In their analysis of how economic growth increases mortality, David Cutler and Wei Huang, of Harvard University, and Adriana Lleras-Muney, of U.C.L.A., found that two-thirds of the effect can be attributed to air pollution alone.

[F] Other research published in the journal Health Economics supports the pollution hypothesis. In their analysis of the Great Recession in Europe, José Tapia Granados of Drexel University and Edward Ionides of the University of Michigan found that a one-percentage-point increase in the unemployment rate is associated with a one percent lower mortality rate for respiratory illnesses, as well as reductions in mortality for cardiovascular disease and heart conditions, which are known to be sensitive to air pollution. In countries where the recession was more severe — the Baltic States, Spain, Greece and Slovenia — respiratory disease mortality fell 16 percent during 2007-2010, compared with just a 3.2 percent decline in the four years preceding the recession.

[G] Other factors contribute to rising mortality during expansions. Occupational hazards and stress can directly harm health through work. Some studies find that alcohol and tobacco consumption increases during booms, too. Both are associated with higher death rates. Also, employed people drive more, increasing mortality from auto accidents.

[H] Some recent work suggests that economic booms may have become less deadly and busts more so in recent years. This could be a result of less polluting production in modern, expanding economies, or of better medical care for those with conditions sensitive to pollution. Safer roads and cars, and less driving under the influence of alcohol and other substances, could also play a role.

[I] Other analysis shows that although smaller economic booms increase mortality, larger ones decrease it. Japan's economic booms in the 1960s and 1970s are associated with longer life spans there, for example. Serious and lengthy downturns — like the Great Depression — are associated with shorter lives, even as smaller ones lengthen them.

[J] In total, there's little question that long-term economic growth broadly improves the human condition. But not everyone enjoys the gains equally.

In the short run, economic expansions can cut short the lives of some.

From *The New York Times*

ANSWER

16. 答案：[E]

解析 這句話的economic growth can bring people higher income, it also cause a lot of air pollution（經濟增長能給人們帶來更高的收入，但也製造了很多空氣汙染問題）可以從段落[E]中的 But a surging economy does more than generate greater income. An industrial economy also pumps out more air pollution as more goods are produced（但是快速的經濟增長不僅帶來了更高的收入。工業經濟製造更多產品的同時也會製造更多的空氣汙染）看出，故選[E]。

17. 答案：[I]

解析 這句話的核心是small economic growth increases mortality（小的經濟增長增加死亡率）與段落[I]中的smaller economic booms increase mortality意思一致，故選[I]。

18. 答案：[F]

解析 該句中有一個核心詞彙economic recession（經濟衰退），出現在了段落[F]中，且reduces mortality（降低死亡率）與段落[F]中的respiratory disease mortality fell 16 percent during 20072010, compared with just a 3.2 percent decline in the four years preceding the recession意思相一致，故選[F]。

19. 答案：[C]

解析 根據該句中的unemployment and mortality在文章 [C]段中有體現，且句子中there is a relationship between unemployment and mortality與該段落中的found a similar relationship between joblessness and mortality相一致，因此選[C]。

20. 答案：[G]

解析 該句中出現了核心詞彙factor以及affect mortality during booms，可從段落[G]中的Other factors contribute to rising mortality during expansions（在繁榮時期其他因素增長了死亡率）體現，故選[G]。

Passage 5

21. The island will bring a lot of benefits to the locals without being swamped.
22. The resort islands and the islands with lots of inns are very different in terms of treatment.
23. Tourist taxes can be used to protect Maldives projects, but local residents don't know how the money is planned.
24. Storms and sea water have a very bad impact on the buildings in Maldives.

25. The disappearance of Maldives will cause great losses, not just the disappearing resorts.

[A] GURAIDHOO, Maldives — From the foyer of his small guesthouse some 100 feet from the shoreline, Mohamed Nizar, 52, was wondering how long his business could remain viable.

[B] Last year, during an unusually nasty storm, water snaked through the narrow streets of Guraidhoo, a small island in the Maldives, pooling around the floor of the three-room house and chasing away guests. Down along the beach, the picture was even worse. Erosion of the shore has become so severe, he said, that the owner of a neighboring guesthouse stakes plastic jerrycans in the sand to curb flooding during sea swells.

[C] "What is the lagoon now used to be the football field on this island," Mr. Nizar said on a recent afternoon. "I have to leave this guesthouse if it keeps eroding. I am sure of it." "What is the lagoon now used to be the football field on this island, "Mr. Nizar said on a recent afternoon. "I have to leave this guesthouse if it keeps eroding. I am sure of it."

[D] Guesthouses have proliferated across this archipelago in the Indian Ocean, as the Maldives shifts away from catering to the über-rich and welcomes budget-conscious travelers. But unlike resort islands, which spend millions of dollars on constructing sea walls, dredging sand and hiring marine biologists, islands with small-scale guesthouses are mostly reliant on the government for protection from shore erosion and rising seas, which many on Guraidhoo attribute to climate change.

[E] Residents say the funds for conservation projects are available in the form of tourist taxes, paid through business owners to the government. The problem, they say, is that it is unclear where the money is going — or whether it ultimately can save the world's lowest-lying country.

[F] "If the Maldives don't exist, we're not losing just 400,000 people," said Maeed Mohamed Zahir, the director for advocacy at Ecocare, an environmental organization based in Malé, the capital. "We're losing a nationality, an identity, a cultural history, a language, a script," he added. "We're losing the beaches. We're losing the coconut palms. We're losing everything."

[G] Now, with guesthouses injecting cash into local economies and providing greater employment opportunities outside the resort industry, many hope this new revenue generator is here to stay. That is, of course, if the islands remain above water.

[H] In 2015, to help fund conservation and waste management projects in the Maldives, the government passed a bill levying a "green tax" on tourists visiting resorts. For every night booked, tourists pay $6. Last year, guesthouses, which were initially exempt from the policy, were added to the list of green taxpaying businesses at a discounted rate of $3 a night.

From *The New York Times*

ANSWER

21. 答案：[G]

解析 根據這句話中的The island will bring a lot of benefits to the locals（這個島嶼會給當地人帶來很多好處）可從段落[G]中的with guesthouses injecting cash into local economies and providing greater employment opportunities outside the resort industry（民宿為當地經濟帶來了現金流，還在度假村行業之外提供了更多的工作機會）體現出來。

22. 答案：[D]

解析 這句話的關鍵是提到了resort islands和the islands with lots of inns之間的不同，這可以從文章的第四段中But unlike resort islands, which spend millions of dollars on constructing sea walls, dredging sand and hiring marine biologists, islands with small-scale guesthouses are mostly reliant on the government for protection from shore erosion and rising seas（不像那些高級度假村所在的島嶼可以花費數百萬的美元建造海堤、疏浚泥沙、雇用海洋生物學家，遍布民宿的島嶼則主要靠政府來防止海岸侵蝕和海平面上升）看出，故選[D]。

23. 答案：[E]

解析 這句話的關鍵是Tourist taxes（旅遊稅），只有在段落[E]中有體現。

24. 答案：[B]

解析 該句話中提到了暴風雨和海水對馬爾地夫建築的影響，可從文章的[B]段中體現出來，例如 Last year, during an unusually nasty storm（異常強烈的暴風雨）和pooling around the floor of the three-room house（淹沒了這個三居室的地板）以及owner of a neighboring guesthouse stakes plastic jerrycans in the sand to curb flooding during sea swells（一家民宿的老闆在沙子下埋下塑料容器防止漲潮的時候淹水）。故選[B]。

25. 答案：[F]

解析 該句話提到了馬爾地夫消失會引起損失，這與文章中[F]段落的If the Maldives don't exist和 we're not losing just 400,000 people相吻合，因此選[F]。

Passage 6

26. The intense theatrical spirit of Yogyakarta has created many artists, whose unique style has brought them very high returns.

27. The city has a variety of activities on weekends almost every weekend, including formal and informal activities, and if you walk into the business block, it will give you a different feeling.

28. The city is remote, but the organization still actively condemns extremism and intolerance in the world.

29. Yogyakarta serves as the rural center of power and art to provide official ceremonies and some routines.

30. Java has a wealth of court art, and these traditional cultures have undergone many hardships and have not disappeared.

[A] After the tropical thunder rolls across south Java comes the rain, and each drop has a character. Some sweep across the bamboo roof in high-pitched volleys, and some plop into the puddles one by one, luminous, like silver. Others hit the dried banana leaves with a solid, resonant thunk.

[B] In early Java, they heard music in these sounds and rhythms. They refined it over the centuries into a complex, ethereal form of auditory theater that needs as many as 10 instruments at once, so expansive in tones and harmonies that it cannot fit into any Western style of notation. By now you hear gamelan all over this ancient capital, from the airport public address system to the marbled palace of the local sultan.

[C] All of Java's courtly arts, including shadow puppetry and classical dance, first flourished Yogyakarta. They made this small city the heartland of traditional Javanese culture, protected during colonization, wartime, occupation, revolution and years of authoritarian rule. And now, as Indonesia's voters turn away from the past and reach out for an uncertain but promising future, Yogyakarta has emerged as one of the world's most vibrant centers of artistic innovation and risk-taking.

[D] This remote provincial city could even play a part in healing a terror-weary world. Not long before the recent attacks in Jakarta, it was here that the world's largest Islamic organization started a global campaign to repudiate extremism and intolerance, from the madrasa named for a local saint who preached a pluralistic, tolerant form of Islam in the 16th century. There's even a Muslim academy for transgendered people here, the only one in the country.

[E] Little known in the West but familiar throughout Southeast Asia, the city known simply as Yogja (pronounce the 'Y' as 'J') has been a royal center of art and power since the eighth century, even after Dutch colonials made Jakarta the capital. With several major universities, it has always attracted an artsy, intellectual crowd. As an ancient city and the last remaining sultanate in the country, it has long nurtured the presentations that, for Javanese, give symbolic form to everything from official ritual to the routines of daily life.

[F] Mr. Miroto was born and raised in this city, where dance class is required in high school. Since then he has toured the world and won praise with acclaimed choreographers such as Pina Bausch and Peter Sellars.

閱讀實踐──整體掌握文章

His own dancing draws on the rich vocabulary of classical Javanese movement, pulling together its rapid, angular, formal phrases into fluid, emphatic statements of personal experience rather than collective myth. Rather than remaining in Berlin or Los Angeles where he studied, he started the Miroto Dance Company, building an arts campus around this high-roofed studio, clad in aged coconut trunks. A performance here may start on a traditional stage or outdoors, on a terrace that lets dancers overflow across the nearby stream, wandering among torches and foliage, or splashing in a pool fed by a waterfall.

[G] The theatrical spirit runs so strong in Yogyakarta that it has energized the figurative arts as well. Local painters such as Agung Kurniawan, the duo known as Indieguerillas, and the puppet maker and cartoonist Eko Nugroho offer an emphatic, whimsical yet brutal approach that can deliver scabrous commentary on politics and pop culture. As contemporary art of Southeast Asia attracts more attention all over the world, these locals have become global stars, with prices soon to follow.

[H] With the national dance institute based here, there are events almost every weekend, ranging from formal productions to pop-up events. Just this year, the weekly dance performance at the kraton features a rotating series of the area's top troupes. Don't be deterred by the scruffy entrance to the kraton off the bustling shopping district of Malioboro Street; once you are inside, it gets much nicer, with uniformed guides.

From *The New York Times*

ANSWER

26. 答案：[G]

解析 這句話中的關鍵詞是theatrical spirit（戲劇精神）出現在段落[G]中，且段落[G]中的these locals have become global stars, with prices soon to follow（這些當地藝術家成了全球明星，其作品的價格也跟著上漲）與該句中的very high returns相關，故選[G]。

27. 答案：[H]

解析 該句中提到了這個城市在周末有很多活動，與段落[H]中的With the national dance institute based here, there are events almost every weekend, ranging from formal productions to pop-up events（因為國家舞蹈學院坐落在這裡，這個城市幾乎每個周末都有很多活動，從正式的到臨時的活動應有盡有）相聯繫，這句話中的different feeling指的就是走進商業街區和入口的不一樣的感覺。

28. 答案：[D]

解析 根據該句話中的關鍵詞彙，remote（偏遠），organization（組織）以及extremism and intolerance（極端主義和不寬容行為），可與這篇文章中段落[D]

的內容吻合。

29. 答案：[E]

解析 該句話中的official ceremonies（官方典禮）是關鍵詞，可從段落[E]中找出official ritual，又因段落[E]中的Yogja has been a royal center of art and power與該句中的serves as the rural center of power意思相近，因此[E]正確。

30. 答案：[C]

解析 這句話中的court art，出現在這篇文章的段落[C]中，又因 段落[C]中的They made this small city the heartland of traditional Javanese culture, protected during colonization, wartime, occupation, revolution and years of authoritarian rule（他們讓這個城市成為爪哇傳統文化的心臟，在經歷了殖民、戰爭、占領、革命和多年的專制統治後依然被保存）與句子中的have not disappeared意思一致，因此[C]正確。

Passage 7

31. Some patents didn't take place because of the flawed patent system.
32. Because the patent system does not bring innovation and prosperity, it is not worth the money.
33. The patents were originally used to spur innovation, but here they are a profit-making tool for some people.
34. Patents on agriculture are not as promising as people think, and agricultural productivity is growing as slowly as ever.
35. Some examples prove that we cannot abolish the patent system.

[A] Ideas fuel the economy. Today's patent systems are a rotten way of rewarding them.

[B] In 1970 the United States recognized the potential of crop science by broadening the scope of patents in agriculture. Patents are supposed to reward inventiveness, so that should have galvanized progress. Yet, despite providing extra protection, that change and a further broadening of the regime in the 1980s led neither to more private research into wheat nor to an increase in yields. Overall, the productivity of American agriculture continued its gentle upward climb, much as it had before.

[C] In other industries, too, stronger patent systems seem not to lead to more innovation. That alone would be disappointing, but the evidence suggests something far worse.

[D] Patents are supposed to spread knowledge, by obliging holders to lay out their innovation for all to see; they often fail, because patent-lawyers are masters of obfuscation. Instead, the system has created a parasitic ecology of trolls and defensive patent-holders, who aim to block innovation, or at least to stand in its way unless they can grab a share of the spoils.

An early study found that newcomers to the semiconductor business had to buy licenses from incumbents for as much as $200m. Patents should spur bursts of innovation; instead, they are used to lock in incumbents' advantages.

[E] The patent system is expensive. A decade-old study reckons that in 2005, without the temporary monopoly patents bestow, America might have saved three-quarters of its $210 billion bill for prescription drugs. The expense would be worth it if patents brought innovation and prosperity. They don't.

[F] Innovation fuels the abundance of modern life. From Google's algorithms to a new treatment for cystic fibrosis, it underpins the knowledge in the "knowledge economy". The cost of the innovation that never takes place because of the flawed patent system is incalculable. Patent protection is spreading, through deals such as the planned Trans-Pacific Partnership, which promises to cover one-third of world trade. The aim should be to fix the system, not make it more pervasive.

[G] One radical answer would be to abolish patents altogether—indeed, in 19th-century Britain, that was this newspaper's preference. But abolition flies in the face of the intuition that if you create a drug or invent a machine, you have a claim on your work just as you would if you had built a house. Should someone move into your living room uninvited, you would feel justifiably aggrieved. So do those who have their ideas stolen.

[H] Today's patent regime operates in the name of progress. Instead, it sets innovation back. Time to fix it.

From *The Economist*

ANSWER

31. 答案：[F]

解析 這句話中的flawed patent system（有缺陷的專利系統）出現在段落[F]中。

32. 答案：[E]

解析 這句話中的patent system does not bring innovation and prosperity（專利制度沒有帶來繁華與創新）與段落[E]中的The expense would be worth it if patents brought innovation and prosperity. They don't（要是專利制度給人帶來了創新與繁榮，錢就花得值，然而並沒有）意思吻合，所以[E]正確。

33. 答案：[D]

解析 這句話中出現了patents（專利）和spur innovation（刺激創新），與段落[D]中的Patents should spur bursts of innovation意思相吻合，因此選[D]。

34. 答案：[B]

解析 這句話中的agricultural productivity is growing as slowly as ever（農業生產力和以前一樣緩慢增長）與段落[B]中的the productivity of American agriculture continued its gentle upward climb, much as it had before意思一致，故選[B]。

35. 答案：[G]

解析 這句話中的Some examples（一些例子）與段落[F]中的machine（機器）和house（房子）的例子相吻合。

Passage 8

36. If the participants found lying to their advantage, they will choose to deceive each other. Then researchers will observe the intensity of the reaction in the amygdala.

37. Sometimes the researchers asked subjects to lie to study their brain activity.

38. People will find themselves doing bad behavior when the story gets larger and larger.

39. The beginning of small lies may prompt people to make up bigger lies later.

40. As the brain becomes more and more numb, the initial negative emotional signals associated with lying will gradually diminish.

[A] People who tell small, self-serving lies are likely to progress to bigger falsehoods, and over time, the brain appears to adapt to the dishonesty, according to a new study.

[B] The finding, the researchers said, provides evidence for the "slippery slope" sometimes described by wayward politicians, corrupt financiers, unfaithful spouses and others in explaining their misconduct.

[C] "They usually tell a story where they started small and got larger and larger, and then they suddenly found themselves committing quite severe acts," said Tali Sharot, an associate professor of cognitive neuroscience at University College London. She was a senior author of the study, published on Monday in the journal Nature Neuroscience.

[D] Everyone lies once in a while, if only to make a friend feel better ("That dress looks great on you!") or explain why an email went unanswered ("I never got it!"). Some people, of course, lie more than others.

[E] But dishonesty has been difficult to study. Using brain scanners in a lab, researchers have sometimes instructed subjects to lie in order to see what their brains were doing. Dr. Sharot and her colleagues devised a situation that offered participants the chance to lie of their own free will, and gave them an incentive to do so.

[F] A functional MRI scanning device monitored brain activity, with the researchers concentrating on the amygdala, an area associated with emotional response. Participants in the study were asked to advise a partner in another room about how many pennies were in a jar. When the subjects believed that lying about the amount of money was to their benefit, they were more inclined to dishonesty and their lies escalated over time. As lying increased, the response in the amygdala decreased. And the size of the decline from one trial to another predicted how much bigger a subject's next lie would be.

[G] Participants in the study were asked to advise a partner in another room about how many pennies were in a jar. When the subjects believed that lying about the amount of money was to their benefit, they were more inclined to dishonesty and their lies escalated over time. As lying increased, the response in the amygdala decreased. And the size of the decline from one trial to another predicted how much bigger a subject's next lie would be.

[H] These findings suggested that the negative emotional signals initially associated with lying decrease as the brain becomes desensitized, Dr. Sharot said.

[I] Functional imaging is a blunt instrument, and the meaning of fluctuations in brain activity is often difficult to interpret. Dr. Sharot agreed that the study could not determine exactly what type of response the decreased activity in the amygdala represented. "We know for sure it's related to lying," she said. "Whether it's their negative emotional reaction, that's only speculation, based on the parts of the brain we looked at."

[J] But the researchers included numerous checks on the study's results and replicated some parts of it before publication. The research was led by Neil Garrett, a doctoral student at University College London at the time. Dan Ariely of Duke University and Stephanie C. Lazzaro of University College London were also authors of the report.

[K] The new study, he said, provided one way of doing that, and showed the importance of considering the emotional component of dishonesty.

From *The New York Times*

ANSWER

36. 答案：[G]

解析 這句話的意思是：若受試者發現撒謊對自己有利，他們就會選擇欺騙對方。然後研究人員就會觀察到杏仁體裡反應的強弱。這句話的內容可以從段落 [G]中的When the subjects believed that lying about the amount of money was to their benefit, they were more inclined to dishonesty and their lies escalated over time（當受試者覺得就硬幣數量撒謊對自己有利時，會更傾向於對對方撒謊，隨著時間的推移，他們的謊言也會逐漸升級）看出。

37. 答案：[E]

解析 這句話中出現了subjects to lie to study their brain activity（受試者撒謊來研究他們的腦部活動）與段落[E]中的researchers have sometimes instructed subjects to lie in order to see what their brains were doing（研究者有時讓受試者撒謊以此來觀察其腦部活動）意思相近。

38. 答案：[C]

解析 這句話中出現了bad behavior（不良的行為）與段落[C]中的severe acts（惡劣的行為）的意思是一致的，且這句話中的story gets larger and larger與段落[C]中的tell a story where they started small and got larger and larger 意思一致，故選[C]。

39. 答案：[A]

解析 這句話中出現了small lies和bigger lies之間的關係，根據文章的內容，這句話與段落[A]的內容People who tell small, self-serving lies are likely to progress to bigger falsehoods（說一些利己的小謊言的人們可能會編造出更大的謊言）是吻合的。

解析 這句話中的As the brain becomes more and more numb（隨著大腦變得越來越麻木）與段落 [H]中的as the brain becomes desensitized的意思相一致。

Passage 9

41. Almost every table has a plate of meatballs, which needs to be seared for a while and requires two hours to braise.
42. The chicken roll tastes sweet. I like this dish very much, but the guests at other tables seemed to like it just fine.
43. The guests will drink a bowl of free soup before dinner, and the more it tastes, the stronger it gets.
44. The eggs are not fully dispersed, but they can also be seen flecks of white, which can be fried until they are unevenly brown and quickly out of the pan.
45. The salty flavor of the turnip spreads out like the color of a rose through dark glasses. It reminds me of the situation when I jump into the sea and get out of the water, half of which comes from smell and half comes from taste.

[A] It was the only ingredient in the omelet on my plate at Mama Lee, a small, plain-spoken Taiwanese restaurant in Bayside, Queens. The eggs had been beaten loosely, so flecks of white still showed, and hustled from the pan when patchy bronze. Inside, they were studded with tender nubs of turnip, yielding with a quiet crunch.

[B] Nothing else had been added, not even salt. "Everything is in the turnip," said Mei Lee, the restaurant's eponymous owner. The root's briny flavor was diffuse, like a tint of rose in sunglasses. It made me think of surfacing after a plunge in the sea, that half-taste, half-scent of salt.

[C] In Taiwan, you would categorize this dish as xiao chi: small eats. It's not fancy and not meant to be. And still I wanted to write ode upon ode to it.

[D] "This is simple, home-style food," Ms. Lee insisted. She is a no-nonsense figure in apron and bandanna, comfortingly bossy. Twice, she scolded me gently for ordering too much, concerned for my health.

[E] Every meal begins with a generous, free bowl of soup, which, on my visits, was a clear broth made from pork bones that at first tasted like nothing but grew stronger with each spoonful.

[F] Eventually nearly every table holds a plate of the enormous meatballs known as lion's heads, rough spheres of ground pork bound by egg and mottled with ginger and garlic. They are seared briefly, then braised for two hours until they emerge as soft as physically possible without falling apart. At the touch of chopsticks, they calve like glaciers.

[G] According to legend, three-cup chicken earned its name from a 13th-century recipe improvised for a hero's last meal, with one cup each of sesame oil, soy sauce and Shaoxing wine. Here, a more complex calibration anoints boneless hunks of dark thigh meat, which acquire a seal the color of caramel in the wok and arrive shining, adorned with garlic and swooning leaves of Thai basil.

[H] Salt-and-pepper chicken is sweeter, the skin more fluffy than crackly. As for the chicken roll, listed under Special Dishes, it has no chicken: The filling is fish paste, ground pork and carrots, infiltrated by five-spice, folded inside bean-curd skin, and fried. This also skews sweet, and comes with ketchup. Its appeal remains a mystery to me, but people at other tables seemed to like it just fine.

[I] Restaurant hours are erratic, so call ahead. The staff members take a "rest," as the sign in the window puts it, from 4 to 5 p.m. On weekends, the food often sells out by 7:30 p.m. If Ms. Lee is not feeling well — "I used to have good health, but this restaurant gives me lots of pressure" — she will take the day off. Last year, she closed the restaurant for four months so she could spend time with her parents in South Korea.

From *The New York Times*

ANSWER

41. 答案：[F]

解析 該句話中出現了meatball，以及which needs sear for a while and two

hours to braise，也就是大肉丸的做法，因此其指的是段落[F]中的They are seared briefly, then braised for two hours until they emerge as soft as physically possible（簡單地煎一下然後燜兩個小時直到它們變得非常軟），也是指的大肉丸的做法，選[F]。

42. 答案：[H]

解析 這句話中的關鍵詞彙chicken roll（雞肉捲）以及seemed to like it just fine出現在段落[H]中 This also skews sweet, and comes with ketchup. Its appeal remains a mystery to me, but people at other tables seemed to like it just fine（這道菜偏甜，有番茄醬，對我來說，它的吸引力仍然是個謎。但是其他桌的客人只覺得它還好）。

43. 答案：[E]

解析 這句話中的drink a bowl of free soup before dinner（在飯前喝一碗湯）出現在段落[E]中。

44. 答案：[A]

解析 這句話中的but they can also be seen flecks of white（還能看到蛋白）與段落[A]中The eggs had been beaten loosely, so flecks of white still showed的意思吻合。

45. 答案：[B]

解析 這句話中的The salty flavor of the turnip spreads out like the color of a rose through dark glasses（大頭菜的鹹味會散開，就像透過墨鏡看到的玫瑰顏色一樣）與段落[B]中的The root's briny flavor was diffuse, like a tint of rose in sunglasses意思是一致的。

Passage 10

46. Some researchers believe that the demise of dinosaurs has nothing to do with asteroid impact and they will eventually be replaced by mammals.

47. The nutrient content of ferns and gymnosperms is very low, which need take a long time to digest, causing sauropods to grow in size.

48. The researchers believe that if the asteroid does not hit the earth, it is likely to produce a suffocating atmosphere for months or years.

49. An asteroid, 15 kilometers in diameter, hit the earth and caused many disasters.

50. Some researchers believe that a new crop of grasslands on earth will increase the presence of hoofed animals and herbivores and predators that prey on them.

[A] It was the kind of cataclysm that we can scarcely imagine. When an asteroid 15km-wide (nine miles) slammed into planet Earth 66 million years ago, it struck with a force equivalent to about 10 billion Hiroshima bombs. A radioactive fireball seared everything for hundreds of miles in every direction and created tsunamis that sped halfway around the globe. Even the atmosphere may have started to burn, and no land animal more than 25kg (55lb) would survive; in fact, around 75% of all species became extinct. The so-called 'non-avian' dinosaurs didn't have a hope, and only the small, feathered flying dinosaurs we know today as birds would make it through.

[B] But what if history had taken a different course? What if the asteroid had missed or arrived a few minutes earlier? That is the scenario suggested by researchers featured in The Day the Dinosaurs Died, a recent BBC documentary. These scientists – including geologist Sean Gulick of the University of Texas – argue that if the asteroid had arrived mere moments earlier or later, rather than hitting the shallow waters of Mexico's Yucatan Peninsula, it would have plunged into the deep sea of the Pacific or Atlantic oceans, absorbing some of the force and limiting the expulsion of sulphur-rich sediments that choked the atmosphere for the months or years ahead.

[C] Had that been the case, there would still have been a catastrophe and extinctions, but some larger dinosaurs may have survived. Pondering the course of this alternative timeline is an intriguing thought experiment that dinosaur scientists are only too enthusiastic to speculate about. Would dinosaurs be here today? What new dinosaurs might have appeared? Would dinosaurs have developed human-like intelligence? Would mammals have remained in the shadows? Would humans have evolved and – as depicted in Disney's 2015 film The Good Dinosaur – found a way to survive alongside them?

[D] Some researchers argue that, even without the asteroid, the reign of the dinosaurs may already have been ending. "I take a slightly unorthodox view that dinosaurs were doomed anyway because of cooling climates," says Mike Benton, a paleontologist at the University of Bristol in the UK. "They had just about held their own to the end of the Cretaceous, but we know that mammals were diversifying... and dinosaurs had already been declining for 40 million years." Benton believes mammals would still have replaced the dinosaurs. He is an author of a 2016 paper suggesting dinosaurs were slower than mammals at replacing extinct species.

[E] Assuming dinosaurs had survived, what factors might have shaped their evolution? Climate change might have perhaps been the first big hurdle. An event known as the PalaeoceneEocene Thermal Maximum, 55 million years ago, saw average global temperatures reach 8C hotter than today, and rainforests spanning much of the planet.

[F] Another trend in the later Cretaceous was the rise of flowering plants or angiosperms. During the Jurassic, most plants were ferns and gymnosperms (which include ginkgoes, cycads and conifers). These tend to be less nutritious than angiosperms, and the huge size of sauropods may have been driven by the processing time and gut size needed to digest them efficiently.

[G] Another major event, about 34 million years ago at the Eocene-Oligocene boundary, was the separation of South America and Antarctica. This caused a circumpolar current to develop, leading to the formation of the Antarctic ice cap and cooling and drying the world. During the Oligocene, and later the Miocene, grasslands then spread across great swathes of the planet.

[H] "Slender-legged, fast-running, herbivorous mammals became common – in the past you could amble or leap off and hide, but you can't hide in the open grasslands," Holtz says. This is when, in our history, we started to see a burst in the diversity of hoofed, grazing animals and the carnivores that preyed upon them.

From *The New York Times*

ANSWER

46. 答案：[D]

解析 這句話中的關鍵詞Some researchers 和 mammals，與段落[D] 中的 Benton believes mammals would still have replaced the dinosaurs（本頓認為即使沒有小行星撞擊，哺乳類仍然會取代恐龍）意思相一致。

47. 答案：[F]

解析 該話中出現了The nutrient content of ferns and gymnosperms is very low（蕨類植物和裸子植物的營養成分很低），與段落[F]中的These tend to be less nutritious than angiosperms, and the huge size of sauropods may have been driven by the processing time and gut size needed to digest them efficiently（這些植物比蕨類植物營養低，由於消化時間和消化所需的腸道尺寸來有效地消化食物促使了蜥腳類恐龍體型的增大）吻合，因此選[F]。

48. 答案：[B]

解析 這句話是在假設小行星沒有撞擊地球的情況（if the asteroid does not hit the earth），這個話題出現在段落[B]中，與What if the asteroid had missed or arrived a few minutes earlier?（假如小行星錯過了地球，或者提早幾分鐘來到又會怎樣？）相吻合，所以選[B]。

49. 答案：[A]

解析 該句中的15 kilometers in diameter是解題的關鍵，其是用來介紹那顆小行星的，出現在段落[A] 中，從When an asteroid 15km-wide (nine miles) slammed into planet Earth 66 million years ago 這裡可以看出，15公里寬就是

指的其直徑，選[A]。

50. 答案：[H]

解析 這句話中的hoofed animals and herbivores and predators that prey on them（有蹄類動物和捕食它們的食肉動物）出現在段落[H]中，與see a burst in the diversity of hoofed, grazing animals and the carnivores that preyed upon them（看到有蹄類和食草類動物以及捕食它們的食肉動物變得活躍）意思相一致，而grazing animal與herbivores意思一樣，因此選[H]。

Passage 11

51. The exceptional skill was gained through the persistent hard work, exceptional motivation.

52. Exceptional circumstances contributed to exceptional performances.

53. Learning how to use Microsoft's software created an inertia in Microsoft's favour.

54. The key to success not only rely on one's own performance, but also depend on good fortune.

55. Circumstance is also an important aspect for a successful man.

[A] Bill Gates is a lot luckier than you might realise. He may be a very talented man who worked his way up from college dropout to the top spot on the list of the world's richest people. But his extreme success perhaps tells us more about the importance of circumstances beyond his control than it does about how skill and perseverance are rewarded.

[B] We often fall for the idea that the exceptional performers are the most skilled or talented. But this is flawed. Exceptional performances tend to occur in exceptional circumstances. Top performers are often the luckiest people, who have benefited from being at the right place and right time. They are what we call outliers, whose performances may be examples set apart from the system that everyone else works within.

[C] Many treat Gates, and other highly successful people like him, as deserving of huge attention and reward, as people from whom we could learn a lot about how to succeed. But assuming life's "winners" got there from performance alone is likely to lead to disappointment. Even if you could imitate everything Gates did, you would not be able to replicate his initial good fortune.

[D] For example, Gates's upper-class background and private education enabled him to gain extra programming experience when less than 0.01% of his generation then had access to computers. His mother's social connection with IBM's chairman enabled him to gain a contract from the then-leading PC company that was crucial for establishing his software empire.

[E] This is important because most customers who used IBM computers were forced to learn how to use Microsoft's software that came along with it. This created an inertia in Microsoft's favour. The next software these customers chose was more likely to be Microsoft's, not because their software was necessarily the best, but because most people were too busy to learn how to use anything else.

[F] Microsoft's success and market share may differ from the rest by several orders of magnitude but the difference was really enabled by Gate's early fortune, reinforced by a strong success-breeds-success dynamic. Of course, Gates's talent and effort played important roles in the extreme success of Microsoft. But that's not enough for creating such an outlier. Talent and effort are likely to be less important than circumstances in the sense that he could not have been so successful without the latter.

[G] One might argue that many exceptional performers still gained their exceptional skill through hard work, exceptional motivation or "grit", so they do not deserve to receive lower reward and praise. Some have even suggested that there is a magic number for greatness, a ten-year or 10,000-hour rule. Many professionals and experts did acquire their exceptional skill through persistent, deliberate practices. In fact, Gates' 10,000 hours learning computer programming as a teenager has been highlighted as one of the reasons for his success.

[H] But detailed analyses of the case studies of experts often suggest that certain situational factors beyond the control of these exceptional performers also play an important role. For example, three national champions in table tennis came from the same street in a small suburb of one town in England.

[I] This wasn't a coincidence or because there was nothing else to do but practise ping pong. It turns out that a famous table tennis coach, Peter Charters, happened to retire in this particular suburb. Many kids who lived on the same street as the retired coach were attracted to this sport because of him and three of them, after following the "10,000-hour rule", performed exceptionally well, including winning the national championship.

From *The New York Times*

ANSWER

51. 答案：[G]

解析 文章中[G]段裡多次出現exceptional skill，且根據many exceptional performers still gained their exceptional skill through hard work, exceptional motivation和through persistent, deliberate practices可得知，與句子中through the persistent hard work, exceptional motivation最匹配，都表達了獲得卓越技能

的方法，故選[G]。

52. 答案：[B]

解析 在[B]段中，Exceptional performances tend to occur in exceptional circumstances是本段的主旨句，與句子中 Exceptional circumstances contributed to exceptional performances（卓越的環境造就了卓越的成就）吻合，故選[B]。

53. 答案：[E]

解析 該句話中出現了Microsoft's software和inertia關鍵詞，與段落[E]中This created an inertia in Microsoft's favour.（這就形成了一種對微軟有利的惰性）相匹配，而且段落中第一句也提到 Microsoft's software，故選[E]。

54. 答案：[C]

解析 該句話中performance和good fortune是關鍵詞，出現在段落[C]中，根據performance alone is likely to lead to disappointment（完全是憑藉自身的能力，那可能就會失望而歸）和you would not be able to replicate his initial good fortune（也無法複製他當初的好運）可知，成功的秘訣不僅依靠自身能力，而且依靠好運氣，故選[C]。

55. 答案：[F]

解析 在段落[F]中，多次出現success，根據關鍵詞circumstance定位到段落[F]中，Talent and effort are likely to be less important than circumstances（與環境相比，天賦和努力或許就顯得沒那麼重要了）和he could not have been so successful without the latter（如果缺乏有利的環境，他就無法取得這麼大的成功）可知，環境因素對於成功來說依然非常重要，故選[F]。

Passage 12

56. A face-to-face language exposure is very important when learning a language for young children.
57. Caretakers who speak a foreign language can provide some benefits for the child in studying that language.
58. The child can learn the two different languages.
59. The language ability of children is gained through a good deal of effort and massive exposure to that language.
60. Learning a different language can help the language ability of children.

[A] Highly competent bilingualism is probably more common in other countries since many children growing up in the United States aren't exposed to other languages. But the steps along the road toward bilingualism can help a child's overall facility with language. And early exposure to more than one language can confer certain advantages, especially in terms of facility with forming the sounds in that language.

[B] But parents should not assume that young children's natural language abilities will lead to true grown-up language skills without a good deal of effort. Erika Hoff, a developmental psychologist who is a professor at Florida Atlantic University and the lead author of a 2015 review article on bilingual development, said: "For everybody trying to raise a bilingual child, whatever your background and reason, it's very important to realize that acquiring a language requires massive exposure to that language."

[C] Pediatricians routinely advise parents to talk as much as possible to their young children, to read to them and sing to them. Part of the point is to increase their language exposure, a major concern even for children growing up with only one language. And in order to foster language development, the exposure has to be person-to-person; screen time doesn't count for learning language in young children — even one language — though kids can learn content and vocabulary from educational screen time later on. "For bilingual development, the child will need exposure to both languages," Dr. Hoff said, "and that's really difficult in a monolingual environment, which is what the U.S. is."

[D] Pediatricians advise non-English-speaking parents to read aloud and sing and tell stories and speak with their children in their native languages, so the children get that rich and complex language exposure, along with sophisticated content and information, rather than the more limited exposure you get from someone speaking a language in which the speaker is not entirely comfortable.

[E] Parents come up with all kinds of strategies to try to promote this kind of exposure. Some families decide that each parent will speak a different language to the child. But the child will be able to sort out the two languages even if both parents speak them both, Dr. Hoff said. "There is certainly no research to suggest that children need to have languages lined up with speakers or they get confused." On the other hand, that rule could be a way of making sure that the non-English language is used.

[F] If a child grows up with caretakers who speak a foreign language — perhaps a Chinese au pair or a French nanny — the child may see some benefits down the road in studying that language. But if a child grows up speaking that second language — Korean, say — with cousins and grandparents, attending a "Saturday School" that emphasizes the language and the culture, listening to music and even reading books in that language, and visits Korea along the way, that child will end up with a much stronger sense of the language.

From *The New York Times*

ANSWER

56. 答案：[C]

解析 在段落[C]中出現了the exposure has to be person-to-person，此句話剛好與句子中的a face-to-face language exposure相對應，都是表達面對面的語言接觸之意，在段落[C]中Part of the point is to increase their language exposure（這樣做的一個原因是增加他們接觸語言的機會）可知，面對面的語言接觸對幼兒的語言學習很重要，故選[C]。

57. 答案：[F]

解析 該句中Caretakers和foreign language是關鍵詞，在文中可以對應到[F]段落，根據If a child grows up with caretakers who speak a foreign language（如果一個孩子成長期間有一個說外語的看護人）和the child may see some benefits down the road in studying that language（對孩子將來學習相應語言是有益處的）可得知，外語看護人對孩子學習相應語言有益，故選[F]。

58. 答案：[E]

解析 根據段落[E]中 the child will be able to sort out the two languages even if both parents speak them both（即便父母都是兩種語言同時使用，孩子也是能應付的），與句子中3內容相符合。

59. 答案：[B]

解析 該句中the language ability 是核心詞彙，出現在段落[B]中，而且young children's natural language abilities will lead to true grown-up language skills without a good deal of effort（兒童天生的語言能力，不需經過艱苦的努力就能轉化為真正的成人語言技能）和acquiring a language requires massive exposure to that language（要想掌握一門語言，必須大量接觸這門語言）可得知，兒童的語言能力需要通過大量努力和大量的接觸獲得，故選[B]。

60. 答案：[A]

解析 根據段落[A]中 the steps along the road toward bilingualism can help a child's overall facility with language（在獲取雙語能力的過程中，對一個孩子的整體語言能力是有幫助的）和early exposure to more than one language can confer certain advantages（盡早接觸超過一種語言也可以帶來某種優勢）可得知，學習不同的語言有助於提高兒童的語言能力，因此與句子內容相符。

Passage 1

[A] Technology is opening up more possibilities.

[B] Definitions of supply-chain finance abound and its scale is hard to pin down.

[C] Once approved by Sainsbury's, its invoices are loaded onto the supermarket's supply-chain finance platform, run by Prime Revenue, an American company.

[D] No bank is involved, though the firm has recently teamed up with Citigroup.

[E] Suppliers, of course, have always needed finance for the gap between production and payment.

[F] Smaller local banks, however, may lose out as the market expands, and suppliers spurn them to borrow more cheaply from larger lenders.

[G] However, not every bank will win. The smaller fry in the world's supply chains just might.

[H] More banks are setting up programmes.

In 2015 Kiddyum, a small company from Manchester that provides frozen ready-meals for children, won a contract from Sainsbury's, a big British supermarket chain. Jayne Hynes, the founder, was delighted. But sudden success might have choked Kiddyum's cashflow. Sainsbury's pays its suppliers in 60 days.

In fact Kiddyum gets its cash within a few days. (1) The Royal Bank of Scotland (RBS) picks up the bills, paying Kiddyum early. Kiddyum pays a fee which, Ms Hynes says, is a small fraction of the cost of a normal loan. Sainsbury's pays RBS when the invoice falls due. (2) Traditionally, they could borrow on their own account, or sell their receivables—unpaid invoices—at a discount to businesses known as factors. Modern supply-chain finance, now some 25-years-old, also lets suppliers piggyback on the creditworthiness—and lower borrowing costs—of big corporate customers. Cash replaces receivables on their balance-sheets. Buyers can lengthen payment terms (from 60 to 90 days, say), knowing suppliers are less likely to fail for want of cash. Banks acquire good-quality assets.

(3) But it is agreed that it is growing fast. BCR Publishing, which reports on the industry annually, estimates that at the end of 2014 banks and factoring operations had € 40bn-50bn ($48bn-60bn) of "funds in use". Thomas Olsen of Bain, a consulting firm, reckons (on a broader definition) that the market is

expanding by 15-25% a year in the Americas and by 30-50% in Asia, with food and retailing among the most active industries. Naveed Sultan, who heads Citigroup's trade-finance and treasury divisions, says supply-chain finance is the fastest-growing area of his trade business.

Unmet demand looks enormous. Even domestic supply chains are extensive. A new study by Mercedes Delgado of MIT's Sloan School and Karen Mills of Harvard Business School finds that American firms supplying other firms employ 44m people. Of those, employers of 26.8m are involved in international trade. So far financing programmes have largely focused on big corporations and their first-tier suppliers. Among the obstacles to growth are know-your customer and anti-money-laundering rules. The Asian Development Bank estimates the annual global "finance gap" in trade finance, a related field, at $1.5trn. Anand Pande, head of supply chain finance at iGTB, which provides technology to banks, calls supply-chain finance "a land of unrealised promise".

That is true for both banks and borrowers. Eric Li of Coalition, a research firm, forecasts that this year large banks' revenues from programmes instigated by big buyers will be $2.8bn, 28% more than in 2010. If supplier-led finance is included, growth has been just 18%, far less than for lending volumes. Margins have been squeezed. The market is fragmented, Mr Li notes. After the financial crisis, many banks cut back their foreign operations.

Banks are not, in fact, being overthrown by technological upstarts—as, say, high-street retailers have been by Amazon. Symbiosis is the rule. Two big banks, HSBC and Santander, have allied with Tradeshift, an invoicing, finance and procurement network that connects over 1.5m buyers and suppliers worldwide. HSBC has also joined forces with GT Nexus, a global supply-chain management platform. Banks can tap into a new pool of customers; companies in the tech firms' networks can find finance more easily. (4)

More is in the pipeline: banks are exploring, for example, how blockchain technology might align the flow of data and money more closely with the flow of goods. Bain's Mr Olsen sees several business models emerging, some led by single banks, some by groups of them, and others by platforms, big companies and e-commerce firms such as Amazon and Alibaba. (5)

From *The Economist*

ANSWER

1. 答案：[C]

解析 該空格前的內容是In fact Kiddyum gets its cash within a few days（事實上，Kiddyum在幾天內就能得到現金），空格後的內容提到了Sainsbury's pays RBS when the invoice falls due（當發票到期時森寶利需要支付RBS費用），而發票不是憑空出現的，根據選項[C]項的內容連接了前後的內容。

2. 答案：[E]

解析 該空格於段落的首句，後面的內容指的是獲得資金鏈的方式，根據選項，[E]的內容可引導出具體的獲得方式。

3. 答案：[B]

解析 由空格後的but可知後面的內容與空格處的內容是轉折的關系，but後的內容是：「人們一致認為，它正在快速增長」，因此前面的內容應表現出「不同」，縱觀選項只有[B]項是在說供應鏈金融的定義有很多，很難對其下定義，後面就緊跟but後的內容，符合文章意思。

4. 答案：[F]

解析 該空格的位置是在段落的最後，要與前面的內容有關聯或者起承上啟下的作用，該段落的大致意思是在講述銀行沒有被科技新秀推翻，用匯豐銀行和桑坦德銀行作了例子；以及銀行可以通過各種方式找到融資。根據選項，[D]、[F]、[G]和[H]提到了銀行，可先排除[D]，因該段沒有出現Citigroup（花旗銀行），[H]項的意思是：更多的銀行在制定方案，顯然與該段落的意思不一致，[G]項的Not every bank will win，其中的win沒有可指代的意思，只有[F]中的Smaller local banks是與匯豐和桑坦德這些大銀行相比的較小銀行。

5. 答案：[G]

解析 該空格的位置是在段落的最後，由該段落中Bain's Mr Olsen sees several business models emerging, some led by single banks, some by groups of them, and others by platforms, big companies and e-commerce firms such as Amazon and Alibaba，可知銀行出現了新興的商業模式，一些是由單一銀行主導，一些是由銀行集團領導，另一些是電子商務公司，根據選項提及銀行的只有[G] 和[H]，[G]項中的not every bank will win指的就是並不是每一家公司都能達到提到的這三種模式，因此選[G]。

Passage 2

[A] We do it more if we see other people doing it.

[B] Over all, I found that I struggled more with the small instances of honesty, rather than the big.

[C] Could upping my personal honesty light up a pleasure center in my own brain?

[D] My social media self wasn't a lie, but if I was going to focus on truly honest behavior, it seemed better not to indulge too much.

[E] She lost interest about halfway through my explanation, which was OK. with me.

[F] My journal pointed these instances out to me rather starkly.

[G] My plan was to jot down different instances throughout the day where I had to make a choice about honesty and notice how it felt.

[H] After all, the brutal truth can be painful, but people need to know it if they are to improve their performance, especially in a work or school situation.

I've been keeping an honesty journal for the past several months. With honesty much in the news lately — you might even say honesty is having a cultural moment — I wanted to reflect on my own. My 6-year-old daughter once told me that telling the truth made her feel "gold in her brain." (6)

(7) The day I started the journal, the same 6-year-old daughter asked me during her bath if the cat really went to sleep last year, and if that actually meant that I had killed him. I rinsed her hair and sighed, wondering if I should wait to start this honesty project until my children were grown. But I braved it and told her that yes, I had made the choice for him to die, because he was suffering and I wanted him to be at peace. (8)

It struck me that the choice to lie or be honest was often a choice between two equally undesirable things. Telling my daughter the truth did not make me happier, but lying wouldn't have either.

Still, I wondered about those little lies we tell to avoid hurting people's feelings. Researchers at the University of California San Diego Emotion Lab are looking at "prosocial" lies — the white lies we tell to benefit others, like telling an aspiring writer their story is great because you want to be nice and encourage them, when in reality you know it needs work and will meet rejection. A recent study at the lab suggests that we are more likely to tell a prosocial lie when we feel compassion toward someone, because if you feel bad for someone, the last thing you want to do is hurt them with the truth. These lies feel better in the short term, but they often do more harm than good in the long. (9)

(10) So, when a client accidentally paid me twice for a project — sending a duplicate $1,000 check a week after they'd already paid me — there was no internal debate. It was $1,000, so obviously, I notified the client. But when the McDonald's drive-thru cashier gave me an extra dollar in change and the line had been SO long and all I wanted was a Diet Coke and my kids were acting crazy in the back seat and why was this stupid McDonald's always so slow anyway... It was a different story. Even though I gave the dollar back, I almost didn't, because an extra dollar was such a small thing and seemed somehow justified. Had I not been focused on honesty, I'm not sure I would have given it back.

Even though honesty felt like a struggle, I started to like how it felt. Research from the University of Notre Dame has shown that when people consciously stopped telling lies, including white lies, for 10 weeks, they had fewer physical ailments (like headaches) and fewer mental health complaints (like symptoms of depression) than a control group that did not focus on honesty.

　　When people were more honest, they also tended to feel better about their relationships and social interactions, the researchers found. This rang true for me, mostly because I felt better about myself. I like the saying, "Everybody wants the truth, but nobody wants to be honest." I didn't always want to be honest. But I wanted the truth, and this focus on honesty helped me feel that I was doing my part.

From *The New York Times*

ANSWER

6. 答案：[C]

解析 該空格的位置是在段落的最後，因此這句話需要跟段落的意思相聯繫，該段落中出現With honesty much in the news lately — you might even say honesty is having a cultural moment — I wanted to reflect on my own（由於最近的新聞中有很多關於誠實的話題——你甚至可以說誠實迎來了文化上的敏感時刻——我也想反思一下自己的誠信情況）以及My 6-year-old daughter once told me that telling the truth made her feel "gold in her brain（我六歲的女兒有一次告訴我，實話實說讓她覺得她的「腦袋裡有金子」），根據選項可知[C]項中的upping my personal honesty以及in my own brain與其有著相聯繫的內容。

7. 答案：[G]

解析 該空格的位置是起承上啟下的作用，空格後的內容是記日記後發生的事情，因此該空的內容要與空前的誠實和空後的日記有關，根據選項[G]正確，jot down意為「記下，寫下」。

8. 答案：[E]

解析 該空格的位置是在段落的最後，要求與該段落的意思相聯繫，該段講的是作者與女兒之間發生的事情，根據選項[E]中的she可知指的是作者的女兒。

9. 答案：[H]

解析 該空格的位置是在段落的最後，前一句話是These lies feel better in the short term, but they often do more harm than good in the long（短期來看，這些謊言會讓人感覺良好，但假以時日，它們造成的傷害會大於它們帶來的好處），講述的是謊言揭穿後的傷害，也就是殘酷的真相，後面的句子要與這個有聯繫，[H]中的the brutal truth can be painful與其意思一致。

10. 答案：[B]

解析 該空格的位置位於首句，可知是對該段落的總結或者為了引出下文，可根據該空後的內容判斷，這段話主要講述的是「我」與客戶以及「我」與麥當勞之間1美元的事情，根據選項與[B]中的small instances意思一致，故選[B]。

[A] Once you commit the time and emotional energy to get your butt in the chair to write, you face a daunting task — figuring out what to write about.

[B] Instead, look at times you've struggled or, even better, failed.

[C] The best applications and the weakest don't come to committee.

[D] A girl wrote about her feminist mother's decision to get breast implants.

[E] But in a personal essay, you want to express more nuanced thinking and explore your own clashing emotions.

[F] I went to a developing country and discovered poor people can be happy.

[G] They allowed the writer to explore the real subject.

[H] If the subject doesn't matter to you, it won't matter to the reader.

Picture this before you plop yourself down in front of your computer to compose your college application essay: A winter-lit room is crammed with admissions professionals and harried faculty members who sit around a big table covered with files. The admissions people, often young and underpaid, buzz with enthusiasm; the professors frequently pause to take off their glasses and rub their eyes.

These exhausted folks, hopped up from eating too many cookies and brownies, have been sitting in committee meetings for days after spending a couple of months reading applications, most of which look pretty similar: baseball = life, or debate = life, or "(11)".

They wade through long lists of candidates, state by state, region by region. (12) It's the gigantic stack in the middle that warrants discussion.

The truth is, most essays are typical. Many are boring. Some are just plain bad. But occasionally one will make an admissions officer tear down the hallway to find a colleague to whom she can say, "You have to read what this Math Olympiad girl said about 'Hamlet.' "Your goal is to write an essay that makes someone fall in love with you.

Here's a tip: choose a topic you really want to write about. (13) Write about whatever keeps you up at night. That might be cars, or coffee. It might be your favorite book or the Pythagorean theorem. It might be why you don't believe in evolution or how you think kale must have hired a PR firm to get people to eat it.

A good topic will be complex. In school, you were probably encouraged to write papers that took a side. That's fine in academic work when you're being asked to argue in support of a position. (14) In an essay, conflict is good.

While the personal essay has to be personal, a reader can learn a lot about you from whatever you choose to focus on and how you describe it. One of my favorites from when I worked in admissions at Duke University started out, "My car and I are a lot alike." The writer then described a car that smelled like wet dog and went from 0 to 60 in, well, it never quite got to 60.

Don't brag about your achievements. (15) Failure is essayistic gold. Figure out what you've learned. Write about that. Be honest and say the hardest things you can. And remember those exhausted admissions officers sitting around a table in the winter. Jolt them out of their sugar coma and give them something to be excited about.

From *The New York Times*

ANSWER

11. 答案：[F]

解析 該句位於雙引號裡，也就指的是申請文書的內容，也可指的是申請文書的話題，根據選項，[F] 可作話題使用。

12. 答案：[C]

解析 根據該空格後面的句子，It's the gigantic stack in the middle that warrants discussion（值得討論的是中間那一堆不上不下的申請），[C]項中的The best applications and the weakest（最好的和最弱的申請）與其緊密相連。

13. 答案：[H]

解析 該空格前面的句子是choose a topic you really want to write about（選擇一個你真正想寫的話題），接下來的句子應該是圍繞著「話題」展開，根據選項，[H]中的subject與其內容一致，且這句話的內容If the subject doesn't matter to you, it won't matter to the reader（如果這個話題對你來說不重要，那麼讀者也不會覺得有多重要）是對空格前面句子的具體解釋。

14. 答案：[E]

解析 該空格前面的句子裡有分類，如in school以及in academic work，根據選項可知[E]中的But in a personal essay（個人）可與其相呼應，故選[E]。

15. 答案：[B]

解析 該空格後有一個關鍵詞failure，是從前句引申出來的，因此選[B]，instead後的建議也與前句 Don't brag about your achievements（不要誇耀你的成就）所要表達的意思相關。

Passage 4

[A] Many large grocery store chains across the U.S. offer free birds and other dinner items if you spend over a certain amount.

[B] Create a budget and decide what's important.

[C] If you want to save money, you need to have a plan in place.

[D] If you want an organic look, use autumn leaves and pinecones from your yard to create centerpieces.

[E] Tell your guests to bring something to share.

[F] The company compiled the dating by asking 1,000 participants, ages 18 and up, how they plan to celebrate.

[G] Experiment with spices from your kitchen that you would normally overlook.

[H] Costco also offers low-cost basics like cooking oil and baking powder.

Thanksgiving is the holiday for appreciating fine wines and good food with family and friends. But overindulging can be pricey. The average consumer will spend approximately $97.55 this Thanksgiving on non-travel related expenses, according to a recent survey by LendEDU, an online marketplace for student loan refinancing. (16)

This, of course, is only an estimate and does not include name brand products or anything fancy. Toss in side dishes, desserts and booze and the price only goes up. (17)

1. Party

First, decide what kind of event you're going to have. If you're hosting a party, have a potluck. (18) "It's the spirit of the holidays," says Andrea Woroch, a consumer and money-saving expert. "People want to help." And if you're the guest, don't show up empty-handed. Websites like Offers.com and Groupon. com have deals on gift baskets and flower arrangements.

2. Menu

(19) No one ever eats the cranberry sauce? Leave it off the menu and save both time and money. Instead of offering guests three variations of dessert, just pick one. "Planning out the menu by person is expensive," Lempert says. "If you try to do everything for everyone, you're going to waste a lot of money." Instead, he recommends making a list of who's coming over and what dietary restrictions each person has to ensure you're making the right amount. "You're not saving any money if you're throwing away a lot of food," Lempert says. Butterball has a cooking calculator to help you determine the right amount of food per person.

And don't wait until a week before Thanksgiving to start shopping. Stores are more likely to have the products you want the earlier you shop since quantities often run out the closer you get to any kind of event, Lempert notes. That means you might end up shopping at a more expensive store out of convenience.

3. Wine

Whole Foods has gotten a bum rap as the leader in "whole paycheck" spending. But it has a surprisingly affordable selection of wine and beer deals if you buy in bulk, including a 10% case discount when you purchase six or more bottles. Cost Plus World Market, which has locations around the U.S., also offers similar case discounts. "You can get the Two Buck Chuck at Trader Joe's," Demer says, referring to the chain's Charles Shaw brand. "But if you want good quality wine for cheap, then go to Whole Foods."

4. Decorations

Get crafty by making your own Thanksgiving decorations. Dollar stores across the U.S. have the best prices on supplies. (20) Once the holiday is over just throw them away without the hassle of storing them for next year.

From USA Today

ANSWER

16. 答案：[F]

解析 這句話前的內容LendEDU對普通消費者的一個調查，該空格的內容需要與此有聯繫，根據選項[F] 的內容是說這個公司對多少人進行了調查，故[F]正確。

17. 答案：[C]

解析 該空格前的內容是在普通消費者在感恩節這天的消費情況，空格後的內容是省錢的計劃，根據選項[C]可作為承上啟下的作用。

18. 答案：[E]

解析 該空格前的一個單詞是potluck（家常便飯），空格處應是對此的理解，根據選項[E]的內容符合，即讓客人自己帶食物。

19. 答案：[B]

解析 該空格所處的位置是位於句首，因此可根據後面的內容得知，後面的第一句的內容是如果客人不吃小紅莓醬就不把這個食物放進菜單裡，也就是說這個食物是不重要的，對於預算就能降低一些，根據 選項[B]項符合。

20. 答案：[D]

解析 這段話中主要講的是裝飾，根據選項[D]的內容符合，提到了裝飾。其意思是：如果你想要一種有機的外觀，那就用你的院子裡的秋葉和松果來做裝飾。故選[D]。

Passage 5

[A] We have a concept for this, an event where anyone joins in, and everyone here is at home.

[B] Two subway lines, the F and the 6, are within a 10-minute walk.

[C] Guests can also order from the menu and have their meal served in the garden.

[D] The group welcomes visitors to their headquarters in an out-of-the-way, bunker like concrete building.

[E] The Ludlow, opened in June 2014, includes the hard-to-book restaurant

Dirty French, which is from the same team as Carbone and Parm.

[F] In a search like this, it's hard not to run into street posters on rap events.

[G] Its stylish décor included a black and cream silk rug, with a series of varied patterns, adorning the dark wood floors;

[H] Additional items and room service are also available but for a charge.

From $295.

The 175-room, 20-story Ludlow is one of the latest arrivals to downtown Manhattan's well-established chic hotel scene, which includes the Mercer, Sixty SoHo and Crosby Street hotels. The hoteliers Ira Drukier, Richard Born and Sean MacPherson, who own several other boutique hotels in New York City together, such as the Jane and the Bowery, bought the abandoned red-brick building from a real-estate developer and spent two years fashioning it into luxury accommodations with a contemporary design. (21) The property also has a lovely garden with six tables and brick walls partly covered in ivy, as well as heating, allowing it to remain open year-round.

The Ludlow is in the heart of the Lower East Side, one of the city's most desirable areas for the hip and youthful set. New York institutions like Katz's Deli and Bowery Ballroom are within walking distance. And it is near hot-ticket restaurants and bars, bakeries and indie boutiques. (22)

There are 10 room categories ranging from a Studio Full to the Penthouse Suite. Our 235-square-foot Studio Queen had a large window overlooking lively Essex Street, which was great for people-watching. (23) cream-painted wood beams; an oversize round brass chandelier, handmade in Marrakesh; and a charming, tiny round white-marble table with two purple velvet chairs and a dark wood bed with a comfortable queen mattress.

Snug but aesthetically fun, the bath had robes from the trendy Parisian fashion label Maison Margiela white tiled walls, black-and-white checked floors and a white marble sink with brass fixtures and a large brass mirror. The shower stall had a rain-shower head, and though the water pressure was moderate at best, the toiletries from the luxe brand Red Flower made up for it.

Besides the garden, there's a lobby lounge with a limestone gas fireplace, oversize chandeliers, Moroccan rugs and vintage furniture. A small but airy gym is on the 20th floor. The intensely popular bistro Dirty French is on the entry level of the hotel, and hotel guests are given priority reservations. (24)

A continental breakfast, part of the room rate, is offered at Dirty French starting at 7 a.m. seven days a week. The three choices are served à la carte, and include a plate of in-season fruit such as pluots and papayas, a pastry basket from the French bakery Balthazar and yogurt with granola. (25)

The Ludlow wins high marks for its neighborhood feel and is a smart choice for travelers looking for an authentic sense of place away from the crowds.

From *The New York Times*

ANSWER

21. 答案：[E]

解析 該句的位置是在段落的中間，因此可從段落中找出關鍵的詞和句子來選擇匹配項，該段落是通過介紹曼哈頓市中心的繁華酒店引出了勒德洛酒店好的條件，接下來的內容是對勒德洛酒店的介紹，空格處的內容就包含在其中，根據選項，[E]中的The Ludlow, opened in June 2014（勒德洛酒店2014年6月開業）就是對這個酒店的介紹，因此選[E]。

22. 答案：[B]

解析 該空格是在段落的結尾，這就需要先把握段落的整體意思，這段話是在介紹勒德洛酒店的地理位置，例如is in the heart of the Lower East Sid（位於下東區的中心地帶）和within walking distance（幾步之遙），根據選項，[B]的內容與其內容一致。

23. 答案：[G]

解析 該句子的特點是空格後cream-painted的首字母沒有大寫，因此該句話的內容與後面的內容是並列的關係，後面的內容cream-painted wood beams; an oversize round brass chandelier（米黃色橫梁；馬拉喀什手工製作的大型圓形黃銅吊燈）是在介紹房間的特點，所以該空的句子也需要是這個內容，根據選項，[G]正確。

24. 答案：[C]

解析 該句子位於段落的最後，應與這個段落有關係，而這段話講述的是這個酒店包含花園、休息室、健身房，以及與其相關的具體細節，選項中，[C]的Guests can also order from the menu and have their meal served in the garden（客人也可以在菜單上點餐，要求將其送至花園用餐）可以看出是與此段講述的內容聯繫。

25. 答案：[H]

解析 該空格所在的段落是在介紹這個酒店的早餐是包含在房價內的，有三道菜，也就是說這三道菜是免費的，根據選項[H]中的內容Additional items and room service are also available but for a charge（額外的點餐和客房服務也可以，但是要收費）與其緊密聯繫。

Passage 6

[A] But her larger ambitions go unrealized. At first it seems that she, too, has wasted her potential.

[B] Though conventionally "successful," he dies at 50 believing himself a failure for not following through on his original life plan.

[C] But that doesn't mean their lives will lack significance and worth.

[D] The most meaningful lives, I've learned, are often not the extraordinary ones.

[E] Connecting and contributing to something beyond the self, in whatever humble form that may take.

[F] A part of that involuntary, palpitating life, and could neither look out on it from her luxurious shelter as a mere spectator, nor hide her eyes in selfish complaining.

[G] Much like a meaningful life, the completion of this book is hard won and requires effort.

[H] Rather than succumb to the despair of thwarted dreams, she embraces her life as it is and contributes to those around her as she can.

Today's college students desperately want to change the world, but too many think that living a meaningful life requires doing something extraordinary and attention-grabbing like becoming an Instagram celebrity, starting a wildly successful company or ending a humanitarian crisis.

Having idealistic aspirations is, of course, part of being young. But thanks to social media, purpose and meaning have become conflated with glamour: Extraordinary lives look like the norm on the internet. Yet the idea that a meaningful life must be or appear remarkable is not only elitist but also misguided. Over the past five years, I've interviewed dozens of people across the country about what gives their lives meaning, and I've read through thousands of pages of psychology, philosophy and neuroscience research to understand what truly brings people satisfaction. (26) They're the ordinary ones lived with dignity.

There's perhaps no better expression of that wisdom than George Eliot's "Middlemarch," a book I think every college student should read. At 700-some pages, it requires devotion and discipline, which is kind of the point. (27) The heroine of the novel is Dorothea Brooke, a wealthy young gentlewoman in a provincial English town. Dorothea has a passionate temperament and yearns to accomplish some good in the world as a philanthropist. The novel's hero, Tertius Lydgate, is an ambitious young doctor who hopes to make important scientific discoveries.

Both hope to lead epic lives. Both Dorothea and Tertius end up in disastrous marriages - she to the vicar Mr. Casaubon, he to the town beauty Rosamond. Slowly, their dreams wither away. Rosamond, who turns out to be vain and superficial, wants Tertius to pursue a career lucrative enough to support her indulgent tastes, and by the end of the novel, he acquiesces, abandoning his scientific quest to become a doctor to the rich. (28)

As for Dorothea, after the Reverend Casaubon dies, she marries her true love, Will Ladislaw. But her larger ambitions go unrealized. At first it seems that she, too, has wasted her potential.

This is Eliot's final word on Dorothea: "her full nature, like that river of which Cyrus broke the strength, spent itself in channels which had no great name on the earth. But the effect of her being on those around her was incalculably diffusive: for the growing good of the world is partly dependent on unhistoric acts; and that things are not so ill with you and me as they might have been is half owing to the number who lived faithfully a hidden life, and rest in unvisited tombs."

It's one of the most beautiful passages in literature, and it encapsulates what a meaningful life is about: (29)

Most young adults won't achieve the idealistic goals they've set for themselves. They won't become the next Mark Zuckerberg. They won't have obituaries that run in newspapers like this one. (30) We all have a circle of people whose lives we can touch and improve - and we can find our meaning in that.

As students head to school this year, they should consider this: You don't have to change the world or find your one true purpose to lead a meaningful life. A good life is a life of goodness - and that's something anyone can aspire to, no matter their dreams or circumstances.

From *The New York Times*

ANSWER

26. 答案：[D]

解析 該空格處的這段話中出現了Yet the idea that a meaningful life must be or appear remarkable is not only elitist but also misguided（然而，有意義的人生必須非比尋常，這種觀點不僅是精英論者，還是誤導性的）與選項[D]中的The most meaningful lives, I've learned（我終於明白，最有意義的人生）相呼應，空格後的they指的是那些有意義的人生。

27. 答案：[G]

解析 該空格處於段落的中間，前面的內容是通過引用理論引出了一本書的內容，選項[G]的內容是the completion of this book（讀完這本書），符合段落意思，空格後接著對書本的內容作介紹。

28. 答案：[B]

解析 該空格位於段落的最後，其句子要與該段落的內容有聯繫，這段話都是在講述特蒂斯對婚姻夢想的失敗，根據選項[B]的內容與其相關，其中的he指的就是特蒂斯。緊接著下一段在講多蘿西婭的失敗之處，剛好對這一段話中的首句Both Dorothea and Tertius end up in disastrous marriages（多蘿西婭和特蒂斯的婚姻都是不幸的）作了解釋。

29. 答案：[E]

解析 由該空格前的encapsulates what a meaningful life is about（總結了一個有意義的人生是怎麼樣的）可知該空格處是在陳述一個道理，且這段話開頭的it指的是前一段落的內容，因此這句話的內容可從前面的段落中得出線索，and that things are not so ill with you and me as they might have been is half owing to the number who lived faithfully a hidden life, and rest in unvisited tombs（你我之所以不那麼悲慘，一半的原因是因為人們以忠實和隱居的方式生活，然後安息在無人過問的墳墓中），從這裡可知其實是在宣揚一種不求聞達的態度，與選項[E]中的in whatever humble form（以任何謙卑的形式）相呼應。

30. 答案：[C]

解析 該空格的位置位於段落的中間，前面的句子是Most young adults won't achieve the idealistic goals they've set for themselves（大多數年輕人都不能實現自己設定的理想主義目標），且這篇文章的主旨是在告誡人們默默無聞不是一件不好的事情，因此選項中的[C]可以在此給人們一點信心。

Passage 7

[A] With a group of about a dozen others, they each took three or four flights during two hours on the dunes.

[B] As in many places we go in Japan, I was impressed by the number of fit elderly people who could keep up with the rest of us.

[C] That makes it a very relaxing place for a getaway.

[D] They also tried paragliding, carrying their parachutes on their backs on the walk from the boardwalk to the dunes.

[E] While Japan's system of shinkansen, or bullet trains, makes travel around the country extremely convenient, no lines stop in Tottori.

[F] There are even camels to ride.

[G] My son and husband caught on quickly, though they both had some spectacular wipeouts that left their faces covered in sand.

[H] The husband and wife who worked behind the counter told us of a "secret" beach, so we decided to skip Uradome and explore.

Shortly after I posted a picture on Instagram from the sand dunes of Tottori on the west coast of Japan, a friend from Brooklyn commented, "Where is this?" The subtext: This could not possibly be Japan, right?

With its steep hills of creamy golden sand and vast expanses ruffled into scalloped patterns by the wind, Tottori evokes a scene out of the Sahara. (31)

Although these dunes are not the largest in Japan (those are in Aomori, in the north, and used for military exercises), the sand dunes of Tottori are the largest that are accessible to visitors.

But even in Japan, the dunes are more famous for their literary connotations than as a travel destination. They were the setting for Kobo Abe's classic novel "The Woman in the Dunes," but among Japanese tourists, Tottori, the least-populated region in Japan, ranks just 43rd among 47 prefectures in attracting visitors.

(32) We live in Tokyo, a city of immense crowds and towering buildings. But when I took a walk with my daughter along the dunes, it was easy to leave behind any sign of other people.

One reason for Tottori's absence of tourists is its relative isolation. (33) But it is just over an hour by plane from Tokyo Haneda Airport, and there is a convenient bus that connects the airport in Tottori to the center of the modest city.

Most hotels and restaurants are in the center of town, and the dunes are reachable by city bus as well as taxis. As the Tokyo bureau chief for The New York Times, I had come to report on the Sand Museum, where artists from around the world assemble every year to build massive sculptures from the distinctively moldable sand. The museum is open to the public from April through early January, and it is a delightful place to marvel at what sand can do in the hands of skillful artisans.

The dunes are protected as a national park, and there is no charge to climb them. It's a great workout for the thighs — in some places the sand reaches 165 feet. (34)

Although the dunes stretch for 10 miles along the coast, most visitors seem to stick to a fairly narrow area, climbing a steep hill next to a lagoon. Even the people watching was fun: We saw a man climbing in a business suit with a briefcase, as well as a group of millennials dressed in pink bodysuits kicking around a pink ball. And, well, why not?

Those who want more of that flying feeling can get their feet off the ground at Tottori Sakyu Sand Board School (like snowboards, but for sand) or try paragliding with the Tottori Sand Dunes Paragliding School.

For sand boarding, you get a board, a helmet and about two minutes of instruction in how to bend your knees, grab your thighs and slide down a steep slope that bottoms out at the ocean. (35)

From *The New York Times*

ANSWER

31. 答案：[F]

解析 該空格位於段落的最後，要與該段落的內容有關係，該段中的Tottori evokes a scene out of the Sahara（鳥取市讓人覺得這裡是撒哈拉），這裡表明

閱讀實踐 —— 整體掌握文章

鳥取市給人一種震撼的感覺，根據段落，選項[F]中 的There are even camels to ride（這裡甚至還有駱駝可以騎），是對其的另一個驚訝，因此選[F]。

32. 答案：[C]

解析 該句子是該段落的首句，要麼與前一段話有聯繫，要麼是對該一段落的總結，該空格後的內容講述的是東京的人群很擁擠，但和女兒一起走在沙丘上時卻很輕鬆，根據選項，[C]的內容適合放在句首，that指的是前一段中提及的這個地方在日本遊客心中排名相對較低，致使客流量少而帶來的輕鬆感，relaxing place與後面的作者與女兒散步的悠閒場景相呼應。

33. 答案：[E]

解析 該空格是這段話的第二句，該段落後面的內容明顯是對第一句話的解釋，第一句話的意思是：鳥取市遊客罕至的原因之一是它相對偏僻，根據選項，[E]解釋了鳥取市相對偏僻的原因，因此選[E]。

34. 答案：[B]

解析 該空格位於該段落的最後一句話，說明要與前面的內容有聯繫，該空格前的內容是：沙丘位於一個受保護的國家公園，但爬沙丘不收費。爬沙丘對大腿是很好的鍛鍊，有些高達165英尺。根據選項，[B] 的內容the number of fit elderly people who could keep up with the rest of us（身體健康的老年人能趕上剩下的我們）指的就是爬沙丘時的狀態，與其內容相聯繫。

35. 答案：[G]

解析 該空格位於該段落的最後，要與前面的內容相聯繫，前面講述的是滑沙前需要的一些準備動作，根據選項，[G]的內容與其緊密聯繫，說的是作者的兒子和丈夫很快學會了（這些準備動作），但是他們的臉也被埋進沙子裡過，場面很壯觀。

> **Passage 8**

[A] Regulations are adapting to this shift: all but seven states have adopted net-metering policies, which credit solar-enabled homes and businesses for the excess energy they feed back into the grid.

[B] Their cost has fallen so quickly that in many places retail electricity customers are saving money by placing panels on top of their houses or businesses; 200,000 have done so in the past two years.

[C] Third, they could split energy used and consumed into separate transactions, meaning that a solar customer sells all his energy to a utility before buying what he needs.

[D] After a fierce campaign their call was rejected, though the regulator approved a small solar surcharge. Georgia Power also proposed a fat tariff; it too was defeated.

[E] It will simply eliminate some marginal projects. And by then there may be a revival of Ivanpahstyle solar-thermal plants, as energy-storage technologies improve and utility firms look to them to provide steady power throughout the day.

[F] Its backers compare it to the nearby Hoover Dam; an astronaut claims to have spotted it from the international space station.

[G] Last year it represented 29% of new electricity capacity, behind only natural gas at 46%.

[H] Scientists are now pretty sure that there are two kinds of clock at work in the body.

Though dazzling, Ivanpah and large plants like it will not generate much of this growth. The federal loan guarantees that allowed their creation have expired. More important are photovoltaic solar cells, a rival technology that converts sunlight directly to electricity. (36)And there is a lot of room to grow. "There's no market saturation in any state; not even close," says Lyndon Rive of Solar City, a solar-installation firm. Even David Crane, the boss of NRG, co-owner of Ivanpah, says that photovoltaic installations are the future.

A bigger test will come in 2017, when the federal government's solar-investment tax credit drops from 30% to 10% (unless Mr Obama can convince Congress otherwise). Still, says Shayle Kann at GTM, this will be no "death knell"; (37)

(38) At least 22 states allow consumers to buy the electricity produced by solar panels that a third party installs on their homes. This lets people take advantage of solar's savings without having to pay the hefty up-front installation costs. In 2013, third-party-owned systems accounted for most solar installations in California, Arizona, Colorado and Massachusetts.

Some utilities grumble that customers who benefit from net metering escape the costs of maintaining the grid they depend on. Last year Arizona Public Service, the state's biggest electric firm, urged regulators to slash the savings that new solar customers would derive from net metering. (39)

Julia Hamm of the Solar Electric Power Association identifies three ways regulators could help utilities cope with these changes. First, they could demand monthly infrastructure fees from solar users. Second, they could list every component of value separately rather than wrapping the cost of infrastructure maintenance, for instance, into usage charges. (40)

Still, while user-generated solar power makes utilities skittish, many have rushed to embrace it on the supply side. In 2013 they installed roughly 4,100MW of solar capacity, up from 2,390MW in 2012. Renewable portfolio standards, which in 30 states force utilities to generate a certain share of their electricity from clean sources, are part of the reason. But so is hard economics: low installation and labour costs, clean power delivery at peak midday hours and a hedge against fuel-price volatility.

From *The Economist*

ANSWER

36. 答案：[B]

解析 該處空缺出現在段落的中間，要從空缺前面和空缺後面找線索。空缺前面的句子中出現了 More important are photovoltaic solar cells. 空缺後面用and there is a lot of room to grow. 和 photovoltaic installations are the future.七個選項中，選項[B]中出現的Their cost has fallen so quickly和in the past two years. 與空格前後關鍵訊息相呼應，所以選項[B]正確。

37. 答案：[E]

解析 該處空缺出現在段落的最後，理應從空缺前面和下一段句首中找關鍵詞。空格前關聯詞為A bigger test，tax credit drops from 30% to 10%，death knell。選項[E] it will simply eliminate some marginal projects中的it就是指空格前文所述，所以選項[E]正確。

38. 答案：[A]

解析 該處空缺出現在段落的開始，需要在空缺後半部分找關鍵詞。空格後句中「至少22個州允許消費者購買第三方安裝在他們屋頂的太陽能電池板產生的電……」的關鍵詞為At least 22 states, buy the electricity，installation costs，選項[A] 中all but seven states，adopted net-metering policies，credit solar-enabled homes and businesses中恰好與之對應，因此，正確答案為[A]。

39. 答案：[D]

解析 此處空缺在段落末尾，應在空缺前的句子中尋找關鍵詞。空格前的關鍵詞是Some utilities grumble 和 urged regulators to slash the savings，選項[D] 中fierce campaign their call was rejected，a small solar surcharge以及proposed a fat tariff正與之對應。所以選項[D]正確。

40. 答案：[C]

解析 此處空缺在段落末尾，應在空缺前的句子中尋找關鍵詞。從空格前可找到關鍵詞First，Second 可知只有選項[C] Third與此對應。所以選項[C]正確。

Passage 9

[A] a neologism that describes the lackluster performance of foggy-brained, sleep-deprived employees, with sleep programs like Sleepio.

[B] His first, the Re-Timer, a pair of goggles fitted with tiny green-blue lights that shine back into your eyes, aims to reset your body's clock.

[C] I want to reunite humanity with the sleep it is so bereft of.

[D] Sleep entrepreneurs from Silicon Valley and beyond have poured into the sleep space.

[E] The product, called Dreem, has been beta-tested on 500 people (out of a pool of 6,500 applicants, Mr. Mercier said) and will be ready for sale this summer.

[F] poor sleep will make you fat and sad, and then will kill you.

[G] You can hear the loons and the wind through the fir trees, and there's the weight of 10 blankets on top of me because it's a cold night.

[H] Mr. Mercier sent me his Dreem headset, a weighty crown of rubber and wire that he warned would be a tad uncomfortable.

At M.I.T.'s Media Lab, the digital futurist playground, David Rose is investigating swaddling, bedtime stories and hammocks, as well as lavender oil and cocoons. Mr. Rose, a researcher, an inventor-entrepreneur and the author of "Enchanted Objects: Design, Human Desire and the Internet of Things," and his colleagues have been road-testing weighted blankets to induce a swaddling sensation and listening to recordings of Icelandic fairy tales — all research into an ideal sleep environment that may culminate in a nap pod, or, as he said, "some new furniture form."

"For me, it's a swinging bed on a screened porch in northwestern Wisconsin," he said. "(41) We're trying a bunch of interventions."

Meanwhile, at the University of California, Berkeley, Matthew P. Walker, a professor of neuroscience and psychology and the director of the Sleep and Neuroimaging Laboratory there, is working on direct current stimulation as a cure for sleeplessness in the aging brain. Dr. Walker is also sifting through the millions of hours of human sleep data he has received from Sense, a delicately lovely polycarbonate globe designed to look like the National Stadium in Beijing that measures air quality and other intangibles in your bedroom, then suggests tweaks to help you sleep better.

"I've got a mission," he said. "(42)" Sense is the first product made by Hello Inc., a technology company started by James Proud, a British entrepreneur, for which Dr. Walker is the chief scientist.

In Paris, Hugo Mercier, a computer science engineer, has invested in sound waves. He has raised over $10 million to create a headband that uses them to induce sleep. (43)

That is when Ben Olsen, an Australian entrepreneur, hopes to introduce Thim, a gadget you wear on your finger that uses sound to startle you awake every three minutes for an hour, just before you go to sleep. Sleep disruptions, apparently, can cure sleep disruption (and Mr. Olsen, like all good sleep entrepreneurs, has the research to prove it). It is his second sleep contraption. (44) He said that since 2012, he had sold 30,000 pairs in 40 countries.

For years, studies upon studies have shown how bad sleep weakens the immune system, impairs learning and memory, contributes to depression and other mood and mental disorders, as well as obesity, diabetes, cancer and an early death. (Sedated sleep — hello Ambien — has been shown to be as deleterious as poor sleep.)

The federal Centers for Disease Control and Prevention calls sleeplessness a public health concern. Good sleep helps brain plasticity, studies in mice have shown; (45) It is also expensive: Last year, the RAND Corporation published a study that calculated the business loss of poor sleep in the United States at $411 billion — a gross domestic product loss of 2.28 percent.

From *The New York Times*

ANSWER

41. 答案：[G]

解析 該空格位於引號內，該空格前的內容是：它是威斯康星州西北部一個包有的紗窗的露臺上的一張搖擺床，該空的句子要與這句話相聯繫，根據選項[G]的內容適合，指出在這個地方睡覺時的所感。

42. 答案：[C]

解析 整篇文章都是講述睡覺，因此這裡的mission也應該跟睡覺有關，且這句話是他自己的想法，根據選項，[C]項的內容符合句意。

43. 答案：[E]

解析 該空位於段落的最後，該空的關鍵在於前面的He has raised over $10 million to create a headband that uses them to induce sleep（他籌集1000多萬美元創造了一款用聲波誘導睡眠的頭帶），根據選項[E]的內容正確，The product指的就是頭帶，後面是對這款產品其它方面的介紹。

44. 答案：[B]

解析 該空的關鍵在於空格前的It is his second sleep contraption（這是第二款睡眠裝置），與選項[B]中的His first, the Re-Timer, a pair of goggles（第一款產品Re-Timer是一副護目鏡）相呼應，選[B]。

45. 答案：[F]

解析 該空處的句子是在分號前，可知要與前面的內容並列，前面講述的是研究結果，根據選項，[F] 項中的poor sleep與分號前的good sleep相呼應，也是研究結果中的某一項。

Passage 10

[A] It also used data about deaths from any cause, which might have included automobile or other accidents unlikely to have been affected by sedentary time.

[B] and how much time, if any, they had spent exercising (mostly with walks).

[C] Even in this short time frame, there were deaths.

[D] And they have questioned whether gender, race or weight might alter how sitting affects us.

[E] In the meantime, consider setting an alert on your phone or computer to ping every half-hour and remind you that now would be a good time to get up and move.

[F] More hopefully, the study also suggests that we might be able to take steps to reduce our risks by taking steps every half-hour or so.

[G] But interestingly, the risk of early death did drop if sitting time was frequently interrupted.

[H] You can grab something from the printer, or simply walk across the room to talk to a colleague face-to-face.

Too much time spent in a chair could shorten our lives, even if we exercise, according to a study that uses objective measures to find the links between lengthy sitting time and death among middle-aged and older adults. (46)

Most of us almost certainly have heard by now that being seated and unmoving all day is unhealthy. Many past epidemiological studies have noted that the longer people sit on a daily basis, the likelier they are to develop various diseases, including obesity, diabetes and heart disease. They also are at heightened risk for premature death.

This association between sitting and ill health generally remains, the past science shows, whether people exercise or not.

But most of these studies have relied on people's memories of how they spent their time on any given day, and our recall about such matters tends to be notoriously unreliable. The studies also usually have focused on the total number of hours that someone sits each day. Some scientists have begun to wonder whether our patterns of sitting — how long we sit at a stretch and whether, when, and how often we stand up and move — might also have health implications. (47)

So for the new study, which was published this week in Annals of Internal Medicine, scientists from Columbia University in New York City and many other institutions turned to an extensive database of existing health information about tens of thousands of Caucasian and African-American men and women 45 or older who were part of a study of stroke risk.

Accelerometers are, of course, an objective measure of how much and often someone sits, exercises or otherwise moves about. The scientists pulled the records for the accelerometer group.

281

They then stratified these participants into various groups, depending on how many hours per day each person had sat, as well as how long each of the bouts of sitting had continued, uninterrupted — 10 minutes? 30 minutes? 60 minutes? more? — (48)

Finally, they checked these records against mortality registries, looking for deaths that had occurred within about four years of the participants having worn the accelerometers and completed other health tests.

(49) About 5 percent of the participants of all ages had died during the follow-up period. (The scientists discarded any data from people who had died within a year of their testing, since they might have had an underlying illness that increased their fatigue and prompted them to sit often.)

The scientists then found strong statistical correlations between sitting and mortality. The men and women who sat for the most hours every day, according to their accelerometer data, had the highest risk for early death, especially if this sitting often continued for longer than 30 minutes at a stretch. The risk was unaffected by age, race, gender or body mass.

It also was barely lowered if people exercised regularly. (50) People whose time spent sitting usually lasted for less than 30 minutes at a stretch were less likely to have died than those whose sitting was more prolonged, even if the total hours of sitting time were the same.

The results also indicate that if you must be chair-bound for much of the day, moving every 30 minutes or so might lessen any long-term deleterious effects, he says, a finding that adds scientific heft to the otherwise vague suggestion that we all should sit less and move more.

From *The New York Times*

ANSWER

46. 答案：[F]

解析 該空格是在第一段的最後，空前講述的是：一項研究發現即便鍛鍊身體，久坐也會導致壽命縮短，根據選項，[F]中的the study also suggests that（這項研究也顯示）可知是連接前面的內容，因此選[F]。

47. 答案：[D]

解析 空格所處的第4段內容是科學家要研究的內容，第9段是研究的結果，相較之下在第四段中缺少了age, race, gender or body mass這樣的話題，根據選項[D]正確。

48. 答案：[B]

解析 該研究得出的一個結論是It also was barely lowered if people exercised regularly（就算定期鍛鍊，這一風險幾乎也沒有降低），因此研究的內容是需要跟鍛鍊有聯繫，而在這段中只涉及了人們每天坐幾個小時以及每次持續不間斷地坐多久，故空格處的內容需要涉及鍛鍊，根據選項[B]正確。

49. 答案：[C]

解析 該空格處於段落的首句。該空後的句子是大約有5%的人在隨訪期內死亡，這應該是對前一句的解釋，根據選項，[C]項的內容可作其的總結句。

50. 答案：[G]

解析 該空格處於段落的中間，空前講述的是：就算定期鍛鍊，死亡的風險也沒有降低，空後的意思是：每天坐相同時間的情況下，久坐被打斷的人們比那些每次坐的時間長的人壽命高，那麼如何從前一句話引導到後一句的內容呢，就需要一個過渡句，根據選項，[G]的內容合適，but是對首句話的轉折，也引出了久坐被打斷的概念。

Passage 11

[A] it also helped to remember that people were often more forgiving than you might think.

[B] This is easier said than done, though, so how exactly do you change your behavior and learn to embrace your mistakes?

[C] Typically, it manifests as confusion, stress, embarrassment or guilt.

[D] Psychologists call this cognitive dissonance — the stress we experience when we hold two contradictory thoughts, beliefs, opinions or attitudes.

[E] If it is clear to everybody that you made a mistake, digging your heels in actually shows people your weakness of character rather than strength.

[F] Our confirmation bias kicks in, causing us to seek out evidence to prove what we already believe.

[G] On the other hand, research has shown that it can feel good to stick to our guns.

[H] And we make our partners, co-workers, parents and kids really, really mad at us.

Despite your best intentions and efforts, it is inevitable: At some point in your life, you will be wrong.

Mistakes can be hard to digest, so sometimes we double down rather than face them. (51) The car you cut off has a small dent in its bumper, which obviously means that it is the other driver's fault.

(52) For example, you might believe you are a kind and fair person, so when you rudely cut someone off, you experience dissonance. To cope with it, you deny your mistake and insist the other driver should have seen you, or you had the right of way even if you didn't.

"Cognitive dissonance is what we feel when the self-concept — I'm smart, I'm kind, I'm convinced this belief is true — is threatened by evidence that we did something that wasn't smart, that we did something that hurt another person, that the belief isn't true," said Carol Tavris, a co-author of the book Mistakes Were Made (But Not by Me).

"Dissonance is uncomfortable and we are motivated to reduce it," Ms. Tavris said.

When we apologize for being wrong, we have to accept this dissonance, and that is unpleasant. (53) One study, published in the European Journal of Social Psychology, found that people who refused to apologize after a mistake had more self-esteem and felt more in control and powerful than those who did not refuse.

Feeling powerful may be an attractive short-term benefit, but there are long-term consequences. Refusing to apologize could potentially jeopardize "the trust on which a relationship is based," Mr. Okimoto said, adding that it can extend conflict and encourage outrage or retaliation.

Another study, from the Stanford researchers Carol Dweck and Karina Schumann, found that subjects were more likely to take responsibility for their mistakes when they believed they had the power to change their behavior. (54)

The first step is to recognize cognitive dissonance in action. Your mind will go to great lengths to preserve your sense of identity, so it helps to be aware of what that dissonance feels like. (55) Those feelings do not necessarily mean you are in the wrong, but you can at least use them as reminders to explore the situation from an impartial perspective and objectively question whether you are at fault.

Similarly, learn to recognize your usual justifications and rationalizations. Think of a time you were wrong and knew it, but tried to justify it instead. Remember how it felt to rationalize your behavior and pinpoint that feeling as cognitive dissonance the next time it happens.

From *The New York Times*

ANSWER

51. 答案：[F]

解析 該空格位於這個段落的中間，與前後的內容都要有所聯繫，空格後的內容是舉的一個例子，可對該空格的選擇提供線索，The car you cut off has a small dent in its bumper, which obviously means that it is the other driver's fault（你插隊而擋住的後面的車上的保險桿上有一個小凹痕，這顯然意味著是那個司機的錯）這句話可印證選項中的[F]，即 Our confirmation bias kicks in（我們的認知有所偏移），causing us to seek out evidence to prove what we already believe（我們會尋求證據來證明我們所相信的），與前一句的內容也有聯繫。

52. 答案：[D]

解析 該空格後的例子可作為該題的線索，其意思是：你可能認為自己是個善良、公正的人，所以當你粗暴地插到其他人前面時，便會經歷這種失調。根據選項，這裡的善良、公正和粗暴地插到其他人前面與[D]項中的hold two contradictory thoughts, beliefs, opinions or attitudes（持有兩種相互衝突的想法、信仰、意見或者態度）吻合，因此選[D]。

53. 答案：[G]

解析 該空格位於段落的中間，前面指的是：為錯誤道歉就得接受這種失調，這令人不快，空後的內容是「不接受道歉會令人感覺強大」，這中間缺少一句話來過渡，根據選項[G]項的內容合適，on the other hand指的是不為錯誤道歉會讓人感覺良好的這一方面，這兩句話也是對立的兩個方面，故選[G]。

54. 答案：[B]

解析 該空格位於段落的最後，根據下一段的第一句The first step is to recognize cognitive dissonance in action（第一步是要認識到行動上的認知失調），空格前的內容只是在講述一個研究結果，那麼如何引出這句話呢？選項[B]項的內容how exactly do you change your behavior（如何做能改變你的行為），指出了要如何做，可引出The first step。

55. 答案：[C]

解析 該空格前的內容是so it helps to be aware of what that dissonance feels like（所以了解失調的感覺是怎樣的會有所幫助），後面又指出Those feelings（這些感受），因此這中間的內容是具體的感受，根據選項，[C]的內容符合。

Passage 12

[A] Buy some old-fashioned alarm clocks for your bedside table and Put your cell phones in a basket in the kitchen.

[B] More than one-third of the 143 women in the study said their partner responded to notifications mid-conversation.

[C] And consider eliminating phone use in the car so that you can use that time to talk to your partner about whatever is on your mind.

[D] The conflict between phone love and human love is so common, it has its own lexicon.

[E] I love talking with you, but when you're constantly checking your phone it's hard to have a great conversation.

[F] When one partner constantly checks his or her phone it sends an implicit message that they find the phone (or what's on it) more interesting than you.

[G] They find us dates (and sex), entertain us with music and connect us to friends and family.

[H] Couples need to form an alliance and decide together what are the new rules.

We have an intimate relationship with our phones. We sleep with them, eat with them and carry them in our pockets. We check them, on average, 47 times a day — 82 times if you're between 18 and 24 years old, according to recent data.

And we love them for good reason: They tell the weather, the time of day and the steps we've taken. (56) They answer our questions and quell feelings of loneliness and anxiety.

But phone love can go too far — so far that it can interfere with human love — old fashioned face-to-face intimacy with that living and breathing being you call your partner, spouse, lover or significant other.

(57) If you're snubbing your partner in favor of your phone it's called phubbing (phone + snubbing). If you're snubbing a person in favor of any type of technology, it's called technoference. A popular song by Lost Kings even asks: "Why don't you put that [expletive] phone down?"

In a 2016 study published in the journal Psychology of Popular Media Culture, 70 percent of women revealed that smartphones were negatively affecting their primary relationship. (58) One out of four said their partner texted during conversations. The women who reported high levels of technoference in interactions with their partners were less happy with their relationships and with their lives overall.

It's not just women who are feeling dissed. Dr. Roberts, who is a professor of marketing at Baylor University, asked 175 men and women questions about their partners' smartphone use. Nearly half of respondents, 46 percent, reported being phone snubbed (phubbed) by their partner. People who reported higher levels of phubbing also reported higher levels of relationship conflict.

In our quest to be connected through technology, we're tuning out our partners and interrupting a kind of biological broadband connection.

If you're feeling frustrated by phone interference in your relationship, talk to your partner but be positive. "Emphasize the benefits of being more connected," Ms. Bell said. Rather than dictate to your partner what they should or should not do, try an approach such as, "(59)"

Here are some suggested ways to break up with your phone long enough to connect with your partner.

Designate "no cell" zones in your home. With your partner, decide which areas of your home, such as the living room and the kitchen, should be technology-free. (60)

Try a phone-free bedroom for one week. Yes, it's fun to check Twitter just before bed, or when you're sleepless at 2 a.m., but you might be more likely to converse with your partner if the phone were elsewhere. And just the act of favoring your relationship over your phone sends a clear message to your partner.

From *The New York Times*

ANSWER

56. 答案：[G]

解析 該空格的段落內容是And we love them for good reason（我們愛手機的很多理由），這段話的最後一句話They answer our questions and quell feelings of loneliness and anxiety（它們回答我們的問題，平息孤獨和焦慮的心情）也是愛手機的理由，故選項[G]的內容符合該段落的意思。

57. 答案：[D]

解析 該空格後面的內容是If you're snubbing your partner in favor of your phone it's called phubbing (phone + snubbing)（如果你偏愛手機忽略伴侶，這種行為叫作電話冷遇（電話 + 冷落），空格的內容要與此有關，根據選項[D]項的中的it has its lexicon（它有了自己專門的詞彙）與這些專有詞彙phubbing和technoference相呼應。

58. 答案：[B]

解析 根據該空格前後的內容70 percent of women revealed that（70%的女性透露）以及空格後的 one out of four said（四分之一的人都表示）可知，該空展示的內容還是跟研究發現的內容有關，根據選項，[B]的內容one-third of the 143 women in the study said（143名女性重的三分之一表示）與其要表達的意思一致。

59. 答案：[E]

解析 該空格的內容可從Rather than dictate to your partner what they should or should not do, try an approach such as（而不是規定你的伴侶應該做什麼或者不應該做什麼的解釋，比如你可以嘗試），可知該空的內容是在教你怎樣表達才算正確的方式，根據選項，[E]的內容體現出了告誡之後所應表現的話語，也體現出了talk to your partner but be positive（跟伴侶談談但要以積極的態度），故選[E]。

60. 答案：[C]

解析 最後這兩段的首句是作者給出的兩點建議，因此該空格的內容要與Designate "no cell" zones in your home（在家裡指定一個無手機區域）相關，根據選項，[C]項的內容符合。

Passage 1

As the $1.6 trillion Infrastructure Modernization Bill moves through Congress, a wide swath of public advocacy groups is assuring that the focus of rebuilding remains on proven, sustainable technologies that can move the country away from its dependency on fossil fuels.

The American Society of Civil Engineers has estimated that $1.6 trillion is needed to bring the nation's infrastructure up to the level enjoyed by other industrialized nations.

Brice Terra is a spokesperson for Rebuild Sustainably, a group that formed when the funding bill was initiated, and that now counts nearly 400,000 members. The group has helped keep public pressure on senators to aim high in crafting the rebuilding bill. "We must minimize environmental impact with dense yet fully livable cities, convert rural suburbs back to farmland, and provide access to services rather than just sheer mobility," said Mr. Terra.

Under pressure from their constituencies, lawmakers on both sides of the aisle are pushing for a version of the bill that frees the U.S. from dependence on fossil fuels.

"We don't want a patch that just preserves business as usual," said Rahm Emanuel, Representative of Illinois, who has been leading the push for sustainable rebuilding in the Senate. "Rather, true convenience must be our top priority."

"What we've realized is that we need to move away from the automobile," said Senator Richard Shelby, Republican of Alabama. "We need to transition the United States to a more convenient, livable, economical, and enjoyable way of life."

Mr. Blumenauer cited as instrumental to the bill's passage the widespread public outrage which began in reaction to $10 gasoline prices and was quickly channeled by groups like Rebuild Sustainably. "When gas hit $3.50 back in March 2008, people drove 11 billion miles less per month than they had the year before," said Blumenauer. "When it hit $10, people realized that the problem wasn't high gas prices — the problem was gas. Fortunately, we Americans have always had the imagination and will to meet challenges."

From *The New York Times*

1. Why do the public advocacy groups say that the work being rebuilt needs sustainable technology?

[A] Because these technologies can help countries to reach the level of other countries.

[B] Because it can wean the country off fossil fuels.

[C] Because this is very helpful to the development of the country.

[D] This is to enhance the confidence of the public.

2. Which is Terry's opinion?

[A] He wants to form a group when the funding bill was initiated.

[B] He tries to help the public put pressure on the senator.

[C] He argues that by establishing the infrastructure of the state, the state will reach the level of other countries.

[D] He thinks that people should reduce the impact on the environment and the city that is suitable for living.

3. What can we learn from the third and the fifth paragraph?

[A] The purpose of Mr. Terra is different from Mr. Emanuel.

[B] The two speakers hope to promote sustainable reconstruction.

[C] The American way of life is more convenient and economic than other countries.

[D] People in the United States want to reduce the production of cars.

4. What is the attitude of Mr. Blumenauer in the last paragraph?

[A] Prejudicial   [B] Negative   [C] Positive   [D] Averse

5. Which of the following is true according to the text?

[A] The construction of infrastructure will cost a lot of money.

[B] Brice Terra opposes sustainable reconstruction.

[C] More and more people pay more attention to life style and environment.

[D] People realized that the event was caused by high oil prices.

ANSWER

1. 答案：[B]

解析 根據問題中的public advocacy groups sustainable technologies可將其定位至第一段，文中出現sustainable technologies that can move the country away from its dependency on fossil fuels，從該句可知永續科技可使國家擺脫對化石燃料的依賴，而[B]項中的wean off表示「逐步減少對……的依賴」，故選[B]。

2. 答案：[D]

解析 問題中詢問的是特拉先生的主張，出現在文章的第三段，[A]說明了組織成立的時間，並不能表明是特拉先生的主張，可排除；[B]項中的「幫助公眾對參議員施加壓力」，指的應是這個組織的人，而不僅僅指的是特拉；[C]項與特拉先生無關；[D]的內容與文章中的We must minimize environmental impact with dense yet fully livable cities, convert rural suburbs back to farmland（我們必須盡量減少對環境和密集但適宜居住的城市的影響，將農村郊區改造成農田）意思相一致。

3. 答案：[B]

解析 第三段是有關布萊斯‧特拉，第五段是有關拉姆‧伊曼紐爾，他們兩個都跟可持續重建有關，因此[B]項的意思可從中看出來，因為他們都是為了可持續重建，所以他們的目的是一樣的，[A]不正確，[C]項的意思只是文章中理查‧謝爾比的主張，[D]項無法得知。

4. 答案：[C]

解析 從文章中出現的句子we Americans have always had the imagination and will to meet challenges（我們美國人一直有想象力和迎接挑戰的能力），可知布魯曼紐爾先生是以一種自豪的心態説的，因此是積極向上的，選[C]，averse 意為「不樂意的」。

5. 答案：[A]

解析 根據文章的內容，Brice Terra is a spokesperson for Rebuild Sustainably，指的是布萊斯‧特拉是可持續建設的發言人，排除[B]；[C]項的「越來越多人」沒有在文章中體現；[D]項應是天然氣，故選[A]。

Passage 2

Now scientists have discovered fossils of the oldest mammals related to mankind.

Researchers have found two teeth from small, rat-like creatures that lived in the shadow of the dinosaurs.

[▲A]

They are the earliest undisputed fossils of mammals belonging to the line that led to human beings.

They are also the ancestors to most mammals alive today, including creatures as diverse as the blue whale and the pigmy shrew.

[▲B]

Dr Sweetman, a research fellow at Portsmouth University, identified the teeth but it was undergraduate student, Grant Smith who made the discovery.

Dr Sweetman said: Grant was sifting through small samples of earliest Cretaceous rocks collected on the coast of Dorset as part of his undergraduate dissertation project in the hope of finding some interesting remains. [▲C]

Quite unexpectedly he found not one but two quite remarkable teeth of a type never before seen from rocks of this age.

I was asked to look at them and give an opinion and even at first glance my jaw dropped!'

The teeth are of a type so highly evolved that I realised straight away I was looking at remains of Early Cretaceous mammals that more closely resembled those that lived during the latest Cretaceous - some 60 million years later in geological history.

In the world of paleontology there has been a lot of debate around a specimen found in China, which is approximately 160 million years old. [▲D]

This was originally said to be of the same type as ours but recent studies have ruled this out. That being the case, our 145 million-year old teeth are undoubtedly the earliest yet known from the line of mammals that lead to our own species.

From *The Daily Mail*

6. According to paragraph 1and 2, scientists have discovered that this mammal
[A] lived in harmony with the dinosaurs
[B] is the ancestors of the mouse
[C] is associated with humans
[D] has two small teeth

7. Look at the four triangle [▲] that indicate where the following sentence could be added to the passage.

The findings are published today in the Journal, Acta Palaeontologica Polonica, in a paper by Dr Steve Sweetman.

Where would be the sentence best fit?

8. The word dissertation in the second sentence of paragraph 6 in the passage refers to

[A] thesis   [B] research   [C] test   [D] practice

9. Why does author say "I was asked to look at them and give an opinion and even at first glance my jaw dropped" in paragraph 8?
[A] To make the article become interesting.
[B] To elicit the following.
[C] To prove that they lived during the latest Cretaceous.
[D] To prove this amazing discovery.

10. The word paleontology in the first sentence of paragraph 10 in the passage refers to

[A] biology   [B] archeology   [C] paleontology   [D] psychology

ANSWER

6. 答案：[C]

解析 這個問題詢問的是有關這種哺乳動物，[A]項指的是「與恐龍和諧相處」，沒有體現；[B]指的是「是老鼠的祖先」，這個不正確，文章中只是說

「像老鼠」；[D]項指的是「有兩顆小的牙齒」，不正確，因為科學家只是發現了兩顆牙齒，small是對這種哺乳動物的形容，故選[C]。

7. 答案：[B]

解析 這句話中的the findings應是對前面發現的總結，根據文章，[A]項的位置把前後的發現給隔開了，這句話不適合這裡，[C]項前的內容是格蘭特在做的事情，與findings無關，[D]項前的內容講述的是一個標本存在爭論，與findings無聯繫，故只有[B]項的位置適合。

8. 答案：[A]

解析 這個詞位於這句話中as part of his undergraduate dissertation project（作為大學生_____項目），dissertation在這裡是「論文」的意思，與[A]項的意思一致。

9. 答案：[D]

解析 這句話的前後的段落意思都是在圍繞著新發現的這個化石展開，「我」的反應是even at first glance my jaw dropped（驚訝到掉了下巴），說明這個發現真的是驚人，所以[D]正確。

10. 答案：[C]

解析 這篇文章整篇都是在講化石，且後面出現了160 million years old的specimen，所以這個詞的意思是古生物學，與[C]項的意思相近。

Passage 3

After long and often bitter debate, Congress has passed legislation, fiercely fought for by labor and progressive groups, which will limit top salaries to fifteen times the minimum wage. Tying the bill to a plan of overall reform of the U.S. economy, the bill echoes a similar effort enacted by President Franklin Roosevelt in 1942, which was followed by the longest period of growth for the middle class in U.S. history.

"When C.E.O. salaries remain stable thanks to high taxation of high salaries, there's little incentive to take big risks with shareholders' money, and the economy remains in a steady growth mode," said Senator Barney Frank, one of the bill's co-sponsors. "But when C.E.O. salaries can fly through the roof, there's a very strong incentive for C.E.O.s to rake in massive dividends, often at the cost of the company's, and the country's stability."

The first time the U.S. implemented a maximum wage was in 1942, when President Roosevelt said that "no American citizen ought to have an income, after he has paid his taxes, of more than $25,000 a year," the equivalent of $315,000 today.

Some version of a maximum wage law was in effect until 1980. Before 1964, income over $400,000 in today's dollars faced a 91 percent federal tax rate, and the top-bracket tax rate never dipped below 70%. Under Reagan, the top tax rate slid down to 28 percent — a shift that is now understood to have been one of the prime contributors to the mortgage meltdown and other market failures.

The current minimum wage is $5.85 ($12,168 annually) making the new maximum wage $182,520/ year. Any amount over that will be taxed at a rate of 100 percent.

The Center on Executive Compensation is an industry-backed group based in Washington whose goal is to tell corporate America's side of the executive pay story. Richard Floersch, the center's chairman and the chief human resources officer at McDonald's, defended high salaries. "Most companies", he said, "are dedicated to a very strong executive compensation program with very strong principles around pay for performance."

In the two days since Mr. Floersch made these comments to a reporter, the Center on Executive Compensation has dissolved. A statement on their website now reads: "We have decided that in light of recent changes in economic policy, and the failure of hedge fund managers and banks to prevent massive losses despite their astronomical pay, our Center has lost its relevance." The statement also acknowledges the problems caused by Fannie Mae and Freddie Mac executives falsifying profits of $9 billion so their firms would appear attractive to investors and then, instead of being fired, receiving retirement packages upwards of $10 million.

From *The New York Times*

Questions 11-14

Do the following statements agree with the information given in reading passage. Write

YES   if the statement is true

NO   if the statement is false

NOT GIVEN   if the information is not given in the reading passage

11. The shift of the top rate is believed to be one of the causes of the mortgage crisis.

12. Most companies' pay systems are strictly governed by national policies.

13. Many corporate chairmen have very strong principles around pay.

14. As the country's economy grows steadily, the rate of purchase of the fund will be higher and higher.

Questions 15-17

Answer the question below. Choose

NO MORE THAN FOUR WORDS AND / OR A NUMBER from the passage for each answer.

15. How many times is the maximum wage limited to the minimum wage?

16. What is the factor that leads to mortgage meltdown and other market failures?

17. What are many companies committed to?

18. What about their company for investors?

ANSWER

11. 答案：YES

解析 該句話中的mortgage crisis（抵押貸款危機）與文章第四段中的mortgage meltdown意思是一致的，該句的最高稅率的轉換與第四段的a shift that is now understood to have been one of the prime contributors to the mortgage meltdown and other market failures相呼應，故應是YES。

12. 答案：NOT GIVEN

解析 文章中並沒有涉及companies' pay systems（公司的薪酬制度）受到 national policies（國家政策）的嚴格管理。

13. 答案：NO

解析 該句的have very strong principles around pay出現在文章的倒數第二段， 但是文章中出現的 是Most companies，而不是Many corporate chairmen，因此 錯誤。

14. 答案：NOT GIVEN

解析 該句中的the rate of purchase of the fund（基金購買率）沒有在文章中提 到。

15. 答案：fifteen times

解析 文章第一段中出現which will limit top salaries to fifteen times the minimum wage，因此是十五倍。

16. 答案：top tax rate

解析 根據文章第四段的最後一句Under Reagan, the top tax rate slid down to 28 percent — a shift that is now understood to have been one of the prime contributors to the mortgage meltdown and other market failures，因此是最高 稅率的轉變導致了mortgage meltdown and other market failures。

17. 答案：executive compensation program

解析 根據文章第六段中 "Most companies", he said, "are dedicated to a very strong executive compensation program with very strong principles around pay for performance，因此是executive compensation program。

18. 答案：attractive

解析 文章的最後一段出現so their firms would appear attractive to investors and then, instead of being fired，因此是吸引力。

Passage 4

The attack had the hallmarks of something researchers had dreaded for years: malicious software using artificial intelligence that could lead to a new digital arms race in which A.I.-driven defenses battled A.I.-driven offenses while humans watched from the sidelines.

But what was not as widely predicted was that one of the earliest instances of that sort of malware was found in India, not in a sophisticated British banking system or a government network in the United States.

Security researchers are increasingly looking in countries outside the West to discover the newest, most creative and potentially most dangerous types of cyber attacks being deployed.

As developing economies rush to go online, they provide a fertile testing ground for hackers trying their skills in an environment where they can evade detection before deploying them against a company or state that has more advanced defenses.

The cyber attack in India used malware that could learn as it was spreading, and altered its methods to stay in the system for as long as possible. Those were "early indicators" of A.I., according to the cyber security company Dark trace. Essentially, the malware could figure out its surroundings and mimic the behavior of the system's users, though Darktrace said the firm had found the program before it could do any damage.

"India is a place where newer A.I. attacks might be seen for the first time, simply because it is an ideal testing ground for those sorts of attacks," said Nicole Eagan, the chief executive of Darktrace.

In the case of attacks carried out by a nation-state, companies in the United States can hope to receive a warning or assistance from the federal government, while companies elsewhere will often be left to fend for themselves.

Cyber security experts now speculate that a February 2016 attack on the central bank of Bangladesh, believed to have been carried out by hackers linked to North Korea, was a precursor to similar attacks on banks in Vietnam and Ecuador.

That hackers managed to steal $81 million from the Bangladesh Bank generated headlines because of the size of the heist. But what interested cyber security experts was that attackers had taken advantage of a previously unexplored weakness in the bank's computers by undermining its accounts on Swift, the international money transfer system that banks use to move billions of dollars among themselves each day.

The malware discovered by Darktrace researchers stopped short of being a full-fledged A.I.-driven piece of software. It did, however, learn while it was in the system, trying to copy the actions of the network in order to blend in.

As internet use has expanded in Africa, Mr. Liska said, his company has noticed an increase in so-called spear-phishing attacks in which hackers appear to be testing their skills in English- and French-speaking African countries. Spear phishing employs messages that appear innocuous but contain dangerous malware. They are one of the most popular forms of cyber attacks, though they largely depend on the attackers' ability to hone a message that can fool a victim into opening a link or attachment.

He said that in the spear-phishing tests his company had found, attackers appeared to be testing their language, but did not include the actual malware in the link, what he described as the payload.

From *The New York Times*

19. What is the characteristic of cyber attacks that researchers worry about?
[A] Human can watch from the sidelines the defensive measures based on artificial intelligence.
[B] Malicious software using artificial intelligence may compete with offensive means of artificial intelligence in a digital contest.
[C] The defense measures of artificial intelligence can sometimes be defeated by malicious software.
[D] Not mentioned.

20. Why do cyber attacks usually occur in developing countries?
[A] Because these countries are always using the Internet to spread knowledge.
[B] Because these countries don't have sophisticated banking systems or networks.
[C] Because hackers can test their own technology to attack countries with advanced defenses.
[D] Because developed countries can get help from the government.

21. Which of the following can express the meaning of Liska?
[A] The expansion of the Internet has increased fraud.
[B] Hackers only like to test their skills in an English-speaking country.
[C] Spear phishing is the hacker's favorite form of network attacks.
[D] Spear-phishing found by Liska's company is not malware.

22. What can we learn from the article?
[A] Malicious software is completely led by artificial intelligence.
[B] Cyber security experts are interested in developing countries attacked by hackers.
[C] Malware has the ability to learn after intrusion into the system.
[D] None of the above is true.

23. Which of the following can be used as the title of this article?
[A] Developing countries become experimental sites for cyber attacks.
[B] Comparison of cyber attacks in India with other countries.
[C] Measures taken by countries in the face of cyber attacks.
[D] Consequences of various countries after cyber attacks.

ANSWER

19. 答案：[B]

解析 該題的回答在於第一段中malicious software using artificial intelligence that could lead to a new digital arms race in which A.I.-driven defenses battled A.I.-driven offenses while humans watched from the sidelines.（人工智慧的惡意軟體可能導致一種新的數據軍備競賽，這指的是人工智慧的惡意軟體與以人工智慧為主的進攻手段之間的競賽，而人類只能站在一旁觀看），該句話的意思與選項[B]的內容相一致。

20. 答案：[C]

解析 在文章第四段中they provide a fertile testing ground for hackers trying their skills in an environment where they can evade detection before deploying them against a company or state that has more advanced defenses（為駭客們提供了的試驗沃土，檢驗自己的能力然後對其他更具有先進防禦性的公司或者國家發動攻擊），因此是因為發展中國家的防禦能力相對較弱，[C]項的表述與這句話的意思相一致。

21. 答案：[D]

解析 根據最後一段中的He said that in the spear-phishing tests his company had found, attackers appeared to be testing their language, but did not include the actual malware in the link（他說他的公司在測試中發現釣魚軟體只是在測試語言能力，連結中並不包含惡意軟體），因此[D]項的意思與其一致。

22. 答案：[C]

解析 在文章倒數第三段中出現It did, however, learn while it was in the system, trying to copy the actions of the network in order to blend in（然而，它確實在系統中學習，為了融入試圖複製網絡的行為），這裡的it指的是惡意軟體，[A]項應為不是完全被人工智慧引導的軟體，[C]的has the ability to learn與其意思相一致。

23. 答案：[A]

解析 若想從選項中選出這篇文章的題目就需要把握整篇文章的大意。這篇文章中第四段出現了As developing economies rush to go online, they provide a fertile testing ground for hackers trying their skills in an environment where they can evade detection before deploying them against a company or state that has more advanced defenses（由於發展中國家急於上網，這就為駭客們提供了試驗的沃土，檢驗自己的能力然後對其他更具有先進防禦性的公司或者國家發動攻擊）以及第六段 simply because it is an ideal testing ground for those sorts of attacks（僅僅是因為（印度）為這種攻擊提供了理想的測試地），所以這篇文章的題目是[A]。

Passage 5

The Great Barrier Reef in Australia has long been one of the world's most magnificent natural wonders, so enormous it can be seen from space, so beautiful it can move visitors to tears. But the reef, and the profusion of sea creatures living near it, is in profound trouble.

Huge sections of the Great Barrier Reef, stretching across hundreds of kilometers of its most pristine northern sector, were recently found to be dead, killed last year by overheated seawater.

More southerly sections around the middle of the reef that barely escaped then are bleaching now, a potential precursor to another die-off that could rob some of the reef's most visited areas of color and life. [▲A]

The damage to the Great Barrier Reef, one of the world's largest living organisms, is part of a global calamity that has been unfolding intermittently for nearly two decades and seems to be intensifying. In the paper, dozens of scientists described the recent disaster as the third worldwide mass bleaching of coral reefs since 1998, but by far the most widespread and damaging.

The state of coral reefs is a telling sign of the health of the seas. Their distress and death is yet another marker of the ravages of global climate change. [▲B]

If most of the world's coral reefs die, as scientists fear is increasingly likely, some of the richest and most colorful life in the ocean could be lost, along with huge sums from reef tourism. In poorer countries, lives are at stake: Hundreds of millions of people get their protein primarily from reef fish, and the loss of that food supply could become a humanitarian crisis.

Globally, the ocean has warmed by about 1.5 degrees Fahrenheit since the late 19th century, by a conservative calculation, and a bit more in the tropics, home to many reefs. An additional kick was supplied by an El Nino weather pattern that peaked in 2016 and temporarily warmed much of the surface of the planet, causing the hottest year in a historical record dating to 1880.

It was obvious last year that the corals on many reefs were likely to die, but now formal scientific assessments are coming in. The paper in Nature documents vast coral bleaching in 2016 along a 500-mile section of the reef north of Cairns, a city on Australia's eastern coast.

Bleaching indicates that corals are under heat stress, but they do not always die and cooler water can help them recover. [▲C] Subsequent surveys of the Great Barrier Reef, conducted late last year after the deadline for inclusion in the Nature paper, documented that extensive patches of reef had in fact died, and would not be likely to recover soon, if at all.

The global reef crisis does not necessarily mean extinction for coral species. The corals may save themselves, as many other creatures are attempting to do, by moving toward the poles as the Earth warms, establishing new reefs in cooler water.

But the changes humans are causing are so rapid, by geological standards, that it is not entirely clear that coral species will be able to keep up. [▲D]

Within a decade, certain kinds of branching and plate coral could be extinct, reef scientists say, along with a variety of small fish that rely on them for protection from predators.

From *The New York Times*

24. Why does the author say "But the reef, and the profusion of sea creatures living near it, is in profound trouble" in paragraph 1?
[A] To point out the trouble of reefs and a large number of marine creatures
[B] To emphasize the destructiveness of human beings to the ocean
[C] To elicit the actual situation of the reef
[D] To explain the relationship between reefs and a large number of marine creatures

25. The word bleaching in paragraph 2 is closest in meaning to _____.
[A] decolorizing   [B] improving   [C] reducing   [D] changing

26. According to the passage, coral reef is a sign in that _____.
[A] it adds color to the ocean
[B] it can feed a group of marine creatures
[C] any life can exist as a signal
[D] it can show changes in global climate

27. Look at the four triangle [▲] that indicates where the following sentence could be added to the passage.

And even if the corals do survive, that does not mean individual reefs will continue to thrive where they do now. Where would the sentence best fit?

28. The word kick in paragraph 6 is closest in meaning to _____.
[A] news   [B] blow   [C] reality   [D] evidence

ANSWER

24. 答案：[C]

解析 這句話是第一段話的最後一句，通常是對這段話內容的解釋或者引出下一段話，第二段話講述的是很多珊瑚礁死亡，出現了白化現象，因此這句話的目的是為了引出下一段，即珊瑚礁的具體實際情況。

25. 答案：[A]

解析 這個詞的意思可從接下來的這句話中推測出：a potential precursor to another die-off that could rob some of the reef's most visited areas of color and life（這會是大面積死亡的徵兆，可能讓最受遊客喜愛、充滿色彩和生命的珊瑚礁區域消失），因此是與色彩有關，[A]項的意思與其最為接近，意為「變白，漂白」。

26. 答案：[D]

解析 這個問題中的coral reef is a sign可以在第四段中體現，The state of coral reefs is a telling sign of the health of the seas. Their distress and death is yet another marker of the ravages of global climate change（珊瑚礁的狀況是可以顯示海洋健康狀況的一個有說服力的跡象。它們的危機和死亡也是全球氣候變化的指標），根據選項，[D]項的意思與其最接近。

27. 答案：[D]

解析 這句話的意思是：即使珊瑚確實可以存活下去，也不意味著個別的珊瑚會在其目前生長的地方長存，[A]所在的段落講的是發現珊瑚死亡和白化的情況，[B]處段落指的是珊瑚礁是海洋和全球氣候變化的信號，[C]處的段落指的是白化的含義，以及珊瑚出現白化就意味著基本死亡，只有[D]處的段落和上一段是在講述珊瑚會不會存活的問題，[D]處的段落是在對前一段內容的反駁。因此選[D]。

28. 答案：[B]

解析 該詞前面那句話指的是全球海洋溫度上漲，有很多珊瑚礁生存的區域的溫度也上升了，該詞所處的句子指的是聖嬰現象讓全球表面溫度也暫時升高，這兩個都是不好的消息，因此 kick在這裡可譯為「打擊」，與選項[B]中blow意思最為相近，都可意為「……對……的打擊」。

Passage 6

A mother has blasted one of this year's must-have Christmas toys in a scathing online post. Mother Ciara Umar, from Stockton-on-Tees, County Durham, took to Facebook to criticise the L.O.L. Surprise! Big Surprise, describing it as a "waste of money".

The £60 toy contains a collectible doll and 49 other separate gifts to unwrap, including some encased within bath bombs.

However, Mrs. Umar was left disappointed when she bought one for her daughter Elisa and took to Facebook to warn other parents.

Her post has gone viral and has been shared by more than 7,000 times since it was uploaded on Friday. It has also received dozens of comments from shocked parents who said they would think twice before buying the toy for their own children.

In her post, with a 'feeling annoyed' tag, she says: 'So Elisa got the Big LOL Surprise today. I would definitely not recommend if you don't want to waste your money. The pic on the right is all you get just pre warning yas (bucket not included).

She shared the post with an image of the "surprise" toys which included some small plastic dolls and a handful of miniature doll accessories.

Ciara later added: "I was mortified when I saw the contents. Don't get me wrong, she was over the moon opening them and had five baths with the bath bombs, but then just went back to her iPad. The novelty wore off within 15 minutes."

"She got what was in the picture then there was five more surprises in the bath bombs. It's an absolute waste of money, it's not even a full ball either, it's only half a ball as the back is flat."

More than half a million of the smaller LOL toys have been sold in the UK since it was launched in March and it is now the nation's best-selling toy.

The limited edition Big Surprise has proved so popular that some retailers have set a limit of one ball per customer.

However many who read Mrs Umar's post explained they would no longer be buying one for their child's Christmas.

Christine Ruddy said: "That's disgraceful, what a disappointment...won't be getting one now." Kelly Sawyer added: "I'll tell my friend, her little girl is obsessed to have one. That's terrible, and I thought the Hatchimal was a rip-off."

But not everyone feels the same and others have commented on Ciara's post to say they'd be happy to spend the money to bring a smile to their children's faces.

Nicola Mack said: "Oh I know they are totally not worth the money. Olivia has her heart set on this, it's all she's asked for, I'd have a really unhappy little girl on Christmas morning if Santa doesn't bring this."

"It really is a lot of money for what you get, but I would pay this just to see the smile on her face."

A brand spokesperson said: "LOL Surprise is currently the best-selling toy in the UK and a number of other countries. Prices range from £5.99 for the LOL Tots to £59.99 for the Big Surprise."

From *The Daily Mail*

Questions 29-33

Answer the question below.
Choose NO MORE THAN FOUR WORDS AND / OR A NUMBER from the passage for each answer.

29. What's the attitude of the mother after she bought the toy for her daughter?

30. What did the other parents say to the company after seeing the post?

31. What does the surprise toy contain?

32. What is the most unsatisfactory thing for Ciara?

33. What caused retailers set the limit of one ball to per customer?

ANSWER

29. 答案：disappointed

解析 文章第四段的這句話提到However Mrs Umar was left disappointed when she bought one for her daughter Elisa，因此買完玩具後剩下的是失望。

30. 答案：they would think twice

解析 這題詢問的是其他父母看到這則貼文後，對那個公司說了什麼。這個問題可以從第五段中It has also received dozens of comments from shocked parents who said they would think twice before buying the toy for their own children得知，因此答案是they would think twice。

31. 答案：some small plastic dolls

解析 根據文章中第七段的She shared the post with an image of the 'surprise' toys which included some small plastic dolls and a handful of miniature doll accessories，因此答案是some small plastic dolls and a handful of miniature doll accessories（小型塑膠娃娃和一些迷你娃娃配件），因不能超過4個詞，故用some small plastic dolls。

32. 答案：it's an incomplete ball

解析 西亞拉抱怨到具體的細節呈現在第九段it's not even a full ball either（它也不是一個完整的球），因此答案為it's an incomplete ball。

33. 答案：limited edition Big Surprise

解析 這個問題的答案在倒數第八段The limited edition Big Surprise has proved so popular that some retailers have set a limit of one ball per customer，因此是因為限定版大驚喜。

Passage 7

Zaro Bates operates and lives on a 5,000-square-foot farm on Staten Island, which may make her the city's only commercial farmer-in-residence. But instead of a shingled farmhouse surrounded by acres of fields, Ms. Bates lives in a second-floor studio in a midrise apartment complex built on the site of a former naval base overlooking New York Bay.

The farm itself sits in a courtyard between two buildings at Urby, a development with 571rental apartments that opened in Stapleton last year. Ms. Bates draws a modest salary and gets free housing, which sounds like a good deal until you discover how much work she has to put in.

The 26-year-old oversees a weekly farm stand on the complex premises from May through November and donates to food banks. In her repertory? Some 50 types of produce — greens, summer vegetables, flowers, herbs and roots. She does this with help from her business partner and husband, Asher Landes, 29.

Let the doubters doubt.

"A lot of people instinctively call it a garden, but we really try to manage it for a commercial market," Ms. Bates said. "It's funny that people have different kinds of notions of what a farm is. Some people think it needs to have animals, that it needs to have acreage. We intensively crop this space so that we can produce for market, and that's why we call it a farm."

Farming, of course, is a New York tradition. In the late 1800s, loam and livestock were predominant north of Central Park and in what is now the East 50s.In "Win-Win Ecology," Michael L. Rosenzweig argues that ecological science has rooted itself in the common ground of development and conservation: the use of rich natural resources in places where we work and live.

Farms like Ms. Bates's, in addition to more traditional farmland, have been around for quite some time. Thomas Whitlow, an associate professor of horticulture who specializes in urban plants at Cornell University, Ms. Bates' salma mater, said that in the 1940s some 40 percent of fresh market produce in New York was grown in victory gardens.

"Certainly, urban populations in general are very adaptable as conditions change," Dr. Whitlow said. "They can change within the space of a year. Just a hundred years ago we were almost a hunter-gatherer society and did indeed have farming in major metropolitan areas."

Ms. Bates had hardly seen farmland as a child. Her parents, who moved to Carroll Gardens, Brooklyn, in the early 1990s, rarely took the family upstate. They had the backyard of their home, but no green thumbs between them. The yard was a play space.

After graduating from the College of Agriculture and Life Sciences at Cornell, where she studied developmental sociology, Ms. Bates volunteered as a groundskeeper at the Kripalu Center for Yoga and Health in Stockbridge, Mass.

"That was the first time that I drove a tractor, did wood chipping, shoveled heaps of snow in the Berkshires winter, then planted in the springtime and just worked outside with a team of people through the seasons," she said. "That was my first experience with that type of work and really falling in love with that."

From *The New York Times*

34. Why does Zaro Bates live in a studio in a high-rise residential area?

[A] Because the environment of the farm is not suitable for living.

[B] Because the farm is very remote, and the city is far from the farm.

[C] Because this place can overlook New York Bay.

[D] Because she manages the farm, she can live in this free house.

35. What can we learn from the paragraph 5?

[A] This farm is thought to be a garden because it contains a lot of plants.

[B] People have different opinions about what a farm should be like.

[C] There are a lot of vegetables that are grown intensively on this farm, which is enough to supply the whole city.

[D] The farm is large, so she employs an employee.

36. What were north of Central Park and in what is now the East 50s used for?

[A] Domestic animal

[B] A beautiful manor

[C] Growing and producing crops

[D] Not mentioned

37. Which is the correct term for this farm like Bates's?

[A] This kind of farm is popular with many people.

[B] The farm like Bates's has been around since the 1940s.

[C] Its forms are more diverse than more traditional farms.

[D] The farm is rooted in ecological conservation.

38. When did Bates fall in love with planting?

[A] In 1940s

[B] After she graduated

[C] In the early 1990s

[D] When she was young

ANSWER

34. 答案：[D]

解析 該題問的是為什麼紮羅·貝茨住在高層住宅區裡，引申為：為什麼不住在農場的木瓦農舍裡，這個問題可以定位在文章的前兩段中，選項[A]中的environment沒有出現在文章中，[B]項指的是農場不優越的地理位置，與第二段中The farm itself sits in a courtyard between two buildings at Urby, a development with 571rental apartments that opened in Stapleton last year（農場位於爾比的兩棟建築之間，這是斯泰普爾頓去年開盤的地產項目，共有571座出租公寓）不符，而從Ms. Bates draws a modest salary and gets free housing（貝茨女士領著微薄的薪水並得到了這一個免費的住房）看出，這個地方不是她能選擇的，故只有[D]正確。

35. 答案：[B]

解析 這段話的內容指出的是人們對於一個農場的定義不一樣，所以有的人把這個農場稱為花園，可以從第五段中的It's funny that people have different kinds of notions of what a farm is看出，與[B] 項的內容一致。

36. 答案：[A]

解析 根據文章第六段中的內容Farming, of course, is a New York tradition. In the late 1800s, loam and livestock were predominant north of Central Park and in what is now the East 50s（當然，種植業是紐約的傳統。在19世紀末沃土和家畜在中央公園以北和現在被稱為東50s的地方占優勢）可知livestock與[A]項中的domestic animal意思是一致的，故選[A]。

37. 答案：[B]

解析 根據文章倒數第五段中的內容said that in the 1940s some 40 percent of fresh market produce in New York was grown in victory gardens（在1940年代，紐約新鮮市場大約40%的農產品來自於勝利果園），且Farms like Ms. Bates's have been around for quite some time（像貝茨女士這樣的農場已經存在了很長一段時間），説這種農場已經有了就是指的前面的1940年代的勝利果園，故與[B]項的內容相近。

38. 答案：[B]

解析 根據文章最後一段，That was my first experience with that type of work and really falling in love with that，從這裡可以看出她愛上種植，而時間列在前一段中，After graduating from the College of Agriculture and Life Sciences at Cornell，因此是在她畢業後，選[B]。

Passage 8

The classic description of the sensation of a heart attack is that it's like a heavy weight crushing your chest accompanied by a feeling of overwhelming anxiety. In films people clutch their chests, show panic in their eyes and then fall to the floor. And it can happen just like that. But not always.

[▲A]Heart attacks occur when the supply of blood to the heart becomes blocked, usually by a blood clot. [▲B]Despite what's happening in the body, sometime people feel no chest pain at all, which means they delay getting help. [▲C]Sometimes this is known as a silent heart attack. A study published in 2016 found this could happen in as many as 45% of heart attacks. [▲D]

The data for this research started being collected in the late 1990s and since then the diagnosis of heart attacks has improved, so the figure would probably not be as high today, but every year there are still some people who, at the time, had no idea they were having a heart attack.

There are also patients who knew that they were ill, but not why. They feel pain in the jaw, neck, arms, stomach or back and feel short of breath, weak or light-headed. They might sweat or vomit. It's the combination of symptoms rather than the severity of chest pain that allows for a diagnosis.

It is often said that these heart attacks without chest pain are more common in women, leading women to delay getting help and reducing their chances of survival. In order to establish whether this really is the case, researchers in Canada in 2009 set out to measure the symptoms of a heart attack systematically, by studying 305 patients undergoing angioplasty. This is where a blocked blood vessel is re-opened by inflating a small balloon inside it. The procedure can briefly mimic the symptoms of a heart attack, so while the balloons were inflated patients were asked to describe what they could feel. They found no differences between men and women in terms of chest discomfort, arm pain, shortness of breath, sweating or nausea, but women were more likely to have pain in the neck and jaw in addition to chest pain.

The findings of other studies have been inconsistent, sometimes finding that men and women are equally likely to experience chest pain, others that it's more common in men. Sometimes the issue is confused by researchers including other diagnoses alongside heart attacks in the same study. So in 2011 a review was conducted, with the sole aim of establishing whether there is a difference in the symptoms experienced by men and women.

Studies from the US, Japan, Sweden and Germany, UK and Canada were all included, the largest involving more than 900,000 people. The data was taken from the best 26 of these studies, combined and re-analysed. They concluded that women are less likely than men to present with chest pain and more likely than men to have symptoms such as fatigue, nausea, dizziness or fainting and pain in their neck, jaw or arms. With both sexes, the majority still experienced chest pain, but a third of women and almost a quarter of men had heart attacks without having any symptoms in their chest, making it hard for them to realise what's happening to them.

If you don't know how serious your symptoms are, naturally you're less likely to go for help. People wait on average between two and five hours.

A new study has sought to find about more about people's thought processes in making what can be a life-and-death decision to go to a doctor. In-depth interviews with a small number of women who'd had heart attacks revealed that half knew something was wrong and immediately went for help. Three had vague symptoms which began as mild, but then got more intense, prompting them to the doctor. But the remaining people had no idea their symptoms were to do with their heart and didn't tell anyone else, deciding to wait and see.

So the lesson is that a crushing chest pain is very serious and could indicate a heart attack, but so could a collection of other symptoms, therefore we need to consider the possibility of a heart attack even when it doesn't seem quite like in he films.

From *The New York Times*

39. Look at the four triangle [▲] that indicate where the following sentence could be added to the passage.

Even with mild chest pain, many assume they have indigestion and only discover later that they've had a heart attack after an electrocardiogram in hospital shows damage to the heart. Where would be the sentence best fit?

40. The word nausea in the eighth sentence of paragraph 5 is closest in meaning to?

[A] diarrhea   [B] vomiting   [C] naupathia   [D] headache

41. Why does author say "The findings of other studies have been inconsistent" in paragraph 6?

[A] To show the unprofessionalism of other studies

[B] To elicit a special study conducted in 2011

[C] To emphasize the correctness of the results of this study

[D] To draw data from other studies

42. According to the passage, all of the following are mentioned as a reason why people cannot get treatment in time EXCEPT

[A] People think about their finances before they go to the hospital.

[B] People have misconception about the symptoms of their bodies.

[C] People's bodies are just vague symptoms.

[D] People do not understand what's happening in the body.

43. According to the passage, if patients have no symptoms, _____.

[A] they think their discomfort is due to indigestion

[B] they'll know they're sick

[C] they go to the hospital regularly

[D] they will not seek help immediately

ANSWER

39. 答案：[C]

解析 這句話的意思是：即便出現輕微的胸痛，很多人也會認為他們僅僅是消化不良，但隨後他們會在醫院心電圖測試中發現實際上是心肌梗塞在作祟。」空格所處的這段話的首句是Heart attacks occur when the supply of blood to the heart becomes blocked, usually by a blood clot（由於血栓阻塞血液向心臟供血就會出現心肌梗塞），後面的內容是對其的解釋，因此其可作為總結句。這句話所放位置的線索可以從Sometimes this is known as a silent heart attack（有時這被稱為「沈默」心臟病）找到，這裡的this指的就是前面的情況，而silent指的是出現的輕微胸痛在心電圖上可看出是心肌梗塞在作祟，故選[C]。

閱讀實踐──整體掌握文章

40. 答案：[C]

解析 該詞nausea與文章中提到vomit（嘔吐）是不一樣的，故可排除[C]，[A]項的意思是「腹瀉」；[D]項的意思是「頭痛」；[C]項的意思是「噁心」，nausea與其意思一樣，都表「噁心」。

41. 答案：[B]

解析 這題的問題是為什麼作者要說「其他研究的發現缺乏一致性」，這句話後面的內容展示了研究結果不一致的表現，但並沒有出現在4個選項中，接下來的內容是引出了2011年為此而專門做的研究，與[B]項的內容一致。

42. 答案：[A]

解析 這個問題可以引申為哪一個不能作為人們不能及時得到救治的原因，[B]項中的misconception（誤解）指的是心肌梗塞的症狀被認為是消化不良；[C]項指的是通常情況下認為不會為了輕微的症狀而就醫，根據倒數第二段But the remaining people had no idea their symptoms were to do with their heart and didn't tell anyone else, deciding to wait and see（剩下的人不知道這些症狀與心臟相關，也沒有告訴身邊任何人，而是決定等等再看）可看出；[D]的內容可以從第二段Despite what's happening in the body, sometime people feel no chest pain at all, which means they delay getting help（儘管身體內出現了病症反應，病人卻對此一無所知，從而使他們無法及時得到救治）得知，故選[A]。

43. 答案：[D]

解析 這個問題問的是：如果患者沒有症狀會怎麼樣，根據文章中倒數第四段的最後一句，had heart attacks without having any symptoms in their chest, making it hard for them to realise what's happening to them.（有著心肌梗塞卻沒有症狀，使他們很難知道自己已經發病），也就是不會立即尋求幫助，故選[D]。

Passage 9

"Turn your face toward the sun, and the shadows will fall behind you."

"Every day may not be good, but there is something good in every day."

Researchers are finding that thoughts like these, the hallmarks of people sometimes called "cockeyed optimists," can do far more than raise one's spirits. They may actually improve health and extend life.

There is no longer any doubt that what happens in the brain influences what happens in the body. When facing a health crisis, actively cultivating positive emotions can boost the immune system and counter depression. Studies have shown an indisputable link between having a positive outlook and health benefits like lower blood pressure, less heart disease, better weight control and healthier blood sugar levels.

Judith T. Moskowitz, a professor of medical social sciences at Northwestern

University Feinberg School of Medicine in Chicago, developed a set of eight skills to help foster positive emotions. In earlier research at the University of California, San Francisco, she and colleagues found that people with new diagnoses of H.I.V. infection who practiced these skills carried a lower load of the virus, were more likely to take their medication correctly, and were less likely to need antidepressants to help them cope with their illness.

The researchers studied 159 people who had recently learned they had H.I.V. and randomly assigned them to either a five-session positive emotions training course or five sessions of general support. Fifteen months past their H.I.V. diagnosis, those trained in the eight skills maintained higher levels of positive feelings and fewer negative thoughts related to their infection.

An important goal of the training is to help people feel happy, calm and satisfied in the midst of a health crisis. Improvements in their health and longevity are a bonus. Each participant is encouraged to learn at least three of the eight skills and practice one or more each day. The eight skills are:

■ Recognize a positive event each day.

■ Savor that event and log it in a journal or tell someone about it.

■ Start a daily gratitude journal.

■ List a personal strength and note how you used it.

■ Set an attainable goal and note your progress.

■ Report a relatively minor stress and list ways to reappraise the event positively.

■ Recognize and practice small acts of kindness daily.

■ Practice mindfulness, focusing on the here and now rather than the past or future.

Dr. Moskowitz said she was inspired by observations that people with AIDS, Type 2 diabetes and other chronic illnesses lived longer if they demonstrated positive emotions. She explained, "The next step was to see if teaching people skills that foster positive emotions can have an impact on how well they cope with stress and their physical health down the line."

She listed as the goals improving patients' quality of life, enhancing adherence to medication, fostering healthy behaviors, and building personal resources that result in increased social support and broader attention to the good things in life.

Gregg De Meza, a 56-year-old architect in San Francisco who learned he was infected with H.I.V. four years ago, told me that learning "positivity" skills turned his life around. He said he felt "stupid and careless" about becoming infected and had initially kept his diagnosis a secret.

"When I entered the study, I felt like my entire world was completely unraveling," he said. "The training reminded me to rely on my social network, and I decided to be honest with my friends. I realized that to show your real strength

閱讀實踐──整體掌握文章

is to show your weakness. No pun intended, it made me more positive, more compassionate, and I'm now healthier than I've ever been."

From *The New York Times*

Questions 44-48

Complete the following sentence according to the passage, using no more than four words from the passage for each other.

44. There's no question that brain activity affects _____.

45. The function of these eight sets of skills is to_____.

46. The extra benefit of this training is_____.

47. Dr. Moskowitz wanted to teach people skills that cultivate positive emotions to test whether they can affect_____.

48. Gregg De Meza realized that showing your real strength is _____.

ANSWER

44. 答案：body

解析 這句話可以溯及到文章第四段的There is no longer any doubt that what happens in the brain influences what happens in the body，因此可用body來回答。

45. 答案：help foster positive emotions

解析 這題的答案可以溯及至第五段Judith T. Moskowitz, a professor of medical social sciences at Northwestern University Feinberg School of Medicine in Chicago, developed a set of eight skills to help foster positive emotions，故可用help foster positive emotions來回答。

46. 答案：improvements in their health / longevity

解析 這個問題可以溯及至文章的第七段Improvements in their health and longevity are a bonus，故可選擇這兩個的任意一個。

47. 答案：their physical health

解析 這句話可以溯及至文章的倒數第四段The next step was to see if teaching people skills that foster positive emotions can have an impact on how well they cope with stress and their physical health down the line，因回答不能超過4個詞，故選擇their physical health。

48. 答案：showing your weakness

解析 這句話可以溯及至文章的最後一段，I realized that to show your real strength is to show your weakness，這裡的前後都用到了to，但是在問題中前面沒有to，那麼後面也不用to，故要用 showing your weakness。

Passage 10

One year after giant pandas graduated from endangered to "vulnerable," a welcome designation after 28 years, Chinese scientists have sobering news: The animal's natural habitat in China is in serious danger.

In a study published in Nature Ecology & Evolution on Monday, researchers report that suitable panda habitats have significantly and steadily declined since 1990, the year the International Union for the Conservation of Nature first classified the animals as endangered. That could make any gain in China's wild panda population a short-lived conservation victory.

Logging, human encroachment, road construction and agriculture have conspired to divide panda habitats into tiny sections, a process known as fragmentation, the study said.

Ouyang Zhiyun, a professor of environmental science at the Chinese Academy of Sciences, and his colleagues studied 40 years of satellite data to reach their conclusions, and are urging the Chinese government to take specific steps to restore panda-friendly environments.

Giant pandas are a national icon of China, the only place in the world where they live outside of captivity. Years of Chinese government efforts to reverse their dwindling numbers, such as the restoration of bamboo forests and establishment of national habitat reserves, helped bring the animals back from the brink. They were declared no longer endangered in September 2016 after population estimates reached 1,864 — not counting cubs. That's up from a low of about 1,200 in the 1980s.

But even with that good news came a warning: Climate change and other factors could devastate the pandas' habitat in the longer term, rendering any population surge a temporary victory, the IUCN said. Exacerbating the problem is the fragmentation of China's panda population, confined now to just six mountain ranges and about 30 isolated groups, 18 of which contain no more than 10 individuals.

From *The New York Times*

49. Which sentence is the thesis statement in this passage?
[A] That's up from a low of about 1,200 in the 1980s.
[B] Giant pandas are a national icon of China, the only place in the world where they live outside of captivity.
[C] The animal's natural habitat in China is in serious danger.
[D] That could make any gain in China's wild panda population a short-lived conservation victory.

50. According to the study, which of the following has no effect on the habitat of giant pandas?

[A] Road construction
[B] Agricultural activities
[C] Population size
[D] Logging

51. Which of the following sentence can serve as a summary of the fifth paragraph?
[A] Other countries keep giant pandas in captivity.
[B] Chinese government should take action to protect giant pandas.
[C] The giant panda was identified as an endangered animal again.
[D] Pandas are not endangered animal currently.

52. Which sentence is true according to the last paragraph?
[A] Climate change doesn't affect on the habitat of giant pandas.
[B] Climate change has great influence on the habitat of giant pandas.
[C] Climate change has little impact on the habitat of giant pandas.
[D] Climate makes the same effect as human activity on the habitat of giant pandas.

53. What can we learn from the passage?
[A] The habitat of giant pandas affects on the growth of giant pandas.
[B] Some races of the giant panda have been extinct.
[C] The suitable giant panda habitat has increased.
[D] China is the only place for giant pandas to live.

ANSWER

49. 答案：[C]

解析 這篇文章是一篇說明文，文章的主旨句出現在開頭段，即：中國的大貓熊自然棲息地正處在嚴重危險中。其它三個選項都是圍繞這個主旨展開的一些說明。

50. 答案：[C]

解析 文章的第三段提到：伐木活動，人類侵入，道路建設和農業活動在破壞大貓熊的棲息地，而選項[C]的「人口數量」沒有提及，故為答案。

51. 答案：[D]

解析 選項[A]「其它國家有圈養的大貓熊」和[B]「中國政府應該採取行動保護大貓熊」在該段中沒有提及，故可排除；選項[C]「大貓熊再次被認定為瀕危動物」與原文的They were declared no longer endangered相反，[D]與訊息一致。

52. 答案：[B]

解析 在最後一段中提到：氣候變化和其它因素，從長期來看，會毀壞大貓熊的棲息地。由此可知氣候變化對大貓熊棲息地的影響是很大的，選項[B]符合題意。

Part 1
Part 2
Part 3

53. 答案：[A]

解析 最後一段提到了大貓熊的分散化，而並沒有提到大貓熊的種族滅絕，故排除[B]；文中第二段提到適合大貓熊居住的棲息地在不斷減少，選項[C]中的「增加」與此訊息相反，故可排除；選項[D]的意思是「中國是世界上唯一適合大貓熊居住的地方」，這在文中沒有提及，而且不符合事實。選項[A]「大貓熊棲息地對大貓熊的數量有影響」與本文的主題相符，故選[A]。

Passage 11

閱讀實踐——整體掌握文章

Revisions in the Physician Payments Sunshine Act (S.2029) will now make it a Class D federal felony for physicians to accept more than $25 annually in gifts or other rewards from pharmaceutical companies or biological product and medical device manufacturers.

The legislation targets offending individual physicians, hospitals, schools, and other medical institutions that deal directly with patients. [▲A]

Patients' rights and medical ethics groups, like the New England Medical Ethics Commission in Boston, are exultant. "It's not like the A.M.A. or [pharmaceutical trade association] PhRMA were ever going to comply with their own stated standards, [▲ B]" says Patty Williams, Director of Communications for the commission. Williams is referring to the American Medical Association's 1991 guidelines on gifts to physicians from industry, which stemmed a tide of blatant gift-giving in the 1980s, but have been criticized for allowing new byways for abuse: free lunches and dinners, travel and honoraria, and the hemorrhaging of complimentary pens, coffee mugs, and other product-related paraphernalia into doctors' offices.

"What we really need is a sea change in the medical profession wherein physicians realize that it isn't O.K. to get gifts or fill our offices with advertisements for products. It demeans patient care," says Mount Sinai School of Medicine professor Dr. Joseph Ross. [▲C] While some programs, which scrutinize pharmaceutical company information and sales practices, have been in place for several years in states, their effect is limited by the willingness of doctors to abide by ethical standards. But they believe that more people will benefit from this legislation in the future. [▲D]

From *The New York Times*

54. According to paragraph 1and 2, the legislation can
[A] Offend medical device manufacturers.
[B] Let people know about the doctor's income.
[C] Increase financial transparency between physicians and pharmaceutical

manufacturers.

[D] Build trust between doctors and patients.

55. The word scrutinize in the paragraph 4 is closest in meaning to

[A] Build   [B] Seperate   [C] Collect   [D] Investigate

56. Look at the four triangle [▲] that indicate where the following sentence could be added to the passage.

It also makes it a federal offense for medical industries to circumvent customary gift-giving practices through third parties, such as lawyers and insurance companies, or via "educational" events. Where would be the sentence best fit?

57. Why does author say "The legislation targets offending individual physicians, hospitals, schools, and other medical institutions that deal directly with patients" in paragraph 2?

[A] To draw a specific example

[B] To emphasize that this legislation basically guarantees the rights of patients

[C] To explain the causes and the time of the legislation

[D] To demonstrate the actual impact of regulations

58. The word *their* in the fifth sentence of paragraph 4 in the passage refers to

[A] Information

[B] Pharmaceutical company

[C] Doctors

[D] Programs

ANSWER

54. 答案：[C]

解析 問題詢問的是這項立法能夠怎麼樣，[B]和[D]的意思並沒有在文章中説明出來，[A] 項指的是Offend medical device manufacturers（打擊醫療器材製造商），但這個法案不是為了醫療器材製造商建立的，而是為了讓內科醫生與醫療器材商之間沒有送禮行為，與[C]項的financial transparency（財務透明度）意思相近，故選[C]。

55. 答案：[D]

解析 根據動詞後面的內容pharmaceutical company information（製藥公司訊息），可排除[A]和[B]，而後面提到因為醫生的道德標準使效果受到限制，而文章中的立法是為了規避這些不好的行為，因此[D]項合適。

56. 答案：[A]

解析 這句話的意思是：這也使得醫療行業規避了通過第三方贈送禮品的做法，如律師和保險公司，或通過「教育」。這句話的主要內容指的是某事物使醫療行業的行為得到了規範，因此適合[A] 處，it 指代的是前面的legislation。

57. 答案：[B]

解析 這句話的意思是：該法案的目標是打擊直接與病人打交道的個體醫生、醫院、學校和其他醫療機構，其只是目標不能證明其實際影響，排除[D]；該句話的後文也沒有直接的例子證明這個觀點，排除[A]；[C]項的time沒有體現。故選[B]。

58. 答案：[D]

解析 their指的是複數可排除[B]，their後面的意思是其效果受到了限制，將[D]項的「計劃」放在 該句中符合文章意思，即該計劃實施的效果受到了限制。

（Part 1 / Part 2 / Part 3 閱讀實踐——整體掌握文章）

Passage 12

The Faroe Islands, a remote archipelago that juts out of the cold seas between Norway and Iceland, doesn't even appear on some world maps. But as of last week, the verdant slopes, rocky hiking trails and few roads of the 18 islands are on Google Street View — and a team of cameratoting sheep helped get them there.

When the islands' tourism board decided last year that it wanted to get the company's attention, it knew it would need an unusual pitch. It also knew that its rugged terrain would not be easily traversed by those Google cars that ply city streets worldwide, snapping photos. So it strapped solar-powered, 360-degree cameras onto the backs of a few shaggy Faroese sheep and began uploading the resulting, and very breathtaking, images to Street View itself.

The whole sheep idea — which the tourism board called "Sheepview 360" — was not such a stretch. Sheep are a big deal in the Faroe Islands, an autonomous nation within the Kingdom of Denmark whose name translates to "islands of the sheep." The islands' distinct breed is believed to have been imported by Norse settlers in the 9th century, and today about 80,000 sheep live there, far outnumbering the 50,000 people. Tourism official Levi Hanssen said most Faroese have some connection to raising sheep, about one-third of which are slaughtered for meat; the others are used for wool and dairy products.

And although all the sheep are owned, they roam freely — usually.

"It's not very easy putting cameras on sheep," Hanssen, the content manager for VisitFaroeIslands.com, said in an interview. "We would just stand there, and they would stand there and look at us. You have to, in some way, get them to move."

Last week, the Faroe Islands made its debut on Google Street View. Most images ended up being captured by humans, and they included all public roads and hiking trails. But Hanssen said the tourism board decided to leave some spots out to preserve a bit of the islands' mystery.

Sheepview was charming, but it was at heart a marketing bid — and a successful one, said Hanssen, who said it had a "PR value we could never have bought ourselves." Hotel reservation rates, the country's primary yardstick for measuring tourism, are up at least 10 percent this year, he said. Visitors tend to be outdoorsy types, but the islands are also increasingly attracting gourmands who come for "really good, locally sourced food," Hanssen said.

The tourism board has moved on to a new, sheep-free effort to get Google Translate to include Faroese, which descends from old Norse.

As for the sheep that made Street View happen? They retired from filming, Hanssen said. He wasn't sure, however, whether any ended up as someone's locally sourced dinner. "Their job," he said, "was done."

From *The Washington Post*

Questions 59-63

Do the following statements agree with the information given in reading passage. Write

YES   if the statement is true

NO   if the statement is false

NOT GIVEN   if the information is not given in the reading passage

59. The Faroe Islands are very remote, and the islands' tourism board decided to attach cameras to the sheep in order to attract the attention of the company.

60. The different species of sheep are thought to be introduced by settlers from Iceland.

61. They suggest putting this high-tech product on its back.

62. The sights of all the islands in the faroe islands were exposed by the camera on the back of the sheep.

63. This kind of marketing tool increases the number of tourists.

ANSWER

59. 答案：YES

解析 這句話可以從文章的第一段和第二段看出，例如，The Faroe Islands, a remote archipelago （法羅群島，一個偏遠的群島）以及it strapped solar-powered, 360-degree cameras onto the backs of a few shaggy Faroese sheep，所以這句話正確。

60. 答案：NO

解析 這句話中的settlers from Iceland（冰島定居者）不正確，在文章的第三段中的是Norse settlers（挪威定居者），因此不正確。

61. 答案：NOT GIVEN

(解析) 這句話與文章沒有關聯。

62. 答案：NO

(解析) 在文章的第六段中出現了But Hanssen said the tourism board decided to leave some spots out to preserve a bit of the islands' mystery（但漢森表示，旅遊局決定留下一些景點不被展示進而保留島嶼的神秘感。），因此並不是所有的景觀都被暴露，故不正確。

63. 答案：YES

(解析) 根據文章的倒數第四段，Visitors tend to be outdoorsy types, but the islands are also increasingly attracting gourmands（遊客往往喜歡戶外活動，但這些島嶼也越來越吸引美食家），因此指的是遊客數量的增長，故這句話正確。

Passage 13

Relieving stress and anxiety might help you feel better — for a bit. Martin E.P. Seligman, a professor of psychology at the University of Pennsylvania and a pioneer in the field of positive psychology, does not see alleviating negative emotions as a path to happiness.

"What makes life worth living," he said, "is much more than the absence of the negative." To Dr. Seligman, the most effective long-term strategy for happiness is to actively cultivate wellbeing.

In his 2012 book, "Flourish: A Visionary New Understanding of Happiness and Well-Being," he explored how well-being consists not merely of feeling happy (an emotion that can be fleeting) but of experiencing a sense of contentment in the knowledge that your life is flourishing and has meaning beyond your own pleasure.

To cultivate the components of well-being, which include engagement, good relationships, accomplishment and purpose, Dr. Seligman suggests these four exercises based on research at the Penn Positive Psychology Center, which he directs, and at other universities.

Identify Signature Strengths

Write down a story about a time when you were at your best. It doesn't need to be a lifechanging event but should have a clear beginning, middle and end. Reread it every day for a week, and each time ask yourself: "What personal strengths did I display when I was at my best?" Did you show a lot of creativity? Good judgment? Were you kind to other people? Loyal? Brave? Passionate? Forgiving? Honest?

Writing down your answers "puts you in touch with what you're good at, "Dr. Seligman explained. The next step is to contemplate how to use these strengths to your advantage, intentionally organizing and structuring your life around them.

Find the good

Instead of focusing on life's lows, which can increase the likelihood of depression, the exercise "turns your attention to the good things in life, so it changes what you attend to," Dr. Seligman said. "Consciousness is like your tongue: it swirls around in the mouth looking for a cavity, and when it finds it, you focus on it. Imagine if your tongue went looking for a beautiful, healthy tooth." Polish it.

Make a Gratitude Visit

Think of someone who has been especially kind to you but you have not properly thanked. Write a letter describing what he or she did and how it affected your life, and how you often remember the effort. Then arrange a meeting and read the letter aloud, in person.

Respond Constructively

That is, instead of saying something passive like, "Oh, that's nice" or being dismissive, express genuine excitement. Prolong the discussion by, say, encouraging them to tell others or suggest a celebratory activity.

"Love goes better, commitment increases, and from the literature, even sex gets better after that."

From *The New York Times*

Question 64-68

Summary

Complete the following summary of the paragraphs of the passage, using no more than two words from the passage for each other.

In Seligman's view, the most effective long-term strategy for happiness is to cultivate happiness actively. He believes that four kinds of __64__ are needed to cultivate happiness. First of all, find the signature advantage, in order for you to know how to take advantage of these and deliberately use them to __65__ your life. The second is to look for the good in life. This requires you not to __66__ the bad things, but to transfer it to the good things that will lower your possibility of developing __67__. Then, try writing a thank-you note to someone who has not received your thanks. The final exercise is to be constructive. In other words, don't say something passive or dismissive when you talk to someone, but show __68__.

ANSWER

64. 答案：exercises

解析 根據文章第四段的內容Dr. Seligman suggests these four exercises based on research at the Penn Positive Psychology Center, which he directs, and a other universities可知是four exercises。

65. 答案：organize / structure

解析 根據文章第六段的內容The next step is to contemplate how to use these strengths to your advantage, intentionally organizing and structuring your life around them，因此可用organize或者structure。

66. 答案：focus on

解析 根據文章第七段的內容Instead of focusing on life's lows, which can increase the likelihood of depression, the exercise "turns your attention to the good things in life, so it changes what you attend to，因此是focus on。

67. 答案：depression

解析 根據文章第七段的內容Instead of focusing on life's lows, which can increase the likelihood of depression（不要把註意力集中在生活中不好的事情上，它們可能會增加你患憂鬱症的可能性），而該空格指的是關注好的事情的結果，那當然是降低患憂鬱症的可能性，故用depression。

68. 答案：genuine excitement

解析 根據文章倒數第二段的內容That is, instead of saying something passive like, "Oh, that's nice" or being dismissive, express genuine excitement，因此是展示genuine excitement。

易人外語 系列 **E0011**

零基礎學英文閱讀，一本就掌握：
3 步驟漸進練習╳ 52 篇閱讀訓練╳ 49 篇考題演練

英文菜鳥別慌張，入門基本文法架構全解析，上手快狠準！

作　　　者	許唐、林軒
總 編 輯	黃璽宇
主　　　編	吳靜宜、姜怡安
執 行 編 輯	林妍珺、李念茨
美 術 編 輯	王桂芳、張嘉容

初　　　版	2019 年 05 月
出　　　版	含章有限公司
電　　　話	（02）2752-5618
傳　　　真	（02）2752-5619
地　　　址	106 台北市大安區忠孝東路四段 250 號 11 樓 -1

定　　　價	新台幣 360 元／港幣 120 元
產 品 內 容	1 書

總 經 銷	昶景國際文化有限公司
地　　　址	236 新北市土城區民族街 11 號 3 樓
電　　　話	（02）2269-6367
傳　　　真	（02）2269-0299
E-mail:	service@168books.com.tw

歡迎優秀出版社加入總經銷行列

港澳地區總經銷	和平圖書有限公司
地　　　址	香港柴灣嘉業街 12 號百樂門大廈 17 樓
電　　　話	（852）2804-6687
傳　　　真	（852）2804-6409

▶本書部分圖片由 Shutterstock圖庫、123RF圖庫提供。

含章 Book站

現在就上臉書（FACEBOOK）「**含章BOOK站**」並按讚加入粉絲團，
就可享每月不定期新書資訊和粉絲專享小禮物喔！

https://www.facebook.com/hanzhangbooks/
讀者來函：2018hanzhang@gmail.com

國家圖書館出版品預行編目資料

零基礎學英文閱讀，一本就掌握：3 步驟漸進練
習╳ 52 篇閱讀訓練╳ 49 篇考題演練 / 許唐、林
軒著 . -- 初版 . -- 臺北市 : 含章有限公司 , 2019.05
　　面；　公分（易人外語：E0011）
ISBN 978-986-97266-7-2（平裝）

1. 英語　2. 讀本

805.18　　　　　　　　　　　　　108001517